JUL 1 3 2017

CATALYST

A **ROGUE ONE** NOVEL

BY JAMES LUCENO

THE ROBOTECH SERIES
(As Jack McKinney,
with Brian Daley)

THE BLACK HOLE TRAVEL
AGENCY SERIES
(As Jack McKinney,
with Brian Daley)

THE YOUNG INDIANA
JONES CHRONICLES
The Mata Hari Affair

STAR WARS
Cloak of Deception
Darth Maul: Saboteur (eBook)
*The New Jedi Order—Agents
of Chaos I: Hero's Trial*
*The New Jedi Order—Agents
of Chaos II: Jedi Eclipse*
*The New Jedi Order:
The Unifying Force*
Labyrinth of Evil
*Dark Lord: The Rise
of Darth Vader*
Millennium Falcon
Darth Plagueis
Tarkin

STANDALONE NOVELS
Head Hunters
A Fearful Symmetry
Illegal Alien
The Big Empty
Kaduna Memories
The Shadow
The Mask of Zorro
Rio Passion
Rainchaser
Rock Bottom
Hunt for the Maya
*Looking-Glass: The Adventures
of 3Sky and Flint*

CATALYST

A **ROGUE ONE** NOVEL

JAMES LUCENO

DEL REY • NEW YORK

Written in partnership with Leland Chee, Pablo Hidalgo,
Matt Martin, and Rayne Roberts of the Lucasfilm Story Group.
With special thanks to Gareth Edwards and the screenwriters
and producers of *Rogue One: A Star Wars Story.*

2017 Del Rey Mass Market Edition

Published in the United States by Del Rey, an imprint of Random House, a division of Penguin Random House LLC, New York.

DEL REY and the HOUSE colophon are registered trademarks of Penguin Random House LLC.

Originally published in hardcover in the United States by Del Rey, an imprint of Random House, a division of Penguin Random House LLC, in 2016.

This book includes the short story "Voice of the Empire" by Mur Lafferty, which was originally published in *Star Wars Insider* magazine #170.

ISBN 978-1-101-96700-3
Ebook ISBN 978-1-101-96701-0

Printed in the United States of America

randomhousebooks.com

9 8 7 6 5 4 3 2 1

Del Rey mass market edition: May 2017

For Udi Saly and Liz Conover, "bonfire hearts."
May the Force be with you infinitely.

THE DEL REY

STAR WARS

TIMELINE

THE DEL REY

STAR WARS™

TIMELINE

A long time ago in a galaxy far, far away. . . .

For years, the Clone Wars have raged across the galaxy. Countless worlds have been ensnared in the conflict between the Galactic Republic and the Separatist army led by the devious Sith Lord Count Dooku. While rumors spread that the Separatists are nearing completion of a superweapon, fear grips the Republic. In response, Supreme Chancellor Palpatine has tasked a secret team of researchers with perfecting a battle station for the Republic:

the Death Star.

PART ONE

LIFE DURING WARTIME

1

PRESSURE

"WHAT IF . . ."

It was as much as Galen Erso got out before falling silent and pacing away from the alphanumeric data field that hovered above the holoprojector. Galen's fragment of a question also seemed to hang in the air, and his fellow researchers in the control room stopped what they were doing to regard him in palpable expectation. One of them, Nurboo, broke the pregnant silence.

"You've a new idea, Galen? Should we delay the test?"

Galen either didn't hear him or didn't care to. He stood motionless for a moment, his gaze unfocused, then resumed his determined pacing, mumbling numbers and calculations to himself.

A second Valltii gave his large and hirsute head a doleful shake. "It's no good, we've lost him."

From across the room, Tambo's gravelly voice shushed him.

"Can't you see he's thinking?"

Galen's pose certainly said as much. His head was

lowered, eyes and lips narrowed, and his thick arms were folded across his chest, as if clutching something to himself. The new idea, perhaps.

Standing just over 1.8 meters tall, he was broad-shouldered and well developed, despite having spent most of his thirty-odd standard years in earnest rumination and reflection, often scribbling the results of all that thinking on whatever was handy. His hair was uncombed, falling around his face in heavy strands in a way that made him dashing in sunlight, dangerous in the dark.

Lyra finally pushed herself out of her chair and ambled over to him.

"What if . . ." she said in a patient, leading way.

Everyone in the control room took it as a good sign when the thumb and forefinger of Galen's left hand went briefly to the corners of his mouth, stretching the skin.

"We're getting there," Lyra said. She loved it when Galen went so deep that he essentially disappeared from the world, going where few could follow, to his own private hyperspace.

A few centimeters shorter than him, she had a high forehead and layered auburn hair that just reached her shoulders. Arching brows and a slightly down-turned mouth gave her a somewhat somber look, though she was anything but. She and Galen had wed on Coruscant almost five years earlier, and she was every bit her husband's equal in appeal, with the physique of a natural athlete, honed by a lifetime of exploration on dozens of remote worlds. Bundled up in a coarse sweater and baggy trousers, Lyra affected a colorful earflapped cap made of local yarn, and she wore it well.

The only humans among the research group, they were a long way from the Core, and even farther from the conflict that had recently erupted between the Republic and the Confederacy of Independent Systems, the so-called Separatists. The six stout Valltii they had lived and worked with for the past four standard months had large round faces and mouths made for chewing meat. Beneath lustrous growths of facial hair, their skin was as blue as the glacial ice that covered half the planet. Galen and Lyra conversed with them in a pidgin of Galactic Basic and the indigenous language, which was guttural and filled with lengthy words that were confounding to humans. With an ear for mimicry, Lyra did better with the language than Galen did.

She was on the verge of goading him again when he blinked as if remembering who or where he was, and his attention returned to the data field.

She smiled lightly. He was back.

Reviewing the lengthy differential equations top to bottom, Galen stepped closer to the field, as if there were something to be discerned behind it or along its faintly oscillating edges.

"Assis," he said finally, addressing the droid on the far side of the holoprojector.

"Yes, Dr. Erso."

"Line four. Change the coefficient to five and recalculate."

The TDK-160 research-assistant, a reconfigurable

droid that just then was standing on two slender alloy legs, complied and sent the results to the holotable.

Everyone kept their attention on the field while the quotient groups, coefficients, and derivatives began to shift.

The control room was designed to house technology rather than living beings. Lined with humming machines, it lacked windows and was always colder than it had any right being. Heat was pumped in through ducts high overhead, but the room's real warmth came from its having acquired a lived-in look through long months of research and experimentation. No one minded the unpacked crates stacked in the corners, the empty food containers piled on Nurboo's worktable, or the litter of backup data storage devices. As cluttered and claustrophobic as it was, it was more hospitable than just about anywhere outside.

Thick walls broken by sliding entryways kept out the worst of the cold. A rear doorway accessed a ramp leading to a labyrinth of corridors that connected disparate parts of the facility, a few of them wide enough to accommodate compact utility speeders. Elsewhere were banks of computers and analyzers, plotting boards, comm stations, even a rudimentary HoloNet transceiver for extraplanetary communications.

It wasn't Lyra's kind of place at all, but she had formed fast friendships with Galen's colleagues, and Vallt was home for now.

Most of the ignition facility lay far below them, where gases were compelled to mingle and intense heat was generated. There, too, was the superheated ion-plasma reactor and the superconducting coils that cooled it, along with the hydrothermal autoclaves in which enormous crystals were synthetically grown. The fusion plant itself could power Vallt's entire northern continent, and one day it might, but that wasn't its present purpose. The goal was to generate outbursts of raw power that could be harvested, stored in capacitors, and doled out sustainably to worlds in need. The place hadn't come cheap even in prewar credits, and Zerpen Industries, headquartered in an autonomous system in the Outer Rim, was still awaiting a return on its investment.

"The equation won't resolve," Nurboo said when the data field began flashing as if beside itself in confusion.

Galen addressed the droid once more. "Assis, go back."

The original integrals and summation symbols returned to the field, and Galen studied them for a long moment.

"Is that a smile?" Tambo asked. "Lyra, is he smiling?"

Instead of retasking Assis, Galen leaned into the field and began to wave his arms in the air like an orchestra conductor or magician, altering the calculation. When the field had transformed and stabilized, everyone gathered around the holotable to scrutinize the results.

"That's a fine number," one of the Valltii said.

"An elegant solution," another pronounced.

"Shall we conduct the test now?"

The six of them scattered to their workstations and

instruments, exchanging comments and suggestions as they went about their responsibilities with renewed enthusiasm.

"The boule is in place," Easel reported, referring to the synthetic crystal.

Galen fixed his gaze on the central display screen.

Nurboo cleared his throat. "Test sequence initiated."

Illumination in the control room dimmed briefly as deep below them immense pressure was brought to bear on a massive crystal that had been grown only two months earlier. The synthetic gem had been modeled on an actual kyber, which Zerpen had gone to great lengths and cost to acquire. Relatively rare, the so-called living crystals were almost exclusively the property of the Jedi, who seemed to regard the kyber as sacrosanct. Finger-sized ones powered their lightsabers, and larger ones were rumored to adorn the ornate façades of their isolated temples.

"Results show a piezoelectric effect of point-three above previous," Nurboo said.

The researchers watched Galen, who was shaking his head back and forth.

"No?" Tambo said.

"We should be seeing a much larger increase." Galen firmed his lips and scowled at no one in particular, wrestling with what might have gone wrong. "The unit cell stacking in the synthetic isn't stable enough. We'll have to run a spectrographic autopsy and begin again. The entire batch of boules might be flawed."

It was nothing they hadn't been through countless

times, but disappointment hung in the cool air regardless.

Galen returned to his thinking pose.

"We could try applying more pressure," Easel suggested in the gentlest way. "Perhaps return the crystal to the vapor chamber and introduce a new dopant."

Galen glanced around him, dubious and distracted. He had his mouth open to reply when a short chime issued from the control room comm station.

"Main gate," one of the Valltii said.

Lyra rolled her chair over to the comm suite and watched the monitor. A meter of fresh snow had fallen during the night, and the air still swirled with flurries. The subsurface heaters that usually kept the principal access road clear had malfunctioned, so snow was piled high in windblown drifts from the gate all the way to the facility entrance. Where Lyra expected to see a taqwa-hauled supply sled waiting, the monitor showed a dilapidated military troop carrier. The word *taqwa* translated as "snow-strider," although the approximation provided no hint of the quadrupeds' innate ferocity.

"The troop carrier hails from the Keep," Nurboo said from over her shoulder.

"Iron Gauntlet Legion," Easel added. "The camouflage eddies are distinctive."

Uncertainty furrowed Lyra's brow. The sight of the military vehicle filled her with sudden misgiving. "What would soldiers want at this hour?"

"Another request to provide power for their base?"

Nurboo tried to make light of the situation. "And here I was hoping for a food delivery."

Galen joined them at the comm suite. "Whatever the reason, we'll be our usual courteous and accommodating selves."

"If we must," Tambo said.

Lyra blew out her breath in resignation. "I'll see to it."

She had just begun to rise when Nurboo nimbly placed himself in her path. "You'll do nothing of the sort. You've been spending entirely too much time on your feet."

A second Valltii agreed. "You haven't been resting enough."

Her eyes darted back and forth between them, a tolerant smile tugging at her lips. "Keep your lab coats on, boys, I'm only going down to let them in."

"One of us will go in your place," Nurboo insisted.

"All of a sudden I'm more delicate than one of your ice figurines?"

"And more precious."

Lyra's smile broadened. "That's sweet of you to say, Nurboo, but I already have a mother. Fortunately, she's about twenty parsecs from here, and the last thing I'm going to do is let all of you start falling over yourselves to keep me a prisoner—"

A second chime from the comm suite interrupted her. The main gate attendant's face appeared on the central screen.

"What do the soldiers want, Rooni?" Lyra asked toward the mike.

Rooni said something she couldn't make out, so she swung back to Nurboo and the others. "Will all of you stop your clucking! It's like a henhouse in here." When they fell silent, she turned back to the mike. "Say again, Rooni."

"King Chai is dead," the Valltii said. "Phara now rules the Keep."

"Marshal Phara lacked the military support to overthrow King Chai," Nurboo said, his expression worried. "There must be some mistake."

"Unless she received support from the Separatists," Tambo said.

"The Separatists?" Nurboo tried to make sense of it. "Why would Count Dooku want to wade into Vallt's internal affairs?"

No one spoke for a moment, then Easel looked from Nurboo and Tambo to Galen. "For Galen," Easel said. "The Separatists want his research. Phara must have promised to deliver him into their custody."

Nurboo's eyes widened, and his whiskers stood on end. "It's the only explanation," he told Galen. "Count Dooku wants that big brain of yours."

Galen made his lips a thin line. Close to Lyra's ear, he said: "The war has caught up with us."

Lyra felt the truth of it in her chest. The safe bubble they thought they had created was bursting. For the first time in as long as she could remember she was frightened, not so much for herself or Galen, but for the future she had imagined. "Is it true, Rooni?" she said toward the microphone. "Are the soldiers here for Galen?"

Rooni's big bushy head returned a slow nod. "Marshal Phara has appropriated all extraplanetary concerns. The facility is today the property of Vallt."

"Zerpen will have something to say about that," Galen said.

"Perhaps," Rooni allowed. "But you and Lyra need to leave immediately and let Zerpen Industries deal with Phara."

"You must heed Rooni's advice," Nurboo said. "Phara wouldn't have dispatched a troop carrier unless she means business."

Galen regarded the Valltii for a moment, then shook his head. "Leave here how, exactly?"

"The tunnels," Easel said. "If you go now, you'll have time enough to reach your ship and launch."

Galen gazed around the room in clear dismay, refusing to give ground. All the months of research just to make a start. How could Phara take this away from him? Didn't she realize what Vallt and so many other worlds stood to lose by interrupting his work?

Nurboo drew himself up. "Galen! The two of you are wasting precious time."

Galen nodded with reluctance and turned to the droid. "Assis, you're coming with us."

"I expected no less, Dr. Erso," the droid replied.

Nurboo stepped forward to urge the three of them toward the control room's tunnel access ramp. "Hurry! Trust that we'll do our best to delay the soldiers."

Lyra smirked good-naturedly. "With what, your data styluses? That's almost worth waiting around to see."

Nurboo's blue face fell. "We're as able-bodied as the soldiers, Lyra."

Galen grew serious. "Don't give them any reason

to mistreat you. Remember, it's me they want, not you."

"The troop carrier has cleared the gate," Easel said from the comm suite.

Lyra began to hurry though the control room, hugging everyone goodbye. "Not that I'm going to miss the smell of fried circuitry and stale food," she said when she got to Nurboo.

"Promise you'll comm us," he said. "We expect to see many, many holoimages."

"We'll get this sorted out," Galen said, trying to sound optimistic. "You're not through with us yet."

"Yes, yes," Nurboo said, all but pushing him through the door. "But let's save this discussion for when you're safely on the far side of Vallt's pathetic excuse for a moon."

A compact speeder bobbed at the base of the ramp. The air was much colder, and the din of the underground machinery echoed from the stone walls. The principal tunnel ran from the facility all the way to the starship hangar, with dozens of branches leading to remote outbuildings and subsidiary power stations.

Assis's legs telescoped and it stepped adroitly into the speeder's forward socket. When Galen and Lyra had clambered into the rear bench seat, the droid contracted and wedded itself to the controls.

"All speed, Assis," Galen said, "we've a ship to catch."

Assis's head rotated toward him. "Then hang on, Doctor."

The skimmer shot forward, pinning Galen and Lyra against the cushioned seatback, semicircular illumination arrays lighting portions of the tunnel as the speeder advanced. But they hadn't reached the first fork when the droid brought the vehicle to an abrupt stop.

"What is it, Assis?" Lyra asked.

The droid's head rotated. "There is movement ahead, in both the main tunnel and the power station fork. More than twenty Valltii. All of them on foot."

Galen wasn't surprised. "They're onto us," he said quietly. He glanced around him, focusing on a hatchway in the tunnel wall. "Assis, where are we exactly?"

The droid responded immediately. "Beneath the south station equipment room."

Galen turned to Lyra, holding her gaze. "We need to go the rest of the way on the surface."

Lyra's brows went up. "You're kidding, right? We won't make half a kilometer in that snow."

Galen clamped his hand on the TDK droid's sloping shoulder. "Assis is going to take us."

Assis actually stirred. "I fear that I'll only slow you down, Dr. Erso."

Lyra nodded in sudden understanding. "The twin-tread module."

Galen gave her hand an affectionate squeeze. "Let's hope that everything's where we left it."

Abandoning the speeder, the three of them raced for the hatchway.

The hatch opened on a short flight of metal stairs

that ended in the south station equipment room. Lyra knew precisely where to find the coats, gloves, boots with toe bindings, and long wooden skis. While she tossed clothing to Galen, versatile Assis contracted its limbs and lowered itself atop a pair of continuous tracks adapted for snow travel. Buttoned into a long coat with a fur-lined hood, Galen affixed ropes to projections on the droid's now boxy body.

Lyra raised the door, and the cold walloped them into a brief silence. A blast of wind-driven flurries cycloned around the three of them.

"We'll take it slowly," Galen said while he clipped his boots to the skis.

Lyra shot him a look. "Not you, too. Who tore whose knee on that Chandrila downhill?"

He looked momentarily chastised. "Excuse me for showing concern."

She gave a final tug to one of her gloves and clomped over to him. Linking her arms around his neck, she pulled him close and kissed him firmly on the lips. "You can show as much concern as you want." She eased back, then added, "Just another adventure, right?"

"More of an experiment."

She kissed him again. "I love you."

Lyra pulled the hat down onto her head and cinched the collar of the jacket. Assis moved out into the fresh snow on its treads, the ropes grew taut, and all at once the trio was tearing across the rolling treeless terrain toward the docking bay four kilometers away. Despite the late hour Vallt's primary was a mournful blur moored low on the horizon, its customary location at that time of year in the northern latitudes. The surface snow had melted slightly, and they skied just outside the deep double-track left by Assis's module. The lights of the facility had just disappeared behind them when the first projectile rounds sizzled past. Galen glanced over his shoulder in time to see two groups of Valltii riders converging behind them in close pursuit. A slight shift in the breeze carried the sound of the taqwas' hoofed feet thundering through the snow.

"Assis, we have to beat them to the hangar!" Galen shouted.

"Easy for you to say, Doctor, when it's me they're shooting at!"

Galen grimaced. It was true: With his big brain suddenly up for grabs, Galen Erso was too valuable to harm.

The droid accelerated, Galen and Lyra bent low on their skis behind, the pace and the cold air sending tears streaming down their cheeks. The Valltii riders continued to fire their antique rifles even as they began to fall farther and farther behind. By the time the docking bay came into view Galen, Lyra, and Assis were out of range, but their pursuers were whipping their snow-striders with abandon in an effort to catch up.

Encouraged, Assis called all it could from the tread module, and in moments the hangar dome was looming before them, Zerpen's sinuous logo emblazoned on the curved side.

In the wan light, Galen scanned the final stretch of

snow. "No sign of prints or tracks," he said. "We're going to make it."

Short of the dome, Lyra let go of the rope and hurtled for the main hatch, bringing herself to an expert stop at the exterior control panel. By the time Galen slid to a less elegant standstill, the hatch was up and the interior of the hangar was illuminating. Their small, sleek spacecraft sat silently under spotlights. Unclipping from the skis, they plodded through a thigh-high drift that had formed in front of the hatch.

"Prep the ship," Galen told Lyra in a rush. "I'll get the dome opened."

"Watch out for falling snow."

"And me, Dr. Erso?" Assis asked, the tug ropes still dangling from its torso. "What would you have me do?"

Galen glanced briefly at the approaching riders. "Remain here and secure the entry behind us." He crouched somewhat to address the droid directly. "You have your instructions if this doesn't work."

"I will execute your orders, Dr. Erso."

Galen and Lyra hurried inside—he for the dome controls, she for the ship. Hitting the switch that opened the roof, Galen raced to join Lyra, but neither of them had advanced more than a few meters when a rope net as heavy as a trio of taqwas and just as coarse dropped from somewhere overhead, propelling them into each other and trapping them underneath.

"I'm guessing you didn't figure this into your calculations," Lyra said, struggling to rise to her knees.

Galen tried to extricate his right arm from the leaden mesh, escape and safety just out of reach. Anger raged

in him. The Valltii had engineered the net to fall as
soon as the roof retracted. How could he have failed to
foresee such a crude trap? Or had he deliberately led
them into it? "Looks like we made a bad call."

"Back on Coruscant, you mean."

Assis was reconfiguring itself to lend a literal hand
when the sound of galloping animals and guttural
voices infiltrated the dome. In short order, eight shaggy
big-footed taqwas exhaling breath clouds paraded
through the hatch and began to pick their way carefully around the deployed net. Bearing the brand of
Marshal Phara on their rumps, they had long necks,
sharp teeth, and doleful eyes. The riders were thickset
males dressed in boiled-leather long coats and hide
boots, the cheeks above their thick beards polished by
Vallt's blizzards to a cerulean sheen. One of them dismounted from a wooden saddle and doffed a wool
cap as he approached Galen.

"Thank you for not disappointing us, Dr. Erso,"
he said in the indigenous tongue.

Galen gave up on freeing his arm and allowed himself to sag to the hangar's cold hard floor. "Good job
covering your tracks."

The black-eyed rider went down on one knee in
front of him. Small blood-red beads were braided
into his iced whiskers, and he smelled of smoke and
rancid butter tea. "We strung the net two days ago.
Last night's snowfall favored our plans. But don't feel
too bad, you would never have reached here by way
of the tunnels, either."

"So we learned."

"I am an innocent party to all this!" Assis said

from just inside the hatch, back to bipedal mode and displaying two short arms. "I was pressed into service and had no choice but to follow orders!"

Without standing, the rider turned to his cohorts. "Muzzle that droid."

Two riders dismounted to carry out the command.

Galen heard the sound of a restraining bolt being hammered into the droid's torso. "Lyra's the innocent party," he snapped. "Get her out from beneath this thing."

The same riders who had silenced Assis lifted a corner of the weighty mesh and helped Lyra to her feet, but made no move to free Galen.

"You are under arrest by order of Marshal Phara," the lead rider told him.

"On what charge, exactly?"

"Espionage. Among others."

Galen looked him in the eye. "Two weeks ago you and I sipped tea together, and now you're arresting me."

"Things change, Dr. Erso. My orders were to capture you. Marshal Phara will decide your guilt or innocence." He stood and faced one of the mounted soldiers. "Ride to the facility and send the troop carrier to deliver Dr. Erso to Tambolor prison."

2

ISOLATION

TWO GUARDS IN BRISTLY JACKETS and bulky fur caps led Galen from the stone-walled cell into a room with plaster walls and a high arched ceiling. Sapwood crackled in the mouth of a large fireplace, and oily smoke from torches set in wall sconces lazed in the air. Behind a large scarred desk sat a sturdy woman wearing a belted brown uniform. Her hair was parted in the middle, slicked down with what might have been lard, and fell in two precise braids linked and entwined with colored yarn. Argent rings adorned her fat blue fingers, and her nose was pierced by a small blood-red stud. Her eyes were a shiny black, enlivened by the wad of stimulant berries she had packed in one glossy cheek. She motioned him to the rickety chair that faced the desk.

Galen extended his free hands to her. "Are you certain you don't want to shackle me?"

Her grin revealed large dark-stained teeth. "I don't think you can do much harm in here, Dr. Erso," she said in the local tongue. "Unless of course the Republic implanted you with some sort of secret weapon."

He lowered himself onto the chair. They had kept him on ice for two local weeks, though he had been permitted a brief visit with Nurboo. His friend had promised to try to convey a handwritten message to Lyra, wherever she was being held.

"You have some odd notions regarding the Republic's capability."

She spread her hands in a kind of shrug. "The tragedy of living on the Outer Rim, Doctor." She paused, then said: "I am Chieftain Gruppe. Have you been comfortable? Is there anything you need?"

Galen rubbed the growth that covered his cheeks and chin. "A razor. A hot bath. An extra blanket."

"I'll see to it that you receive them." She turned to one side to spit a stream of black fluid into a pot on the floor.

"I thought Vallt had laws against false arrest, Chieftain."

"New constitution," Gruppe said in an offhand way. "Essentially we're free to do just about anything we wish—anytime, anywhere, and to anyone."

"I'm certain you'll be a wealthy landowner before you know it."

"An ancillary benefit, to be sure."

Galen gazed up at the leaky ceiling and water-stained walls. "You could patch those leaks with a bit of permacrete."

She turned slightly in the chair to follow his gaze. "No one informed me that you are a stone setter in addition to being an energy researcher, Doctor."

Galen gave vent to his anger. "Where is Lyra, Chieftain? What have you done with her?"

She smiled tightly. "In safekeeping. Resting comfortably."

"When will I be allowed to see her?"

Gruppe leaned back in the chair. "That depends entirely on you."

His expression hardened. "Perhaps you don't understand—"

"I understand completely, Doctor. How many of your months remain before the child is due?"

"Approximately two—unless you've placed her in danger."

She waved in dismissal. "The child is yours?"

"Of course the child is mine."

"I ask only because it is my understanding that the human women of Coruscant no longer carry or deliver their own progeny—that they hire others to do that for them."

"Not on the Coruscant I know."

"You're not one who dwells in the clouds then?"

"Lyra and I have a small apartment on the campus of one of the universities."

Gruppe considered this. "An individual of your standing?"

"I demand to be with Lyra for the birth, Chieftain," he said with force.

"And you will be, Doctor. We're not barbarians, after all." She gazed at him for a long moment. "We've met, you know. Three months back at the ball King Chai threw when he welcomed Zerpen to Vallt."

"You'll excuse me if I choose not to remember."

Her brows knitted. She turned to loose another stream of liquid into the pot and wiped her mouth on the sleeve of her drab uniform. "I'm sure you must feel like one of the rodents you use in your experiments—"

"I don't use animals in my research."

"Be that as it may, you've no need to remain here. The length of your confinement is completely in your hands. You could walk out of here today and return to the company of your wife."

Galen smiled without mirth. "And all I need to do is confess to being a spy for the Republic and agree to swear my allegiance to the Separatists." He shook his head. "I'm sorry, Chieftain, but I'm merely a researcher in the employ of Zerpen Industries. I don't work for the Republic, and I'm certainly not about to work for Count Dooku."

"Science doesn't take sides, is that it?"

"Well put."

"With galactic affairs as they are, there's little profit to being neutral, Doctor."

Galen tilted his head to regard her frankly. "I can only wonder what Count Dooku offered Vallt's new leadership. Perhaps he promised to tug this world a bit closer to your star."

Gruppe's shoulders heaved. "Trade, respect, fair representation in the Confederacy. All that we weren't receiving as a member world of the Republic."

"It's all bluster, Chieftain. Like the winds here. You'd be better off going about your business without aligning yourselves with either side. Take that to Marshal Phara."

"To what end, Doctor? To continue lives of leaky roofs, cold beds, and rancid tea? Perhaps you think we don't yearn for the things readily available to the Core and Mid Rim worlds. Or is it that you prefer to keep Vallt primitive and secluded? A museum exhibit for Coruscant's elite tourists."

"And if the Separatists lose this war? What happens to Vallt then?"

"For a man who claims not to take sides you seem to have a fixation on winners and losers."

"I don't care one way or the other. But you're mistaken to believe that Vallt will profit when this war has run its course." He paused, then said: "How do you think Zerpen will respond when they learn that you've seized their facility? They've invested a lot of time and credits in Vallt."

"We anticipate that they will be eager to renegotiate the terms of the original contract."

"And I'm expected to be a bargaining chip in this renegotiation."

"Something to that effect, yes." She fell briefly silent, then said: "What can you tell me about the Republic military?"

"Not a blessed thing, thankfully."

"Where did the clone army originate?"

Galen stared at her and laughed. "Who do you take me for?"

"How long have Chancellor Palpatine and the Jedi Order been planning this war?"

"You're wasting your time, Chieftain. You'll have to ask them."

Gruppe leaned over to spit, then inserted a large purple berry into the cud in her cheek. "By all accounts your research has been very productive."

"We're making progress."

"In energy enrichment."

"Thanks to Vallt's abundance of natural resources and what was King Chai's generosity, yes."

"I'm told that you are actually growing crystals."

"Yes," Galen replied. "It's a complicated process, but if we can succeed in growing crystals that yield results, we may be able to supply inexpensive power to developing worlds."

"Like Vallt."

"Like Vallt."

"Isn't it true, though, that energy can be employed in many ways? In the same way it can provide illumination for a city, it can be used to power weapons of mass destruction."

"If I thought that Zerpen was engaging in weapons research, I wouldn't be working with them."

"Truly?" She mulled it over. "You have many friends here who say that we should simply banish you or turn you over to your superiors at Zerpen. But in fact, Doctor, you're too valuable to be returned; especially now, in light of these accusations of espionage. You might be inclined to rescind your neutrality and lend your notable talents to the Republic. You see the dilemma in which we find ourselves."

"Obviously I've failed to make myself understood, Chieftain."

"Perhaps. But time is hardly a precious commodity on Vallt, so we don't mind wasting it, as you so colorfully put it. Time enough for an inquest, followed by a trial before the Tribunal. And all the while away from your wife. I can certainly appreciate your position, but I would have thought you would want a better life for your child." She paused to blow out her breath. "Well, Marshal Phara is taking the matter under advisement. Should your innocence be established you will of course be permitted to leave Vallt."

Galen shook his head in elaborate disappointment. "There's a test we run at the ignition facility. We subject certain crystals to intense pressure in order to entice them to produce a kind of electrical current. Conversely, those same crystals can be made to shrink in size when excited by an external current. I'm trying to determine which of the tests I'm being subjected to just now."

Gruppe's eyes clouded over; then she smiled with what struck Galen as genuine warmth. "You're an odd sort of being, Dr. Erso."

"You're not the first to make that observation, Chieftain."

"You seem to take pride in being stubborn."

"I only know one way to be."

Gruppe took a deep breath. "It must be difficult to live with."

He tried to read her. "Having principles?"

"No." She tapped the side of her head, clearly indicating Galen's. "All that deep thinking."

Lyra's hands were shaking as she unfolded the letter Nurboo had delivered. Handwritten on parchment of the sort the Valltii used, the message filled both sides of the stiff sheet. The wide margins on one side were crammed with drawings of faces and figures, interspersed with fragments of equations, as if Galen was multitasking—one part of him writing to her while another part sought to solve some calculation spinning through his head. She had to turn the sheet ninety degrees each way and upside down to decipher some of the jottings. The reverse side was covered top-to-bottom and edge-to-edge with Galen's near-microscopic scrawl. His handwriting was almost as indecipherable as his theories about crystals and their potential to provide inexpensive power, but years of transcribing Galen's personal notes had allowed her to interpret both.

The letter began:

> I have learned—from Chieftain Gruppe, who has interrogated me on three separate occasions so far—that you are, in her words, "in safekeeping" in the northern wing of the Keep. As luck would have it, I can see a bit of that architectural monstrosity from the small crazed window in my room—my cell, really—though I have to perch myself precariously on a three-legged stool I set upon the hard slab of my sleeping platform, and what with the pale winter light I'm left staring directly into the smudge of Vallt's distant primary. Even so I try to imagine the room you inhabit and hope that you have reason from time to time to peer across the city at Tambolor, your gaze alighting on my candlelit cubicle.

In fact she hadn't done that because she hadn't known where he was being kept. But now that she did she eased herself out of the plush chair at the foot of the broad bed and moved slowly to the bay window, one hand supporting her ever-expanding belly. Wiping frost from the bubbled glass, she peered out across the courtyard and across the blockish hand-built city beyond. Central to the courtyard sat an enormous statue of a taqwa rider dressed in cape and helmet, with a war club raised in his right hand. High above, a dozen broad-winged fliers were wheeling in the monochrome sky. In the city, a few Valltii could be glimpsed going about their business: a scattering of beast-drawn sleds maneuvering through the city's maze of frost-heaved lanes. The imposing prison sat on a tableland far to the east and resembled the Keep in many ways, as it had served as the palace in a bygone era. Lights flickered in some of Tambolor's lower-story windows, but the upper stories, all the way to the exaggerated roof—too steep even for snow to accumulate for very long—loomed black as night. Which level, which cell? she wondered. Why hadn't Galen provided her with an appointed time to look, so that he could wave a candle in his window and she would know where he was and that he was all right?

She lowered herself onto the soft cushion of the bay's window seat and as she did the baby stirred and either kicked or elbowed her, which made her smile and wish all the more that Galen was with her so she could press his hand against her abdomen to feel the life within. One of her handmaidens was a midwife, and she was excited by the prospect of witnessing and assisting in a human birth. Giddy as children and loyal to Phara only when the marshal's henchmen were within earshot, the handmaidens were as eager to meet Galen as Lyra was to hug him to her.

Lifting the message into the meager light, she continued reading.

> As prison cells go mine isn't too bad. It's remarkable what the Valltii can do with stone, and this room, this entire building really, is about as impressive an example of worked stone as I've seen anywhere on- or offworld. The walls are a meter thick, the high ceiling a flawless geometry of ovoid arches, the massive columns left raw and unadorned, as if to call attention to the skill of the masons who raised them. The corridors are filled with the incessant sound of hand chisels at work.
>
> There are, of course, the bars that seal me inside, the dim light, the odors, and the daytime chutes of snowmelt running down the walls from the sloping roof. When the temperature plunges at night I can almost ice-skate across the tiled floor. I have, though, discovered some interesting patterns and faces in the growths of algae and moss, even in the arrangement of the unhewn stones, some of which I include here for your amusement. Plus I have been running all make and manner of calculations in my head. The strict routine of toilet

breaks and meals of starchy root crops is allowing me to make a lot of headway.

But enough about me and my predicament.

Chieftain Gruppe has also assured me that you are being treated well, but how can I know for sure? Nurboo, when he visited to collect this missive, said that he hadn't been able to ascertain anything about your living conditions or, more important, the state of your health. Your remark about that downhill trip on Chandrila stirred many recollections of that expedition, and how crucial your knowledge of the wilderness was to our survival. Can you recall the interior of that cave as lucidly as I can—the stalactites, the drip water, the extraordinary view over the glacier? We have had some times, haven't we; some amazing experiences. Adventures! And just as we've always managed to get out of tight spots, we'll get out of this one. We just need to hold out and trust.

Once more she raised her eyes from the sheet as memories tugged her from the present. It was so like Galen to go off on tangents. In his usual fashion, he was deliberately misremembering. He'd had as much to do with ensuring their survival as she had. Even with a torn knee he had stoked the fire, helped prepare their meals, melt snow for cooking. He was forever underselling himself, downplaying his innate strength and power. She recalled the first time she'd set eyes on him on Espinar, thinking: *If this guy was any more magnetic, pieces of metal would fly across the room and start sticking to him . . .*

She went back to reading.

> I take full responsibility for this imbroglio—unlike Chandrila, which really wasn't my fault. (I will also lay the blame on those cheap bindings.) You were reluctant to come to Vallt and in retrospect I should have listened to you. It was only a matter of time before Vallt aligned itself with the Separatists, and I should have seen that coming. Well, perhaps I did and simply refused to acknowledge it. For the research, of course, and—you have to admit—we have forged some lasting friendships these past months. Then there is the crystal research itself, and the discoveries the team has made. We're onto something big with this last batch of kyber synthetics; I can feel it. There's no telling at this point what the limits are: power enough to supply enriched and renewable energy for entire continents, certainly. Perhaps for entire worlds. I do ache to get back to the facility to continue the work. Research is the only thing I'm good at, and I'm determined to provide for you and our child. I lament that that seems a long shot just now.
>
> But enough about me again!

What I really ache to do is hold you, and I will do whatever I must to be with you when you deliver our child. Chieftain Gruppe has said over and over that I hold the key to our freedom. It is contingent merely on my agreeing to work for the Separatists rather than for Zerpen. All these false charges of espionage will be dropped, and we can go back to living as we were just weeks ago. And this is where I have to ask you: Should I simply accept their terms? I will do it—for your sake, for the sake of our unborn daughter. You need only say the word. Take solace in the fact that my mind remains free—to dwell on you from afar. Until we are together once more. All my love.

She frowned as she set the letter down alongside her on the cushion. He knew full well that she would never tell him to act against his principles. But where it might strike some as a kind of ploy—a shifting of the responsibility for his decision onto her to keep himself from being held accountable—she understood that he meant every word of it. She picked the sheet up to reread, her eyes brimming with tears by the time she reached the end. As painful as it was to read, the letter had been the first she had received from him in years and she cherished it.

* * *

Assis came to with a start.

Its optical sensors registered that a Valltii soldier with long and bejeweled mustachios had removed the restraining bolt a different soldier had installed . . . 27 local days, 18 divisions, and 6.23 fragments earlier.

It was still just inside the entrance of the domed docking bay in which Dr. Erso and Lyra had been netted. A Zerpen spacecraft rested on a sheen of ice that had formed since their capture. Several soldiers were circling the craft at the moment, their breathing forming small clouds in the frigid air. One was clearly aware of the sounds of Assis's restart and self-diagnostic, but was paying it no mind. Assis's alloy extremities were rendered slightly brittle by the cold. Its relays and conductors were slow to warm.

As per Dr. Erso's programmed commands, the TDK-160's sensors reached out in search of devices with which it could communicate. It found the spacecraft's hypercomm transceiver and entered into a jaunty dialogue with it.

While the two machines spoke, Assis's intelligence ran through various scenarios regarding its fate once the Valltii determined that it had executed Dr. Erso's task. One scenario had it undergoing a full memory wipe and rebuild; another, a full dismantle and recycling; a third, commendation by those it served and to whom it belonged.

A relationship with the craft's hyperspace communications suite established, Assis relayed audio and visual data regarding Dr. Erso's arrest and the com-

mandeering of the research facility by soldiers loyal
to Vallt's new government, which the transceiver in
turn relayed to the appropriate parties in a burst
broadcast.

All of this occurred in the blink of an eye.

3

SECRET WEAPONS

ON A WORLD AS POPULOUS as Coruscant where the guest list for an invitation-only event could run to the tens of thousands, the mixed-species gathering of 150 beings taking place in the Strategic Planning Amphitheater at the summit of the Republic Center for Military Operations raised the definition of *exclusive* to new heights. Not a standard year earlier, before the start of the war and the Republic's still-astonishing acquisition of a Grand Army of clone soldiers, the very notion of a Strategic Advisory Cell would have been viewed as just another ruse by members of the Senate to fatten themselves on the rich drippings of the bloated Republic coffers. Now, in light of intelligence regarding the state of the Separatist war machine, the committee was seen—certainly by the assembled insiders—as crucial to Republic efforts to counter and defeat the Confederacy of Independent Systems.

Lieutenant Commander Orson Krennic, the person largely responsible for remodeling and expanding the building, was seated halfway between the amphithe-

ater's rounded stage and the tiered balconies reserved
for a few select senators and representatives of the
industrial cartels that had remained loyal to the Republic: Corellian Engineering, Kuat Drive Yards, Ren-
dili StarDrive, and the like. Just turned thirty, Krennic
was of average height, with bright-blue eyes, narrow
lips, and wavy light-brown hair. Recently transferred
from the Corps of Engineers to the cell's Special
Weapons Group, he wore the same white tunic affected by some members of the intelligence and security services.

Seating in the room hadn't been assigned by rank,
species, or order of importance, but Krennic was determined to move himself closer to the wings of the
stage where Supreme Chancellor Palpatine's right-
hand man, Mas Amedda, sat with several of his gaud-
ily attired key advisers in front of a curved windowwall
that looked out on the southern sprawl of Coruscant's
Senate District. In the months since the weekly briefings had begun, Krennic had managed to advance ten
rows toward his goal, and was confident of reaching
it by the first anniversary of the Battle of Geonosis.

The room contained as many uniforms as not.
Seated to Krennic's left was the chief of naval intelligence and to his right the director of COMPOR—the
Commission for the Protection of the Republic. Elsewhere were high-ranking members of the military,
structural engineers, starship designers, and theoretical and experimental physicists. Many of them were
near- or nonhuman—a handful of the latter immersed
in tanks of liquid or wearing transpirators that supplied the atmospheric gases native to their homeworlds.

Krennic knew some of the scientists as associates on the War Production Board, others merely by reputation.

As the room began to quiet, he leaned slightly to one side to gaze between two ruddy, small-horned heads at the thin-limbed alien scientist who was speaking from the front row.

"Vice Chancellor Amedda and esteemed colleagues, I am pleased to announce that phase one of the project has been completed."

A male Parwan, Dr. Gubacher was a specialist in artificial intelligence who worked closely with the Jedi in designing surveillance and espionage droids. Pressed to the apparent voice box of Gubacher's dome-shaped head was a device that rendered his sibilant utterings in fluent Basic.

"If you'll direct your attention to the holoprojector . . ."

Most did; others enabled small devices built into the armrests of many of the chairs that replicated the 3-D data issuing from the massive center stage unit. Personal comlinks were not permitted in the amphitheater, and even the projectors were quarantined from the HoloNet.

A gleaming metallic ring hung above the stage, motionless against a backdrop of stars.

Gubacher raised himself on tentacle legs to regard the ring for a moment, then twirled to face the control booth in the amphitheater's uppermost tier. "Please provide the alternative view." He waited for the ring to become vertical in the field. "Ah, that's better. Now please expand the field so that the ring can be viewed in context."

As the ring diminished in size, warships, construction vessels, asteroids, and the starlit rim of a desolate-looking planet began to appear in the field.

Gubacher gestured to the ring. "One hundred and twenty kilometers from pole to pole. In itself, an incredible achievement."

Applause erupted in the amphitheater, and even Mas Amedda proffered a gratified smile. Having spent time at the construction site, Krennic felt that the holovid didn't do justice to the work in progress above the planet Geonosis. But the holo would have to suffice, since few members in the amphitheater had been allowed to visit the project. The wedge-shaped *Venator*-class Star Destroyers on view, as well as many others scattered through the Geonosian system, were there to deny entry to any unauthorized visitors.

"What you see is the product of countless hours of construction work undertaken by machines," Gubacher continued, "most of which are newly designed, and some of which are controlled by sentient operators stationed in our orbital command habitats, as can be seen"—he indicated three bright specks in the holofield—"here, here, and here." Turning to the control booth, he said: "Please project aspect two."

Murmurings and their analogs in a variety of languages issued from the audience while the field disappeared. In its place resolved a panorama of the red planet's asteroid belt, replete with construction vessels of all classifications—miners, transports, tenders, tugs—coming and going like a swarm of vespids building a nest.

"Our quarry, if you will," the Parwan said, "sup-

plying us with metals, organic materials, even supplies of water. Similarly viable asteroids have been
towed and tractor-beamed to the site from throughout the field, and in some instances from fields surrounding the star system's gas giants."

The holovid shifted again to display a view of
massive orbital platforms, busy with ship traffic.

"Once the ores are mined," Gubacher went on,
"they are hauled to foundries in synchronous orbit
for the production of durasteel and other structural
metals. By cannibalizing the battle droid factories
Baktoid Armor built on the surface, we were able to
have the foundries up and running soon after the start
of asteroid mining." Once more he signaled the control booth. "Please project the original schematic."

A sphere with a massive northern hemisphere con-
cavity appeared above the holoprojector.

"Our goal," Gubacher said, "the mobile battle station."

It was Supreme Chancellor Palpatine himself who
had presented the schematic to the Strategic Advisory
Cell at the second briefing. But in fact the battle station wasn't a product of Republic research and development; it had originated with the Separatists. The
captive Geonosian leader, Poggle the Lesser, maintained that Count Dooku had provided Poggle's hive
with the basic plans, and that the Geonosians had
merely refined them. To the best of Poggle's knowledge, the Separatists had no project of their own in
the works. However, most cell members had refused
to take the Geonosian at his word. Intelligence had
high confidence that Dooku's forces, in league with

various corporations allied to the Confederacy, were in the process of constructing a battle station somewhere in the galaxy, and an extensive search was under way to locate and destroy that secret site. Krennic considered the evidence specious, but rejecting the possibility out of hand would have jeopardized Republic funding for the project, regardless of the authority that had been ceded to Palpatine by the Emergency Powers Act. If the battle station was as potentially potent as scientists had determined it to be, then it was vital that the Republic get theirs built first.

There were lingering questions as to how the original schematic had fallen into Republic hands, though most accepted that the plans had been found during or shortly after the second Battle of Geonosis—not however by the Jedi, who were neither represented on the committee nor aware of the project. Even Gubacher had been required to sign the Official Secrets Act and was going to have to keep his slit-mouth shut when dealing with members of the Order.

"With our prime meridian now complete," the alien scientist was saying, "we can proceed with the fabrication of a temporary equator, along with a series of latitudinal bands to rough in the sphere. As these bands are secured from pole to equator, construction of the hull will commence, along with the partitioning of individual interior sections. These cabinspaces will be clad, sealed, and pressured in order to permit the use of sentient laborers in addition to droids."

"Where will this sentient labor force come from?" someone down front asked.

Gubacher pirouetted toward the voice. "Various options are being explored."

"I've seen workforce estimates ranging in the millions," the same person said.

An alien seated a few rows in front of Krennic spoke before Gubacher could respond. "The cell subcommittee is considering providing the Kaminoans with a template to grow a labor force of clones adapted for deep-space work."

Before anyone else could jump in, all two meters of Mas Amedda rose to his feet, banging his figure-headed staff on the floor in a call for silence. "I want to caution everyone present not to get ahead of themselves. An adequate supply of workers will be found when the need arises."

Krennic focused his gaze on the splendidly robed Chagrian vice chancellor, who had his pink-rimmed eyes narrowed and his large head angled so that his two impaling horns were pointed straight at the audience.

He steeples his fingers when he has doubts about what is being presented. His dangling lethorns quiver when he is engaged. His forked tongue darts out when he equivocates . . .

Gubacher called for holoimages of a Trade Federation starship to be displayed alongside the schematic. Republic engineers had postulated that the battle station had been inspired by the central control orb of the decades-old *Lucrehulk*-class transport.

"Imagine, if you will, the twin arms of the Lucrehulk as the eventual equator of our battle station. Save that ours will be a kind of trench in which will be housed docking and hangar bays, tractor beam generators, projectors and emitter towers, turbolaser emplacements, and mooring platforms for ships of the fleet. Shield projectors and communications arrays will be distributed all across the armored surface, analogous to colonies. This will allow us to devote the entire interior space—except for a habitable crust several kilometers thick comprising command centers, armories, maintenance blocks, and such—to the fusion reactor, the hyperdrive and sublight engines, and of course the weapon itself."

Krennic watched Amedda, whose long-taloned fingers caressed his chin as he began to circle the projected images, which were more than twice his substantial height.

"What is the status of the weapon?" the Chagrian asked.

Gubacher swiveled to someone seated nearby and motioned with his willowy upper limbs. "Professor Sahali, perhaps you should speak to that."

Lead scientist of the Special Weapons Group, the man who stood to tackle the question was nearly as wide as he was tall, and sported a floppy hat and a pair of goggle-like glasses.

"As regards the weapon," he began in a thick Outer Rim accent, "even the schematic is vague. We suspect, however, that the Geonosians envisioned making some use of the focusing dish to house a weapon capable of evaporating planetary atmospheres, or perhaps disrupting planetary cores."

"Does such a weapon exist?" Amedda asked, stopping to look down at Sahali. "Is it even within our scope to create one?"

"Since the very inception of the Republic there has been no need for such research," Sahali made clear, "let alone funding. That said, following the Naboo Crisis of just eleven years ago, Republic Special Weapons Group developed plans for an automated battle-moon asteroid."

"I believe there were also plans for a torpedo siege platform," someone said.

Sahali acknowledged the remark with a curt nod. "Needless to say, Vice Chancellor, neither of the projects made it past the design stage."

"I should think that those were mere toys compared with this," Amedda said, gesturing to the battle station schematic.

"Quite so," Sahali said.

"The weapon will prove to be our greatest challenge," Gubacher said. "The hypermatter reactor, the drives, all the rest, are merely elaborations of the armaments our finest engineering firms have been able to provide to Star Destroyers and other vessels. But the weapon . . . the weapon won't merely be a larger version of the turbolaser. It will be something that has yet to be seen."

Amedda turned to him. "How long will it take to develop this . . . marvel of technology? I need an estimate."

Gubacher's dome of a head rolled in uncertainty. "Very difficult to say. Many of the greatest minds in the Republic are working on it. Nevertheless, the weapon will require something truly novel in the realm of energy enhancement. A breakthrough of, dare I say, galactic proportions."

Krennic sat back in confident repose, convinced that fate had supplied the means for him to move to the front row.

"Let's not stand on ceremony, Lieutenant Commander," Mas Amedda said, welcoming Krennic at long last into his spacious office in the Senate Dome. "Please be seated."

Krennic assessed the room and took the best seat. "Thank you, Vice Chancellor."

"I apologize that I've not been able to meet with you sooner."

Krennic replied with a dismissive flick of his hand. "I know you've been busy. The war and all . . ."

He'll steeple his claws.

Amedda steepled his long fingers and appraised Krennic from across the expanse of alloy desk. "My aides tell me that your visit has something to do with the project."

Krennic fed him a beaming smile. "Everything to do with the project."

"Which component—precisely?"

"The weapon."

The Chagrian's bulbous lethorns didn't disappoint; they quivered, which suggested engagement. "Well, then, I'm very sorry I couldn't meet with you sooner."

Krennic had never spent personal time with the vice chancellor. They had been in many a room together, and Krennic had observed him out and about, at the opera before the war and in the Senate Building and elsewhere on numerous occasions. Krennic's invitation—in effect his orders—to join the Strategic Advisory Cell had originated with Amedda, though Krennic doubted that the Chagrian had any memory, or perhaps even any knowledge, of that.

Ever since he had been transferred from the Corp of Engineers and required to swear to innumerable security oaths, Krennic's life had been transformed. He naturally assumed that his personal comlink was tapped; that his close friends, remaining family members, and past and present lovers had been interviewed; that his every search on the HoloNet was monitored and evaluated. Though he wore a white tunic, publicly he was still a member of the Corps of Engineers; only his associates in the cell were aware of his duties as coordinator of the Special Weapons Group. The new assignment had also required a return to school to suffer through intensive courses on the weapons Rothana, Kuat, and others had built for the Kaminoans to equip the Grand Army, and on the weapons Baktoid, Hoersch-Kessel Drive, and others were engineering and producing for the Separatists. On graduating he had supervised a brain trust of research experts who reported directly to the upper echelon of the Republic military. As vice chancellor, Mas Amedda didn't have any real authority over him, but Krennic thought it useful to pretend that he did, if only to establish their relative standing.

"If this concerns the weapon," Amedda was saying, "you should have spoken up at the briefing."

Krennic nodded. "Perhaps I should have, but I felt that this matter is better discussed privately."

A slight tremor shook Amedda's dangling lethorns. "Well, here we are."

Krennic plunged in. "Dr. Gubacher was right to say that many of the finest minds in the Republic are working on developing the battle station's principal weapon—all except one."

The tremor in Amedda's fleshy growths grew more sustained.

"His name is Galen Erso."

Amedda pressed his claws together. "Erso. Should I be familiar with him?"

"You can't be expected to know everyone."

"My sphere is politics, after all, not science and technology."

In fact, Amedda's sphere was overseeing the Republic slush fund and placating Palpatine, Krennic told himself. But if the Chagrian wanted to play, he was game.

"Galen Erso is one of the Core's most renowned polymaths. A theoretician, a mathematician, an engineer and experimental physicist. At present he is the preeminent authority on crystals and their use in supplying enhanced power."

Amedda showed him a blank look. "Crystals?"

Krennic nodded. "For the past ten years he has been experimenting with many types. But his recent research has focused on the kyber crystal."

Amedda's expression didn't change. "I have a passing familiarity. My understanding is that kybers are exceedingly uncommon."

"They are—especially large ones." Krennic sighed dramatically. "If the Jedi Order could be persuaded to share information, things might be different."

He'll show the tip of his forked tongue.

Amedda wet his lips. "These kyber crystals are important to the Jedi?"

"Among other uses, the crystals power their light-sabers."

"Well, no wonder then. The exclusivity must frustrate this Galen Erso to no end."

"That's exactly why he has been attempting to synthesize them."

Amedda's ice-blue eyes widened. "That seems a bold enterprise. I have heard the kyber described as a living crystal."

"I've heard the same."

"But what makes you think that Erso's research would have some bearing on the battle station weapon?"

Krennic took a breath. "I'll confess that I'm not acquainted with the state of his current research. But Special Weapons has evaluated his earlier research, and there are indications that Erso's theories could lead to a new direction in energy enrichment. We're studying ways to adapt the research."

"To weaponize it, you mean."

"More accurately. However, we need a complete understanding of his work—not to mention access to his current research on synthesis."

Amedda took a moment to parse it. "How is it that you know Erso, Lieutenant Commander?"

"We became friends on Brentaal as students in the Futures Program."

Amedda offered a tell that reeked of skepticism.

"You were in the gifted program?"

Krennic let the slight slide. "For a period of time— before being offered a position in the design regiment of the Corps of Engineers."

"Ah, yes," Amedda said, sinking back into his big chair. "If memory serves, your team is responsible for many of Coruscant's military headquarters." He fell silent, then said: "Do you believe that the Separatists are working on a battle station?"

Krennic rocked his head. "Dooku has left plenty of clues to that effect—massive procurements of certain rare resources, computer intrusions to acquire scientific data that have since been redacted and quarantined—including much of Galen Erso's published research."

Amedda thought about it. "Why wasn't Erso approached to join the cell when it was inaugurated?"

"At the time he was already under contract to work for Zerpen Industries."

Amedda glowered. "Neutralists—and yet profiting from both sides of this contest." He waved the issue away. "Then we simply need to induce Erso to break his contract."

"Unfortunately, we learned recently that Dr. Erso is languishing in a prison on Vallt."

Amedda's anger returned. "Why of all worlds is he on Vallt? You realize that Vallt has gone over to the Separatists?"

"I do. But Vallt was a Republic member world

when Dr. Erso agreed to oversee Zerpen's onworld facility. A deal was cut with Vallt's former leadership that allowed for mining and construction in return for a very generous aid package."

"A poor choice regardless," Amedda said. "Why was he arrested?"

"Trumped-up charges of espionage."

"Perhaps to compel him to change allegiances?"

"As we see it."

Amedda gave his head a somber shake. "Vallt teetered on the edge for a decade. As former chair of the Senate, I served on a committee with Vallt's representatives, and even then they were a disaffected group, complaining about being ignored by the Republic. And now the military has staged a coup and affiliated itself with the Separatists." He paused to regard Krennic. "How did Zerpen react to Erso's arrest?"

"Republic Intelligence has of course been monitoring Zerpen. Several standard weeks ago, a burst transmission was intercepted, sent apparently by hypercomm from a Zerpen ship on Vallt to the company headquarters in the Salient system, alerting them to the seizure of the facility and the arrest of Dr. Erso."

"What was their response?"

"Zerpen planned to take action, but we've asked them to stand down from making any overtures."

"Who is *we* in this instance?"

Krennic smiled lightly. "I took it upon myself, Vice Chancellor."

Amedda interlocked his fingers and leaned forward, lowering his horns. "For what purpose, Lieutenant Commander?"

Krennic took the menacing posture in stride. "It's my belief that a rescue by us will go a long way toward persuading Dr. Erso to share his research with the Special Weapons Group."

Amedda retreated somewhat. "Why does he need to be persuaded? You said yourself that he was in the Republic Futures Program. He should be more than willing to comply and cooperate."

"Except that he's something of a pacifist. A conscientious objector, if you will."

Amedda blew out his breath in disdain. "If that's true, then we needn't worry about him serving the Separatists. Let him rot in prison."

The Chagrian's change in posture told Krennic that he was in danger of losing Amedda unless he acted quickly, so he altered his approach.

"Under normal circumstances I would agree. However, the one sticking point is that Dr. Erso's wife was pregnant when they left for Vallt, and unless something untoward has happened, she is close to delivering the baby by now."

Amedda took a moment to respond; his lethorns stirring slightly. "Are you suggesting that those in charge on Vallt might use Erso's wife and child as methods of persuasion?"

"We are at war, Vice Chancellor. Anything's possible. And if the Separatists are indeed working on a battle station . . ."

Amedda nodded slowly in understanding. "I see what you're getting at. Still, I'm prone to let this lie—or perhaps allow Zerpen to take the lead on freeing Erso."

"Again, I'm inclined to agree. But I've an idea for having it both ways."

Amedda's lethorns quivered, and he regarded Krennic with intensity. "Somehow I expected you might. But I don't want the details, Lieutenant Commander. And I insist that you take care to distance yourself to ensure full deniability."

"Naturally."

"If in the end Erso's research moves us closer to engineering a weapon for the battle station, then you will have not only my gratitude, but also that of Supreme Chancellor Palpatine and the Republic itself."

Krennic restrained a smile. "We all play our part, Vice Chancellor."

4

BEGINNINGS

THE BABY'S FIRST CRIES ECHOED off the high walls of Lyra's chamber. As was customary on Vallt, a birth within the walls of the Keep was regarded as a cause for jubilation—more so in that the birth of the human child coincided with the first day of the spring season. From the courtyard below, rocket bombs were launched into the night and a small crowd that had learned of the birth and braved the arctic temperatures was celebrating, gathered around fires and stalls selling skewers of grilled meats and root vegetables, with many of the men seated on low benches quaffing glasses of strong homebrewed alcoholic drinks.

Jyn, as Galen and Lyra had named her, had been placed on her mother's still-heaving chest by one of the midwives, to be soothed by her warmth and familiar heartbeat.

It had been a long labor, but not especially difficult, and Lyra had been a champ throughout, even when she was snarling at anyone close by. Pale and drenched in sweat after all the hours, she nevertheless seemed to be in better shape than Galen, who was still processing the experience.

He asked himself: Was there actually some benefit to having been captured? Just about anywhere else, he and Lyra would have been surrounded by well-meaning but all-business droids in an environment so sterile as to be lifeless.

Was it bizarre to feel *gratitude*?

Lighter by a couple of kilos and as fully bearded as most of the Valltii—in a transparent effort to leave him closer in appearance to his captors, Chieftain Gruppe had never come through with the promised scissors or razors or depilatories—Galen had been released from his cell the moment Lyra's water had broken, and been transferred by a taqwa-drawn sled to the Keep chaperoned by two prison guards whom he assumed would return him to the prison as soon as Jyn's cries yielded to sleep.

The midwife who had swaddled Jyn brought Galen out of his reverie.

"You can remain with Lyra and the child or give them a few moments to rest."

Lyra nodded to indicate that rest was preferable.

He gazed at her. "I don't know if I have the strength to leave."

"Don't fret," one of the handmaidens said, "you'll be permitted to stay for the night."

In naked relief, Galen leaned over to kiss Lyra on the forehead, Jyn on the crown of her head. She was a beautiful girl, a good weight and size and very healthy, according to the midwife who had assessed her. Dark curls were plastered to her scalp, and Galen could already see that she had her mother's mouth.

Two of the doting handmaidens escorted him to the chamber's massive wooden door. In a room directly across the wide hallway, Nurboo, Easel, Tambo, and the rest of his colleagues from the Zerpen facility were waiting to congratulate him with embraces and hard claps on the back—and of course to get him drinking. All of them were eager to see Jyn but the midwives wouldn't permit it, calling them rumpled, germ-ridden, miscreant wizards—though all in fun.

From out of nowhere a mug was pressed into Galen's hand and quickly filled with a viscid white liquid and the toasts began, with long swallows following each of them. Galen was near drunk in no time, which would have been the case even if he had been consuming his accustomed calories and hadn't been awake for the past twenty local hours. The drinks, the torchlight, the cheery faces of his friends worked the most nourishing kind of magic on him.

"I thought you were going to name her after me," Nurboo said.

"Now, how would that sound?"

"I'll have you know that Vallt has as many female Nurboos as it does males."

Galen didn't doubt it. Nurboo—like Tambo and Easel—was a day designation. The entire planetary population chose among scarcely two dozen names.

"Perhaps the next child?" Nurboo persisted.

"I'll confer with Lyra."

Everyone fell suddenly silent. Galen turned to find Chieftain Gruppe standing behind him. Her stern face broke into a broad grin and she embraced him harder than the others had and accepted a flagon of the homebrew, which she downed in one lengthy swallow.

Galen knew the danger of feeling affection for one's jailer, and had gone to great lengths to maintain a safe emotional distance from Gruppe or any of the others. And yet tonight he felt a warmth spread through him that had less to do with the alcohol than a sense that he was among family. As reckless as it was, he had formed a strong bond with the Valltii—even his captors, even with Gruppe.

"You know we're not your enemy," she said after a loud, appreciative belch.

"I'm trying not to think of you that way, but the walls of my cell keep reminding me that I'm a prisoner."

"It's simply circumstance."

Galen showed her a wry smile. "Even so, Chieftain, no one likes to be a victim of that."

She returned a solemn nod. "A short time ago Vallt was a Republic member world; now it supports the Separatists. And yet, what does any of that have to do with us?"

"It certainly had a lot to do with my ending up in Tambolor prison."

Her eyes narrowed in begrudging agreement. "Our deal with the Separatists seemed reasonable enough at the time: support for the coup in exchange for our turning you over to their custody. Now, however, we're not sure we want to lose you."

More manipulation? Galen wondered. "I've grown on you, is that it?"

She snorted a laugh. "Your co-workers maintain that the research has continued in your absence. Have you considered simply working for us, Galen—for Vallt? Converting the facility into a power station to supply the Keep and the entire city?"

"I'm not certain how that would be perceived by Zerpen."

"Yes, I've read the terms of your contract. No involvement in local matters, let alone local politics.

"Unfortunately true."

"And yet where is Zerpen now? Why haven't they reached out to us?"

"Do they even know?" Galen asked.

Gruppe laughed and clapped him on the shoulder. "The laboratory droid—Assis—was debriefed. We know all about the burst transmission sent to Zerpen in the Salient system."

Galen frowned. "Then I've no idea why they haven't reached out."

"Again, we are not your enemy. We have nothing against you personally. Our issues are with the Republic Senate and Palpatine."

"I also have issues with them."

"Then where is the harm? Remain with us, help Vallt develop, raise your child away from the strife and noise of the Core. We've come to think of you as one of our own. Especially now that Jyn is a Valltii, a citizen of our world."

"You pose a good argument, Chieftain."

She poured him another drink. "Rumor has it that the Tribunal will be hearing your case shortly, and"—she lowered her voice—"that you will be exonerated."

Galen stared at her, afraid to get his hopes up. "And then?"

"Your confinement in Tambolor will come to an end. You and Lyra and the baby will be reunited."

"And permitted to leave Vallt?" he asked with caution.

"It is too early to promise that. Perhaps Marshal Phara will grant you absolution. A pardon." Gruppe's shoulders heaved in an elaborate shrug. "Eventually there will be another coup, a new leader. This is the way of all worlds, not only Vallt."

"The vicious circle."

Gruppe sniffed and called for another flagon. "Who knows, Galen, maybe Count Dooku or your Palpatine will find a way to break the cycle, once and for all."

Two white-armored clone troopers escorted Has Obitt from the cofferdam that linked his small freighter to the Republic Cruiser. He had thought about turning tail the moment the cruiser had appeared on the scanners, but declining an invitation from a warship that had placed itself directly in his path hadn't seemed the brightest idea.

"When do I get to learn where I'm going?" he hazarded to ask the clone troopers.

"When you get there," the one on his left said.

Has smirked. "You guys are never less than predictable."

"Yeah, we're made that way," the other clone said.

A native of remote Dressel, Has was a dark-complected, tall, and hairless humanoid with a furrowed face and a deep cranial groove that ran from the bridge of his nose all the way to the nape of his thick neck. He had been told by humans that his mouth was disproportionately large, but that he had soulful eyes. The rest of him was similar enough to humans that they weren't uncomfortable in his company—nor he in theirs.

The clone troopers led him down several broad corridors and through several right-angle turns until they arrived at an open hatchway, which they flanked after motioning him into the cabin beyond. A human officer was standing inside, slightly shorter than Has, but erect and sinewy, with light-brown hair and a narrow face humans probably considered handsome. He wore a white tunic over black pants tucked into lustrous knee boots. In a corner of the observation bay behind the human Has could see the short wings and broad fantail of his ship, aboard which his new crew had to be wondering what their captain had gotten them into.

"Welcome aboard, Captain Obitt," the officer said.

"Thank you." Has's uneasy inflection turned it into a question. "Commander . . ."

"Krennic. Lieutenant commander actually, but thanks for noticing."

The human seemed slightly out of place aboard the cruiser—his uniform was all wrong—so Has allowed himself to relax. Probably another request for information about Separatist ship movements or distribution. Has made a point to glance around him. "My first time aboard one of these," he said in a casual way.

"And?" Krennic said, as if hanging on Has's reply.

"Uh, impressive to be sure, but cold."

Krennic's brows beetled in interest. "Do you mean cold as in chilly or cold as in austere?"

"Austere?"

"Severe. Lacking in comfort," Krennic explained.

"Well, I haven't really seen enough of the ship to comment—"

"Perhaps we can arrange for a personal tour after we're done here," Krennic said, cutting him off. "It's for sale, in any case."

Krennic's dead-serious tone made the remark even more outlandish. "A bit out of my league."

Krennic adopted a look of surprise. "Don't tell me business hasn't been good."

Again, the disparity between the words and the tone left Has feeling slightly flummoxed. "Business has been all right."

Krennic frowned. "Just all right? Are you saying that that supply run to Ryloth didn't earn out? Or that the jump to Hellenah to deliver munitions didn't pay off? Certainly that clever workaround at Christophsis turned a profit."

Has started to reply, then thought better of it and

began again. "I'm not too proud to admit when I've been outsmarted."

The corners of Krennic's mouth went up. "Good for you. Pride is an overvalued quality."

"You obviously know more about me than I do about you."

"Indeed I do, Captain. But let's even things up, shall we? What is it you wish to know about me?"

Has decided he had nothing to lose by asking. "I guess I'd like to know which Republic agency I'm dealing with, since your uniform tells me this isn't your ship."

"Very observant of you. I'm with the Corps of Engineers."

Maybe, Has thought. But that wasn't the full answer.

"Have you by chance ever put in at Regalia Station?" Krennic said.

"You probably already know that I have."

Krennic smiled broadly. "We're beginning to understand each other. Regalia is mine. Not mine, of course, but I was chief of the design and construction teams. Have you been to Coruscant recently?"

"Not recently, no."

"I'll give you a list of which of my works to visit on your next stopover."

It was Has's move, but he declined. "What does the Corps of Engineers want with me? When you hailed us, you said something about a friendly chat."

"I'm sorry, have I said something to contradict that?"

Has waited.

"It's simply that I have a proposition for you."

Has wished he could plug his ears. Providing intelligence was one thing, but *propositions* usually led to trouble. "We're only taking small jobs at the moment."

Krennic was undeterred. "I'd classify this one as small, as these things go."

Has exhaled with purpose. "Look, Commander, I'm just a smuggler trying to earn a living, like a thousand others in this sector alone."

Krennic appraised him. "You're actually going to play the humble card? Has Obitt, who has worked with the Jedi Order on several occasions? Who has earned a reputation as a pilot to trust with all make and manner of cargoes? Who has extricated himself from any number of tight spots?" He paused briefly, then added: "Who is known to make periodic deliveries to Merj?"

Has said nothing.

"You're aware of course that Merj is a Separatist world, aren't you, Captain?"

Has swallowed and found his voice. "We don't deliver anything in the way of weapons or proscribed merchandise. Strictly equipment and supplies."

Krennic scowled. "I'll give you that one. But I want to know how these allegedly innocent supplies are delivered."

Has shook his head. "I don't follow."

"Walk me through it," Krennic said. "You arrive at Merj . . ."

"Merj spaceport control clears us to land," Has began. "We land. We off-load the supplies—"

"Do you actually carry them off or do you use droids?"

"We do it ourselves."

"With lifters?"

"We use antigrav containers. Two crewmembers to a container, and normally no more than four containers each delivery."

"How large are the containers?" Krennic motioned to the office bench seat. "As large as this?"

Has considered the question. "They're standard repulsorlift containers. Two meters by one meter, one-point-five deep."

"Do you conduct them into the research facility that adjoins the spaceport, or do you hangar them?"

Has's curiosity increased apace with his anxiety. "We guide them in. Why are—"

"You're in and out?"

"Usually, yes."

"How many personnel on the ground?"

Beads of sweat were forming on Has's grooved brow, but he managed to keep from wiping them away. "At the port? Six, sometimes as many as eight or ten."

"Are the containers inspected?" Krennic pressed.

"Infrequently," Has said, eager to be done with it now. "At least, not lately."

"What about when you leave?"

Has added new wrinkles to his face. "Why would they?"

"Yes or no?"

"Early on, yes, they were inspected," Has said with

more force than he intended. "Now that we're regulars, no."

"Very good, Captain." Krennic's spirited smile returned. "I, along with a couple of my comrades, would very much like to become members of your crew—provisionally, of course."

Has's heart sank, and he compressed his plump lips. "Commander, Merj has been a good deal for me. I don't want to do anything to jeopardize a relationship that took a long time to build."

Krennic glared at him. "You don't want to jeopardize your popularity with the Separatists. Is that what you're telling me?"

Has groped for clarification. "I try to steer clear of taking sides. I'm just a—"

"Yes, yes," Krennic said in dismissal, "we've been through all that. But suppose I could promise you that, in exchange for your service, the Republic would be willing to overlook some of your more questionable activities."

It wasn't the first time the offer had been made, but Has understood that this one couldn't be refused. "Get out of jail free, is that it?"

"We'll simply shrug and look the other way."

Has asked the question he didn't want to. "What if I decide the job's not for me?"

Krennic swung to the observation bay and stretched out his arm. "Pick a planet."

Has stared at him. "What, any planet?"

"The one you want your remains shipped to, Captain." Krennic's laugh ended as quickly as it began, and he took a few steps in Has's direction. "You're wondering just what you've gotten yourself into, is that it?"

"Wouldn't you be?"

Krennic whacked him playfully on the upper arm. "The big time, Has. The big time."

5

HOSTAGES TO FORTUNE

WHEN HAS OBITT HAD TOLD Krennic that he and the handpicked members of his team were going to have to wear transpirators while on Merj, Krennic assumed that caustic vapors from the Morseerian laboratory complex posed a health risk. That, however, wasn't the reason.

"Morseerians are methane breathers," Has explained.

Krennic reproached himself for having forgotten, but had ultimately decided that breath masks wouldn't affect the operational status of the mission. And in the end, masks became critical to the finalized plan.

Has had also informed Krennic that Morseerians didn't distinguish among human faces, so they wouldn't be able to recognize undercover clone troopers. Yet he was surprised to find that the team Krennic had assembled was made up of non-clone special ops soldiers assigned to Republic Intelligence. Perhaps members of the Corps of Engineers received only limited combat training, and Krennic refused to allow himself to be ordered around by clones. Whatever the case, the direct action operatives chosen by the lieutenant commander were former Republic Judicials who had participated in numerous peacekeeping operations before the war and plenty of mobility missions since. The six were commanded by a young Coruscanti named Matese, who was a skilled sniper and demolitions expert—and may or may not have been responsible for the assassination of several high-value targets throughout the Core. Tall and layered with muscle, Matese was as humorless as they came, but Has observed that he never questioned Krennic's orders and was clearly capable of getting any job done.

Has had yet to make peace with having been drafted into Republic service, despite Krennic's assurances that he expected nothing more than grudging cooperation. Has's crew was even unhappier about being replaced, until Krennic had doled out enough slush-fund credits to finance a few standard weeks of R&R on Ralltiir, where the crew exchange had been made.

The *Good Tidings,* Has's able and agile light freighter, was perfect for slipping through blockades, equipped with a Class Two hyperdrive and a pair of infrequently used but meticulously maintained laser cannons. Krennic had performed a thorough inspection and sensor sweep on boarding the ship, and was comforted to see firsthand that Has handled the *Good Tidings* with a skill sharpened through decades of piloting. Has's easy rapport with Merj's spaceport control agents also convinced Krennic that he was as trusted as any smuggler could be.

Matese and the rest of the rangers were dressed in versions of the environment suits Has and Krennic were wearing. Sophisticated comlinks had been engineered into the design of the transpirators that covered their mouths and noses. The cargo—already packed into the cushioned interiors of the antigrav shipping containers the crew would guide through customs into the Separatist research complex—was made up of chemical reagents, laboratory equipment, and vacuum-packed vials of live viruses.

Krennic had expressed concern that an all-human crew would arouse suspicion among the immigration and customs agents, but Has had guaranteed that he had employed human crews in the past, and that there was no need for worry. In fact, the Morseerian spaceport officials—four-armed bipeds with translucent skin and conical heads covered with multihued scales—did little more than glance at the shipping manifests Has provided and rap their knobby knuckles on one of the alloy containers. Cleared through customs, the eight-member group steered the cargo through hermetically sealed doors and into a wide corridor that led to the research complex. Has had already provided detailed intel on the number of officials to expect, as well as the layout of the arrivals area and the corridors beyond, and Krennic complimented him, commenting that what he glimpsed along the route was almost identical to the picture he had formed in his mind.

Unhappily, the ease of their entry did little to allay Has's unrelenting dread.

As they maneuvered the containers deeper into the complex, holosigns in several languages including Basic began to appear, warning visitors away from restricted areas and cautioning against possible contamination.

The team's destination was the biotics research lab, where three Separatist scientists were known to be overseeing the creation of a biological warfare agent aimed at infecting the clone army. A final set of airtight doors opened into the laboratory itself, where the trio of Morseerians were waiting, clearly impatient to unpack what Has had delivered from a warehouse across the stars. Enthusiasm grew as they removed each flimsiplast-wrapped item from its memory-foam bed, handling everything as gingerly as they might a newborn baby.

"Wonderful," one of them said in Basic, gesticulating with his upper pair of arms. "You were able to procure the Saloflex."

"Eighty-nine percent pure," Has told him through the mask enunciator.

"Perfect, perfect. Your professionalism never fails to impress us."

Has grimaced behind the mask, and could feel Krennic's eyes on him. Just what the lieutenant commander needed to hear: that Count Dooku's Separatists could always count on Has Obitt to deliver.

The rangers moved into position while the Morseerians were preoccupied. On Matese's subtle hand gesture, one member of his command activated a microdevice that dazzled the lab's security cams, while another armed a triggering device implanted in his wrist.

By then, the tallest of the three Morseerians had found and extracted Krennic's surprise: a cylinder no larger than a fire suppressant canister, fitted with a single flow valve.

"What is this?" the alien virologist asked Has. "This isn't on the manifest."

"Look again," Has said. "All we did was load the cargo."

A second Morseerian turned the device about in his lower hands and looked hard at Has.

"Captain, what's going on here?"

Through his earbead Has heard the high-pitched undulating whine of the weapon initiator, and watched as a cloud of white neuroparalytic gas vaped from the canister, quickly filling the room and immobilizing the Morseerians. One tried desperately to sound an alarm, but Matese was on him before he had moved a meter. The other two researchers simply crumpled to the floor. Immediately the rangers went into action, tearing the foam inserts from the shipping containers then hauling the researchers to their feet and lowering them into the now empty antigravs, as if preparing them for burial.

"We need to provide them with methane as soon as we get them aboard the ship," Has said. "Otherwise they'll die."

Krennic dismissed the warning with a negligent wave of his hand. "The containers are rigged to supply an atmospheric mix. That will have to do for now."

"This one's too tall for the container," one of the rangers said.

"Fold him in there," Matese ordered.

Has tried to intervene. "No one is supposed to get hurt!"

Krennic shot him a gimlet look and waved him back. "Get with the program, Has. We're not going to break him."

Has restrained himself from saying anything more. *Getting with the program* was precisely what he *didn't* want to do, and the reason he'd become a smuggler in the first place. Up until now he had devised his own program, and suddenly he was taking orders.

On a nod from Krennic, the team began to conduct the containers out the way they had come in: through sliding doors and along corridors until they had returned to the customs area. They were meters from exiting onto the landing zone apron when one of the customs agents called to them, gesturing to the final container—the very one into which the tall Morseerian had been folded.

"Something's hanging out there," the agent started to say when he realized that it was a three-fingered hand. Efficiently then, he drew a serious-looking sidearm from its holster and leveled it at Matese. "Open it."

Matese, though, had already sprung into action, and felled the Morseerian with a stiff-fingered blow to the windpipe before he could utter another word. Quick to react, the rest of the customs agents drew their weapons and the rangers dived for cover behind the antigrav containers. Alarms began to blare and additional Morseerians, armed to the teeth, began to spill through the doorway of an adjacent building.

Has flattened himself to the ground as blaster bolts streaked overhead and ricocheted, the rangers returning fire from a host of carefully concealed weapons. Has saw three customs agents go down, holed through and through. Then Krennic's voice battered his eardrums.

"Change of plans! We'll have to make do with two!"

Has couldn't make sense of it until he saw Matese steering the telltale shipping container directly into the thick of the advancing customs agents. Without warning the rest of the rangers dropped to the apron, and a blinding flash leached all color from the immediate world.

The shaped charge built into the antigrav container made mincemeat of half a dozen Morseerians and rendered most of the others unconscious. On his belly at the edge of the blast, Has took some of the brunt of it and regained consciousness to find Matese and Krennic dragging him across the apron toward the ship while the rest of the team was maneuvering the two remaining containers into the *Good Tidings*' forward cargo bay.

"No one was supposed to get hurt," Has stammered as Matese picked him up and deposited him in a heap on the cold deck of the hold. "No one was supposed to get hurt . . ."

The last sight he saw before lapsing back into unconsciousness was Krennic's eyes beaming above the transpirator.

"The unpredictable nature of deception," Krennic told him through the mask mike. "But congratulations, Has. You're a full-fledged operative of the Republic now."

It was just dawn when Lyra was stirred from sleep and told that she had been ordered to leave the Keep at once. None of the handmaidens could tell her why, and two of them were sobbing uncontrollably. Lyra dressed while one of the Valltii swaddled six-month-old Jyn in blankets, kissed her, and pressed her into Lyra's arms. She hugged each of them tightly, and left them wailing on the landing as she was escorted down the stairs by a pair of guards. Outside, despite the sun being much higher in the sky than it had been only a month earlier, the air was chill, whipped by a persistent northern wind, and she shivered as she was ushered to the waiting carriage.

"Where are you taking us?" she asked.

She hadn't expected an answer, and so was ill prepared when the driver said:

"Tambolor prison."

Her heart pounded. Were she and Jyn being transferred there? Had Galen's continued refusal to swear fealty to the new regime resulted in imprisonment for the three of them? Far worse, had Galen been slated for execution?

Had all of them?

Uncertainty preyed on her as the carriage trundled

through the city streets; then the prison rose into view, cold and forbidding. She had gazed at it so often from her chambers in the Keep that drawing to a stop in front of the detested place felt unreal, like a bad dream.

The tall gates swung open and suddenly Galen was standing alongside the carriage, bracketed by two prison guards, looking much thinner than she allowed herself to admit and wearing a beard as long as a bib. The guards, however, made no effort to restrain him when he shuffled to her, embracing her and Jyn for a long moment.

"I've dreamed of this moment," he said, stepping back to take them in. His eyes went to Jyn. "Let me hold her."

Lyra passed Jyn to him. Carefully he peeled away the swaddling that masked her face and smiled more broadly than Lyra had ever seen him smile. Jyn stirred in his arms, and Lyra said: "She remembers you, Galen."

"She's beautiful," he said, inspecting her face. "Her eyes have changed color."

Lyra nodded. "They're sort of flecked."

"Stardust," Galen said. "That's what's in her eyes."

"Galen, what's happening?" Lyra risked asking. "Why have we been brought here? They're not going to—"

"I haven't been told anything. They took me out of my cell before dawn."

"The same with us. I'm worried."

"Don't be." He showed her his grimy hands. "See?

No restraints. And no one has brandished a weapon at me all morning."

Lyra didn't find much relief in it. "Could they be sending us somewhere else? Is there a worse prison?"

Before he could reply, one of the guards ordered Galen up into the carriage.

He did as instructed, and the drivers snapped their whips over the heads of the lead taqwas, which set off at a brisk pace. The carriage's wooden wheels bounded over bumps and ruts, and Lyra inadvertently bit down on her tongue. When Tambolor had disappeared from view, Galen raised himself up on the bench seat to take a look around.

"We're heading for the spaceport."

Lyra's eyes widened. "You don't think—"

"I don't want to jinx anything by thinking."

Lyra held her breath as the circular landing zone came into view below them, only to have her hopes dashed. Fifty or more Separatist battle droids stood in formation at the edge of the field, commanded by a male Koorivar sporting a tall cranial horn and a richly cloaked uniform. The lackluster drop ship that had delivered them sat off to one side.

Galen looked stricken. "I guess Phara changed her mind about handing me over to Count Dooku."

Lyra fought back tears. From one prison to another. Would the Separatists use her and Jyn to coerce and ultimately break Galen, forcing him to join the war?

Opposite the battle droids were several taqwa riders, including Chieftain Gruppe, dressed in her signature brown uniform and wearing an earflapped cap tugged down over her braided hair. When the carriage had drawn to a halt and Galen and Lyra had climbed down, Gruppe dismounted and approached.

"I'm almost sorry to see you go," she told them.

"Not as sorry as I am," Galen said with a mix of anger and disappointment. "What happened to the charges being overturned and our being allowed to leave?"

Gruppe grinned. "You misunderstand, my friend."

As if on cue, a starship appeared high overhead and began a very controlled descent toward the landing zone. Trained to take down surveillance drones and small craft, a dozen sky-kings followed it down.

The Koorivar uttered a barely audible command and the battle droids brought their rifles to port arms.

Galen squinted at the emblem emblazoned on the light freighter's underbelly. "Zerpen!"

Lyra put the edge of her hand to her brow and followed his gaze. "Since when does Zerpen fly anything that ragged?"

Galen ignored the question. "I knew they wouldn't forget us."

Lyra gave her head a shake, as if to make sure she wasn't dreaming. She hugged Jyn closer as the Zerpen vessel settled on its trio of landing gear, blasting everyone with grit. The boarding ramp lowered and a sole figure in a white environment suit similarly emblazoned with the company logo descended to the pad. Lyra felt her jaw drop, and when she turned to Galen she saw that he, too, was agape.

"Orson Krennic?" she whispered.

He nodded, seemingly incapable of speaking or looking away.

"But—"

"We need to play this by ear," Galen managed.

The Koorivar commander and Chieftain Gruppe met Krennic halfway, and the three of them stood regarding one another for a long moment.

Krennic looked around with purpose before speaking. "Which of you is in charge?"

Gruppe answered him in Basic. "Marshal Phara has granted me authority to settle this matter."

"And you?" Krennic said to the Koorivar.

"I'm here to make certain you honor the terms of the exchange."

Krennic sniffed with clear purpose and took a few steps back toward the boarding ramp. "Please deboard our guests," he called up into the ship.

Lyra watched closely as a muscular human appeared, similarly attired in Zerpen garb, followed by a pair of distressed-looking four-armed humanoids wearing elaborate breath masks and enviro-suits, and a Dressellian whose big eyes darted every which way while he and the human escorted the humanoids to where Gruppe and the Koorivar were standing.

The Separatist commander appraised the humanoids. "Identify yourselves."

"I am Dr. Nan Pakota," the taller of the masked aliens said. "This is my colleague, Urshe Torr."

Gruppe turned to Krennic. "I need further confirmation."

Krennic opened his jacket and pulled out a datapad, calling Gruppe's attention to something on the display screen. "Satisfied?"

Gruppe nodded and the Koorivar followed suit.

Krennic handed the datapad to the chieftain. "Yours to keep."

Gruppe dropped the datapad into one of her coat pockets and motioned to where Galen and Lyra were standing. "I don't suppose there's any need to introduce you."

Krennic grinned and sauntered over to them. Reaching for Galen's hand, he said: "Dr. Erso, I'm so relieved to find you in good health." He turned to Lyra while he was still pumping Galen's hand. "And Mrs. Erso, and—oh, my, is this the child?"

Lyra had her mouth open to respond but nothing emerged.

"May I have a peek?"

She removed the wrappings that covered Jyn's face.

"Precious! She looks just like you!"

Businesslike once more, Krennic returned to Gruppe and the Koorivar. "Speaking for Zerpen Industries, I must say that this has been a regrettable incident—as was the Republic's abduction of two Separatist researchers. But we are glad to have been in a position to broker their release, as well as that of Dr. Erso and his family, who should never have been subjected to so much as harsh words, let alone imprisonment."

Gruppe shrugged. "War gives rise to all manner of irascible behavior." She glanced at Galen. "Personally I can add that it has been a privilege getting to know Galen Erso, and I hope that he and Lyra will find it in their hearts to forgive our inhospitality."

"I'm working on it," Galen said.

"Remember that Jyn is a Valltii citizen," Gruppe said.

Krennic's eyes narrowed in distaste, and he swung to the Dressellian. "Ready the ship, Captain. The sooner we're off this wretched world, the better." Glancing at Galen, he gestured offhandedly to the boarding ramp. "Dr. Erso, if you and your wife would be so kind as to hurry aboard."

"I hope that your journeys are fruitful," Chieftain Gruppe called out as Galen and Lyra were climbing into the ship.

Once inside, Krennic whirled Galen into an embrace. "How wonderful to see you after all this time!"

"Orson, I don't under—"

"Not now," Krennic interrupted, stepping back but continuing to grip Galen's biceps. "I'll explain everything in due course, but right now there are more important matters to attend to."

Everyone moved into the main cabin, where three other humans with close-cropped hair were seated at various duty stations. All eyes were on them as Galen and Lyra strapped into one of the acceleration couches. Lyra cradled Jyn close.

"Contact Commander Prakas as soon as we lift off," Krennic told the comm tech as he was strapping in. "Tell him to give us just enough time to get up the well."

The freighter lifted off and rocketed into Vallt's pale sky. Galen turned his attention to the cabin's starboard-side viewport as stars began to reveal themselves.

"Brace yourselves for evasive action," Krennic warned.

Galen twisted slightly in the direction of the viewport. A sudden shift in the starfield was followed by a brief glimpse of a Separatist warship bristling with weapons; then the darkening sky came alive with crisscrossing hyphens of laserfire.

"Ha! So much for honoring the terms of the exchange!" Krennic shouted.

Lyra pressed Jyn more tightly to her chest as the freighter was jolted by fire. A flash of nova-bright light filled the viewport and the freighter rolled over onto its port side, its belly peppered with debris.

"Hold tight!" Krennic shouted above the sound of Jyn's crying. "There may be other enemy ships in the area."

Clamping his arm around Lyra's shoulder, Galen cut his eyes to the viewport once more and glimpsed a dagger-shaped Republic cruiser appearing out of hyperspace. Simultaneously, a voice issued from a comm station speaker.

"Lieutenant Commander, we're in position."

Krennic swiveled toward the console. "Right on schedule, Prakas! There were droids and a *Settie*-class drop ship on the surface, though it might be in the air by now. When you're done with them, target the Keep."

"Orson, no!" Lyra said in an anguished voice. "It's done. It's over with!"

"Not quite," Krennic said without looking at her. His gaze favored Galen. "A strike will give the pro-Republic legions an opportunity to reclaim power.

What's more, we promised Zerpen that they'd get their ignition facility back."

"They're harmless, Orson," Galen said, "Separatists or no."

Krennic's look was patronizing. "Perhaps. But we're at war, and they're on the wrong side."

Galen was still shaking when the freighter made the jump to hyperspace. The thought of Gruppe and so many others immolated by bolts of starfire left him weak-kneed and nauseated. Lyra had to be feeling the same, and he couldn't bring himself to meet her dejected gaze.

Free of his harness, Krennic stood, ripped the Zerpen logo from his tunic, and tossed it out of sight. "We have to put some meat back on those bones of yours," he said as he crossed the cabin to Galen, "but I think I could get used to the beard." Finally, he turned to Lyra. "Obviously they kept you in more civilized confinement. And the child—"

"Jyn."

Krennic rolled it over on his tongue and shrugged lightly. "She's healthy?"

"Very."

"Well then, there's something to be said for the Valltii."

"A lot can be said for them, Orson," Galen told him.

"You'll have to fill me in at some point. But I promised you an explanation." He sank into a chair from which he could address both of them. "Because of the espionage charges leveled against you, Zerpen was reluctant to enter into negotiations with Vallt's new regime—the *late* Marshal Phara, one can hope. For all Zerpen knew, you actually were a Republic agent all along. I realize how that must sound, but you know how these faceless profit-driven corporations can be. So naturally the Republic stepped in to intervene. Zerpen agreed that we could portray ourselves as emissaries if we agreed to expedite the return of their facility."

"This was a Republic operation?" Galen said in patent disbelief.

"It was. I'm genuinely surprised that Count Dooku didn't commit more forces to oversee the exchange, but I'm not going to complain about a bit of unexpected good fortune."

Galen's face looked bloodless. "Orson, I don't know how to thank you."

Krennic smiled lightly. "Well, we couldn't let you molder in prison on some desolate world. I could imagine what you had to be going through—the position you were in—and I decided to do the thinking for you. I hope you won't hold it against me."

Galen was shaking his head back and forth. "But all these resources—just to free us. I don't feel right about it."

"Now who's being ridiculous? Besides, this operation was sanctioned at the highest levels."

Galen looked up, blinking in disbelief. "I'm surprised to hear that anyone in power is even aware of me."

"Once I explained fully who you are and what

happened, I was instructed to take whatever steps were necessary to bring you home."

Galen's expression became quizzical. "But you're still with the Corps of Engineers, aren't you?"

"Of course. But my role has expanded—considerably—what with the need for space stations, armaments, ships of the fleet."

"Was firing on the Keep part of the arrangement?" Lyra asked in no uncertain terms.

Krennic eyed her for a moment before responding. "Let's just say that the Supreme Chancellor was very troubled by Vallt's turn to the Separatist side."

She held his gaze until he looked away.

Galen blew out his breath. "We tried to avoid being caught up in all this, and look at the end result."

"You didn't pull the trigger on Vallt, Galen."

"I might as well have."

Krennic's eyes narrowed perceptibly. "If you're determined to beat yourself up about it, I can't stop you. But the sooner you get used to being back in the real world, the better."

"Meaning what, exactly?" Lyra said in the same harsh tone.

He looked at her askance. "Meaning that this war only ends when we win it, in whatever way we can."

"And the losers?" Galen said.

Krennic sighed. "Up to a point that will be for them to decide."

The three of them fell silent, until Galen asked: "Are we headed to Coruscant?"

Krennic rose from the chair and nodded slowly.

"Ultimately. But there's something you need to see first."

Has brought the *Good Tidings* out of hyperspace a safe distance from Grange and unclipped from the chair's restraints. "Can you handle this?" he asked Matese, who occupied the copilot's seat.

"Trust me, Obitt, I got it."

Krennic had mentioned that Grange was the scientist's homeworld, and Has was curious to gauge Dr. Erso's reaction to what he was about to confront. When Has entered the freighter's main cabin, Krennic, Erso, and his wife—their child in her arms—were standing at the starboard viewport staring aghast at the battle raging on all sides of the planet. Republic and Separatist warships were going at it high above Grange's dun, leafy-green, and seafoam surface, explosions blossoming in space and along the starlit curve of the agrarian world.

Has noticed that the frail scientist's right hand was twitching, almost as if he were writing in the air. He was clearly in poor health after several standard months of confinement, and the sight of Grange being taken apart wasn't doing him any good.

Just the way Krennic wanted it, Has was certain.

"Your homeworld has been under siege for the past two standard months," the commander was explaining. "Unfortunately, we can't risk getting any closer without becoming involved. The Republic dispatched what forces could be spared, but the Separatists had a good lead on us, and now we're getting our heads handed to us."

"Why Grange?" Erso said. "Grange has nothing."

Has had heard the question asked more times than he could count, and the answer was always the same.

"Grange has resources," Krennic said. "It's well situated for jump points to remote sectors. And for Count Dooku the war has become a numbers game. The more worlds he brings into the Confederacy, the more he weakens the Republic. No world is immune— not even yours."

Erso looked even more distressed. "Is it this bad everywhere?"

"Worse," Krennic said.

Erso's wife, Lyra, glowered at him. "You seemed to have no problem contributing to it at Vallt."

Krennic's shoulders hunched, but he didn't respond.

Has smiled to himself, taken by Lyra's spunk. In a physical match between her and Krennic, he might have put his credits on Lyra.

"The Separatists will never prevail," Erso was saying. "Surely it's only a matter of time."

Krennic answered without turning from the horrid view. "The Republic is doing what it can with what it has, but the designers of the Grand Army failed to prepare for every eventuality, and in many cases we've found ourselves outgunned or outnumbered. Right now we have a finite number of clone soldiers up against what sometimes seems an infinite number of droids."

"And the Jedi?" Lyra asked.

"Also doing what they can. But remember, Dooku is one of their own, and he's a crafty opponent. At times he seems to be able to read our minds, if not simply outguess us. Despite that, many of the Core and Mid Rim worlds are fully committed to preserving the Republic. Several shipbuilding corporations have devoted themselves to providing the Grand Army with advanced weapons and ships. Unfortunately, the research and development isn't progressing as quickly as we would like, and the longer this needless destruction drags on, the worse for everyone. Without a quick victory, the galaxy could die a slow death."

"What will happen to Grange?" Erso asked.

Krennic looked at him over his shoulder. "My best assessment? The Republic will withdraw before we suffer any more losses, and Grange will belong to the Separatists."

Erso paced away from the viewport. "I can't witness this."

Has watched Lyra track and regard her husband, stopping herself from following him. She seemed about to say something when the child began to squirm and fuss in her arms, and Erso swung around to face her.

"She needs to be fed," Lyra told him. "I'll take her aft."

Has pretended to busy himself at the comm station while continuing to eavesdrop on the conversation.

Krennic deliberately waited until Lyra was out of earshot to say: "I'm sorry I had to bring you here, Galen, but I felt that you needed to see this for yourself. And turning your back to the view won't alter anything. Your homeworld is caught in the middle of this thing, and people are dying by the tens of thousands."

Krennic the tactician, Has thought. His sly way of getting Erso to get with the program; to, what, lend his genius to the war effort? If that was the case, Krennic had misjudged him.

"And people wonder why I want no part of this," Erso said without moving.

The commander frowned. "I don't think you've thought this all the way through, Galen. You may think you're removed from the war, but you're not. Do you know that Zerpen Industries is one of the corporations that has been serving both sides?" Krennic motioned to Has. "Ask our captain. He knows."

When the scientist looked at him, Has nodded, knowing it would be useless to lie in front of Krennic. "I've made a few deliveries on Zerpen's behalf to both Republic and Separatist worlds."

"There you have it," Krennic said, as if proud of himself. "If you really cared about where your funding is coming from, Galen, you'd be out with a pickax looking for kyber crystals instead of proclaiming your neutrality from inside a multibillion-credit synthesizer facility provided by traitors to the cause." Again, Krennic gestured in Has's direction. "Take Captain Obitt, here. He thought he could remain aloof, and now he finds himself forced to take sides."

"*Forced* being the choice word," Has said, showing Krennic a scowl before looking at Erso. "The commander is leaving out a few very important details, but yes, what he says is true. One moment you're going about your business, and the next you're doing someone else's bidding."

The message was lost on Erso, and Krennic merely snorted a laugh; then he moved to stand alongside the scientist. "That's essentially the position the Valltii put you in, wasn't it?"

"They tried. I chose prison."

"For all the good it did, Galen."

Erso made it clear that he didn't like the implication. "At least I could live with myself." He motioned in an offhand way to the view of his smoldering homeworld. "Even this, as tragic as it is, doesn't change my stance on the war."

Has waited for Krennic's counteroffensive.

"My aim in bringing you here has nothing to do with altering your stance," the commander said in a serious tone. "I only want to open your eyes to the truth, Galen. You've been on an enemy world for more than a standard year, and Coruscant has changed in the interim." He paused, then added: "Don't expect to be welcomed back with open arms."

6

BONDING

JYN HAD NURSED HERSELF TO sleep, and Lyra could hear Galen and the others talking in the main cabin, glad not to be a part of the conversation. For her, governments of any stripe would have their constituents believe that they were attempting to remove chaos from the galaxy, that they were trying to make things perfect, when only the Force was perfect. For ordinary beings, life was a constant interplay between order and chaos, day and night, light and dark.

Her reverence for the Force had evolved from an enduring love of nature. Yes, she thought of herself as agile and strong and intuitive, but she understood that her skills were a far cry from those attributed to the Jedi. She did, however, embrace the Order's philosophy of generosity, compassion, and peaceful resolution, and on many a far-flung world she had experienced moments in nature that could only be described as transcendent. It was certainly possible that those peak moments had their basis in belief and emotion, but that hardly mattered; even if she wasn't able to *use* the Force, she could at least *feel* it, and she was content with that. Now what remained to be seen was whether the Force was indeed strong enough to overcome the powers of evil that had swept the Republic into a galaxy-spanning conflict. Could the Jedi triumph, or would evil cast its pall over even the brightest of worlds?

Perhaps Orson was right to have brought Galen to beleaguered Grange. During their early time on Vallt she and Galen had been able to ignore the war, to concentrate on the research and the child growing in Lyra's womb like one of the teams' glittering crystals. But they couldn't keep their heads buried in the snow forever. Now that they were returning to the Core, it was essential that they come to grips with everything that was going on—the truth, as Krennic put it.

Grange had never been a prosperous world, but just forty standard years earlier it had been little more than an outback. Galen had grown up an only child in a poor neighborhood in one of the larger cities. His father had been a merchant, peddling homegrown supplies; his mother, a preschool teacher. Humble roots, it was said. But his mother, the first to recognize Galen's genius, had scraped together enough credits to surround her son with what he needed to keep his mind occupied, especially after he had started school and she understood that he was bored. First, a music synthesizer he was quick to master, then a chemistry set, and finally whatever datacrons she could afford. When credits weren't tight, she would subscribe to a HoloNet service so that he could get a sense of the larger galaxy; that life didn't begin and end on Grange.

Her contributions had the intended effect. By the time he entered secondary school Galen was already excelling in mathematics and the sciences, and his teachers were using the term *prodigy* to describe him. He was learning languages and magic tricks "just because," and he wound up building his own primitive HoloNet transceiver. More important, he was formulating theories and formulas before they were taught, in some cases solving mathematical problems in eccentric ways that surpassed his academic understanding. On several occasions his solutions mystified his instructors, and it was one of those solutions—submitted offworld by a mentor—that drew the attention of scouts of the Futures Program in Grange's sector of space, and then on Coruscant.

Where losing a son to the Core might have been traumatic for some women, Galen's mother could not have been happier for him, for she thought of it as her destiny as much as Galen's that he be surrounded by the galaxy's best and brightest. Hadn't he been born under a rainbow? Grange would have offered nothing more for him than to follow in his father's footsteps and become a merchant. The elder Erso was not as accepting of Coruscant's invitation; nor in the beginning was Galen himself, for he felt as if he already held the entire galaxy in his thoughts. He felt no need to demonstrate his gifts or to be groomed as an academic or scientist. He would have been content to be a merchant, content to explore life and the material world in his own fashion, his mind free to wander where it would, without being beholden to anyone.

He talked a good game, but it was his innate shyness

talking. He had a greater fear of attention than he did failure, refusing even to celebrate his birthday much less receive gifts or acclamation. With romance he was hopeless, pretending disinterest when in fact he was confused by his changing body and how it sometimes took him out of his mind, out of his deep thinking.

He was already enrolled in the Futures Program on Brentaal when he received word that his mother had died after a short illness. Her death and that of his father in a vehicular accident, only a few years later, were brutal blows to his sense of continuity, of permanence.

Shortly after those events he met Orson Krennic.

Orson's name had come up in conversation several times before Lyra actually met him when he began to frequent the Institute of Applied Science in the months preceding the outbreak of the war, and he seemed to be on good terms with many of Galen's former professors and peers.

Though Lyra never saw it, Galen insisted at every turn that Orson was as bright and talented as anyone in the Futures Program, and she still found it difficult to picture them as friends: one who had to be dragged to parties and events, the other whose nocturnal carousing had become legendary in the program.

Orson had gone into government service—Lyra was never clear on whether he had graduated or been dropped from the program—but he had risen quickly to the fore in the Republic Corps of Engineers, supervising the construction of enormous projects, onworld and in deep space. For Galen graduation had been followed by advanced studies, research internships, and teaching positions. By twenty-five he had published prolifically and had earned a reputation as someone destined for greatness. Years earlier it was Orson who had helped Galen land a visiting professorship at the Institute of Applied Science, which came not only with a good stipend, but also with an apartment he didn't need to pay for.

By then Galen had been narrowing his fields of interest and had settled on crystallography and energy enhancement—or, as Galen saw it, crystals had chosen him. As a result, he had begun to travel widely in search of rare crystals, and it was during one of his expeditions that he and Lyra met. She was on Espinar, leading a survey team that had discovered and mapped an extensive cave system, in the depths of which the team had discovered caches of unique crystals formed from rainwater seeping through layers and layers of soil and rock, and sometimes sprouting like radiant teardrops on the tips of stalactites. The crystals turned out not to be kybers or even a class of kyber, but they bore enough similarity to the living crystal to interest the small community of scientists who had devoted themselves to their study. As either luck or fate had had it, Lyra was chosen to guide and provide logistics for the field team Galen assembled. She couldn't to this day say that it was love at first sight or anything close to that—though she did find him attractive and vital from the start.

On Espinar he would sleep until awakened or stay up until told to retire; he would allow himself to go hungry until provided with food or eat until someone advised him to stop. Sometimes Lyra couldn't get a word in edgewise, and at other times Galen wouldn't speak for days on end, preferring instead to seclude himself and write or sketch. He was continually organizing and reorganizing his equipment, and yet he struggled to keep his footing on steep grades. Sometimes when they spoke she would feel as if she were conversing with a droid, though she came to appreciate the breadth of his knowledge and his facility for sustained attention. She began to recognize, too, that what she interpreted as hostility was actually a ploy that allowed him to maintain a safe distance from her while he sorted out what she wanted from him and solved the calculus of their relationship.

The expedition lasted six local months, and by the end of it they were lovers. She had made the first move, but he had gotten the hang of things very quickly. And all at once she occupied the center of his world. She had blazed a path to his heart, and in so doing had allowed Galen to realize that, in fact, he had one.

In the years before the war, Lyra had been concerned that Galen would shift from pure science to military research, but in retrospect she needn't have worried. When many of Galen's colleagues began to accept government handouts for positions, he instead took an offer from Zerpen Industries to continue his research into crystal synthesis and energy enrichment. The last time they had seen Orson was shortly before their departure for Vallt, when they had informed him of Lyra's pregnancy. And now all these months later, who should show up to rescue them but Galen's old school chum.

Still, how could she not be grateful? How could she even allow herself to be suspicious of Orson's intentions—even if he had twisted Galen up inside by bringing him to Grange? He had risked a great deal for them, and if he hadn't come . . .

Well, could even a Jedi know the future?

She listened for a moment more to the muffled conversation. Yes, Galen was tied up in knots. With her maternal instincts running strong, she had to resist an urge to intercede. After all, she wasn't Galen's parent; she was his partner.

Besides, Orson knew the real world much better than either of them did.

Events of the past standard year already crystallizing as memories, Lyra began to drift to sleep with Jyn's warm breath on her cheek, and she thought: If Coruscant was so changed, then perhaps Galen was going to need Orson's help more than ever.

7

IN THRALL TO GRAND IDEAS

"DID WE ACTUALLY SPEND THE whole of the past year halfway across the galaxy?" Galen asked.

"Well, there's that beard of yours," Lyra said, "so we must have been somewhere."

Galen stroked the whiskers Lyra had left behind after trimming and styling the beard to complement his pronounced cheekbones and strong jaw. The two of them were collapsed into cushioned armchairs in the main room of their apartment on the grounds of the Institute of Applied Science, which rose from the heart of one of central Coruscant's finest precincts. Galen had Jyn propped on his left thigh and now he set her gently down on the floor, where she immediately began to work on her crawl.

"Galen, are you sure that's okay?"

He bent down to extend an arm and run his forefinger across the polylaminate flooring. "Clean enough," he said, showing her his fingertip. "Besides, we may as well let her get familiar with the territory."

Lyra smiled as she watched Jyn scurry, then pause to hook a leg under her body and lift herself slightly.

"She'll be walking before we know it. And she's going to be a lot to keep up with."

When Galen didn't respond, she glanced up at him to find him distracted, completely absent. Watching Jyn, his look was at once joyous and anxious, and his thoughts were easy to decode.

"Galen, I'm sorry about the way things worked out. Or didn't."

Her tone brought him back to the moment, and he exhaled slowly. "We were so close to achieving something monumental on Vallt." He gave his head a long mournful shake. "Every time I think about Nurboo and the others, what they might be going through—"

"Don't dwell on it, Galen. There's nothing we could have done to prevent what happened." She sighed with purpose. "I understand, though. Not a day goes by . . ." She let her words trail off, stood and crossed the room so that she could sit beside him, Jyn's interest riveted on a piece of something she found on the floor that Lyra hoped wouldn't end up in her mouth. "Something will turn up."

He showed her a rueful smile. "I'd like to think so. But I've put us in a fix. Zerpen isn't likely to risk bringing me back into the fold right now, and let's face it, without a research position I'm fairly useless."

"You're not useless, Galen. And I'm not exactly incapable of working."

"I know that," he said. "But I feel like I need to make it up to you and Jyn."

"Make what up to us? You better not be blaming yourself for getting thrown into prison."

"I was the one who pushed for accepting Zerpen's

offer. You at least had sense enough to try to talk me out of it."

Lyra turned his face toward hers. "We went into it together, Galen. Now we just need to find a way forward—together."

His eyes brightened somewhat. "I do have an idea."

"Really?" she said.

"I'm going to meet with Orson."

Her smile straightened. "Orson? Why?"

"Thanks to him the three of us are safely back on Coruscant." Galen nodded in Jyn's direction. "We owe him."

Lyra took her lower lip between her teeth. "To a degree, I guess. But despite the role Orson played, it was the Republic that rescued us."

"Okay. Then we owe a debt to the Republic."

Lyra searched his face for clues as to what he had in mind. "I just think you need to be careful around Orson. He still calls himself an engineer, but he's a soldier through and through."

Galen nodded in agreement. "You don't have to worry about my asking him for a job."

"Then what could you possibly have to talk to him about?"

"I'm going to repay our debt by rescuing him."

The scanner that monitored the main entry of the military detention center on Coruscant accessed the coded information contained in the insignia squares affixed to the left breast of Krennic's tunic, and with a chirp of approval the thick door pocketed itself into the partition, allowing him to pass. Two clone troopers stationed inside led him through another door and into the mouth of a brightly lit corridor that sloped toward the turbolift bays that provided passage to the bowels of the building. Krennic knew, because he had supervised the team that had remodeled the place.

He had been back on Coruscant for a standard month, meeting with scientists on the Institute of Applied Science campus and attending strategic planning briefings, after the most recent of which he had received a message from Mas Amedda, saying that they needed to chat. Apprised of Galen's rescue, the Chagrian was probably eager to know when Galen could commence research on the battle station weapon, but in fact Krennic wasn't sure himself. During their journey to the Core and in the time since, he had been careful not to ask Galen directly to participate in the Special Weapons Group; nor had he mentioned anything about the battle station project itself.

What Amedda and the others didn't understand about Galen Erso was that direct approaches seldom worked. Only when Galen was halfway toward persuading himself to do something could he be coaxed the rest of the way. Galen would need to be convinced that it was his destiny to contribute to the battle station, and Krennic was determined to see to it that he didn't miss his calling. He hoped he had planted the seeds and that chaotic Coruscant would provide the water and nourishment.

Until such time, Krennic understood that he had to

continue demonstrating his usefulness to Amedda and Supreme Chancellor Palpatine. Galen's long captivity on Vallt had furnished him with an idea for doing just that, which was why he had come to the detention center to speak with the Geonosian archduke, Poggle the Lesser.

The insectoid alien was waiting behind the rayshield entrance to a windowless and featureless interview room. He had evaded capture during the First Battle of Geonosis only to be taken into custody after the second and brought to Coruscant by the Jedi for interrogation.

"I want all surveillance suspended while I'm in there with him," Krennic told the clone troopers at the entrance to the interview room.

"Do you want to keep the ray shield active?" one of them asked.

Krennic shook his head. "Lower it."

The trooper nodded curtly. "As you wish, Lieutenant Commander."

Poggle was of average height for a Geonosian, with the skull of a long-snouted hominid. His eyes were thick-lidded and unreadable, and from the underside of his muzzle dangled a meter-long organ that was frequently mistaken for a tongue. Insectoid wings sprouted from the bony shoulder blades of a chitinous body that was near impervious to radiation. His two legs were reverse-articulated, and his clawed hands were equipped with dexterous digits.

Since the inception of the Strategic Advisory Cell, Krennic had immersed himself in studying the Geonosian society and learning the basics of the language.

Many of the clicks and whistles and glottal stops still eluded him, but he was proficient enough in conversation to proffer a formal greeting that took Poggle by surprise.

"If you are to converse intelligently in Geonosian," Poggle said in Basic through a translator device, "you will need to focus on lengthening the syllables that make up our words. I had no trouble grasping what you were trying to say, but what you actually said was closer to: 'I greet the knees of your hive and extend my best choices for your willingness.'"

Krennic nodded. "I will strive to improve."

Poggle continued to scrutinize him. "I appreciate the effort, nonetheless."

Krennic lowered himself into a simple chair and folded his hands atop the table that separated him from the archduke. "I am Lieutenant Commander Orson Krennic of the Republic Corps of Engineers."

"An engineer? Not a soldier or an intelligence analyst?"

"No, Archduke. My business, much like yours, is design and construction."

"Then I am curious as to why an engineer would desire to learn our tongue."

"Primarily because I've long been fascinated by your society. For some time I've wanted to congratulate you for introducing autonomous thinking to the battle droids. Central control computers were certainly an outgrowth of the hierarchical structure of Neimoidian society. And we all saw what happened at the Battle of Naboo. The Separatist droid army has come a long way since, and I don't think the Geonosians are given enough credit for that. Even the fact that you are incarcerated here tells me that you are underappreciated by the Separatist leadership, or they wouldn't have allowed you to fall into Republic hands."

"It's true that Geonosis should have been more heavily defended," Poggle allowed.

"I'm certain you had all sorts of unique weapons planned to pad the Separatist arsenal."

"Also true."

Krennic leaned forward and lowered his voice in conspiracy. "What I'm most interested in is the deep-space mobile battle station."

Poggle's wattles twitched slightly as he regarded Krennic. "I know of no mobile battle station."

Krennic sat back, nodding. "I can appreciate why you'd say that. The one I'm referring to is the size and shape of a small moon." He waited, then broke the silence by adding: "You're asking yourself: *Did I or did I not purge all the data on the computers in the Stalgasin war room?* And the answer is, yes, you did. We couldn't get a thing out of the system." He smiled faintly. "But just the same we have learned a great deal about the battle station."

Poggle's reddish skin darkened. "There is no battle station."

"Well, not yet there isn't. I have to ask, though: Was the station yet another example of Geonosian genius, or did Count Dooku or your confederate in this facility, Wat Tambor, provide you with the original design?" Krennic held up his hands before Poggle could reply. "Don't get me wrong, the schematic for the battle station has your flair all over it: the architecture, the superstructure, the parabolic focusing dish . . ." He waited. "Still doesn't ring a bell?"

"I don't know what you're talking about."

"Well, perhaps it's the conditions in this deplorable place," Krennic said, gesturing broadly. "The lack of fresh air and sunlight conspire to scramble one's recollections. Months of solitary confinement begin to work on the brain, and after a while you can no longer discern your memories from your hallucinations. Any sense of how far along Dooku is on building the installation?"

Poggle started to say something but thought better of it.

"Archduke, let's put our cards on the table. I know you've been over this time and again with Republic Intelligence interrogators, and I've listened to every word of the recordings."

Poggle looked dubious. "And you claim to be an engineer."

"It's true, though I admit to being one of high rank and influence. So as one engineer to another, can't you at least abandon the charade and give me some hint as to where the battle station is being built?"

"What good would be served by my talking about something of which I have no knowledge?"

Krennic exhaled with purpose. "All right, then let's talk about something even more pressing, and that is the members of your hive. You know, another thing most beings fail to realize about the Geonosians is that it's in your nature to be industrious. When Baktoid Armor Workshop first approached you about designing droid factories for the Trade Federation, how could you turn that down? A way to keep all your drones and soldiers busy and content. Because the two go hand in hand, don't they: projects and a sense of fulfillment? Anyone with even a passing familiarity with the history of your species knows what happens when there aren't tasks enough to keep everyone occupied. Hives attack hives, hundreds of thousands die needlessly, your vaunted arenas run thick with blood as drones try desperately to improve their status, the cemetery pits overflow with rotting corpses. The rampant agonism prevents your queens from reaching maturity. Surely you of all Geonosians will acknowledge that much, having risen from drone to archduke. And that's what has me worrying about Geonosis in your absence. How quickly will the descent into barbarity occur? Which soldier or drone will rise up to usurp your throne? How soon will your soldiers fly off to found a new colony? Who will see to it that the temperature in the hive queen's chamber remains constant?"

"You have a solution, *engineer*?"

"I do indeed," Krennic said. "And it has everything to do with the battle station you claim not to remember designing, despite what you've already supplied to our intelligence officers. Let's for the sake of argument say that you only threw in with Count Dooku to keep your citizens content and well fed. That you have no real issues with the Republic."

"Let's say."

"And let's further say that the Republic agrees that a productive Geonosian is a happy Geonosian."

"Why would the Republic care?"

Krennic leaned forward once more to lock gazes with Poggle. "Because we want you to build the battle station for *us*."

The pleasure Krennic took in how well he had played the Geonosian archduke was eclipsed by Galen Erso's request to meet privately with him—certainly to solicit Krennic's support in landing a position with the Republic military. It didn't matter to Krennic whether the request was motivated by a sense of gratitude for having been rescued from imprisonment or because Galen had finally come to grips with the fact that his options for employment in any scientific endeavor were few and far between. With Archduke Poggle on board and Galen about to enlist in the cause, how could Mas Amedda and Supreme Chancellor Palpatine fail to be moved by Krennic's ability to take charge and follow through?

The wings of the amphitheater were waiting!

He had already decided on the course he would take with Galen, first by declining to intercede in Galen's affairs—not out of any lack of charity or animosity but because he didn't want to be held accountable for Galen's defying his principles, for altering his *stance* regarding the war. He would, though, allow Galen to argue the point, and gradually accede to his request for a position. Krennic imagined marching Galen directly over to the Strategic Planning Amphitheater to have him swear to a security oath in the presence of Amedda and some of the others, but he knew it wouldn't unfold in that way. Galen would first need to be brought into one of the ancillary battle station programs—defensive shield technology, say, or perhaps hyperdrive research—before becoming a part of the Special Weapons Group.

But all in good time.

Krennic had asked Galen to come to his office in the Corps of Engineers headquarters—an office he himself hadn't visited in standard months—and was waiting behind his desk when Galen was shown in, the scientist heavier by a couple of kilos and his beard trimmed to a presentable length.

Krennic stood, extended his hand, and motioned Galen into a chair. "How good to see you looking healthy and fit again. How are Lyra and . . . the child?"

"Jyn," Galen provided.

"Have all of you adjusted to being back in the Core?"

Galen frowned. "It hasn't been easy—especially being idle."

Krennic adopted a sympathetic expression. "It's difficult to think of you without a project, a team of fellow researchers, a facility in which to work your magic."

"That's precisely why I'm here, Orson. And I hope you'll be open-minded about what I'm about to propose."

Krennic lifted a brow in surprise. "Propose?"

Galen drew a datapad from his pocket and activated it. Instantly the holoimage of an installation of some sort resolved in the air above the desk.

Krennic regarded the 3-D miniature in bafflement. "What exactly am I looking at?"

"Our project," Galen said.

Krennic blinked. "*Our* project?"

"It's a rough design for a new energy facility," Galen went on, "far superior to anything Zerpen Industries has ever built. Some of what you see will have to be reworked, as Zerpen has proprietary rights, and of course I'll need to wait until the terms of my noncompete contract expire, but in the meantime we can get started on assembling a team of the best and brightest and going after funding."

Krennic watched the holoimage revolve, feeling as if his head were doing the same. "Funding?"

"I'm certain you have access to wealthy beings from all sectors," Galen said. "I suppose we could even approach the Republic, if it hasn't allocated everything to the war effort. The point is that in the end— once everyone comes to appreciate the full potential of the energy we'll be able to generate, harvest, and provide—we'll be in a position to dictate terms and amass whatever funds we need."

Krennic realized that his mouth was hanging open and closed it. "Galen, are you actually proposing that we go into business together?"

Galen smiled. "I know I'm asking a lot, as it would mean your having to leave the Corps of Engineers, but we'd be embarking on something so . . . so unprecedented that I'm certain you'll never have cause to look back."

Krennic was speechless. For a brief moment he glimpsed a new destiny opening before his eyes, a window into a future he had never imagined for himself, a path to an entirely different life, and yet just as quickly as the window opened it closed, slammed shut as much by long years of training as by a feeling of trepidation.

"Galen, you can't be serious," he said at last. "Clearly you don't understand my position—"

"But I am serious," Galen cut in. "And I do understand your position. I just think you deserve more than . . . *this*," he added, motioning in a way that took in the Corps of Engineers headquarters.

Krennic swallowed to suppress a sudden defensiveness, a raw desire to tell Galen Erso that *this* was all a sham; to load that datapad of Erso's with the schematic of the battle station and show him what he was really in charge of.

Instead, he said: "I'm flattered and I'm honored, but I'm afraid that my commitment to the Republic comes first and foremost, especially at this time, when the galaxy is divided against itself."

Galen's face fell, but he nodded in understanding. "I wish there was some way to convince you that there are other ways to contribute to peace."

Krennic fixed him in his sights. "As I wish I could convince you," he said with finality.

Staring out the window at the comings and goings of beings on the institute campus, Galen asked himself how he could have felt freer in a prison cell than he did in his own apartment. In his mind's eye he could still take in the view from the barred cell window, the

one that had practically required the talents of a gymnast to behold: fat flakes of snow falling on the tun-
dra, sky-kings performing lazy spirals overhead, the
flickering lights of the city, winter's rippling, wavering
curtains of polar light. And now Coruscant, and a
discontent he had never known; an inability to find
refuge even in his thoughts; to find what one of his
mentors had called *the still point in the turning
world*.

Weeks had passed since Orson's rejection of his
proposal, but Galen still wasn't over it. In retrospect
he realized that he had been grasping at straws; determined to find a swift and easy escape from the quag-
mire in which he found himself. But how could he
have been so audacious as to ask Orson to abandon
the career he had pursued since his earliest days in the
Futures Program? Galen abhorred his commitment to
the Republic military, but Orson plainly had no interest in being rescued.

He turned from the window and moved into the
apartment's main room, careful not to tread on any
of Jyn's toys. With his mind busy in the most useless
ways and the apartment suddenly crowded with
clothes and stuffed animals, mobiles and swing sets—
almost all of it donated by friends whose children had
outgrown those things—he had become compulsive
about trying to impose some sense of order, but there
simply wasn't enough space. So he had turned to his
own possessions—his notes and datacrons and collec-
tions of sample rocks and crystals—and had experi-
mented with arranging everything by category, the
datacrons by order of importance, the crystals by size,

then by color . . . All in an effort to keep from confronting the fact that *he couldn't think*. He couldn't concentrate. Instead his thoughts *churned*, as Lyra used to accuse his feet of doing on hikes through rugged terrain.

He gazed around in near despair. Where he had never had an issue with so-called free time, he was suddenly lost without his research; torn between uncompromising tenderness for Lyra and Jyn and a sense of burden in being able to provide a flawless future for them.

The Vallt he missed no longer existed; nor did the Coruscant he and Lyra had left more than a standard year earlier. Despite the changes war had brought to the Core it might still be possible for them to ride out the conflict here. Even if it meant avoiding HoloNet news reports and steering clear of conversations about war and politics. Surely they could manage that much. Perhaps the war would end as abruptly as it had begun and life would return to normal—or at least to what had been considered normal beforehand.

There had been no word from Zerpen. Orson had affirmed that, what with charges of espionage still hanging in the air, the company was reluctant to contact him. Like Lyra, Orson maintained that an opportunity would eventually present itself, but Galen, normally patient, felt compelled to take charge. The place to begin, he had decided, was with his friends and colleagues at the institute, some of whom he had known since his years in the Futures Program. Many had fled for their homeworlds when war had broken out, but just as many had remained on Coruscant.

Only one, however, had been willing to make time to meet with him; the rest quick to furnish excuses that struck him as more equivocal than clear.

Dressed in a suit two standard years old and already out of fashion, he left the apartment for a lunch appointment with Professor Reeva Demesne in the solarium of the institute's astrophysics building. Coruscant's scrubbed air had a vibrancy it lacked before the war. From the tops of the tallest cloudcutters to the lowest of the Central District's levels, everyone seemed to be actively participating in the defense of the Republic. News reports blared from screens once reserved for advertisements and entertainment. The tiers of traffic lanes were crowded and frenzied. Gargantuan starships landed and launched from the spaceports, the heat from their drives rippling the atmosphere, and military personnel were omnipresent, from uniformed officers of all species to squads of white-armored clone troopers.

The astrophysics building, too, buzzed with activity. Visitors were required to check in at security booths and were sometimes shadowed by small repulsorlift cam droids. Cliques of multispecies researchers and professors hurried about, conversing in hushed tones or finishing one another's sentences with rushed enthusiasm. Other institute denizens seemed completely preoccupied, lost in their own worlds, tapping or speaking notes into datapads as they maneuvered through the bustling corridors, narrowly avoiding collisions with others doing the same. Galen took note that many levels of the building were now restricted to faculty members and staff, with soldiers posted at every egress.

He rode a turbolift to the solarium and spied Reeva seated at a square table by the west-facing windows. The Mirialan's skin was a powdery green, her striking face tattooed in vertical bands of dark diamonds. Her full lips were pigmented in iridescent blue scales. She wore a scarlet robe that reached the floor, and a cowl covered most of her graying hair.

His former mentor stood as he approached and embraced him. "Galen, it's wonderful to have you back on Coruscant. I almost didn't recognize you behind the beard."

He stroked his whiskers as he seated himself. "It's probably time to get rid of it."

"It suits you." She gestured toward the nourishment synthesizers. "What can I get you?"

He shook his head. "I normally skip lunch."

Reeva motioned to her plate of food. "You don't mind . . ."

"Of course not. Good appetite."

"How is Lyra, Galen?"

"Good. Adapting. To being a mother, I mean."

"Ah, yes, the baby."

"Jyn."

She blew out her breath. "How could I forget? I was there when the two of you chose the name! I've too much on my mind lately."

Galen's eyes roamed the sunlit room. "This place has become a hive."

"It's like this all over. The institute is conscripting candidates from university programs even before they graduate. So many people working on so many projects."

"Are you still involved in energy generation and enhancement?"

"No longer."

Galen let his surprise show. "But that was always your passion, Reeva. I was following your research every chance I got. You seemed to be on the threshold of a major advance."

She exhaled in a fatigued way and pushed her plate aside. "Things change."

"So I keep hearing. What are you involved with now?"

She glanced around before answering. "Defensive shield generation. I really can't say a lot about it." A knowing smile lightened the moment. "But I'm sure we'll be able to catch up after the next briefing."

Galen frowned in ignorance. "What briefing?"

She paused for a moment to take his measure. "You're not . . . You haven't joined the defense project?"

He spread his hands in bafflement.

"You haven't signed the Official Secrets Oath?" she pressed.

"I've never even heard of an Official Secrets Oath."

Her eyes shifted. "I'm sorry, Galen, I'd assumed that . . . Well, never mind. You're still with Zerpen then."

"I honestly don't know. The regime change on Vallt apparently left a bad taste in their mouth."

"All the more reason for you to join us."

"Join you in what exactly? Reeva, I can't get a

straight answer from anyone about what's going on. What's become of this place? All these spying eyes and security posts. It feels less like a place for science than a military base."

Reeva firmed her shimmering lips. "You've been away, Galen. The war has altered everything, not only for those directly involved in the conflict, but also for many of us here on Coruscant. Count Dooku shook us awake to a harsh reality, and most of us have traded theory for practicality. Even so, unlimited funding has been wonderful for research."

Galen smirked. "Wars have always been good for innovation. But what's become of our dream of providing renewable energy to shore up microeconomies on developing worlds? To allow them to participate in power production rather than be held hostage to the consortiums?"

"In due time we'll return to that," Reeva said, "and we'll be able to accomplish much more than we ever could before."

Galen was crestfallen. "What's it like—working for the military?"

Reeva's eyes darted again. "My direct contact with them is somewhat limited. I spend my days conferring with colleagues and machines. We calculate, we experiment. We transmit our research."

"These shield generators . . . Are they designed for cities as defensive umbrellas?"

Reeva shook her head. "They're designed for capital ships."

Galen stared at her. "I don't understand. Rothana's ships are capable of withstanding most of what the

Separatists can deliver in the way of laser- or projectile fire."

"Our team is working on protecting something larger—with wider, impregnable coverage."

"Larger than a *Venator*-class Star Destroyer? Is this to parry some new weapons platform Dooku has in the works?"

"So it would seem."

Considering it, Galen prized a marker from his pocket and started to sketch his thoughts onto a napkin. "In the short run you could consider shunting a shield's absorbed energy into a heat sink, then employ neutrino radiators to return energy to the generators and projectors themselves. It's similar to what we've been doing with lasing mediums and crystals. Of course, you need to be careful about overpumping." He continued to sketch. "Maybe multiple shield generators distributed evenly across an entire hull to enhance coverage . . ."

Reeva slid the napkin across the table to regard it. "Interesting . . ."

"Just thinking out loud," Galen said in dismissal. "But this sort of research isn't normally done on Coruscant."

"Our ideas are going to be put to the test in a new facility."

"Am I allowed to know where?"

"I don't even know where it is."

"Official secrets." He sat back, folding his arms across his chest. "It's come to that, has it?"

By way of answer, she said: "All of us need to position ourselves for the future, Galen." And just as quickly she changed the subject. "But listen: A group of us from the old days are having a reunion in a few weeks. Why don't you join us? Bring Lyra. Bring the baby, if you want. I'm certain that a lot of your former schoolmates would love to see you."

"Before everyone ships out for parts unknown, you mean."

Tongue in her cheek, she nodded. "That's a distinct possibility."

8

PUBLIC DISPLAYS OF AFFECTATION

KRENNIC AND VICE CHANCELLOR MAS Amedda left the Strategic Planning Amphitheater together, using a doorway reserved for the highest-level dignitaries. A pair of red-robed guards followed but slowed their pace to drop back as the two began to converse.

"Who authorized you to launch an attack on Vallt?" Amedda said with a snarl of exasperation. He had the tall figure-headed staff gripped in his right hand, and was sporting a shimmersilk cummerbund and an overcloak with padded shoulders—as if his upper torso weren't already wide enough.

"It was a military decision."

"I ask again: On whose authority?"

Krennic looked at him out of the corner of his eye. "You said you didn't want to know any details. Have you changed your mind?"

"I don't want to know. And yet intelligence reaches me and I'm obliged to become involved." Amedda shot him a look. "Who?"

"The admiral in command of that sector. The attack was part of the deal we made with Zerpen, and also a means of safeguarding anything Galen Erso may have revealed to Vallt's Separatist regime regarding the disposition of Republic warships in that sector."

Amedda ridiculed the idea with a reverberating grunt. "Erso wasn't in possession of any intelligence to that effect."

"Just to be sure, then."

"As it happens, the return of Vallt to the Republic has worked in our favor." Amedda's gruff voice lost some of its edge. "I'm told that the world can be used as a staging area for offensives into nearby systems. But let me caution you about the need to respect the chain of command, Lieutenant Commander. Otherwise you risk jeopardizing your position in the cell."

Krennic disregarded the counsel. "I must be allowed to do my job, Vice Chancellor."

"Since when does meeting with the Geonosian archduke fall under your bailiwick?"

Krennic wasn't surprised to learn that Amedda knew of the visit. "The ongoing discussion about the need for a sentient workforce on the battle station gave me an idea, and I chose to follow up on it."

Amedda looked over at him. "Poggle has agreed to provide his drones?"

Krennic nodded once. "He'll make the announcement part of his homecoming."

The Chagrian's grunt signaled endorsement. "Very clever."

They walked in silence for a few moments before Amedda added: "I have briefed the Supreme Chancellor about the rescue of Galen Erso."

Krennic suppressed a smile of satisfaction. "I considered using Lok Durd and Nuvo Vindi in the swap, but I wasn't certain you would sanction their release from confinement. Hence, the two Morseerians—who no longer pose a threat to the Grand Army clones, by the way."

Amedda's free hand stroked the lethorn on that side. "I have been looking into Dr. Erso's research. As you say, he may prove to be of great value to the project."

"I'm glad you agree."

"So why hasn't he been recruited? Why the delay?"

"He's still weighing his options. I suggest we give him more time."

"Time? Are you aware of our recent defeat at Ryloth?"

"I just heard."

"And our losses at Bothawui?"

"Most unfortunate."

"Then I'm sure you'll agree that time is growing short. How can we force his hand?"

"We can't. He's rejected previous offers from the military. The fact that he chose prison over freedom shows that he can't be coerced. He doesn't approve of bureaucracy, and prefers to control as much of his research as possible."

"He was a Zerpen employee," Amedda pointed out.

"Only because Zerpen promised to leave him alone."

"I prefer people without principles," Amedda said. "Is it Zerpen's wish to have him back?"

"Yes, but we've persuaded them not to tender any offers. Dr. Erso was part of the price Zerpen paid for the return of the Vallt facility."

Amedda scowled. "Is there no one who can help us position him? His wife, perhaps."

Krennic shook his head. "Cut from the same cloth, I'm afraid."

"She is not a scientist. Just what is she to him—a minder?"

"A listener. A translator of sorts. Often in charge of transcribing and organizing his notes."

Amedda fairly growled. "Dr. Erso was your idea. Months have elapsed and he continues to elude you. Without the weapon itself, our project is nothing more than a very costly artificial planetoid."

Krennic mulled it over. "Vice Chancellor, I imagine that fishing is a very popular pastime on your homeworld."

"Champala's seas are not what they once were, but yes, of course," Amedda said, clearly wondering where Krennic was going.

"Then you understand the need for a proper lure, the proper bait, even the proper device required to land a catch."

Amedda exhaled through his nose. "To extend your analogy, Dr. Erso may be one of those rare creatures who is not easily attracted to even the most colorful lure or the tastiest bait."

"In his own waters, perhaps. But he's far from those, and swimming directly toward our net." Krennic paused, then added: "Galen Erso is destined to join the project. He just doesn't know it yet."

*   *   *

Krennic had had no plans to attend the Futures Program reunion until he learned that Galen would be attending. The affair was hosted by a wealthy graduate who had served two terms in the Senate and whose apartment suite in 500 Republica was as lavish as any that could be found in Coruscant's most prestigious building.

Many of those present were researchers and scientists involved with various aspects of the battle station project—the drives, shield and tractor beam technology, hypermatter power plant—without a full understanding of what they were working on. As a way of implementing the need-to-know tactics adopted by the cell, research was scattered among thousands of facilities on hundreds of worlds, with all interdisciplinary communication monitored and controlled. An entire branch of Republic security had been created merely to run constant surveillance on key personnel, eavesdrop on off-hours conversations, and capture images for scrutiny and analysis.

Krennic found a vantage point in the room and looked around. With so much drinking going on, he thought, one could almost forget that the Republic was at war.

He wasn't the only one in uniform, as the Futures Program had fed as many graduates into the military as it had academia, the arts, and government service. But few of the officers were risk takers like himself. They were analysts and tacticians, lost in their data banks of information and safe in their hardened headquarters on Coruscant. Most would have remembered him as the one who was always speaking out of turn and yet managed to graduate with high honors.

Abandoning his position, he began to circulate among them, keeping a watchful eye on Galen while affording him ample space to interact with friends and colleagues he hadn't seen in years, many of whom regarded Galen as something of a superstar in scientific circles. A master of the invisible connections between things.

Krennic had originally dismissed Galen as the kind of retiring kid who typically would have been bullied or harassed mercilessly. Little by little, however, he came to appreciate Galen not only for his intellectual superiority, but also for his unique spirit. When called on by a professor, Galen would provide an answer without lifting his eyes from his desk, as if he were busy solving some other problem at the same time or finishing one of his outlandish sketches—with either hand. He had no interest in sports, drinking, flirting, or conquests. He saw the world as if with extrasensory eyes and ears, and had an ability to grasp heady concepts almost instinctively—concepts Krennic sometimes struggled to comprehend. He became fascinated by the prodigy from Grange, and on a couple of occasions had been Galen's protector in fights or brawls.

Adept at reading people, Krennic had made the most of being surrounded by geniuses, and had used his stint in the Futures Program to hone his skills. He devoted himself to learning how to work with academics and scientists; how to put them on the same path and organize them into productive teams. His leadership became as important to a project as their contributions, and he built a reputation as someone who could be the interface between the ones with power and financing and the ones who could calculate and construct and make dreams come true. When it had come time for choosing someone from the Corps of Engineers to head up the Special Weapons Group, the cell had had to look no further than Orson Krennic.

Continuing his perambulation, he saw Lyra Erso speaking with Galen's close friend Reeva Demesne, whom Krennic had drafted into the shield generator program. Having left year-old Jyn with a nanny, Lyra was on her own for a change and a veritable cynosure in a room full of mostly frumpy researchers. When Krennic imagined her, he saw her in rugged boots and hiking shorts and carrying an unwieldy pack on her back; seeing her now in a fashionable skirt and high heels was something of a revelation.

Krennic recalled running into Galen shortly after his return from Espinar several years earlier and being entertained by the crystallographer's bright-eyed confession that he had fallen in love. Galen, who would scarcely raise his eyes when a pretty woman entered a room, in love? It had to be a joke. The thought of Galen's genius being undermined by some grasping creature drove him to distraction. But Krennic couldn't wait to meet the mysterious Lyra—the woman whose mere touch *enchanted* Galen—and when he did he understood what Galen had found in her: his opposite. Each of them drawn to the other's exotic qualities. Still, he hadn't expected the love affair to last more than a couple of months, and was shocked when they wed.

All these years later Krennic still wasn't used to the two of them.

Once he was instrumental in persuading Galen to accept his destiny by joining the project, was Lyra going to be a problem? Thank the stars, that child had come along to keep her occupied and out of his way.

He stopped to listen in on a huddle of people speaking about Galen, and every so often glancing at him. He edged closer to hear a computer engineer named Dagio Belcoze inaccurately recounting the details of Galen's imprisonment on Vallt. An Iktotchi of medium height with a battering-ram forehead and a pair of polished downturned horns, Belcoze was a member of Dr. Gubacher's artificial intelligence team, designing enhanced overseer droids to supervise the battle station labor force. The near-human's big right hand held a drink, and he was ranting that the Republic should simply bomb the Separatist capital world of Raxus out of existence—and that people like Galen Erso were an insult to the goal of victory.

Pushing his way through the huddle, Belcoze staggered up to Galen, who was a centimeter or so taller than Dagio, but lighter by several kilos.

"Here he is," the Iktotchi began in a loud slur. "The prodigal kyber specialist who refuses to join the cause." He spread his fleshy hands. "Perhaps he thinks he's too intelligent to work with the rest of us.

He'd rather work on a Separatist world than serve the Republic."

Even caught by surprise, Galen appeared unperturbed by the allegation. "You're drunk, Dagio," he said. "Which comes as no surprise. What does, is the fact that you're so obviously deluded."

Galen's calm only made Dagio angrier. "The always elusive Erso. I'd like to hear you deny the charges of treason publicly."

Galen shut his eyes for a moment. "I've nothing to deny, and nothing more to say to you."

Krennic spotted Lyra winding through the onlookers to reach Galen as he turned to leave. At the same time, Reeva Demesne saw the situation beginning to escalate and attempted to mediate by stepping between Galen and Dagio and stretching out her arms.

"Gentlemen, please," she said, "this is not an occasion for recriminations."

With a deft sidestep, Dagio outmaneuvered her, took Galen by the shoulder, and spun him around.

"Just what intelligence did you share with them while you were allegedly in custody?"

Galen's face took on sudden color. "I told them what everyone here already knows: that Dagio Belcoze is a second-rate slicer who for years has taken credit for coding written by far more gifted beings."

Krennic moved quickly, placing himself just behind the Iktotchi's left shoulder as Dagio hurled the icy drink directly into Galen's face. Krennic had already discerned that the drink was a diversion, and that Dagio's free hand was cocked and ready to launch. When Galen fell back a step, the Iktotchi fired off a powerful jab aimed at the side of Galen's jaw. Galen, though, was a step ahead of him. Slipping to one side, he raised his arm, assuring that Dagio's punch would deflect off his forearm, then, in a move that caught even Krennic off guard, Galen came in under Dagio's extended arm with a powerful cross that connected solidly with the Iktotchi's cheekbone and sent him stumbling back, confused and bleeding.

A few of Dagio's friends had the wisdom to hold him back, as Lyra was suddenly at her husband's side ready to plant a heel directly into the Iktotchi's forehead.

"Just like old times," Krennic said, stepping carefully to Galen's other side, "except it seems I no longer have to fight your battles."

Galen wiped the drink from his face and nursed his fist. "You never did."

In the ensuing confusion, the room divided into two camps. Adjusting her stance, Lyra slipped her arm through Galen's and began leading him toward the door.

Krennic watched them go.

Galen had been publicly accused of being a traitor, and now humiliated because of his reluctance to serve the Republic. Krennic couldn't have orchestrated it any better had he tried.

9

ANGRY RED PLANET

IT WAS THE RAINY SEASON on that part of Geonosis.
The vast, normally red desert plain had been transformed into a foul-smelling acidic lake that had attracted migratory beasts from throughout the region,
and the cluster of dripstone spires that made up the
Stalgasin hive rose like islands in the mist. The vaguely
circular petranaki arena—a natural butte that had been
decapitated and hollowed—hosted a shallow lake of
its own, composed of the spilled blood of several
thousand drones who had died after three days of
gladiatorial games and had yet to soak fully into the
gritty sand.

Seated among Geonosian aristocrats who had paid
fortunes to revel in being spattered by airborne gore,
Krennic shuddered at the thought of having to spend
what might be a decade on and above the irradiated
world. An astringent smell assaulted his nostrils, possibly the loosed pheromones that were whipping the
assembled crowd of a hundred thousand flightless
drones and winged soldiers to a near frenzy.

The reason for the celebration was twofold: It was

both the Eve of Meckgin and the long-overdue home-coming of the hive's leader, Archduke Poggle the Lesser, whom Krennic had escorted home, traveling by Star Destroyer to the newly established Sentinel Base that safeguarded Geonosis space before transferring to a smaller ship that had carried them the rest of the way. Now the archduke occupied a shell-like podium that had risen from the bowels of the arena and was waiting for the place to settle down so that he could address the multitudes.

Alongside and behind Krennic in the membrane-shaded visitors' boxes were a handful of Supreme Chancellor Palpatine's emissaries and cronies, including Sate Pestage, Ars Dangor, and Janus Greejatus. All, like Krennic, were attired in antirad hydration suits and transpirators, except for the chancellor's bald-headed and ethereal administrative aide, Sly Moore, who wore an invaluable Umbaran shadowcloak that looked as if it had been spun from feathers. Krennic was grateful to see Poggle on the podium at last, certain that another hour of the phantasmagoria would drive him mad.

"How blessed I am by the Creator in being able to join you on an occasion of such spectacle and bravery," the archduke began. "How wonderful it feels to be returned to ever-dramatic Geonosis, harsh but ever welcoming, scoured by the rays of our crimson sun and emboldened by them, blessed to have this corner of space to ourselves so that the Geonosian society has been able take charge of its own evolution and fulfill its destiny."

Poggle had a new staff of office—a kind of crooked

walking stick carved from the tusk of an indigenous carnivorous behemoth—which he lifted into the air to a deafening chorus of clicks and whistles from the crowd.

"It is, in fact, by the good graces of the Republic, whose representatives are today our guests, that I am able to participate."

An angry buzzing rose from the cheap seats. Orray-mounted Geonosian picadors armed with stun poles zapped a few audience members into silence before things could get out of control, but Ars Dangor had his doubts. "I fear we could become appetizers at the drop of a hat," he said to Krennic through speakers built into the transpirators.

As a show of faith, Krennic had ordered the ship's complement of clone troopers to remain aboard, but he was beginning to question his decision. He tried to imagine what it had been like when a couple of Jedi had nearly been butchered in the arena and certainly would have died had other Jedi and a regiment of Grand Army soldiers not arrived in the nick of time, seemingly out of nowhere and taking the galaxy by surprise. Might he be sitting in Count Dooku's seat just now?

Poggle's knobby hands were making calming gestures.

"Yes, yes, it cannot be denied that we have had our differences with the Republic; that two great battles have been fought on our hallowed grounds against the forces of the Republic. But let us pause for a moment to consider the circumstances that led to those conflicts.

"Some of you gathered here today are old enough to remember when Baktoid Armor Workshop came to Geonosis and struck a deal with us to build foundries and produce battle droids and other automata for which we were handsomely rewarded. Then, as ever, we were able to overcome our natural contempt for outsiders in order to fulfill what seemed a noble task.

"Sheltered in remote space, how could we have known that in fully devoting ourselves to that enterprise—for we would never do less—we were serving the interests of a trade cartel that would bring strife to the Outer Rim. Later, too, when Count Dooku came to renew our contract with Baktoid, how could we have known that this human, a former Jedi Knight, had aligned himself with a confederacy of Separatists—a confederacy determined not only to secede from the Republic, but also to cripple the economy of the galaxy by engaging in an all-out war.

"The Republic is not our enemy!"

Wing flapping and whistling erupted from the upper-caste galleries, and the suddenly stirred air wafted the odor of grilled arch grubs into Krennic's breath mask.

"How fitting that on this day celebrating the virtues of industry I should be able to announce the next great undertaking of the Stalgasin hive—and perhaps the greatest it has ever undertaken."

The arena fell eerily silent, tangibly expectant. Even the beasts—the chained reeks and acklays—quieted.

Poggle played to the moment, posing a question.

"How many of you have gazed into the heavens at night and seen something new taking shape above our world? A crescent, a circle, a gleaming ring that is like the portal to another dimension? Many of you have grasped that our asteroids have been supplying the raw materials for the ring, as our dismantled and reassembled foundries have been furnishing the finished products. But how many of you are aware that the ring is an artifact of our hive? That the ring is, in fact, a Geonosian creation?"

Krennic smiled to himself: Poggle was finally taking credit for it.

"We have now been tasked to realize the dream that originated with our designers, in constructing a mobile orb of such size that it will seem to some nothing less than a small moon. This will be the greatest enterprise in which the hive has ever participated, not merely because of the scale but also because the work will necessitate that many of you execute it from inside the orb itself—in space, from where you will be able to gaze down in wonder on our homeworld while you go happily about your assignments.

"Is this not reason for celebration of unprecedented magnitude?"

He gave the crowd ample time to whoop it up, then simmer down.

"I have saved the most important announcement for last," he added in a serious tone. "We have a viable queen—which will shortly mean a doubling of our workforce and the subsequent doubling of our efforts! So let the games continue for another three days. Let blood be spilled and drones prove themselves worthy of escalation. And let us give good cheer to those representatives of the Republic who have helped bring about this miracle of service!"

Krennic's stomach turned at the thought of having to sit through another three days of bloodletting, but a rush of smugness galvanized him.

"Nicer surroundings than for my last interrogation," Galen said after he had taken a seat in the adjutant general's office.

"I was assured that Republic Intelligence treated you very civilly," Wilhuff Tarkin said from his chair.

There was a desk in the room, but Tarkin had motioned Galen to an armchair in a sitting area with a low table centered on an expensive carpet adorned with the Republic symbol. Artwork and datacrons filled the hardwood shelves, and a large window looked out on the Senate Dome.

"I'm referring to my interrogation on Vallt," Galen clarified. "It was bitter cold and the roof leaked. You obviously enjoy a loftier administrative position than Chieftain Gruppe does. Or did, depending on whether she survived the Republic attack."

Tarkin smiled thinly. "I'm told that she did indeed survive. Perhaps she now occupies the very cell you did."

Galen eyebrows went up in surprise. "I'm glad to hear she's alive."

"You two became friendly?"

"You mean as interrogators and their captives sometimes do?"

"I'm simply curious."

Galen snorted. "Simple curiosity doesn't go especially well with this room or your uniform, Commander."

Galen didn't know anything about Tarkin, other
than that he had served in the Republic Navy before
being appointed adjutant general. A tall man some
ten or fifteen years older than Galen, he had sunken
cheeks, a high brow, and a look of penetrating intelligence.

"Let's not get off on the wrong foot, Dr. Erso. This
is an informal interview, not a cross-examination."

"Formal, informal, what's the difference anymore?
Is there a particular cam you wish me to face?"

"You are under no obligation to answer my questions. As I told you, you're entitled to a lawyer—"

"Perhaps we could begin by your answering one of
mine."

Tarkin relaxed in his chair and crossed one knee
over the over. "I'm at your disposal."

"Why am I being prevented from leaving Coruscant? Zerpen's facility on Vallt is now back in operation and I fully expect the company to rehire me."

Tarkin made his thin lips even thinner. "The problem
as I understand it is that Zerpen is still doing business
with worlds in danger of falling to the Separatists, and
we can't risk your being involved in another incident."

"But Vallt has returned to the Republic."

"For the moment. Vallt lies in a very contested sector. It could change hands several times before this
conflict ends, as has happened to many worlds. There
is also, I'm afraid, the ongoing investigation into your
loyalty to the Republic."

Galen made a fatigued sound. "I'm certain you have access to my debriefings by Republic Intelligence and COMPOR."

"I've read them. During those sessions you avowed that you provided no information to Vallt, and that you refused their offer to conduct research for the Separatists. You also stated that you have no interest in conducting research for the Republic."

"I'm a scientist, not an effective."

"No one is asking you to fight on the front lines, Dr. Erso. We have the Grand Army and the Jedi Order for that. What the Republic needs is people willing to support the war effort in other ways."

"Again, I'm not interested in supporting the war in any capacity."

"You hail from a Republic member world that has been left devastated by the conflict. You were educated—at considerable expense—in an elite program founded by the Republic and at a succession of institutions thereafter."

"I don't recall being under any obligation to repay that debt."

"You're not. But let's be frank, Dr. Erso. You see how this looks: a brilliant researcher refusing to lift a finger to help his government?"

"There's a difference between objecting to the policies of the Republic and being a Separatist sympathizer."

"Granted. And yet you feel no allegiance to the Republic?"

"No allegiance to the Republic war machine. If

there's a place for me in energy enrichment, I'll accept the opportunity without hesitation."

Tarkin took a moment to reply. "Your chief area of expertise is crystals."

"Synthetic ones—in place of the ones I'm after."

"The kyber," Tarkin said in a knowing way. "Following up on the original research done by Marsabi?"

Galen drew his brows together in surprise. "To a degree. I'm more interested in what Cuata was doing on Mygeeto and Christophsis before the war placed them in danger."

Tarkin continued to nod. "Zaly had remarkable success in analyzing the internal structure of the kyber. Do you suspect he and other Separatist researchers might be pursuing his findings?"

"It's . . . it's possible."

"Might they have succeeded in weaponizing the research?"

"If they have, the war will soon be over."

"If I recall, Zaly's theory—"

"It's flawed. There is simply no way to contain that kind of power."

"Suppose—"

"You're beginning to sound more like a weapons specialist than a legal authority," Galen interrupted.

Tarkin smiled again. "A passing interest. But make no mistake, Dr. Erso, I'm not trying to recruit you. I'm simply trying to determine if Vallt's willingness to exchange such a brilliant researcher for two rather ordinary ones wasn't engineered to place you back on Coruscant as a double agent."

Galen sniffed. "Finally we come to the real reason I'm not allowed to leave Coruscant."

"What did this Chieftain Gruppe ask of you on Vallt?"

"She asked about the Grand Army—where it came from and how long it was in the planning stages. She asked about Republic weapons, the size of the fleet, the role of the Jedi."

"And you said nothing."

"I had nothing to give them, even if I wanted to."

"Even with your wife suffering as a result, they didn't succeed in turning you."

Galen looked hard at Tarkin. "She didn't suffer."

"You were prevented from seeing each other."

"Lyra is a strong person, with or without me by her side. Perhaps you need to be reminded that it was the *Republic* that rescued me. If I were a double agent, or whatever you're accusing me of being, why wouldn't I be jumping at the chance to work for the military?"

Tarkin didn't speak to that; instead he said: "As it happens, I know a bit about being held captive."

Galen regarded him with interest.

"I spent several weeks in a Separatist facility called the Citadel." He paused to allow it to sink in. "Were you tortured, Dr. Erso?"

"No, I wasn't. You were?"

"Repeatedly."

"I'm sorry—"

"Fortunately I was rescued before my jailers could do their worst. Had the torture continued, well, who knows? The question is: Suppose you are allowed to leave Coruscant and once more fall into enemy hands?"

"I've even less to give them now than before."

Tarkin dismissed it. "Wrong. You have something more valuable than military intelligence, Dr. Erso. You have what's in your head, and we want that to stay there."

Galen returned a despondent nod. "I have a family to support, Commander."

"Perhaps Lyra can find employment in the interim."

Galen allowed his wretchedness to show. "That's hardly the point. I need to be able to carry on with my research. I'm at a loss . . ."

Tarkin sat back, interlocking his fingers and appraising him. "It can't have escaped your attention that you have a powerful ally in Orson Krennic."

Galen raised his eyes from the carpet. "We were acquaintances in the Futures Program. Years ago."

"It's because of your relationship with him that we have decided not to pursue this matter any further."

Galen squinted in uncertainty.

"There will be no inquest or trial. In fact, I'm going to recommend that we close the case on you. You will have to remain on Coruscant until my higher-ups have signed off on this, but I suspect that the process won't entail more than a couple of standard months."

Galen stared. "Months . . ." He rubbed his forehead. "Still, I suppose I should thank you."

"Thank your *acquaintance,* Dr. Erso. But one more question before you leave: Did Lieutenant Commander Krennic offer you a position or a project of any sort?"

"No, nothing. In his own way he simply made the point you've been trying to make. That the war will go on and on and every contribution matters."

"You don't mind that the war will go on and on?"

"Palpatine could have prevented it. Now it's up to people like you to end it."

Tarkin nodded. "And so we shall."

10

THE LONG COMM

THE COMMAND HABITAT ENJOYED THE most all-encompassing view of the construction site: barren Geonosis, the decimated asteroid field and starfields, and the inchoate orb, nurtured and attended to by countless droid and supply ships, its curved super-structure bathed in the rays of the system's flaring primary.

After months of traveling back and forth to the surface, Krennic was never so grateful for artificial atmosphere.

A party in celebration of the completion of the false equator had been held local weeks earlier, although what had been cheered looked more like an antique gyroscope than an actual sphere. Since then a few degrees of the upper hemisphere had been outfitted with latitudinal structural members, and rudimentary layout work had begun on cladding a portion of the curved hull. The construction droids could now devote themselves to fashioning the first interior spaces, which like the equator band would serve as placeholders until such time as actual cabinspaces could be bulkheaded.

Geonosians would be the first to inhabit those immense life-support modules. In the wake of Poggle the Lesser's arena announcement, tens of thousands of drones had been transferred to Orbital Foundry 7, the second largest structure in view from the command habitat. Drones there were currently overseeing production of the enormous pie-slice-shaped concavities that, when assembled, would form the battle station's still somewhat perplexing focusing dish or power well. The drone laborers were lorded over by winged soldiers, but both castes answered to Poggle, for whom had been constructed a separate and lavish suite that was linked by a series of tubular connectors to the foundry. Poggle had also been given a beak-bowed ship of limited range that allowed him to commute to the surface.

The drones were apparently very unhappy with their situation. They had been promised work on the sphere, and were instead being forced to work only on the components of the dish. Poggle, however, dismissed their frustration as beneficial to the endgame of production.

Krennic and the rotund Professor Sahali stood with several members of the Special Weapons Group, watching as one of the wedge-shaped components was being tugged from the foundry's gaping hangar. Three of the slices had been completed, and another six were in various stages of fabrication.

Almost since the inception of the Strategic Advisory Cell no one could agree on the ultimate function of the dish, the construction of which was based on a meticulous study of the Geonosian schematic. Early on, everyone involved in the project had been willing to embrace the notion that function was going to have to follow form. Even their new partner, Poggle, had admitted that the Stalgasin hive hadn't had time to design the weapon before the Battle of Geonosis had curtailed their research.

The plan, in any case, called for assembling the dish in space and maneuvering it by tug and tractor beam into the gargantuan well that had been framed into the sphere's upper hemisphere—the dimple, as some referred to it. The parabolic dish also had to be engineered to telescope away from the hull to facilitate the aiming of the composite beam proton superlaser some of the Special Weapons scientists were proposing.

It continued to puzzle Krennic that Count Dooku hadn't attempted to launch a preemptory strike on the construction site. How had the fact that the battle station schematics were in Republic hands remained a secret? The thinking was that Dooku was too busy working on his own version to worry about what the Republic was doing. In that sense, the project was less about achieving parity than winning the race and being the first to deploy the weapon.

Construction, assembly, and installation of the dish should have been shouldered by the project's structural engineers. But because the dish was considered to be crucial to the station's principal weapon, oversight had fallen to Krennic, who was still in the

midst of trying to make good on his pledge to bring
Galen Erso into the mix.

He had been pleased to learn that the Justice Department had opted to drop the espionage charges
he had arranged to be leveled against Galen. What he
hadn't planned on was Galen's being interviewed by
Wilhuff Tarkin, who had subsequently taken a strong
interest in Galen's plight. Krennic didn't know Tarkin
well, though they had met briefly during Tarkin's stint
as governor of Eriadu, Tarkin's homeworld. The title
governor had stuck, even though Tarkin had since
served as an officer in the Republic Navy. Everything
about the man told Krennic that Tarkin could be
trouble. It was no secret that he enjoyed a close relationship with Supreme Chancellor Palpatine, and that
he was fairly worshipped by many of his former comrades in the Judicials. The only reason Tarkin hadn't
been drafted into the cell on day one was that he
had been imprisoned in a Separatist facility, from
which he had either been rescued or escaped, thus
amplifying both his popularity and his cachet. And
there were rumors to the effect that Tarkin had been
instrumental in convincing Palpatine to move forward
with the battle station—even that he had had a similar weapon in mind even *before* the discovery of the
Geonosian schematics. Serving nominally as adjutant
general for the navy, he was rapidly being brought up
to speed on the status of the battle station, and there
was talk among the members of the inner circle that
Tarkin was being groomed to assume leadership of
the entire project.

Krennic bristled at the thought of having to report to Tarkin, and reasoned that netting Galen was going to be the only way to avoid that. But having that card up his sleeve was different from knowing precisely when to play it.

Staring at the pie-shaped piece of dish, Krennic mulled over Poggle's production philosophy of forcing the drones to perform work that was beneath their skill or caste level as a means of increasing their ultimate output. And an idea came to him.

Why didn't Coruscant have more actual staircases than people-movers? Lyra asked herself as she wound through the throngs in the Central District. It was impossible to get a good workout in a place where she could barely raise her heartbeat, let alone break a sweat. Not on a world where the atmosphere and climate were regulated and artificial gravity was provided at the summits of the tallest structures. Despite the trouble she and Galen had found themselves in on Vallt, Coruscant—even with the threat levels, the false alarms, the real possibility of surprise attacks—was simply too safe. She needed wind and rain, cyclones, quakes, and the threat of avalanches. Unpredictability. Natural forces at work.

She had lost the weight she'd gained with Jyn, but was getting soft after all the months of waiting around for the situation to change. In the months before she and Galen had departed for Vallt, she would often sky-cab to the Jedi Temple grounds and exercise there, basking in the energy of that elegant site, surrounded by a nexus of the Force. Once events leading to the war had begun to ramp up, however, the grounds became heavily patrolled and the atmosphere changed. Now you couldn't even get near the Temple without having a high security clearance.

Had the war affected the Jedi's ability to feel the Force on Coruscant, despite the world's superabundance of sentient life? Were the battles on remote worlds somehow disrupting the Force?

The idea was too frightening to contemplate.

Lyra tried to hurry her pace—exercise was so engrained in her that she needed it as much as nourishment—but there were simply too many beings in her way. Changing course, she ducked into a transit corridor that ended at the southeast corner of Llanter Plaza, where she at last found some breathing space.

Like Galen she was an only child; unlike him, she still had a mother, alive and making ends meet as a fine artist on Aria Prime. Her mother had had to take out loans to finance Lyra's education, which Lyra had paid back by wearing a weighty holocam and hiking on worlds where the terrain was too rough for survey droids—or the costs of employing them prohibitive—to provide 3-D video for various HoloNet providers.

Later she had worked as an environmental impact specialist and a surface verification agent, positions that had eventually led to jobs as a cartographer and a survey team leader. By the time she was twenty-nine she had visited five of the fifty wonders of the Core; six of the thirty wonders of the Mid Rim; and twelve of the twenty-five wonders of the Outer Rim. She had visited several Legacy worlds—environmentally protected worlds—in remote regions, but she had yet to travel through the Inner Core, venture into the Western Reaches, or penetrate more than fifty parsecs into the Unknown Regions.

So many places to see . . .

Marriage had never been part of the plan, to say nothing of a child. But being pregnant with Jyn—especially while in captivity—had made her aware of the Force in a way she imagined the Jedi experienced: a profound connection with life that went beyond mere understanding. And while she supported Galen's research, she was secretly glad that he was no longer attempting to synthesize or create facsimiles of kyber crystals. One might as well try to clone the Force itself, or turn to magic in an effort to simulate the power.

She swung a quick turn into an alley and began to jog before being brought up short by a group of yammering droids bent on enticing her into a holotheater.

As much as she appreciated being out of the apartment, she wasn't enjoying the freedom as much as she had hoped. It was as if she had forgotten something important—that something being Jyn, who on approaching nineteen months old was beginning to chat up a storm and display an early defiant streak. Lyra thrilled at being able to open Jyn's mind, but in fact she felt like she was learning as much as she was teaching.

Maybe the days of feeling entirely on her own were long gone.

As she ambled through a densely crowded shopping district, she tried to recall the last occasion she'd had free time. That would have been several months earlier, on the night of the Future Program's reunion when Galen had gotten into that dreadful dustup. Dagio Belcoze had contacted him a few days later to apologize, blaming alcohol, and Galen had forgiven him. But the Iktotchi's accusations had stung and lingered on in the form of gossip about what had happened on Vallt.

Lyra's support of Galen's decision to avoid military research remained steadfast, but they were now on the edge of falling into serious debt. Worse, Galen was restless and miserable, though he managed to hide his discontent from Jyn, whom he had nicknamed Stardust. Orson Krennic, among others, had promised to find some sort of position for Galen, but no one had come through. Lyra had proposed going to Aria Prime the moment Galen's travel ban was lifted. They could live with her mother, and perhaps wait out the war there.

Meanwhile the conflict was escalating—the worlds of Malastare, Saleucami, and Mon Calamari now in the thick of it—and wherever Lyra ventured on Coruscant she felt as if she was under surveillance. The war had brought tens of millions of refugees to Coruscant, many of whom in the absence of employment opportunities had been forced to live in hopelessly overcrowded relocation centers. Just that morning the HoloNet news had carried a report about a Separatist cell that had been exposed on Coruscant, with several members captured and others killed.

Then there was the cryptic message that had appeared on the screen of her personal comlink one morning from an unknown sender, reading simply: *It's not too late for him to change his mind.* Did the *him* refer to Galen? Had it been sent by Separatist or even Republic operatives? Had the gossip surrounding Galen given birth to it? Was it perhaps from Adjutant General Tarkin, who had actually befriended him?

Though the message might have been meant for someone else entirely, it had rattled her.

She had stopped to look over a window display of hiking shoes and gear when she noticed for a second time the Ryn she had spied earlier while absently appraising a collection of jewelry. The Ryn were a species of itinerant humanoids with white hair and prehensile tails, but it was only the fact that Ryn were such a rarity in the Core that had compelled her to fix on his reflection in the glass. This one was wearing fur boots, a flat cap, and a long red coat. And here he was again, a long distance from when they had first locked eyes.

Lyra's danger senses came alive. The Ryn didn't look threatening, but she didn't like being followed. Quickening her pace, she blazed a twisting trail through the crowds, catching a turbolift just in time to ride it up three levels and another in time to descend one. Stepping out, she glanced furtively in all directions, certain she had given him the slip . . . until she spotted him again, approaching her out of nowhere with his long-fingered hands buried inside his coat.

Glad now that she had left Jyn in Galen's care, she turned and raced deeper into the crowd, then darted into an alley—only to find him coming toward her from the far end. Spinning on her heel, she started back the way she had come, and was amazed to see him in front of her. A swift look over her shoulder confirmed her suspicions: There were two of them, identically dressed and now closing on her from front and rear.

Whirling again, she searched for something she could use as a weapon, as a call for help in that area wasn't likely to draw much more than a passing glance. Were they after valuables they wrongly assumed she carried, or was she facing an abduction or worse?

Were they agents of whoever had left the inscrutable comlink message?

As the pair of Ryn converged, she steeled herself to do what damage she could with her fingernails and feet.

"There's no getting away from us," the one in front said in tone-perfect Basic.

"We'll make it easy for you," said the one behind.

Both of them had their hands hidden, and when they were a meter away they opened their long coats to reveal cleverly designed displays of rings and necklaces, earrings and bracelets.

Lyra stared in openmouthed surprise—and relief— as one of them held up a scintillating pendant, saying with a sudden quiet sibilance:

"Pretty lady, this one has your name on it."

Galen had just finished reorganizing his research notes and was about to check on napping Jyn—a rarity in the Erso household—when the apartment com-link chimed and, when he took the call, a quarter-scale holopresence of Orson genied from the projector.

The signal was shaky and noisy, and Galen began to fiddle with the controls in an attempt to stabilize the vid feed. Orson appeared to be doing the same at his end of the transmission, and ultimately Galen had to downsize the projection to one-eighth scale. As the comm had obviously been routed through an incalculable number of relay stations, the source code was impossible to determine.

"Where in the galaxy are you?" Galen asked after a long moment of adjustments.

"Far from Coruscant."

"Clearly. An engineering project?"

"Massive," Orson said. He was in uniform and standing in front of a ship's viewport. "On an unprecedented scale."

"Military?"

"What do you think, Galen?"

Galen's curiosity was piqued. "An orbital facility or in deep space?"

"A bit of both."

Galen sensed that that was as much as he was going to get by way of explanation. "I'm glad to hear that someone is gainfully employed."

"And how have you been spending your time?"

Galen combed his long hair back with his fingers. "Going stir-crazy."

"Lyra and the child?"

"As good as can be expected under the circumstances. You heard what happened with the Justice Department?"

"I've been briefed."

"It seems I have you to thank again for my not being imprisoned."

"The entire case was without merit," Orson said. "Baseless accusations. I tried to make that clear to Adjutant General Tarkin, but he insisted on launching an investigation."

"Actually, he's been very sympathetic. His hands are tied in terms of rescinding the travel ban, but he's helping in other ways."

"I wouldn't put much stock in what he promises."

"I won't. But he's my only hope right now."

"As it happens, he's not. That's why I'm contacting you. I may have found a position for you."

Galen could scarcely believe what he was hearing.

"It's not much," Orson went on, "but it could end your deadlock."

"Not military—"

"Nothing of the sort. You've heard of Helical HyperCom?"

Galen tugged on his lower lip. "They manufacture personal comm devices."

"HH has a large production facility on Lokori. Right now they're attempting to produce a crystal array to better serve remote areas where communications relays have fallen prey to the war. The Republic is contributing to the research production, as the devices will benefit many struggling member worlds."

Multitasking, Galen called up a galactic map while he listened. "Lokori is near Ryloth."

"Not the most secure destination just now, but well fortified."

"This is unexpected, Orson," Galen said. "Of course I'd have to review the current research and production."

"Director Herbane can send you whatever data you need—assuming you're interested."

"Director—?"

"Roman Herbane. COO or some such title. You'll answer chiefly to him."

Galen fell silent.

"I realize that it must seem like a backward step for someone of your accomplishments," Orson went on, "but isn't there some phrase about sometimes having to take one step back to take two steps forward?"

Galen found his voice. "It's just that I've grown accustomed to supervising my own research and being my own boss . . ."

"I don't want to put you in a situation you'll regret, Galen—"

"You're not, you're not."

"HH will probably leave you to your own devices, in any case," Orson said. "Besides, you can consider the position temporary until something more aligned to your talents and interests comes along."

Galen thought about it. "I'll need to discuss this with Lyra. She's been suggesting we relocate to Aria Prime once the travel restrictions are lifted. Her mother's health is failing."

"Whatever you think best, of course," Orson said.

Galen looked at the map. "Lokori . . ."

"By all accounts a very interesting world—with a much more agreeable climate than Vallt."

"When does Helical need a decision from me?"

"The sooner the better."

Galen blew out his breath. "I've never been good with spontaneity, Orson. Do you have an opinion?"

"My opinion is that you accept the offer. I'll use my influence to make certain you're allowed to leave Coruscant and return to work—even work of a sort that's beneath your station."

Galen nodded for the comlink holocam. "You're placing me further and further in your debt. I don't know how or when I'll be able to repay you."

Orson smiled. "At some point I'll show you the plans for what I'm working on, and you can tell me what you think."

11

MUNDANE SCIENCE

LYRA HADN'T RESEARCHED LOKORI. ON Coruscant she had mentioned the planet to a few friends but had stopped listening when they went into detail. She wanted to be surprised, to be put off her guard. She wanted to be intrigued.

She had showed Jyn a couple of images of where they were headed, but aside from having spent those few months on Vallt, the entire galaxy was new to her.

Even with Krennic's influence and some assistance and encouragement from Wilhuff Tarkin, another three standard months passed before Galen had been able to extricate himself fully from bureaucratic red tape. Then all at once they were done—oaths and contracts had been signed, affidavits delivered, permission to travel granted, apartment sublet—and the next thing they knew they were aboard a passenger ship bound for the Outer Rim, their fares paid for by Helical HyperCom, Galen's new employer. He hadn't told her much about the new position, but Lyra had checked into the company and found it to be above-board, with a good record of contributing to worth-while causes.

The passenger ship shuttle was descending now, and she had her face pressed to the cool transparisteel viewport. The capital city of Fucallpa looked like an enormous flower bed, riotous with colors and shapes. Her gaze took in basketlike structures and spiked domes like outsized succulents; buildings climbing in off-kilter segments with stairways wrapped around them like clinging vines; residential areas that might as well have been horticultural farms, laid out like lobed or pointed leaves.

The indigenous species—also called Lokori—were stalklike insectoids, with stemmed eyes, vestigial wings, and elongated hindquarters from which at one time had extended a second pair of reverse-articulated legs. What struck her from the start, at spaceport immigration and customs, was the Lokori's intrinsic graciousness, evidenced by a to-and-fro motion of the head based on a religious ritual that signaled greeting and gentle acceptance. The locals were immediately enamored of Jyn, whose powerful legs were now carrying her far and wide and whose vocabulary had tripled. A Lokori representative of Helical HyperCom met them outside of customs and showed them to a company landspeeder large enough to accommodate everyone and their few pieces of luggage.

Galen had been quieter than usual during the journey from Coruscant, and as Lyra observed him she knew instinctively that he felt out of his element and unsure. But when he turned to her, perhaps sensing her sideways scrutiny, he smiled.

"What do you think so far?"

"If it's all like this, I'm good," she said. "Better than good."

"What about you, Stardust? Are you having fun so far?"

Jyn nodded, then began to bounce up and down on the speeder's bench seat in a show of enthusiasm. Or maybe she was just picking up on Lyra's obvious hopefulness. In either case, Galen looked at her lovingly and reached behind him to take her hand.

The landspeeder meandered through well-tended streets, coils and curlicues, spirals, arcs, and circles— no grid for Fucallpa—arriving finally at Helical HyperCom's headquarters, which was lackluster and industrial looking by comparison. No effort had been made to mimic the local organic architecture, plus it was surrounded by walls interrupted only by security-post entrances. Inside the cubical main building, Lokori graciousness was replaced by unsettling servitude and a grim sense of duty and obligation.

They were left to wait in a stark room with uncomfortable furniture and bland art adorning the walls. At long last a human woman entered, introducing herself as Roman Herbane's executive secretary. Her long hair was pulled back severely from her high-cheekboned face and tailed halfway down her back. She wore a shimmersilk sheath tailored to accentuate a shapely figure and stylish boots that added centimeters to her height. The smile she forced at Jyn made it seem as if a human child was something new to her. She led the three of them into an expansive office whose windows overlooked a range of thickly forested hills limned against a teal sky.

Herbane was seated behind a large desk, and it seemed to Lyra that he stood only when it occurred to him that he probably should. His expensive suit and sharp-featured face gave him a patrician look. Lyra sensed that Herbane and his secretary had more than a workplace relationship. Galen introduced himself, then Lyra and Jyn.

Herbane's handshake was cool and curt. When he eyed Jyn with what almost seemed suspicion, she picked up on it and decided to hide behind Lyra's legs.

"I hope the journey was pleasant enough," he said, adopting the same smile his secretary used. "I hate connecting through the Dibbik Hub. Such despicable beings, the Toydarians."

Lyra started to say that she found them to be very friendly, but she thought better of it.

"The trip was fine," Galen said. "Uneventful."

"Uneventful is very good these days." Herbane glanced around. "I should offer you a beverage."

Galen waved off the rote proposal, and everyone sat down, except for Jyn.

"Well, then, I assume you've had a chance to review the literature. It would be helpful if you could hit the ground running."

"I did," Galen told him. "You never said if you'd had a chance to look over the notes I sent."

Herbane fidgeted. "Yes, those. To be honest, Dr. Erso, I couldn't make sense of most of it."

"I'd be glad to go over them in detail."

Herbane gawked at him. "You would, would you? Look, let's get something straight from the start, shall we? I'm well aware of who you are and of your various accomplishments in your field. But I've no interest in hearing your theories or engaging in experimentation. We're not reinventing the rocket here. We have a job to do and that's all there is to it."

Galen's expression was quizzical. "Even if that job can be done more efficiently or accomplished at a reduced cost?"

"Just as I expected," Herbane said, putting his hands flat on the desk. "To be blunt, I was against hiring you for this very reason. I expressed as much to my superiors, but you obviously have some very influential friends who convinced them to ignore my concerns and ordered me to accept you. I've put long years into this work and I don't want any trouble. I'm certainly not going to engage you in a battle of wits or intelligence, but for all your scientific papers, degrees, and patents, you're the one sitting there, and I'm the one sitting here."

Galen merely shrugged. "Normalcy has taken leave of the galaxy."

Herbane's jaw dropped a bit and he looked at Lyra. "Is your husband always so confrontational?"

"He speaks his mind," Lyra said.

Herbane turned back to Galen. "We're embarking on a dangerous course, Dr. Erso."

"I don't think so. I just wanted to say that Helical is wasting money using pontite crystals when synthesized relacite would do. Production costs could be halved and bandwidth doubled."

Herbane continued to stare at him. "You're actually going to argue with me your first day on the job?"

"I'm not arguing with you," Galen tried to make clear. "I'm speaking as one colleague to another."

Herbane's face flushed with anger. "I'm not your colleague, Dr. Erso. I'm your boss! Helical Hyper-Com is not Zerpen Industries. We're not researchers; we're providers, and I need you in quality assurance. Unless you feel you can confine your theorizing and speculations to your personal time, I suggest that you save us both a lot of headaches and return to the Core. I'll ask you just this once, Dr. Erso: Can you be a good soldier or not."

"Soldier," Galen said, closing his eyes.

"Worker, employee, however you need to frame it," Herbane continued. "It's a simple question."

From the frying pan to the fire, Lyra told herself.

She restrained an impulse to touch Galen or send him any kind of reassuring message. The job was his choice and she was determined to stay out of it. Jyn was squirming behind her, exhausted. Lyra only realized that she was holding her breath when Galen let his out.

"Tell me what you want done."

Time passed slowly on Geonosis. The only way to relieve the tedium was to shuttle down to the surface, which in fact offered no relief whatsoever. An hour in the heat and stink and the orbital facilities felt heaven-sent.

Krennic had had weeks when he was just trying to get through it.

The last of the pie-slice dish modules had been fabricated, but the dish itself was not yet fully assembled and the upper hemisphere well was still undergoing finishing touches. Droid work on fashioning cabin-spaces in the pole region had also gone much more slowly than anticipated, although a few were fully sealed and habitable, providing work for at least some of the thousands of Geonosian drones who had been ferried upside.

Galen, in the meantime, was ensconced on Lokori, where Krennic suspected—and hoped—that he was even more unhappy and frustrated than he had been on Coruscant. But Krennic viewed the dead-end job with Helical HyperCom as guidance of a sort, a means of directing Galen to his destiny. He had wanted to have Has Obitt transport the Ersos to the Outer Rim—both to keep the Dressellian on the leash and to have him serve as a listening device—but Obitt was suddenly nowhere to be found, and in the end Krennic decided it was best for the family to travel by passenger ship, as normal nobodies would.

He was preparing to contact Galen when his young aide barged into the officers' mess. Lieutenant Oyanta was a tall, pale human, with coal-black hair and eyes with epicanthic folds.

"We've got a problem in the level-one first-stage enclosures," he began. "The drones are dying by the dozens."

Krennic wiped his mouth with a napkin and stood

up. "Did engineering run pressurization and atmospheric checks?"

"All systems are good."

Krennic shook his head in perplexity. "Then what's the issue?"

"Seems there's not enough work for all of them."

"Not enough . . . First Poggle frustrates them by ordering them to perform grunt work, now he pits them against one another for what work there is?"

"Poggle claims to know what he's doing."

Krennic worked his jaw. "It was Poggle who insisted on bringing them up the well before we had work for all of them. How serious is this?"

"Security is warning that the situation could get explosive. There have already been several incidents."

"What sort of incidents?"

"Marines had to draw down on a bunch of drones who refused to follow orders. The enclosures are a mess of blood and guts." Oyanta showed his datapad. "I have video."

"Save it, I just ate." Krennic gestured to his empty plate. "Why aren't Poggle's soldiers overseeing them?"

Oyanta's shoulders heaved in a shrug. "They're standing down."

Krennic grew angrier as he spoke. "This is a security matter. Why am I being dragged into it?"

"Apparently, sir, you're the only one who can reason with the archduke."

"The only one willing to talk to him, you mean."

"And more or less the reverse."

"All right," Krennic said, resigned. "I suppose I'd better make the call."

The two of them exited the mess and set out for the habitat's communications room. When at last they had succeeded in raising Poggle aboard his shuttle, Krennic positioned himself on the holoprojector pad and faced the cam.

"Archduke, we're having a problem controlling your workers," he said. "They're fighting over tasks and refusing to obey orders, and your soldiers might as well be on vacation."

The Geonosian holopresence betrayed no emotion. "I see no problem," he replied in his native tongue.

"They're dying, Archduke—by the dozens."

"Geonosians do not hold life to be as precious as you humans do, Lieutenant Commander. Perhaps you have forgotten how many drones died during the Eve of Meckgin Festival."

"How could I forget."

"That was just for sport and entertainment. Work is a much more serious matter."

"Then why aren't you intervening?"

Poggle's wings stirred slightly. "To derive the most from them, you must be willing to abide their need to compete for tasks."

Krennic glared for the cam. "What are you telling me, that we should just let them fight and die?"

"That is precisely what I'm saying. Rest assured that I absolve your security forces of all culpability should they be required to kill them."

"That's very regal of you, Archduke," Krennic snarled. "But how about offering a solution for *not* having to exterminate our labor force?"

Poggle gestured in haughty dismissal. "Add to

their number and allow them to work it out themselves."

Blaring klaxons in the headquarters building cut short the impromptu lecture Galen had been delivering to some of his Lokori co-workers. He imagined that Roman Herbane would be chagrined to learn that Galen's job of overseeing quality assurance was normally so mindless and repetitive that he had nothing but free time to think and theorize. His equations and words hung in the air as everyone raced to reach the underground shelters.

"Mathematics isn't just science, it is poetry—our efforts to crystallize the unglimpsed connections between things. Poetry that bridges and magnifies the mysteries of the galaxy. But the signs and symbols and equations sentients employ to express these connections are not discoveries but the teasing out of secrets that have always existed. All our theories belong to nature, not to us. As in music, every combination of notes and chords, every melody has already been played and sung, somewhere, by someone—"

It was the second surface attack since he and Lyra and Jyn had arrived. Most of the conflicts were being settled out past Lokori's moons, but Separatist drop ships had once again penetrated the Republic picket line and entered the atmosphere, releasing squadrons of reconfigurable vulture droid fighters. Fortunately the hypercomm production facility was protected by an energy shield provided by a massive but well-protected shield generator situated in the nearby hills, and the labyrinths of service corridors beneath the prosaic buildings were used as evacuation shelters for the entire western district of Fucallpa, including the mostly foreign neighborhood where the Ersos and many other HH employees were housed. In the midst of the earlier raid Galen had fortuitously run into Lyra and Jyn, and had passed a trembling couple of local hours with them until the all-clear had sounded.

It was all the worse because of their growing fondness for Lokori—the sound of clippers and pruners at work on building façades substituting for the incessant sound of stone chisels Galen had heard on Vallt.

He was in search of Lyra and Jyn again when the bombardment began in earnest. From the chatter in the tunnels he learned that the defensive umbrella was taking a thrashing. At a holo station he stopped to watch real-time 3-D video of squadrons of vultures and tri-fighters targeting the shield with concentrated fire in an attempt to overwhelm it, while closer to the hills Republic batteries were doing their best to prevent other fighters from reaching the shield generator itself. The sky was fractured by pulses of raw energy loosed by the reciprocating turrets of the big guns.

Unsuccessful at finding Lyra, Galen retraced his steps through the maze to where he had separated from his co-workers.

"Is there some equation that can put an end to all this, Dr. Erso?" one of the shaken insectoids asked.

Galen set himself down on the floor to join him. "If sentient beings were moved by the same laws that govern nature, there might be. But as we've come to embody entropy, I don't hold out much hope."

A second Lokori countered: "Surely the Jedi have unlocked the secrets of reversing chaos and will be able to outwit nature at its own game."

"The Force derives from nature," Galen said somberly. "Against such chaos, even the Jedi are capable of accomplishing only so much."

12

A COG IN SOMETHING TURNING

JARRED FROM SLEEP BY THE clamorous chirps of his personal comlink, Krennic reached for the device in the dark, thumbed it active, and heard the equally strident voice of his adjutant.

"Sir, we have a full-scale riot in the level-one enclosures," Oyanta said.

Krennic spit a curse through his barred teeth. "I thought we were done with this. What's their issue now?"

"We can't figure out what started it. One moment it was business as usual, the next the drones were destroying all the work they'd completed."

"Destroying?"

"All three months' worth, sir. And they're still on the warpath. Even the marines can't contain them."

Krennic shot to his feet. "Meet me at the comm station. And raise Poggle's ship. With any luck, you'll be waking him up like you did me."

"I'm on it, sir."

Ordering the lights to come up, he threw some

water on his face, stepped into his trousers, and hurried from his quarters.

Incident-free months had gone by. The battle station's parabolic focusing dish was nearing assembly, hull cladding had been added, interior spaces had been bulkheaded and made habitable. Living conditions for the drones had also improved, and every attempt had been made to limit overcrowding. Even the archduke had been especially accommodating—though when not relaying commands to his soldiers, he had confined himself aboard the shuttle with his private contingent of workers.

And now this.

Krennic was at a loss to explain how things had been thrown out of equilibrium. Had Separatist operatives infiltrated saboteurs into the workforce?

His young aide was pacing in front of the unstaffed comm station when Krennic rushed in. Following a brisk salute, Oyanta gestured wildly to the console. "Sir, traffic control reports that the archduke's shuttle has left orbit."

Krennic wasn't sure he had heard him correctly. "Left orbit? When?"

"About the time the riot began."

Krennic bent over the console to scan the monitors. He had assumed that the shuttle was bound for the surface; instead he saw that it was outbound from Geonosis. "Do you have him on the comm?" he barked over his shoulder.

Oyanta gestured again. "Loud and clear."

Krennic enabled the holofeed and swung to the

mike. "Where do you think you're going, Archduke?" he asked in Geonosian.

"I'm sorry to be leaving, Lieutenant Commander, but I have an important engagement."

"Whatever it is can wait, Poggle. Your workers are dismantling everything they put together."

The archduke feigned sympathy. "Try not to be too hard on them. They are simply following my orders."

Krennic's thoughts raced. "Your orders? Have you lost your mind? Get your sorry carapace back here on the double."

Poggle stood tall in the holofeed, his wings slightly extended. "I required a diversion sufficient to occupy your security forces while I engineered my exit."

Krennic muted the audio and turned slightly toward Oyanta. "Comm the flotilla commander. Order him to draw a bead on Poggle's ship."

Oyanta saw to it while Krennic disabled the mute. "What's the nature of this important engagement? Who exactly are you meeting?"

"My comrade, Count Dooku."

While Krennic was absorbing it, Oyanta said: "Captain Frist has the shuttle in target lock."

Krennic grinned for the holocam. "I'm going to give you an opportunity to turn around now and make things right, Poggle. Otherwise you'll be in pieces before you clear the asteroid belts."

Poggle approximated a smile. "Ah, but thanks to your cordiality in providing me with a private retinue of drones, I have full confidence in my ship. You see, while my soldiers were helping you with the battle station, my drones were making significant modifications to the shuttle. I suggest you watch your displays, Lieutenant Commander Krennic."

"Order Frist to open fire," Krennic said.

While he was switching to an exterior view, he saw Oyanta's mouth fall open.

"What is it?"

"Negative engagement, sir. The archduke's shuttle has jumped to hyperspace."

Galen and Roman Herbane were at it again.

"I'm only suggesting that power could be diverted from the production plant to shore up the overtaxed shield generator," Galen was saying. "That will allow us to enlarge the footprint of the defensive umbrella to encompass a greater part of the city itself—perhaps all the way from the western outskirts to Amboo Square and most of the historic center."

"I won't even consider it," Herbane said from behind his desk. "Diverting power will cripple production."

"You're assuming that the facility will survive. More to the point, we owe it to the local population."

Herbane's face wrinkled in derision. "I've heard word that your wife has all but adopted a couple of Lokori from your neighborhood."

"What of it?"

"The locals have already been well compensated for allowing us to produce here," Herbane said. "During the most recent election they were given the chance to vote to raise a shield that would have protected the entire city, and instead corrupt members of the administration decided to refurbish the town hall and their own offices. So don't lecture me on what we owe them."

The air raid on Lokori had never really ended. Over the course of four local months it had waxed and waned. Day and night the skies above Fucallpa bore evidence of the hard-fought battle in near space. Where the planet had been reinforced by elements of the Bright Nebula Fleet, the Separatists had matched the Republic ship for ship.

Time and again Fucallpa was rocked by flights of suicidal droid fighters, which had resulted in thousands of civilian casualties and the devastation of countless buildings.

"A defoliated garden," Lyra had lamented.

She and Jyn had been relocated from Helical HyperCom housing to a safer area well inside the perimeter of the defensive dome, the homey surroundings to which they had just begun to accustom themselves exchanged for the sterile confines of a dormitory at the edge of the company's now seldom-used landing field. Even without being able to airlift product, Herbane had demanded that work continue without interruption, so much so that the warehouses were beyond capacity and shipping containers were stacked all over the grounds.

Rumors circulated of an imminent evacuation of all nonresident personnel at the first instance of a letup in the fighting, but pauses had been so few and far between as to render escape a greater risk than simply hunkering down and trusting that Republic forces would eventually prevail.

Standing on the visitor's side of Herbane's desk, Galen adopted a more conciliatory tone. "Has Helical ordered you not to divert power, or is the decision yours to make?"

"I don't see how that's any of your business, Erso."

"Tens of thousands of lives are at stake."

A massive explosion close by overwhelmed Herbane's reply. The two of them watched from the window as black smoke coiled from the hills and the translucent shield doming the facility began to shimmer and fade.

"The shield generator has been destroyed," Galen said in a quiet voice. "We're all vulnerable now, Roman."

Stricken, Herbane stared at him, seemingly unable to speak.

In the hallway outside the office, Galen ran into one of his co-workers, who told him that the Republic picket line had been dealt a crippling blow. Landing craft had been scrambled to deliver Grand Army companies to the surface, but Separatist troops were already on the ground. Even now, a battalion of battle droids was marching on the city, annihilating everything in its path.

Galen ran off in search of Lyra, whom he found moments later with a helmeted Jyn jammed into a back carrier and gazing over her mother's shoulder. Lyra grabbed a large backpack by the straps and passed it to him.

"The battle droids landed east and north of the

city center," she said in a rush. "That means our best option is to head south into the hills. With the shield generator destroyed, the Seps aren't likely to care about that area. Jyn and I have walked most of the trails through the draws that access the ridge. It's an easy climb, and once we're over the top we can pick our way down into the basin on the far side. There's plenty of good water and small game there, and places for shelter. We have enough food to last for two standard weeks—possibly longer if we economize. The rainy season won't start for at least another three months, and by then Lokori will be retaken by the Republic. Or we could be forced to surrender to whoever's in charge."

"Sounds like you've thought of everything," Galen said.

"You know better than to say that."

Galen shrugged into the heavy pack and they set out, snaking through the labyrinth of underground tunnels and gradually working their way up to the surface and into the streets that radiated out from the facility. Outside of what had been the defensive dome's coverage the destruction was widespread and heartrending. Smoke billowed into a smudged sky, and distant explosions shook the ground. Thousands of Lokori crowded the streets, many of them similarly burdened with packs and supplies. And Lyra wasn't alone in wanting to head for the hills.

They hadn't gone more than a kilometer when the river of refugees was forced to a sudden stop. Word from up ahead trickled back that a phalanx of battle droids was advancing from the west, and so the living stream shifted southeast.

Panic began to mount.

A trio of Republic landers raced overhead, taking heavy fire from hastily installed Separatist batteries. Galen watched as two of the ships sustained direct hits and were reduced to fiery debris, white-clad bodies plunging to the ground. Farther along, they came upon a squad of clone troopers deploying from a carrier that had managed to land.

"There's no exit in this direction," one of them said, waving a gauntleted hand. "All of you need to fall back to the factory."

Lyra shook her head at Galen. "No way, right?"

"No way."

They swung south again, a handful of the insectoids accompanying them, skirting the line where other clone troopers were beginning to dig in and negotiating a clogged alleyway that opened onto a winding highway. They were running now, Galen winded, his legs burning, Jyn silent in the carrier and holding on for dear life. The sky was filled with tracer rounds, red pulses of energy, and blinding explosions. Soot and particles filled the air, and the day grew dark as the sun was eclipsed by smoke. Galen wrapped a moistened kerchief around Jyn's face. The sound of repeating blasters came from their right.

"Battle droids," Galen said.

They turned and ran, only to encounter another dozen of the bipedal monstrosities directly in front of them, marching in step with black blasters raised.

They cut left and increased their pace, running flat-out and breathing hard. Lyra began trying the doors to storefronts they passed, but all were either locked or blocked by piles of organic debris.

Battle droids appeared in front of them again, then behind as they swung around. Blasterfire whizzed through the air. Lokori left and right of them fell to the street.

Protectively, Galen hugged Lyra from behind, Jyn whimpering, with her face pressed to her mother's back.

Lyra dug her booted feet into the base of a slippery debris pile and began to scamper for the top, where it looked as if they might be able to access the leafy roof of a conically shaped building. Galen followed, his work shoes churning in the organic fall, and by the time he caught up to Lyra she was shaking her head. The pile simply wasn't high enough.

They stood together at the base of a sheer wall four meters high without ledges or toeholds and with nowhere to go. Below, battle droids advanced from both ends of the street, killing the few Lokori that remained standing, painting the street green with their blood and joining forces at the bottom of the fall. Everyone Galen and Lyra had run with was on the ground, dead or wounded.

Galen looked down to see one of the droids gaze up at them and communicate something to its brethren. The droids' feet weren't well suited to climbing mounds of organic rubble, but they tried nonetheless, and on realizing they were getting nowhere, they raised their weapons.

Galen's thoughts spiraled. Placing himself in front

of Lyra and Jyn, he lifted his face to the darkened sky and screamed:

"Is there no escape from this madness?"

All at once, as if his voice alone had spawned a miracle, the droids began to power down.

The entire city fell so unexpectedly silent that Galen was as discombobulated as he was comforted. "The central command computer," he sputtered, his eyes leaking tears. "Republic forces took it out. That's the only explanation."

Lyra pressed herself against his back while Jyn cried softly in the carrier. "I don't even need an explanation."

What neither of them knew or could have known was that the war, so abruptly begun three years earlier, was just as suddenly over.

13

KYBER CRYSTAL PERSUASION

FRESH FROM THE CORELLIAN SHIPYARDS, an Imperial Star Destroyer reverted to realspace a thousand kilometers out from the battle station. Because of whom it carried, the ship had been cleared to travel from the Core to Geonosis without having to be granted clearance at Sentinel Base, parsecs distant in another star system. Aboard was Emperor Palpatine, said to be recovering from wounds suffered during an engagement with disloyal Jedi. Traveling with the Emperor was a new addition to the court, a being known only as Darth Vader, masked and caped, clothed in head-to-toe black, and evidently feared by many. But Krennic had to wonder—Vader's eccentric fashion sense notwithstanding—if he was really any more formidable than now Grand Vizier Mas Amedda.

Of greater importance to Krennic was that Wilhuff Tarkin was also known to be aboard the Star Destroyer. Krennic suspected that the reason he himself had been left off the elite passenger list owed to Poggle's escape—even though the archduke was now apparently dead, along with Count Dooku and the rest of the Separatist leadership. Gone, too, were the Jedi generals in their homespun robes, armed with light-sabers and the Force.

Krennic continued to monitor the approach of the Star Destroyer from a bay inside the command-and-control habitat. If nothing else, he had at least managed to get the focusing dish installed in advance of the Emperor's visit.

He watched as a shuttle emerged from one of the capital ship's hangars, hyperspace-capable and as graceful as a long-winged bird of prey.

The war had been won without the battle station; now, however, it was to be put to different use: to eliminate the chance of future conflicts by instilling fear in the hearts of those who would seek to threaten the integrity of the Empire. And yet it still lacked the one special ingredient that would transform it into the weapon it was always meant to be and to elevate Krennic as a result: Galen Erso.

Galen had been sorry to learn that Roman Herbane had lost a limb to blasterfire during the final battle on Lokori and that his executive secretary had sustained fatal injuries. Herbane could easily afford a synthskin prosthesis, but Li-Tan would not be so easily replaced. For all the arguments Galen had had with him, Herbane had simply been a victim of his own stubbornness, lack of foresight, and limited intelligence. Even so, Galen sympathized with the grief the man had to be experiencing.

The memory of the confrontation with the battle droids continued to haunt him.

Helical HyperCom had asked him to consider replacing Herbane as chief operating officer of the production facility, but Galen knew that he lacked the skills necessary for administrative work. More, he yearned to return to pure research. By contrast, he and Lyra and Jyn had grown fond of Lokori, and the offer from HH was tempting. Galen told the president of Helical that he needed time to think about it and had asked for a brief sabbatical.

They were on their way to Coruscant to consider plans for a permanent move to Lokori when Krennic commed, asking that they divert briefly to Kanzi, where he promised to rendezvous with them. He assured Galen that the additional travel expenses would be covered by the Empire.

The Empire.

The galaxy was still reeling from the events of the past few months: the war ended, the Jedi Order disbanded—eradicated, by some accounts—a new and expanded military established to reinforce the limited-shelf-life clones who made up the Grand Army, and ex-supreme-chancellor Sheev Palpatine as self-appointed Emperor.

Galen, Lyra, and Jyn were waiting in the atrium of the Orona Hotel on Kanzi when Krennic marched into the majestic space, dressed in a crisp white uniform and command cap, insignia squares shouting his rank from the tunic, a small contingent of Imperial stormtroopers moving in his wake. An alloy case dangled from his left hand, its pulsing light indicating to

Galen's sharp eye that it would open only for Krennic himself.

Once they had exchanged pleasantries, he led them toward a private room he had reserved, pausing briefly in front of a mural three Bith artisans were laser-etching into a wall of polished stone. The hairless, dome-headed, black-eyed humanoids were working from a detailed drawing that recounted the history of the Republic, from inception to Empire, with a cloaked and cowled Palpatine occupying the crown.

Krennic motioned the Ersos in, and the stormtroopers fell into guard formation outside the door. While Jyn roamed about inspecting the room, Krennic placed the case on a table where it could see and read his coded rank insignia. The case emitted an audible click and whir, unlocking itself, but Krennic left it closed, folding his hands atop the lid.

"I understand that Helical HyperCom has offered you a permanent position," he said to Galen.

"I'm supposed to be thinking it over."

"I hope you plan to turn them down."

"It would be a living," Galen said. "A very good living, in fact."

Krennic laughed, eyeing Lyra, then Galen. "Since when do you two care about credits?"

Galen didn't join him in laughing.

"Well, I have something better to offer, in any case."

Galen and Lyra traded wary looks.

"Let me explain," Krennic said. "Now that the war is winding down—"

"Winding down," Lyra cut in. "It's not over?"

Krennic rocked his head. "Pockets of resistance remain, especially on Umbara. Our forces are engaging in several, shall we say, pacification exercises to bring about a lasting peace. The Emperor has made reparations and reconstruction a priority, and one way he hopes to achieve this is by being able to provide sustainable energy to worlds that have suffered on both sides of the conflict." He gestured with his chin to Galen. "Even your own Grange."

Lyra's brows quirked in a sign of doubt. "This is the same Palpatine who couldn't get anything done as supreme chancellor?"

Krennic stared at her. "He defeated the Separatists."

"With a lot of help."

Krennic dismissed it. "As Emperor he can accomplish what the corrupt prewar Senate wouldn't permit. Project Celestial Power is his vision—his dream."

"Just how is he planning to implement . . . Project Celestial Power?" Galen asked.

"To begin with he has allocated funds for a research facility on Coruscant, which is already under construction in the B'ankor Refuge."

Lyra let her surprise show. "I thought the refuge had been granted to the B'ankora in perpetuity."

Krennic smiled thinly. "The B'ankora have been relocated."

"This research facility is the better offer you mentioned?" Galen said.

"It is. What do you think of the idea?"

Galen exhaled through his nose. "I guess it depends on how I would fit in."

"Fit in?" Krennic said, laughing again. "Why, the Emperor is hoping that you'll accept the position of director of research. Galen, it's precisely the project you approached me with more than a year ago. Your dream as well as the Emperor's."

Galen turned to Lyra in complete astonishment.

"Galen!"

"Orson, I, I don't know what to say . . ."

"You'll say yes if you know what's good for you." He reached across the table to clap Galen on the shoulder; then, smiling slyly, he rapped his knuckles on the lid of the case. "I've something here I suspect will serve as a major incentive." Lifting the lid, he spun the case so that Galen and Lyra could view the contents.

The objects in the case caught the light of the room and refracted it in shifting colors into their eyes.

Lyra's hand went to her mouth. "Are those—"

"Kyber crystals," Galen completed, as if struggling to articulate the words.

"And many, many more where these came from," Krennic said. "In fact, now that the Jedi have been . . . disbanded, the Empire has unrestricted access to worlds that for centuries were accessible only to the Order. Not just these small samples, but enormous crystals. Boulder-sized, I'm told. Even larger."

With care that transcended need, Galen prized one of the translucent crystals from its memory-foam bed and turned it about in his hand. Having hurried over to have a look, Jyn said: "I want one!"

"Maybe someday," Lyra said, gently restraining her from reaching for the case.

Krennic was about to elaborate when a storm-trooper called him from the room, and he excused himself.

Lyra waited until Krennic was outside to place her hand on Galen's forearm. In a hushed but serious tone, she said: "Galen, you know where these came from."

"Mygeeto, perhaps," Galen said, distracted and still fascinated by the colorless kyber. "Possibly Ilum or Christophsis."

"Not their source world," she said. "The size of them, the shape . . ."

He finally turned to meet her wide-eyed gaze.

"These could only have come from Jedi light-sabers."

PART TWO

THE PURSUIT OF PEACE

14

CONGRUENCE

FINISHED WITH HIS BUSINESS DOWNSIDE, Krennic shuttled back up to the sprawling shipyard he'd had a hand in engineering five standard years earlier, which had since suffered the ravages of war. Pocked and scored by turbolaser fire and traumatized by incendiary missiles, the construction and overhaul facility hung like a ruin over equally devastated Kartoosh, itself orbited by a debris cloud made up of shattered vessels and all they had once contained. Maintenance and repair droid ships were at work everywhere, cutting, welding, and grinding, and hundreds of tugs and shuttles were coming and going. In those docks that were still intact, *Venator*-class Star Destroyers and other now superseded ships of the line, many of them designed and built by the Separatists, were being dismantled or retrofitted to serve whatever new purposes they had been assigned. Elsewhere vast arrays of war matériel and arsenals of weapons and munitions were being moved into the cargo holds of transports bound for Imperial depots in faraway systems.

The ship that had carried him to Kartoosh was

berthed at the distal end of one of the yard's longest
docking arms, but instead of returning to it Krennic
had ordered the shuttle pilot to deliver him to an Imperial Star Destroyer undergoing repairs closer to the
hub. Fresh wounds and areas of carbon scoring left
by recent engagements with Separatist holdouts in the
Western Reaches marred the ship's immense triangu-
lar underbelly.

When a tractor beam had eased the shuttle through
a magnetic containment field and into the vast hangar
beyond, Krennic gave a sharp downward tug to his
tunic and led his cadre of borrowed stormtroopers
down the boarding ramp, where the first sight to greet
his eyes was tall and cadaverously thin Wilhuff Tarkin, wearing dress grays and buffed black knee boots,
standing with legs slightly spread and hands clasped
behind his back against a backdrop of several hundred
stormtroopers arrayed in strict formation. A subtle
sideways nod from clean-shaven Tarkin, and the officer standing to his right turned and dismissed the
small army of white-clad soldiers, who fell out as if
on a parade ground.

Krennic smiled lightly as he approached Tarkin, as
if to minimize the show of force the admiral had
taken the trouble to organize. Tarkin would know that
Krennic's stormtroopers weren't his to command, but
Krennic treated them like they were. Even so, the salute he offered Tarkin was nothing short of faultless.

"Must be nice being a legend in your own time,"
Krennic said.

Tarkin vouchsafed a tight smile. "It's not a position
one simply applies for, Lieutenant Commander."

Krennic returned the look. "I'll bear that in mind. Thank you for making time to meet with me."

"Laid up for repairs as we are, I appreciate every opportunity to relieve the monotony."

Krennic glanced around the enormous hangar. "Odd, it's almost intimate compared with what I've grown used to. Still impressive, though."

The sarcasm wasn't lost on Tarkin. "Of course. Your big ball in the sky. Forward motion suits me more than immobility just now."

Krennic pretended seriousness. "Essential when one is still fighting the good fight."

"Better to be productive, in any case, than mired in complications."

Krennic's eyebrow elevated. "Is that the news that's reached you about the project?"

"Is there other news?"

Krennic firmed his lips. "Is there somewhere we can speak in private?"

"This way," Tarkin said, gesturing gallantly for Krennic to precede him.

Leaving the hangar for a broad central corridor, Krennic slackened his pace so that his elder would have no choice but to walk alongside him.

"Apparently I've been misinformed about the state of things at Geonosis," Tarkin commented.

"In fact, we've just entered phase three, with work commencing on the hypermatter reactor and the shield generators."

"And your labor force?"

"With Poggle dead, the hive queen has appointed a new archduke to oversee the soldiers and drones, but the process is nothing more than conciliatory. In effect, the Geonosians now belong to the Empire."

"Then congratulations are in order," Tarkin said, with what struck Krennic as false cheer.

"Success, however, brings new challenges."

"How often the case."

They stopped at a massive viewport to observe a new capital ship—a dreadnought—being inaugurated for launch from its bay.

"Completed in less than a standard year," Tarkin said, as if he had built it himself.

"And yet already obsolete?" Krennic said.

Tarkin glanced at him. "A placeholder. I'm certain, however, that it will do until the battle station is deployed."

The two officers had begun to circle each other as they spoke.

"Our main weapon will have more firepower than ten vessels that size," Krennic said.

Tarkin looked at him out of the corner of his eye. "Should it ever reach completion."

They set off once more, arriving ultimately at what Krennic took to be Tarkin's secondary office. When the hatch slid open, Tarkin motioned him across the threshold into a cool and tastefully furnished cabin. Krennic waited for Tarkin to sit, then took a chair.

"Excuse me for asking, but are you now addressed as admiral, governor, or moff?"

Tarkin had been promoted to admiral before the end of the war, but moff was a new order of rank, conferred by the Emperor on a dozen or so of his most highly valued officers and regional commanders.

"Governor remains my preference."

"Then governor it shall be," Krennic said.

Tarkin regarded him for a long moment, then said: "About these challenges that have brought you here from Geonosis . . ."

"As I said, we're entering a new phase—one that increases the need for raw materials and resources."

"Run out of asteroids, have you?"

Krennic ignored the remark. "It's felt that research sites and mining operations of the size and sort required are best kept concealed from prying eyes, so we've been looking to less populated sectors."

"The Western Reaches, I assume."

Krennic nodded. "After a careful survey, I've selected several worlds suitable for our purposes."

"*You've* selected," Tarkin said.

"For the project, yes. Even so, procurement will have to be handled . . . delicately."

"Not the word you would have chosen?"

Krennic shrugged. "The word Vizier Amedda used. He wishes to avoid blowback of any sort that could rile the Senate or stir the spread of anti-Imperial propaganda."

"A reasonable caution, since we certainly don't want anyone looking too closely into what you're up to."

Krennic didn't reply.

"Many of the mining companies that were in league with the Separatists have concessions on dozens of worlds. Why not simply commandeer them?"

"That's essentially what we want to do—with appropriate justification."

Tarkin touched his chin in thought. "The battle station will be the most powerful weapon ever developed."

"Capable of taking on and defeating all comers," Krennic interjected.

"As such," Tarkin went on, "it could become a target for every disenfranchised group between here and Scipio. Thus, great care must be taken to maintain this ruse of yours."

Krennic appraised Tarkin's guarded posture. "If you'll permit an observation, Governor, you seem skeptical."

"I do have reservations," Tarkin said, looking Krennic in the eye. "I'm willing, however, to set aside my doubts for the time being."

"Then I can count on your help?"

"We serve at the pleasure of the Emperor, do we not?"

"We most certainly do."

"Tell me, though, is the Emperor aware of this plan to fabricate justification for appropriating planets?"

"Not yet."

Tarkin snorted again. "Then I'll be certain to inform him."

Safeguarded by thorny space–time anomalies but still close enough to a couple of major hyperspace lanes to permit effortless jumps to lightspeed, arid Rajtiri was said to have birthed and fostered more smugglers than anywhere outside of Hutt space, and the ancient city of Jibuto had prospered as a result. Some indigenous families could trace their smuggling enterprises back twenty generations, and a good deal of the profits accumulated in far-off regions of space had been sent home. Studded with stately spires and parapets and chockablock with colossal domes and pavilions, the city was also known for its profusion of elaborate mausoleums, constructed in honor of the fathers and mothers, sons and daughters who had died in the line of unlawful duty and were hailed as heroes. Large as mansions, the lavish tombs featured towers and tiled cupolas, steeples and belfries, battlements and crenellations, as well as holopresences of the dead and continuously running 3-D epitaphs that were as costly and well produced as mainstream entertainments. The sarcophagi housed inside the ossuaries were never without offerings of fresh flowers or bowls of food and drink supplied by the living.

Owing to the never-ending traffic, Jibuto had hotels, cantinas, and casinos galore, but Has Obitt always eschewed the fancier places for a hole-in-the-wall cantina near the city center known as the Wanton Wellspring. In many ways it was no different from a thousand other cantinas on a thousand other worlds, and Has didn't find it any nastier than the Malicious Moondog on Suba or any more inspiring than the Contented Krayt on Tatooine, but the drinks were strong, the wait staff attractive, and the company generally discreet.

He was seated with two humans and a green-complected Nautolan named Ranos Yalli at a table close to the crowded semicircular bar but far enough from the Twi'lek band so that the four of them could converse without shouting. Has had an iced drink in front of him and suspected he was already on his way to a nasty hangover.

"You'd think there'd be more opportunities now that the Seps are history," the lighter-complected of the pair of humans was saying.

"The war starts to feel like a golden age," the other said, a bald and broad-shouldered Coruscanti named Ribert, "even with all the jumping around we had to do."

"One mess to another," Yalli remarked, carved wooded rings adorning each of his nine head tresses.

Ribert nodded. "It's like no one cares about bargains anymore."

"That's not it," his human cohort argued. "The work's out there. There just aren't enough jobs to go around."

"No wonder things have gotten so competitive," Has said.

Yalli looked at him. "I hear that meiloorun fruit is all the rage in the Sluis sector. What about we divert some of the supplies to make them even harder to get?"

Has flashed him a dubious, drunken look. "Create a black market, you mean."

"Only for starters," the dark-eyed amphibian continued. "Once the growers start feeling the pinch, we levy a tax on them for every kilo of fruit they grow and ship, and we cut back on having to divert the shipments. You know, diversify."

Ribert scowled. "I don't know. Sounds like a lot of effort."

"And really: fruit?" his tall shipmate said.

Has forced a bored exhalation. "I am so sick of this song," he said as the Twi'lek band launched into another cover. "It follows me around like a hungry nerf."

"Maybe you should start your own band," Yalli said.

Has smirked. "Couldn't make any fewer credits than we're making now."

"You obviously don't know bands," Ribert said.

Colleagues and competitors from the old days, they had been drinking all afternoon, drawn together by misery. At the bar, a four-armed humanoid prepared drinks for smugglers sporting turbans, headcloths, loose-fitting outfits, and fancy knives, while around them males and females in seductive attire plied their trades and worked their magic to keep the alcohol flowing. For several standard weeks now, Has had had his eye on a stunning Dressellian barmaid named Woana, who would answer his sidelong glances with an unnerving smile that seemed to say: *You're welcome to try, Has, but be prepared to be shot down in flames.*

Despite the plunge in business, he considered himself lucky to have survived the war. Even after the abduction and rescue op with Orson Krennic had made him unwelcome in Separatist space, he had managed to stay busy. Arrested on Celanon for blockade running, he had been bailed out by the Republic. He had had two freighters shot out from under him, but with Krennic's help had been able to purchase replacements at cost. He lost one crew, gained another; narrowly missed the invasion of Saleucami only to end up smack in the middle of the sneak attack on Roche. The end of the war had found him in Sy Myrthian space doing scut work for a local Hutt. And then the bottom just seemed to fall out, and he had barely worked since. While he had faith in the new galactic order, he made it a point to steer as clear of Imperial confrontations as he did idealistic causes of any sort. Now he mostly operated as a middleman, moving goods between sellers and buyers and making do with meager profits. Then, at his lowest point, who should he hear from but—

Sudden commotion brought him out of self-pity.

Two drunks were arguing either over a temporary companion or a drink—though probably the latter. Both had drawn curving knives from their cummerbunds but were too tipsy to wield them with any precision. Patrons were holding each of them back, more worried about being stabbed by mistake than concerned about the lives of the would-be combatants.

If nothing else, the fight had brought the music to a halt.

"At least some things never change," Has told his companions.

"Yeah, they do," the bald human said.

Yalli gestured. "Watch what happens next."

Has followed the Nautolan's gaze to the front door in time to see two Imperial stormtroopers enter. Advancing on the knife-wielders, they collared each and began to haul them out, to loud booing and colorful curses from the rest of the room.

"Since when's a fight a reason to arrest anyone?" Has said.

"Since the Emperor's given the clones new marching orders," Ribert told him.

"There was a time clone troopers would have started the trouble." Has shook his head. "I mean, it's one thing for the Empire to shut down smuggling routes, but fights?"

The Twi'lek musicians took up where they had left off.

Has had his glass raised to his lips when Yalli said: "I think your guy just walked in."

Has glanced at the door again, recognizing the new arrival immediately, even out of uniform. "That's him, all right."

"Remember to keep us in mind," Yalli added as Has was getting to his feet.

Wobbling somewhat, he eased his way through the crowd to where the Wanton Wellspring's latest patron had taken a seat at a corner table even farther from the band, which Has took as a good sign.

"I hate this song," his contact said as he approached.

Another good sign? Has thought. He grinned faintly and sat.

He hadn't seen Matese since the ops on Merj and Vallt, and seeing him now brought back memories of the human family—the Ersos—he had helped spirit off the latter world. A research scientist who had wanted no part of the war on either side, his feisty wife, and an infant, Has recalled, wondering what might have become of them. Matese still looked like the ranger he'd been then, except for scars that weren't there two standard years earlier, what had to be skin grafts on the right side of his face and neck, and a patch over his right eye.

"You're a hard one to track down, Has."

"Yes, but you found me anyway."

Matese hailed a server. "Buy you a drink?"

Has hoisted his half-full glass. "Still some left." Better not to add to his bleariness, he decided. Not around Matese, anyway.

Matese ordered a double shot and made himself comfortable. "You look good, Has, all things considered."

"You, too."

Matese touched the eye patch. "Lost it on Cato Neimoidia. Just waiting for Veterans Services to cover the cost of an implant."

"You decided not to make it a career?"

Matese shook his head. "Maybe if I'd been regular navy. If I'd stayed in, I'd probably be wearing white plastoid now like some of the academy recruits."

"Have you . . . heard from our former commander?"

Matese studied him. "You mean Krennic?"

Has nodded, wary despite his attempts to hide it.

"Not a peep. I did hear that he made it through the war in one piece. As far as I know he's still with the Corps of Engineers. A builder."

"No contact with him?" Has pressed.

"Not in years. What about you?"

"Maybe six months before the war ended I got

word that he was looking for me, so I made myself scarce."

"Probably for the best."

"That's what I thought." Has relaxed somewhat. "I was just wondering if your reaching out to me was payback from Krennic for services rendered back when."

"Payback?" Matese laughed. "Why would he?"

"Well, he did get me out of jail and help me find two replacement ships, but you're right, why would he?" Has raised his glass in a toast when Matese's arrived. "To Veterans Services."

"To payback," Matese said. He killed the drink in a long gulp and set the glass aside. "How's peace treating you?"

Has's shoulders drooped. "I'm not making what I made during the war."

"Then I may have the remedy for what's ailing you."

Has leaned away from the table. "No harm in hearing you out," he said, certain it was the drink talking.

Matese lowered his voice. "I'm working in one of the depots where Separatist arms are being warehoused."

Has's surprise was genuine. "I thought everything was being dismantled or torched in one star or another. What does anyone need with battle droids when the Empire has Star Destroyers?"

"Not everything is being melted down. I haven't a clue why some of the stuff is being kept, but it is, and no one's checking on it or cataloging it, and it's my guess it'll never get looked at again."

"Okay," Has said slowly and with caution.

"So it's all for sale."

Has gave his head a baffled shake. "Rumor has it the war's over."

Matese ridiculed the idea with a snort. "The war's on pause, Has, and there are groups eager for this stuff so they can be ready when it starts up again."

"That's the remedy—arms-smuggling?" A plosive laugh escaped Has's full lips. "Before you came in, I watched two stormtroopers drag two guys out of here for *fighting*."

"You won't need to worry about Imperials. It's all cleared."

Has studied the former ranger. "How is it all cleared, Matese?"

"The people I work with have a line on everything— patrols, choke points, inspections. Up and down the line everyone gets a fair share of the profits to make sure no one gets caught. All you'd be required to do is make some deliveries."

Has pushed his drink away from him. "I might not be as desperate as I look."

"Sure you are."

"Been checking into my credit reports?"

"Maybe you think you'd do better throwing in with the Hutts or the Crymorah."

Has shook his head. Matese had him all wrong. "Actually, I'm thinking about starting a band."

Matese didn't bite. "Look, all I can tell you is that these ops are a piece of cake. One way or another this stuff is going to end up on the black market or scooped up by criminal cartels. So why not get in on this before that happens?"

Has couldn't resist considering it. "You're talking about moving, what, battle droids, proton torpedoes, ion cannons? My ship's not large enough to carry payloads like that."

"You're getting ahead of yourself. Anyway, we can set you up with a suitable ship if it comes to that. You simply see to the transfers."

"So you want a pilot."

"You're not getting it," Matese said, sounding frustrated. "After a couple of runs I give you a price list. Then you negotiate your own deals with whoever you want. You choose your own crew, your own vessel. You just have to let me know the destination and route so I can get you cleared along the way." Matese nodded toward the table where Has's three companions were still nursing their drinks. "I'll bet your buddies could use the work."

"It's not a question of needing work," Has said. "It's about staying out of prison."

Matese appraised him openly. "So what are you gonna do—find a new profession? Live the life of some downsider who gets excited about seeing an eclipse? Try a run on for size. If it's not for you, you take your profits and get out." He laughed shortly. "Start that band of yours."

15

ON THE SHOULDERS OF GIANTS

Coruscant was most frequently described as a city-world—an ecumenopolis—and while it was true that the fully urbanized eastern hemisphere buildings touched the sky, creating chasms thousands of meters deep, there was an area in the western hemisphere halfway between the pole and the equator where one could still stand on the planet's undisturbed surface; an area where climate control had yet to overrule nature, where the sky wasn't scrubbed clean and storms weren't scheduled or regulated. Originally a stretch of privately owned grassland left undeveloped because of complicated legalities, the area had ultimately been acquired by the former Republic to serve as a sanctuary for a small group of ruminant sentients known as the B'ankora, whose planet had suffered a cataclysmic collision with a meteor. The arrangement had not been designed to be permanent, but in the waning years of the former Republic a benevolent supreme chancellor named Chasen Piian had granted the land in perpetuity to the sole surviving members of the species, and the sanctuary had gradually come to be known as the B'ankor Refuge.

As that region of Coruscant grew up around the refuge, construction droids excavated a rectangle of 5.1 square kilometers down to bedrock, raised two artificial hills, installed a couple of small lakes, brought in soil fertile enough to support copses of shade trees and flowering shrubs, then moved the B'ankora back in so that they could resume their sedentary way of life. As the surrounding monads grew taller and taller, the refuge came to resemble a sunken zoo, but the B'ankora never grumbled about being literally looked down on from all directions.

An Imperial edict enacted immediately after the end of the Clone Wars citing archaic laws of eminent domain removed the ten thousand pure descendants of the original group, not just from the refuge or Coruscant, but from the Core itself, relocating them to similar territory on a dying world in the Mid Rim. The B'ankora's humble structures had been razed, their fields paved over. Most surface trails were erased, and air control stations and surveillance towers erected. A landing field was carved into a stand of towering buildings nearby to facilitate the arrival and departure of researchers and material, and from which starfighters could be scrambled at a moment's notice to enforce no-fly regulations. Much to the aggravation and protest of those Coruscanti who had used the refuge as a recreation area, the recessed rectangle was sealed off to public use. Now the only beings allowed access had been thoroughly vetted by COMPNOR—the Commission for the Preservation of the New

Order—and similar Imperial agencies. On their tunics they wore insignia squares not unlike those worn by members of the Imperial military, providing coded information to security cams and defining the limits of where the wearer could venture.

The repressive security measures struck Galen as exaggerated and unnecessary, even though they had been sold to him and his co-workers as critical to guarding against industrial espionage by rival energy concerns. For him the measures sprang from residual distrust generated during the war years.

Yet another example of the price of peace.

Excepting the security measures, the facility itself was like something out of a dream—one of his own, in fact. The main building was a colossal multilevel cube reminiscent of Helical HyperCom's plant on Lokori; the difference being that the roof of the Project Celestial Power complex was level with the top of the high wall that enclosed the refuge, on all sides of which rose buildings a thousand meters high. Supplies and materials arriving at the nearby landing field were conveyed by airspeeders to much smaller landing zones on the roof, and from those lowered into the facility by means of voluminous turbolifts. The upper levels were mostly reserved for warehousing, while the lower and new sub-bedrock levels were devoted to maintenance rooms, power stations, laser installations, research-and-development centers, laboratories, libraries, and living spaces for a staff of more than twenty-five hundred mixed-species beings.

Both the roof and the expansive front entrance, which was reserved for guests arriving at a secondary landing zone on the grounds, bore the Imperial company logo, which was a bold black circle featuring a smaller circle centered in what could be considered the upper hemisphere.

The symbol notwithstanding, the project had been downplayed in the media. The relocation of the B'ankora and the subsequent construction had received scrutiny early on, but most Coruscanti gradually came to accept that the refuge was now headquarters for an energy research center dedicated to providing renewable power.

Galen had been treated like a luminary when he visited the facility before construction had been completed. Uncomfortable with the attention, he made it known that he didn't want special treatment. He would dress like everyone else, eat in the same commissaries, and his door would be open to anyone with problems or suggestions—even though he had a personal staff dedicated to dealing with employee issues and problem solving. He was required to answer to a six-member board of directors who reported directly to the Emperor's advisory committee. His quarters included an office equipped with a separate library, computer room, and communications suite, linked by turbolift to an elevated residence that had been built expressly for the Ersos, although they had decided to keep their apartment in the Central District as well, if only as a getaway for Lyra and Jyn.

Almost ten standard months to the day of the meeting with Krennic on Kanzi, the facility had had its official opening, attended by political dignitaries and others. Tours had been given, food and drink had been served, speeches had been delivered. Now all that was behind Galen and he had arrived at the refuge, clean shaven and prepped for his initial day of actual work.

Newly delivered to the research lab was the largest kyber crystal he had ever seen.

Suspended from gantries as it was being moved to a huge antigrav platform, the translucent euhedral was the size of a small dwelling, and beyond his wildest imaginings. Gazing up at it while it was being moved, he couldn't determine whether it was in its natural state or had been shaped and polished by unknown tools and hands.

Several of Galen's fellow researchers—all of whom were new to him and clearly as mesmerized as he was—were following the crystal's route through the cavernous room. He had expected to be working with at least a few of his old friends, but, surprisingly, many of the institute crew hadn't returned to Coruscant after the war. Orson had said that some were indeed working for Project Celestial Power, but on diverse worlds where additional research was being done and other facilities were being built. As far as Galen could tell, Orson's role was to oversee the construction of those far-flung installations in accordance with Galen's discoveries.

Like him, his co-workers weren't sure what to make of the giant crystal.

"The faces reveal no evidence of tooling," one of them said, a Gotal with a muzzled face resembling a flower blossom and a pair of thick cranial horns capped with vibration-dampening cozies. "If you look closely, the matrix appears to be in flux—almost like organelles in a living cell."

Galen had already observed that property in his study of some of the finger-sized kybers Orson had provided. The experiments he had conducted in a lab at the Institute of Applied Science had also revealed that close and extended contact with kybers was detrimental to sleep. He hadn't gotten a full night's rest in months, and even on the nights when sheer exhaustion overwhelmed his racing thoughts, the crystals infiltrated his dreams. The Jedi were believed to have been able to establish a kind of rapport with the kybers through the Force. Was it possible that the crystals could affect non-Force-users as well?

Whatever the case, it was no wonder they could never be properly synthesized.

Galen gestured to the kyber as it was being lowered to the antigrav platform. "Do we have any information about the provenance?"

"We do, but the information may be apocryphal," the Gotal said. "The crystal was apparently found on an Outer Rim world where the Jedi had placed it for safekeeping."

"Then it belonged to the Order."

"It may have been their property originally, but—and this is the questionable part—the Jedi are said to have seized the crystal from a criminal group that was preparing to sell it to the Separatists."

Galen was astounded. If the story was true, it suggested that the Separatists had actually been conducting kyber research, perhaps based on Dr. Zaly's early investigations. Given Dooku's Jedi background, of course it made sense. Who better than the Count of Serenno—known to be a master of the lightsaber—to make use of the crystal that powered the weapon to power some sort of superweapon?

Just the thought of it prompted a moment of vertigo. What secrets might be hiding in the Jedi archives? Would he be permitted to access them? Was the outsized kyber before him one of a kind, or were there countless others—and possibly even larger ones? Would he be permitted to visit worlds where kyber veins might exist, kyber lodes? Who would be responsible for mining them? Would the miners be affected with insomnia of the sort he was experiencing? What about the Order's secret temples, which were rumored to be encrusted with crystals of all shapes and sizes . . .

He placed his hand on the repulsor platform to steady himself, stars exploding behind his closed eyelids. He felt as if he were walking on fire.

"Is everything all right, Dr. Erso?" the Gotal asked.

Galen finally turned to the humanoid and forced an affirmative nod. "I want to test the piezoelectric levels before we move on to experimenting with gain mediums or laser pumping."

"We'll make the necessary preparations," the Gotal said.

Galen stared into the depths of the pellucid stone. Could it be cut? Could it be faceted? Could dopants be applied to heighten its conductivity and power output? Could its surface energy be altered?

So many questions, so many questions, so many questions . . .

* * *

"You're the captain?" one of the Imperial storm-troopers said to Has as if refusing to consider that idea.

"Captain Obitt, yes."

The stormtrooper cocked his helmeted head to one side. "All right, follow us."

Has fell into step behind the pair as they began to lead him deeper into the choke point's command station.

Cargo ships entering and leaving certain sectors of the Western Reaches were subject to random checks that had less to do with seizing proscribed goods than ensuring that no one was transporting merchandise carefully controlled by major corporations. A captain had to be ready to show documentation and shipping manifests, and subject his or her ship to boarding parties of civilian inspectors or, in star systems recovering from the war, squads of stormtroopers.

Has's crew had been ordered to remain aboard the ship, which was currently serving as a kind of tug. The proton torpedoes and munitions Has had secured from Matese's contact at an Imperial depot were concealed inside cylindrical modules normally reserved for transporting non-spin-sealed Tibanna gas, which was a costly form of hyperdrive coolant. Inspectors at Imperial blockades usually wanted to check such modules for capacity, leaks, regulatory compliance, and other nettlesome concerns, but there had been none of the usual this time. Once the *Good Tidings V*'s signature had been identified, Has had been instructed to bypass the inspection bays and report directly to choke point command.

One of the stormtroopers was speaking into his helmet microphone as they walked, and a few corridor turns later the three of them were met by a gangly human officer who gestured Has into a cramped office. When the hatch sealed, the Imperial perched himself on the edge of a holotable and gave Has the once-over.

"There's been a slight change in plans," he announced.

Has tried not to slump. It was the very expression he had been waiting to hear since launching from the depot with the contraband. "I can't say I'm completely surprised."

The officer's forehead wrinkled and he snorted a laugh. "Don't get your briefs in a bunch, Captain. Your run's just been made a whole lot simpler." Reaching for the holotable controls, he called up a planetary display. "When you reach Samovar, spaceport control is going to transmit coordinates for your orbital insertion. But instead of tugging your payload down the well, you're going to hold at the insertion point. A couple of haulers will be there to meet you. All you have to do is disengage the canister modules from your ship, and the haulers will convey everything downside."

Has gnawed at his upper lip. "Well, that does make my job easier, except for one thing."

"That one thing being?"

"I'm supposed to receive final payment on delivery of the cargo. Disengagement might not constitute delivery for whoever's on the receiving end."

The officer smiled without humor. "It will. Check your account after you release the cargo. If there's a problem, you order the haulers to hold off, you reengage, and you contact your handler."

Has sat silently for a moment. "Why am I not going down the well?"

"What do you care? Didn't we both just agree that this is easier?"

"I'm not arguing. I'm just curious."

The Imperial frowned. "The sooner you jettison that tendency, the better. It's not good for business. Run your concerns past your handler when you see him next, but learn not to ask questions in the middle of an operation. Get with the program, you understand?"

Has took a moment to respond. "I guess I do."

The same pair of stormtroopers escorted him back to the ship, where he had to reassure the crew that the op was still on course. Even so, Has continued to mull over the new instructions while he took the ship to hyperspace.

Get with the program.

Except for the delivery modification, things were proceeding exactly as Matese had promised. Has took the former ranger at his word about Krennic not being involved, but the whole scam smelled of special ops. Maybe Matese wasn't even aware that he was still working for Krennic. But then what would the Empire have to gain by creating a black market in weapons—unless they wanted to keep the war going for whatever reason? So maybe it was nothing more than vets like Matese and a handful of career Imperials exploiting the weaknesses of a flawed system.

Has brought the ship out of hyperspace a good distance from Samovar. The sublights had just carried them past the planet's outer moon when spaceport control commed, providing data for insertion, orbit, and landing. Has had never visited the surface, but from space Samovar looked pristine—especially for a world in the Western Reaches, where battles between Imperials and entrenched Separatists were still being fought. He knew that several mining concerns once allied to the Separatists still had downside operations, but those were rumored to be low-impact and environmentally conscientious.

Coming up on the insertion point, the ship's scanners found several haulers waiting.

"We're going to disengage from the modules," Has told his copilot, Yalli.

The Nautolan glanced at him. "We're not bringing the cargo in?"

"Change in plans."

"Since when?

"What do you care?"

Yalli shrugged. "Just curious, *Captain*."

The rest of the crew, including Ribert and his lanky pal, saw to disconnecting from the canister modules. Through the forward viewport, Yalli watched the haulers begin to corral the cargo.

"They've got the goods. What's to stop them from cheating us out of the final payment?" he asked.

Has was already checking his account status. When the numbers came up, he beckoned Yalli over to the display screen.

"Stars' end," the Nautolan said, "we just made that much?"

Has couldn't utter a word. The amount was more than he or most of his partners had made during the entire war.

Lyra had given Galen ample time to settle into his new position before following him to the facility. No sooner did she and Jyn enter the research area than the three-and-a-half-year-old was off and running down the corridor.

"I'm not sure how I feel about bringing her grav-board here," she told Galen in a concerned voice.

"A helmet's certainly in order," Galen said. He motioned to the bank of display screens surmounting the communications console. "At least we'll always know where she is."

Lyra took a moment to track Jyn's movements on the screens. "Okay. But we might also want to consider padding the walls."

They kept a further eye on Jyn until convinced she was out of harm's way. Then Galen called up a view of the facility's principal lab. "There's something I've been dying to show you."

Lyra glanced around while Galen was preoccupied. Everything her gaze fell on was shiny and sterile, almost to the point where the facility made Helical HyperCom's plant seem warm by comparison. Galen and the rest of the researchers and staff didn't seem to be bothered by the security measures, and she supposed she would eventually get used to them, but the abrupt displacement of the B'ankora from the refuge continued to rankle.

"Look at this," Galen was saying.

Displayed on the central monitor was an enormous translucent crystal.

"That can't be a kyber."

"But it is."

Galen didn't seem to be able to take his eyes off it.

"In most cases, kybers are brought to the surface by seismic activity—movements along slippage fault lines, and typically only when an oceanic plate is sliding against a continental plate. But even then the movement has to be horizontal. The crystals rise, gathering impurities or other minerals along the way. That's why it has always been said of kybers that they are more often *grown* than mined. The smaller ones can literally be picked up in caves, in streams, in the lava tubes of ancient volcanoes, or sometimes they're found embedded in veins of kyberite, a false kyber. But this one, this one . . . Clearly it was mined, as well as polished, though we haven't been able to identify the source tectonic world. There are traces of a brown rind that must have covered the entire crystal at one time, so it might have been discovered in a massive pod. The source world would have to be remote, one unsuited to settlement or habitation. A world only the Jedi knew about."

Lyra regarded him as he spoke—more, it seemed, to the crystal than to her. He hadn't been sleeping well for months, and he had that mad-scientist look in his weary eyes she'd seen before when he became obsessed with something. At the apartment he had left sketches and enigmatic doodles pinned up all over the place; eerie intertwinings of numerals and obscure figures and mathematical symbols.

"The Jedi's relationship with the kybers—and I use the word deliberately—goes back tens of thousands of years," Galen continued. "Long before that kybers were worshipped for their patterns, and the fact that they're impervious to fire and resistant to hammering—outwardly eternal. Ancient beings associated them with wind, rain, and breath, but the Jedi may have seen them as embodying an aspect of the Force. It's not known how the few extant museum pieces escaped the Order's notice, or why the Jedi weren't allowed to confiscate them."

"Is that what this one is?" Lyra asked. "A museum piece?"

Galen finally turned to her, shaking his head as he did. "This was on its way to the Separatists when the Jedi seized and sequestered it."

Lyra frowned in misgiving. "Doesn't the fact that the Jedi intervened say something about the potential power of the crystals?"

"Of course it does. Remember, Dooku was a Jedi. He knew all about the power of the kyber. From the start the Jedi were determined to keep that inherent power to themselves."

Lyra made a face. "Then couldn't it be that they were protecting the rest of us from that power? Even their lightsabers were just tools for keeping the peace."

"Unfortunately the Jedi are gone," Galen said. "But that shouldn't mean we're obliged to ignore the crystals out of respect for their centuries of service."

Lyra held up her hands. "I only meant that the Jedi never would have wanted that energy to be turned to an evil purpose."

"Of course they wouldn't," Galen said. "And I was concerned about that very thing happening during the war, but not now. This is the Emperor's dream."

Lyra wrinkled her nose. "Can't we just call him Palpatine—in private, I mean?"

Galen ignored that. "For millennia the Jedi had what amounted to exclusive rights to the crystals, except for rare instances when they were discovered by outsiders and found their way onto the black market. I hate to say this, but there's reason to believe that they refused to share the secrets of the crystals out of fear of surrendering some of the power they enjoyed."

Lyra was taken aback. "I don't believe that for a moment."

"It's in keeping with their actions at the conclusion of the war," Galen said in a calmer voice. "Their attempt on the Emperor's life might have been an effort to ensure their elite power and status."

Galen's words were familiar, and Lyra suddenly recalled when and where she had heard them: on Kanzi, shortly after Orson had displayed the kyber crystals and Galen had asked him outright if they had once been used to power lightsabers.

"What of it?" Orson had said. *"They were waging their own separate war and they lost."*

Lyra refused to accept it, and had said as much.

"Are you suggesting that the Emperor would falsify the events that occurred in his office? Have you

had a look at him since his encounter with the traitors? Have you seen what they did to him?"

Galen had intervened, saying that no one was doubting the Emperor's word, but Orson wasn't about to let Lyra off the hook so easily. Addressing her, he had said:

"They doomed themselves by clinging to their outmoded traditions instead of embracing the science of the new age. Think of the good they could have done if they'd been willing to share their secrets instead of allowing themselves to be drawn into a war—against their own principles. But they had no choice once they saw their Order threatened by one of their own."

And now here was Galen, all but mimicking Orson's words when she knew he didn't believe half of what he was saying.

On Lokori, when reports of the events in Palpatine's office and throughout the theater of the war had reached them, both she had Galen had refused to accept the official explanation—the Imperial explanation. The Jedi killed by the thousands, their Temple the scene of a battle, scant survivors scattered to the stars, the Force dispersed . . . She was as heartbroken as if she had lost a family member, and had cried for hours. And yet most beings were so glad to see an end to the war that they accepted the deaths of the Jedi as they did the sacrifices made by the clones of the Grand Army. In what seemed merely standard weeks to Lyra, the Order all but passed into myth, with scarcely a trace of mourning or grief. Orson's *new age* had dawned and the Jedi were relegated to history.

So why the change in Galen? Was he masking his own sadness for what had befallen the Order to justify his feverish desire to unlock the secrets of the kyber? Intent on providing for her and Jyn, fixated on resuming his research, was Galen in danger of losing his way?

His intense gaze had returned to the massive kyber.

"Who knows to what ends Dooku might have put this crystal."

"I can guess," Lyra said carefully, "since Dooku loosed a droid army on the galaxy."

"Dooku was undeniably evil," Galen said without facing her. "But the Jedi also need to be held accountable—even historically—for being insular, and for locking their secrets away. Now we have an opportunity to expose at least some of those secrets."

Lyra shuddered, and somehow Galen picked up on it.

"Our research could lead to a dramatic shift in the paradigm. It's not unreasonable to feel threatened."

"As long as the change is for the benefit of everyone," she managed. "The way the Force is."

He nodded, as if assessing her words. "I'll defer to the Order's sound judgment. We'll investigate with judicious care. But who knows, one day we may even get to the root of the Force itself."

Lyra laughed despite herself. "Now you're really beginning to scare me." She fell silent, then said: "Galen, have you slept at all since you've been here?"

"When I've needed to. You know how I am."

"That's why I'm asking."

He made light of her concern with a negligent wave. "I'll catch up. Right now I couldn't sleep even if I wanted to." He paused to magnify the view of one facet of the kyber. "The internal structure is unlike anything I've seen. It's almost a bridge between organic and inorganic, as close to alive as a stone can be—which I suspect is why the Jedi were able to interact with kybers through the Force. We don't have that option, so science will have to substitute. But it's almost as if the crystals evade our attempts to investigate their properties on a quantum level. They flee from our efforts to analyze them with neutron activation, even plasma mass spectrometry.

"We took extreme care in pumping the crystal with various lasers, and yet still managed to harvest unexpected returns—sufficient to power a modest population center for a standard week. As I explained to Orson, restraint is the challenge facing us right now."

Lyra made no effort to interrupt him, even though the research was beginning to sound more like alchemy or black magic than the science of the new age. She recognized what he was doing: in effect talking to himself in an attempt to reduce his insights to the simplest terms so they could be understood by others. His parents had never attempted to *fix* their compulsive son, and in some sense he had succeeded *despite* his imperfections. In his daily life he would sometimes go out of his way to introduce imperfection—in his drawings, his routines, his attempts at housecleaning— as a means of keeping himself from becoming overly occupied with results. When the habit leaked into his research notes, his theories could seem even more impenetrable.

Frequently there were no words for what was in Galen's mind, which made his formulas and equations intelligible only to a rare few. It wasn't that he didn't wish to see the world as others did; he was unable to. He saw more deeply into things, and was attuned to nature's own musings and inner dialogues.

She backed away from the console to watch him, then backed away a bit more so that she could take in the entire communications station, with its monitors and holoprojectors, and the screens displaying views of the giant kyber from every conceivable angle, and Jyn racing down a corridor. And it struck her that Galen was, in a way, back in prison.

But this time willingly.

Project Celestial Power was a kind of gilded cage.

Krennic listened intently to the surveillance recordings that had been uploaded from the Celestial Power facility on Coruscant to the command module in orbit above Geonosis, pausing the feed several times to replay fragments of Galen and Lyra's conversations.

"I only meant that the Jedi never would have wanted that energy to be turned to an evil purpose," Lyra was saying.

"Of course they wouldn't," Galen said. *"And I was concerned about that very thing happening during the war, but not now. This is the Emperor's dream."*

"Can't we just call him Palpatine—in private, I mean?"

He paused the feed once more and sat back in his swivel chair, bouncing his steepled fingers against his lips in deep rumination.

Just as he'd suspected, Lyra needed to be watched.

16

UNEXPECTED VALUE

THE WANTON WELLSPRING WASN'T THE sort of bar where patrons, regulars especially, were expected to make grand entrances, so Has—arriving for another meeting with Matese—was surprised when the two hulking, snuffling, snout-faced Gamorreans working the door allowed him to cut the line and all but ushered him inside. Maybe it had something to do with his new clothes or the way he was carrying himself that singled him out from the usual pikers looking for pickup work. For indeed everyone in the place, from the daunting Woana, who was coaxing drinks from customers at the bar, to a couple of Twi'lek musicians on break, turned to regard him as he stepped into the main room. Even his competitors took notice. But what should have been a kind of crowning moment was undermined by the looks they ultimately showed him, which were closer to circumspect than congratulatory. Whether stalked or skull-embedded or just spots on a carapace, optical organs followed him as he made his way to the corner table Matese had reserved. The atmosphere was charged with caution, and the few greetings he received were tentative.

Matese had yet to show up, so Has collapsed into a chair, ordered a drink, and tried to make sense of the sidelong glances and the hushed conversations that were so obviously about him they nearly got his ears ringing.

Before the drink arrived, a smuggler he knew only as Molo—a brawny old hand notoriously rumored to have sabotaged more than his share of rivals and currently as down on his luck as any of them—advanced on the table.

"You don't mind if I sit."

Since it wasn't exactly a question, Has simply slid his chair to where he could sit directly opposite the dangerous human in case anything violent went down.

"Happy for the company."

The logo etched into Molo's new ear identified it as the product of a corporation that manufactured cheap replacement organs for war veterans who couldn't afford bacta treatments or synthskin prostheses. Molo's original ear had been given freely in a gesture of deference to a crime syndicate he had inadvertently crossed.

"Spotted your ship at one of the Western Reaches choke points a couple of months back," Molo said. "When you made the big run."

"The big run?"

Molo glanced around. "The rest of your crew out celebrating?"

Okay, Has thought, so word of the Samovar op had spread, which in itself wasn't unusual. Still . . . "Everybody's luck changes at some point."

"That's the way it's supposed to go. But what a lot of us are wondering is how you managed to get in and out without a hitch. I mean, you talk about perfect timing. It's almost like you were tipped off."

Has slid his chair a bit farther out of range of Molo's big fist. "It was just a drop and departure."

"So you weren't warned."

"Warned of what?"

Molo sat back, appraising him openly. "You haven't heard what went down at Samovar?"

Has spread his hands in ignorance. "I've been out of touch."

It was true. Fearing Imperial reprisals following the run, he and the crew had decided to scatter and avoid contact with one another. For Has that had meant a jump to an area of the Outer Rim gaining notoriety as the Corporate Sector, where he could spend some of the credits he had earned. He had only returned to Jibuto at Matese's insistence, relieved not to have found WANTED holos of him posted at every orbital station along the way.

"Imperials discovered a huge cache of arms— munitions and stars know what else. What we hear, a dozen mining concerns have been appropriated and the place is off limits until further notice. That never happens on a Legacy world."

"Legacy world?"

"Legally exempt from exploitation for whatever reasons. Mixed use, low-impact only."

Has didn't bother trying to rein in his bewilderment. "When did all this happen?"

"Almost directly after you left. Local couple of days."

Has shook his head. "It's the first I've heard, Molo."

The human leaned in to the table and lowered his voice. "But we know who did know. Your contact—the one you met with here—someone ID'd him as a former special op."

"He was, but he's a civilian now. Besides, it was just a run. Is that why I'm getting the once-over from everyone in here? You all think I set this up?"

"Once-over? Well, I'll admit that half of us are envious and the other half would like a piece of you, but that's got nothing to do with your being an Imperial sympathizer."

"An Imp—"

Molo motioned him silent. "The half I belong to are hoping you'll bring some of the rest of us in on the action, or at least put in a good word."

Matese entered while Has was still digesting the new information and telling himself to relax. Aware that Has was gazing over his shoulder at the door, Molo turned and smiled. "I'll be giving you some privacy. But think about what I said."

Has nodded repeatedly.

Monitoring Molo's return to his own table, Matese pulled the same chair out and sat down. "What was that about?"

Has glared at him. "When you contacted me you failed to mention anything about what happened at Samovar. A Legacy world, no less."

Matese flinched in amused surprise. "You have

some special fondness for the place, you should have told me beforehand."

Has bit back what he had in mind to say. After all, what was Samovar to him? All he had done was make a delivery. Instead he said: "I like the eye implant."

Matese touched it gingerly. "Didn't have to wait for Veterans Services, after all. Visible and infrared. Comes in very handy."

Has tried again to resist asking, but couldn't help himself. "How did the Imperials learn about the torpedoes we delivered?"

"We have no idea," Matese said. "We ran checks on everyone involved, and no one in our organization gave up any information. Our best guess is that someone on Samovar—some environmental observer—brought it to Imperial attention, not wanting arms on the planet."

Has mulled it over, as if trying to make peace with it. "I guess I can buy that. But why would the Empire appropriate the mining concerns on a Legacy world?"

Matese shrugged. "Beats me. But we're in the clear, so it's business as usual."

"You have another run for me?"

"Why do you think I'm here, Has? I mean, I like you, but not enough that I'm willing to travel just to see you."

"Is there enough work to spread around?"

Matese smiled in understanding. "So that's why the big lug was talking to you. Well, not right now, but maybe down the road. Assuming you're willing to vouch for them."

"I can vouch for some of them," Has said. "So where am I off to this time?"

"You're going back to the Western Reaches. A world called Wadi Raffa."

"Never heard of it.

"Good. Then I don't have to worry about you forming any attachments to it."

Wilhuff Tarkin's Imperial Star Destroyer, *Executrix*, was still holding at Samovar when he received a comm from Coruscant and had it routed to the holoprojector in his cabin. The lawyer representing Samovar's mining conglomerate was a woman named Arsha Lome, who was as strikingly beautiful as a holopresence as she was in real life, and whom Tarkin knew from his days as adjutant general to have as sharp a legal mind as he had ever encountered.

"My clients are steadfast in assuring me that they had nothing to do with the arms shipment your forces discovered," Lome was saying.

Tarkin was standing for the cam, his right hand cupping his left elbow and that hand at his jaw. "That may very well be the case, counselor. We're conducting an investigation into the origin of the arms, who on Samovar procured them, and for what ultimate purpose. I'm confident that the truth will eventually emerge, and that your clients will have their day in court."

"And just when might that be, Governor? A year from now? Two years? My every effort to schedule a preliminary hearing is being frustrated."

"That's something I can't help you with—even for old times' sake."

Red-haired Arsha narrowed her blue eyes. "This has nothing to do with the fact that my clients supplied the Separatists during the war?"

Tarkin adopted a stern look. "The Empire has no need to engage in reprisals of that sort."

"Really. And in the meantime the Empire has run of all mining operations."

"Your clients should be grateful to be free on bail and still employed."

"Still employed but now working for the Empire." Arsha paused for a moment. "I do find it interesting that no sooner does the Empire appropriate operations than all former environment restrictions vanish into thin air." She snapped her long fingers. "As you may or may not know, my clients tried for years to get those Legacy regulations lifted."

"Odd timing, to be sure."

Arsha nodded slightly. "And the seizure has nothing to do with the Empire's unexpected hunger for doonium and dolovite—two of the most important ores mined on Samovar."

"I wouldn't know about that."

She laughed. "Well, if you wouldn't, I can't imagine who would." She fell silent once more, then said: "What sort of game are you playing, Wilhuff?"

Tarkin smiled tightly. "Very nice chatting with you, Arsha. We should catch up the next time I'm on Coruscant."

She sniffed. "Only if we can return to The Cupola—in exchange for your sudden obtuseness."

"I look forward to a wonderful evening."

When the holovid had disappeared, Tarkin went to the viewport to gaze out on previously unspoiled Samovar. Downside, heavy machinery was being off-loaded—augurs, pushbeam transfer equipment, detection sensors, crushers, conveyors and mills. Droids as large as buildings were decapitating mountains, defoliating entire hillsides, stripping soils, and mining operations were already being ramped up. The exploitation of Samovar wouldn't end until every lode deposit had been emptied and every bit of ore extracted down to bedrock. By then the planet's oceans and rivers would be turned to acid by tailings and slurry, its slopes eroded, evergreen forests and clear skies a memory. Some wildlife would survive in remote areas, but not for long. And all for the doonium and dolovite, essential for shielding the battle station's hypermatter reactor core and focusing dish, and eventually its superlaser. Arsha's intuitions were as sound as ever, and she wouldn't be alone in putting two and two together. The media could be controlled, but not entirely. Anyone who was watching closely would surmise that an immense secret project was in the works. At some point, steps would have to be taken.

Necessary evils, some would have it.

And he now counted himself among them.

Mop-up campaigns in the Western Reaches had fully convinced him of the value of the superweapon. The Emperor, the moffs, the Imperial Army of officers and stormtroopers would never be enough to subjugate the entire galaxy. Only *fear* would bring lasting order, and the battle station would come to embody that.

Unfortunately, Orson Krennic wasn't the person to command it.

Tarkin wondered what and how much Krennic wasn't telling him. Keeping from the Emperor his plans to appropriate construction materials for the project was only one sign of his overarching ambition, his impulsiveness, his disdain for authority and the chain of command. No, he simply wasn't the man for the job—but incendiary Krennic was perfectly suited to be the one held accountable for all the setbacks and delays that were bound to plague the project. Exposing him, undermining him, would take very little effort, and yet doing so would pose a great risk to Tarkin, for he knew full well that the Emperor was also eyeing him to assume command and control of the battle station. To avoid having to accept the privilege prematurely, he would have to continue to defer to Krennic until the proper time. Perhaps he would ask Darth Vader to keep an eye on him; he and Vader had partnered successfully on a couple of Imperial missions, and the Dark Lord might just be intrigued enough to get involved.

A short jump away, the bleak future Tarkin envisioned for Samovar was already playing out on Malpaz. It was on Malpaz, under the Project Celestial Power umbrella, that Krennic had constructed a facility intended to make practical application of the research being conducted on distant Coruscant; that was, to weaponize Galen Erso's energy research in order to arm the battle station. It even housed a twin of the massive kyber crystal that was the subject of Galen's current experiments.

Except that things hadn't gone according to plan.

From the safety of his shuttle, Krennic watched a series of powerful, mushrooming explosions reduce what little remained of the duplicate facility to debris and ash. The metropolis that sprawled at the base of the hill on which the installation had been constructed was likewise engulfed in rapidly spreading flames. Worse, a primitive nuclear power plant had melted down during the initial detonations and firestorms, and now a mass exodus was in progress, with hundreds of thousands of mixed-species indigenes fleeing for the far side of the broad river everyone hoped might contain the conflagration. The devastation couldn't have been more crippling had a volcano blown its top in the heart of the city.

"Did we lose anyone?" Krennic asked his aide.

"It's incredible," Oyanta said from the shuttle's comm board, "but the fail-safes allowed everyone to evacuate in time. The locals weren't as lucky."

"Estimate of fatalities?"

"In excess of ten thousand. Radiation from the reactor will likely kill more than the explosions and fires combined."

Krennic worked his jaw. "Who do I blame?"

Oyanta gestured toward the main cabinspace. "The team's assembled."

Krennic squared his shoulders and stormed away. The ten-member team of scientists, which now in-

cluded a couple of former Separatists, was crammed
into the aft cabin, looking nervous and hangdog. A
few of them were gauze-bandaged or slathered in
balms.

"First, tell me that we haven't lost the kyber,"
Krennic said.

"It's all but indestructible," a human member of
the team said. "Once the fire burns out, we can retrieve it."

Krennic nodded. "That will get some of you off
the hook, but one of you needs to explain to me
how a simple experiment could total everything I
built, not to mention an entire city. You had all the
research notes. Was there anything in them you might
have missed or overlooked?"

"The energy output was uncontainable," Professor
Sahali said, obviously speaking for everyone. "The
crystal diffracted the laser instead of supplying the
expected pulse of power. It might as well have been
an out-of-control turbolaser battery."

"Then why didn't the same thing happen at our
sister facility? You had to have misinterpreted the
data or failed to follow procedure."

The Iktotchi specialist, Dagio Belcoze, responded.
"The data are very difficult to construe. If we are in
fact only replicating previous experiments, then our
sister team has to be employing some other method of
harvest and control. Perhaps they used a different
laser or found a way to channel excess output into
storage capacitors. They may be using a different in-
hibition alloy." His downward-facing horns shook as
he spoke. "The data simply aren't specific enough in

many instances, and even where they are specific, the equations are in a kind of shorthand difficult to decipher."

Squat Sahali agreed. "Someone understands the properties of the kyber much better than we do. We'll never be fully successful at weaponization without the original researcher to supervise these experiments."

Krennic growled in exasperation and was headed back to the communications cabin when he realized that Dagio Belcoze was following him.

"What is it?" he said, whirling on the Iktotchi.

"It's clear to me who's behind the research," Belcoze said. "Galen Erso."

Krennic considered refuting it, but instead said: "What if he is?"

"We need him here, with us."

Krennic's nostrils flared. "He's busy elsewhere, Doctor. And I suggest you devote yourself to determining where you went wrong rather than focus on Galen Erso's employment options, so that next time you'll be able to provide me with the expected results."

Belcoze took a step back, as if Krennic's words alone had propelled him; then he turned and hurried to rejoin the others.

Oyanta was standing by the shuttle's viewport.

"It won't do for word of this to get out," he said. "Should we sanitize everything?"

"Can the destruction be made to look like an attack?"

"It already does."

Krennic gave it thought. He supposed he could blame the reactor, blame the locals; contain the survivors in detention camps. What with the radiation it would be for their own good anyway.

"Then leave it be," he told Oyanta finally. "But remove the team."

17

MATERIAL IMPLICATIONS

HAS DESCENDED THE FREIGHTER'S LOWERED ramp and walked to the high bank of the estuary. Shielding his eyes, he looked toward the sea. The offshore breeze was warm and constant, and the crystalline waters moved lazily on the tide. Far out where the inlet met the sea the water was deep blue, and much farther out a range of conical mountains poked from the hazy horizon, as if floating on the brume, the summit of the tallest volcano invisible behind a lenticular cloud. In the middle ground were scattered islands of rock, green and yellow vegetation clinging to clefts, and steep sides carved into isolated sandy coves.

Has turned to the chief of the ground crew that had been on hand to meet him. A short human, she had the look he was becoming more and more accustomed to since having thrown in with Matese: fit, furtive, capable looking, sporting sensibly close-cropped hair. Behind her the five members of her team were helping Has's crew off-load shipping containers from the freighter's forward cargo bay. The ground crew had arrived in a couple of airspeeders with a short train of repulsorlift cargo haulers.

Sparse vegetation sprouted from red clay soil on both sides of the estuary; the sky was as clear as any he had ever seen from below. He knew from coming in that there wasn't a major population center for thousands of kilometers in any direction.

"Choice duty," he said to the crew chief.

"For short stretches. You'd need to be a hermit to want to stay."

"Not much in the way of nightlife."

"Good for lantern bugs." She wiped sweat from her forehead and gestured in a vague way out to sea. "Turlin/Benthic Extraction has a small settlement on the western shore. A rotating mixed-species couple of hundred. Slim pickings as far as company goes, but the drinks are cheap and the food is tolerable."

"That's the extent?"

"No permanent settlements permitted since a group of environmentalists succeeded in having Wadi declared a Legacy world."

Of course, Has told himself. "Turlin/Benthic," he repeated. "Don't know of them."

"Mining consortium. They have a concession for ocean floor extraction."

Has nodded. "I caught a glimpse of their platforms when we came in."

"Mostly a droid operation, but a few living pilots as well."

"What are they dredging up?"

"What I learned when I was hired, the sea has some large areas of polymetallic nodules in the active hydrothermal vents. The vents create deposits that contain ores like doonium, meleenium, dolovite, kammris. T/B uses hydraulic pumps to bring ores to the surface to be processed. The tailings are collected and sent to offworld cleansing centers."

"They care that much about pollution?"

"Like I said, they have no choice, Wadi being Legacy."

"So Turlin/Benthic's the end user of our cargo?"

She stopped what she was doing to smile in a knowing way. "Can't have too many redundant pipe fittings."

"Except they're not pipe fittings."

"Yes, they are," she said in elaborate seriousness. "It says so right on the manifest."

Has forced a laugh that made it appear he was in on the joke.

Wadi Raffa was Samovar all over again. A choke point commander had provided him with landing coordinates and instructed him to come in as gently as possible, employing the freighter's retroturbos rather than positioning thrusters.

He took a moment to monitor the unloading. Everyone seemed relaxed, not worried the way people normally were when arms or spice or other proscribed goods were involved. Because the fix was in. So why couldn't he be happy as well? Was he supposed to worry about the futures of planets like Samovar and Wadi Raffa? Wasn't that the Emperor's job? All Has had to do was follow procedure, take the credits and run, like he always had.

So why was he feeling dirty? And why did his stomach feel like it was tied in knots?

He knew the answer, and knew, too, that there was no value in thinking too deeply about Matese's lies or the Empire's possible reasons for using subterfuge rather than turbolasers to appropriate planets.

"You hauling the containers out to sea?" he asked, trying to sound innocent.

She shook her head. "The platforms are too far out. The cargo's being picked up."

Has searched the sky. "How?"

She prized a pair of macrobinoculars from a case clipped to her belt and offered them.

Pressing them to his eyes, he scanned the horizon, seizing on an object he brought into focus, and exhaling in surprise.

"Is that vessel actually floating on the water?"

She guffawed. "It's like something out of a historical holodrama, right? That's what happens on Legacy worlds. Primitive as it can get."

Has handed back the macros. "How are they going to make the case that a company doing seabed mining on a Legacy world would want ion cannons?"

She narrowed her eyes at him, then looked around as if someone might be listening.

"Protection."

Has wasn't entirely sure if she was in on the plan or not. Maybe she actually worked for the mining company and had no idea that it was all a setup. Or maybe she just didn't want Has to know that she knew.

"Someone takes a sudden interest in this place and

they're going to be put off by a *boat* sporting a couple of Separatist-era ion cannons?"

She shrugged. "Okay. Then maybe the company's worried about deep-sea creatures. Monsters from the seabed."

This human wasn't going to play ball. "You know the one about bringing a vibroblade to a blaster fight?" he commented.

"Is it supposed to be funny?"

"Not for the one who brings the vibroblade."

Lyra was up late transcribing Galen's personal notes, being careful to observe his precise but complex instructions. The research team's notes were compiled by others and transmitted to facilities elsewhere on Coruscant, or offworld for all she knew. As project liaison, Orson was privy to all the latter, but not the former.

Jyn was only meters away in a play area they had created and cordoned off to keep her from wandering too far. Most kids her age would have been asleep hours ago, but Jyn had inherited her father's nocturnal habits and Lyra had given up trying to interfere with her natural rhythms. Luckily for everyone, Jyn was independent and often able to entertain herself, sometimes for hours at a stretch, singing, playing, pretending, as she was doing now.

Light from the surrounding superstructures flooded through the office window, but the view was anything but stimulating. There was only the towering expanse of plasteel wall that enclosed the former ref-

uge grounds and the sky-high buildings that rose
above it. Someone had planted flowering vines at the
base of the wall, but they had yet to climb more than
two meters. Even so, Lyra had made a habit of taking
long walks with Jyn on the grounds, usually at night
when the area around the facility was more gently
lighted, the arcologies and monads notwithstanding—
and despite the feeling of walking on the bottom on
an enormous, waterless swimming pool.

She could feel the facility beating and breathing
around her, though frigid at the core.

Galen was surely still up as well, off somewhere
doing something. When he wasn't directing experiments, he could usually be found in his office, writing
in the air or doing input at a keyboard. Other times
he would resort to entering calculations or notes in
his journal, writing longhand in different-colored inks
as his thinking shifted from one aspect of problem
solving to the next. At the end of such sessions Lyra
would collate the notes by color, then return them to
him for further refinement.

Forced to wear several hats, he alternated between
distracted scientist and harried husband and father,
but in some ways he seemed more content than he
had been in years. He could requisition anything he
needed—lasers, metals, chemicals, consultants, Jedi
datacrons—and the requests would arrive in short
order, no questions asked. Additional crystals of all
sizes continued to flood in, some of them clearly liber-
ated from temples, as they bore minute traces of ad-
hesive, like gems prized from their bezels.

She had grown accustomed to periods like these

when his mind was on fire, when he was physically present but emotionally distant. Frequently she couldn't help but feel that her every attempt to engage him interrupted some inner dialogue or discourse he was attending, and the facility somehow magnified that. At times it seemed as if, in attempting to unlock the secrets of the kyber, he was trying to decode something about himself.

She was willing to accept that the Jedi hadn't scratched the surface of the crystals' power, but she held on to her belief that the Order felt that surface wasn't meant to be scratched. By contrast, what better way to honor the Order's contribution to more than a millennium of service than to use their sacrosanct kybers to provide inexpensive and safe energy to countless worlds. After all, there was no denying that the galaxy was at peace—except for areas where Separatist holdouts were alleged to be entrenched, possibly unaware that the war had ended. Little news from those areas made it to the HoloNet, but she had heard talk to the effect that some distant worlds were still attempting to acquire weapons, but also that the Empire was moving swiftly to curtail those attempts.

"We will do whatever is necessary to ensure an enduring reconciliation," the Emperor had said in a recent and rare public address.

She could only hope that that strong hand would relax once the threats disappeared. Neither optimistic nor pessimistic, she could do little more than hope that Jyn would grow up in more stable times.

She glanced at Galen's multicolored notes and sat back from them, unable to get to the root of her uneasiness. All at once the comm sounded, which was unusual given the late hour. Plus, the display revealed the communication to be from an unknown party and origin point. Thinking back to the message that had found its way to her comlink during the war, she hesitated, but when she accepted the comm, she was delighted to see the face of Galen's friend and onetime mentor, Reeva Demesne.

"Lyra," Reeva said, equally elated, "how lovely to see you."

"You, too, Reeva." Lyra had always been drawn to the Mirialan's dark complexion and exotic facial tattoos.

"I apologize for the late hour, but I decided to take the chance."

"You didn't wake us. I'm working on Galen's notes. But he's not here. I can tell him to contact you—"

"Please do. But tell me first how you've been."

"Good. Everything's fine."

"And Jyn. How is she?"

"I can show you." Lyra trained one of the holocams on Jyn, who was using her toy figures to act out some sort of adventure fantasy.

"Precious. You must both be so proud."

"We are."

"I'm so glad that Galen found a position that suits him."

"It's been exciting, if somewhat daunting."

"I know the feeling, since Galen and I—many of us, in fact—are all serving the same master."

Lyra angled her head in surprise. "You're contributing to Celestial Power?"

"Yes," Reeva said without enthusiasm. "Tell me, Lyra, has Galen heard from Dagio Belcoze recently?"

"Dagio? Why should he? I mean, they made up after their little boxing match, but they were never close friends. As far as I know Galen hasn't heard from any of his old friends. You're the first."

Reeva looked distressed. "It's so strange. I've been trying to contact many of our mutual colleagues without success. Dagio was working on Malpaz . . . It's a bit worrisome actually."

"I can see how it would be," Lyra said. "Where are you, Reeva?"

"I'm on Hypori. I know you're a galactic traveler. Have you ever visited here?" Before Lyra could answer in the negative, Reeva said: "Galen is content with his work?"

Lyra restrained a frown of doubt. "You know him. When the research is going well, he is."

"And he's still working closely with Orson Krennic?"

Lyra took a moment to answer. "Yes, Reeva. Why do you ask?"

"It's just that I see Orson from time to time . . ."

Lyra waited for more, but Reeva fell silent. "I'll tell Galen to contact you, Reeva."

"He doesn't have to. Just tell him that I said hello, and that I hope that we'll have a chance to catch up in person. I'm on Hypori, remember. Hypori."

The comm ended abruptly.

Lyra sat for a long while staring at the empty holofield. Reeva hadn't said all she had wanted to say.

Was she under surveillance in whatever research work she was engaged in?

Lyra replayed the conversation in her head; then thought:

She wants us to know where she is.

Krennic felt like a glorified tour guide as he ordered the shuttle pilot to bring the wide-winged shuttle closer to the battle station's parabolic dish. They had already completed an equatorial orbit as well as a polar one, pausing now and then to examine specific areas of the curved technoscape designated for shield generators and gun towers. Krennic talked nonstop, but thus far neither Grand Vizier Amedda nor any of his flamboyantly attired advisers had asked a single question.

The orb was more completely clad, and a few gun emplacements were under construction in the trench— the battle station's broad equator. Local space was crowded with ships and droids of all classification, with large areas of the hull bathed in light provided by banks of enormous illuminators.

"Do any of you have an interest in visiting some of the interior modules?" Krennic asked.

"Not unless you have a weapon to show us," Amedda said at last.

"Just now the reactor is our priority."

Amedda glowered. "What is the status of the weapon, Lieutenant Commander?"

"We're making slow but steady progress."

The Chagrian showed scorn. "We can accept steady,

but slow is unacceptable. Need we remind you again that this isn't some public works program for Poggle's enslaved descendants? The *weapon* is the priority. The station is nothing without it."

"Weaponizing the research is taking more time than anticipated," Krennic said in a firm voice.

"Then you need to demand more from your scientists."

Krennic made a placating gesture. "We've already eliminated a lot of deadweight. I'm winnowing them down to a core group."

"That's not what I'm referring to. Security is of lesser concern to us than progress—of which we have seen very little." Amedda paused, then added: "We understand that you almost lost your team on Malpaz."

Krennic managed to keep from grimacing. He hadn't known that Amedda had learned of the incident. "A temporary setback. We're reanalyzing the data."

"I'm interested to hear your account of what happened."

Krennic led with a shrug. "The locals mismanaged their nuclear reactor."

"Is that your story?"

"It's a story," Krennic said, refusing to yield.

Amedda had fire in his eyes. "Either you're rushing your team headlong into areas they don't fully understand, or Erso's data are beyond their ken."

Krennic grinned. "You've got a gift for delivering mixed messages, Vizier. Demand more from my team, or exercise caution. Which is it?"

Amedda's forked tongue flicked. "We've given Galen Erso an entire facility. We're providing him with resources and materials from all over the galaxy. We're practically at his beck and call, and still you fail to enlist him." The vizier lowered his horns. "The Emperor is most displeased by these delays. Furthermore, who gave you authority to enlist Imperial forces in the appropriation of mining concerns?"

Krennic squared his shoulders. "It struck me as the most expeditious way of getting what we need."

A low growl escaped Amedda. "You are nothing if not resourceful. But once again you've superseded your authority."

"In the interest of simplicity," Krennic said. "The last time we had this discussion, Vizier, I thought we'd agreed that you were going to allow me to do my job."

"I don't recall agreeing to anything of the sort. In any case, you no longer enjoy the privilege of ignoring the chain of command."

Krennic stared, awaiting elaboration.

"We feel that we have overburdened you," Amedda went on in a falsely offhand way. "You should be attending solely to the weapon, leaving procurement and production to others."

Tarkin, Krennic thought, wondering how Amedda would react to learning that the moff had sanctioned the illegal acquisitions. Not that Krennic would be the one to breach Imperial etiquette and loyalty by revealing that. Not openly, at any rate.

"Until further notice, appropriations operations are suspended," Amedda was saying. "You'll have to make do with materials on hand or find legitimate ways to procure them. As it stands we're going to need to find someone to assume responsibility for what you've done."

"I have some thoughts about that," Krennic said.

"I'm certain you do."

Krennic waited a beat, then said: "I think it would help if you promoted me."

Amedda glared at him. "Is there no limit to your insolence? On what grounds?"

"A promotion would send a clear signal to the scientists and everyone else involved in the project that I'm making headway, and that they need to jump at my command. Rear admiral will suffice."

Amedda forced a fatigued exhale. "Full commander, perhaps. And only on the Emperor's approval."

Krennic inclined his head in a bow.

Clearly the time had come to play his royal card.

18

COMBINATORY PLAY

RYLOTH, OFFICIALLY A PROTECTORATE OF the Empire, was celebrating the anniversary of a major battle against the Separatists during the Clone Wars, but it was as grim a parade as Has had ever attended. No balloons or banners or flag-waving from the viewing stands. Just a couple of thousand native Twi'leks of several colors and head-tail lengths massed behind electrocordons and looking as if they'd been dragged from their residences to bear witness to formations of stormtroopers marching through the streets of Lessu toward something called the Plasma Bridge. The BlasTech-carrying effectives were preceded by a twenty-strong group of indigenes and trailed by Imperial walkers and tanks to the accompaniment of martial music and deafening overflights by squadrons of freshly minted TIE fighters. Anyone would think that the Empire had been responsible for liberating the planet, when in fact it was a homegrown revolutionary named Cham Syndulla, aided and abetted by a couple of Jedi and clone troopers, who had defeated

Skakoan Techno Union foreman Wat Tambor and his legions of battle droids.

Has had arrived just as the festivities were getting started, and was still puzzled as to why Matese had called him halfway across the galaxy instead of meeting at their usual table in the Wanton Wellspring.

More than a month had passed since the delivery to Wadi Raffa. Normally Has was not a follower of the news, but after what had happened at Samovar he had made it a point to learn whether Wadi had suffered a similar fate. Sure enough, a HoloNet service he subscribed to had sent him an article buried among more noteworthy stories reporting that Turlin/Benthic Extraction had been accused of procuring arms. The Legacy world's deep-sea mining operations had been seized by the Empire and the world declared off limits.

Has's freighter was parked at the orbital cordon. Given the TIE fighter aerial display, all downside-bound traffic was on hold. Regardless, the troopers who boarded his ship had been ordered to shuttle him to the surface and deposit him at the local Imperial garrison HQ, in an office that happened to overlook the parade route.

He was standing at the window watching one of the four-legged Imperial walkers clomp by when the office door opened and a nondescript major entered the room, carrying a dossier under his arm. The way the officer sized him up made him think of his first meeting with Orson Krennic, all those years ago.

"Take a seat, Captain," the human said.

Has did, while trying to read the writing on the dossier. "Is Matese going to be joining us?"

The officer looked at him. "It is my sad duty to inform you that Matese is no longer with us."

"No longer with—"

"Dead, I'm afraid."

The news hit Has like a kiloton of concrete. "When? How? I heard from him a standard week ago."

"An industrial accident apparently."

It sounded like code for something untoward, but Has pursued it anyway. "At the depot?"

"I believe so, yes."

Has loosed a sad and suddenly weary exhalation. "Just when he got that ocular implant."

"Pity," the officer said without conviction. "It is also my duty to inform you that all operations are being suspended."

A second kiloton of surprise hit him. "Until when?"

"Indefinitely."

"I just put a hefty down payment on a new freighter," Has said, despite the futility of it. "I've been spreading credits around to help my friends—"

"Regrettable," the officer interrupted. "But these things happen. Here one day, gone the next."

"Like Matese."

"Unfortunately yes."

Has wilted in his chair. "So where does that leave me? And why'd you have me come all this way for a death announcement? You could have commed and at least saved me the fuel."

The human's upper lip curled in distaste; a touch of the new officiousness.

"You are here because I received orders to relay a

personal message that cannot be trusted to comlink, for whatever reasons."

Has raised his eyes. "A message from who?"

"Lieutenant Commander Krennic, of the Corps of Engineers."

Has opened his mouth but no words emerged. He gulped and tried again without result.

"I'm told that you two are acquainted."

"From years ago," Has managed. "But—"

"I can't imagine how or why, but that's not my concern. The commander asks that you report to him on Coruscant soonest." He extracted a military-grade comlink from the dossier envelope and set it on the desk. "You're to use this when you arrive."

Has didn't want to reach for it, but he did, turning it over in his trembling hands. "Coded?"

The officer shrugged. "Also none of my concern."

"Why Coruscant?"

The human took a deep breath, clearly annoyed. "That's for you to know, and for me to remain ignorant about. In this instance, I am merely the messenger."

Sudden commotion outside the window brought both of them out of their chairs. Below a group of chanting Twi'leks carrying placards that read FREE RYLOTH MOVEMENT and THE HAMMER OF RYLOTH had dodged the cordon and were dispersing onto the wide boulevard. Brought to a sudden halt, the nearest company of stormtroopers had regrouped in close-order formation. Still the head-tailed humanoids kept coming. A shouted order from an officer, and the troopers raised their weapons. A follow-up command sent pulses of energy surging over the heads of the protestors, but failed to slow the crowd.

Something told Has that the Empire was about to claim another world.

Krennic had been an infrequent visitor to the facility, so when he told Galen he would be dropping by, Galen was thrilled and demanded that he stay for dinner. Krennic arrived without stormtroopers but in full-dress uniform and with wines for the occasion— both dinner and dessert vintages. Galen was waiting when he set his airspeeder down on the landing zone, and they greeted each other warmly. Lyra and the child joined them in the lobby and the four of them spent more than an hour touring the complex, Galen speaking animatedly about the energy research—as if soliciting Krennic's approval; Lyra, quiet and lagging behind; and the child hurrying ahead of everyone, wearing a toy sword in a scabbard and holding two stuffed animals in her arms.

Night was falling by the time the quartet made their way to the Ersos' comfortable residence, where Krennic opened one of the bottles of wine and Lyra planted her daughter in front of a viewer to watch *The Octave Stairway,* apparently the child's current favorite bedtime story. The view from the living room window was sublime, encompassing a copse of gargantuan trees the B'ankora had planted centuries earlier and, rising beyond those, some of the city-world's newest and most daring skyscrapers.

Krennic could almost forget that they were on Coruscant.

He had hoped Lyra would have come to feel that way, but judging by the surveillance recordings of her conversations with family and friends she was bored and unhappy.

Weeks earlier Krennic had learned that Reeva Demesne had tried to contact Galen, ostensibly to say hello, but in fact to snoop about. Demesne knew nothing of the battle station, but the shield generator program she headed had been folded into the Special Weapons Group, and some of the scattered researchers had begun to compare notes. Fortunately, it was Lyra who had spoken with Demesne, and Krennic had made a thorough study of their conversation. If Lyra had concerns about Galen's research to begin with, then the Mirialan scientist's veiled inquiries had probably doubled them, and before too long Lyra's objections to the program were going to become problematic. Krennic had seen the day coming as far back as the discussion they'd had shortly after the war ended, and recordings of conversations between Galen and Lyra had confirmed that her misgivings had only increased. Demesne had stopped short of alluding to rumors of the weaponizing of Galen's research, but she had made her own concerns about the project almost palpable, and Krennic couldn't allow Lyra's apprehensions to go unchecked. As for Galen, he was so far too seduced by the facility and all it offered to think much beyond the crystals.

Krennic waited until dessert was being served to steer the conversation where it needed to go.

"Are you two happy here?" he asked after they had lifted their glasses in a toast to lasting peace.

The abruptness of his question seemed to catch Lyra by surprise, but Galen was quick to respond.

"It's close to having a dream come true."

He covered Lyra's hand with his own, as if to suggest that she was with him—or was it a subtle signal to her that she exercise caution?

Krennic looked at Galen. "You're receiving all that you need?"

"Supplies arrive daily. I couldn't ask for more."

Krennic smiled and let the silence linger. "I know about the requisitions and supplies, but I'm asking about your personal needs." He gestured broadly. "As nice as this place is, it could strike some as a rather lonely outpost."

Lyra bit back something she was about to say, but Galen was intent on reassuring him.

"We're only hours from anything we lack here. We kept the apartment. Jyn plays with the children of other scientists. Lyra will be homeschooling her."

Krennic addressed Lyra directly, keeping his tone sociable. "I guess we've established that Galen is happy, and it sounds as though the child's needs are being met, but I'm mostly concerned about you."

She flushed. "Me?"

She might as well have said *Since when?*, but Krennic stuck to his script.

"I mean, between motherhood and what you do for Galen, you don't have a lot of time for yourself. I'm simply curious if you're fine with having put your life on hold—temporarily, in any case."

She regarded him frankly. "I haven't put my life *on hold,* Orson. My career, maybe, but certainly not my *life.*"

He showed the palms of his hands. "Maybe I didn't put that right."

"I'll give you the benefit of the doubt. What exactly are you trying to get at?"

Galen was glancing back and forth between the two of them.

"Just this: We have data on what purports to be an extensive vein of kyber crystals on an Outer Rim world. Because of matters we can discuss later, I can't trust just anyone with assaying the extent of the find."

"Do you need a recommendation?" Lyra asked.

"No, I want you to consider undertaking the survey." He gave it time to settle in. "It's not a dangerous assignment. A group of archaeologists already have a small but comfortable research camp set up. You could include one or more of your former teammates if you wish. In fact, it's safe enough for you to take the child along as well."

Galen and Lyra were exchanging shocked looks.

"You should do it," Galen said without question.

Lyra shook her head. "Galen, we need to talk about this—"

"And we will. But I think this would be something wonderful for you. You know I've been concerned about your sacrificing your interests for mine."

"I'm hardly sacrificing myself, Galen. Being here was as much my choice as yours." She looked from Galen to Krennic and back again. "Anything else either of you want to say about my life?"

"You don't need to give me a decision right now," Krennic assured her. "I just want you to consider it."

"I'm serious," Galen told Lyra. "You can't pass this up. Think what an experience like this would mean for Jyn."

Krennic watched her. *Will she ask if he's trying to get rid of her?*

She didn't. Instead she said:

"Orson, do have any idea how long the survey will take?"

Krennic rocked his head from side to side. "You'll know better than I once I provide you with the data. But I suspect not more than a couple of standard months." He looked at Galen. "Can you spare her and your daughter for that long?"

Galen put his lips together and nodded. "We've been separated for longer periods." He didn't mention Vallt, but the implication was clear.

"But your notes," Lyra said.

He touched her hand again. "We'll hold off transcribing them until you return."

Lyra inhaled and blew out her breath, then pushed her auburn hair back from her forehead. "First the facility, now this." She turned to Krennic. "What else do you have up your sleeve?"

New Imperial regulations regarding travel had required Lyra and Jyn to be scanned, interviewed, and subjected to multiple identity checks before being allowed access to the minor landing zone that served the research facility, situated in the heart of the arcologies that walled it to the west.

But the trip didn't seem entirely real until scanners at the sprawling Central District spaceport had cleared them to board the mag-lev that served a portion of the spaceport reserved for the arrivals and departures of private ships. Now here they were threading their way between enormous starships en route to the hangar at which she was to rendezvous with Nari Sable, whom she hadn't seen in person in close to four years.

She had wrestled with accepting Orson's assignment for more than three standard weeks, vacillating between excitement and a sense of vague unease about leaving Galen to his own devices. They had discussed it endlessly, and while he had never been less than encouraging and enthusiastic, she had begun to wonder whether he *wanted her gone*. And maybe that was actually the case; that at this stage of the research he felt that he needed to devote himself fully to it without having to concern himself with her contentment or Jyn's development—precisely the way she often felt at social occasions, worrying about whether he was having a good time. Now, though, all the weeks of uneasiness and indecision were behind her, and she was exhilarated about embarking on an adventure. As the mag-lev came to a stop near the designated hangar, she gave Jyn's hand an affectionate squeeze.

"This is going to be so much fun."

Jyn nodded. "Is Papa going to miss us?"

"He sure is. Do you think he'll remember to eat?"

"Mac-Vee will make him eat."

Their nanny and housekeeping droid.

"You're right, Mac-Vee won't let him miss a single meal."

They were wearing backpacks and dressed in serviceable outfits, though Jyn had insisted at the last minute on wearing a helmet that made her look like a starfighter pilot. Their luggage had been delivered ahead of time and was now at the mercy of droids responsible for moving everything from the terminal to the private hangar.

As they hastened across the concrete apron toward the hemispherical building, Nari Sable emerged, dressed in a sleeveless belted tunic and lace-up boots, looking as if she had just arrived from the Outer Rim. Seeing Lyra, she quickened her pace, smiling broadly; as soon as she reached them, she pulled Lyra into a tight hug and kissed her on both cheeks.

"It's been way too long," she said into Lyra's ear.

"I know. Let's promise not to let that happen again."

Still smiling, Nari backed out of the embrace to appraise Lyra, running her fingertips over her old friend's face. Lyra took note of the faint lines around Nari's eyes, the result of having spent too much time in harsh starlight, touches of premature gray in her hair, creases forming at the corners of her mouth. She was thin but still muscular, and her green eyes shone with the vitality of someone half her age. Then Nari's gaze fell on Jyn and she withdrew another step, her hand in front of her mouth in surprise.

"She's your twin! Except for the helmet."

"Do you want to see what's in my backpack?" Jyn asked, already shrugging out of it.

Nari went down on one knee in front of her. "I sure do. But let's wait until we board our ship, okay?"

"I brought macrobinoculars, too."

"You did? That's great, sweetie, because we're going to need them. As soon as we're inside, I want to see everything."

"Okay," Jyn chirped.

Nari stood up and gestured toward the hangar. "Come and see our ride." She put her arm around Lyra's shoulders as they walked.

The two had been fast friends since childhood, though Nari was twice the athlete Lyra was—a runner, gymnast, old-school adventurer. Like Lyra, she had a history of serial relationships, but unlike Lyra, she had stuck to decisions made as a teenager to neither marry nor have children. Lyra thought of her as the woman she might have been had she taken that other fork in the road. Their different paths aside, they had shared many adventures, exploring, surveying, and mapping. Nari had been her maid of honor at the simple wedding that included Reeva Demesne as a guest. She had made Alderaan her home during the war, but—with exploration back to full tilt—had worked steadily since, and even had access to a survey company starship. Lyra had been lucky to catch her between jobs, and on Coruscant, no less.

The interior of the hangar was lit brightly enough for Lyra to get a good look at the ship. A compact freighter, it was lozenge-shaped with a wide fantail and a dorsally mounted cockpit. It needed paint and body work, but appeared serviceable.

"All of our equipment is already onboard," Nari was saying. "They even provided us with a recording droid."

Lyra nodded noncommittally. "Rough around the edges, but we've been in far worse."

"No kidding. It's well maintained and it looks a lot better on the inside. The pilot is charming. He's Dressellian."

The revelation didn't exactly stop her in her tracks, but the combination of Dressellian *and* pilot did make her blink.

Although it wasn't until she spied him coming down the ramp that she understood why.

"Welcome aboard, Lyra," he said. "I don't know if you remember me, but—"

Lyra gaped openly. "Of course I remember you."

Nari's fine brows knitted. "You two already know each other?" She thought for a moment. "I guess that makes sense—"

"It's not what you think."

"Not what I think?" Now her brows went up. "Should I give you some privacy?"

"No, you need to hear this," Lyra said more strongly than she meant to. She turned back to the Dressellian. "I'm sorry, I don't remember your name."

"Has Obitt."

She nodded. "Obviously you still have a connection with Orson Krennic, Has."

"Actually I don't—or at least I didn't until a few weeks ago. I've been mostly on my own since . . .

back when. Freelancing, you know. The commander contacted me to see if I was available to pilot you to Alpinn, and I said yes."

Lyra remained dubious. "Freelancing what, exactly?"

"Merchandise. Supplies. Meiloorun fruit."

"Then you're not a spy."

Nari was glancing back and forth between them. "Does one of you want to catch me up?"

Lyra glanced at her. "Has was the pilot who flew Galen, Jyn, and me off Vallt during the war."

Nari nodded in comprehension. "Where you were arrested."

"Yes. But Has and Orson came to our rescue, isn't that right?"

Has nodded. "I was just the pilot, Lyra."

"And you're still just a pilot."

"Commander Krennic doesn't want to give the impression that the survey is an Imperial mission, or that it has anything to do with the Imperial military."

"Give the impression . . . I need to hear from you that it's not an Imperial mission."

"It's nothing of the sort," Has said. "That's why we're using my ship and not traveling with an escort of stormtroopers. This way we can avoid being targeted by insurgents—of any stripe." He looked at Jyn. "Your daughter has grown into a beautiful child."

Lyra relaxed somewhat. "Thank you, Has."

Has bent down to speak to Jyn. "You were just a baby when we met. I'm very glad to see you again."

Jyn made no effort to conceal her inspection on his

nonhuman features, especially the deep groove in his cranium. "Do you want to see what's in my backpack?"

Lyra snorted. "Maybe I'll feel better about this once all of us unpack."

19

CLOSED INTERVAL

KRENNIC DELAYED HIS RETURN TO Geonosis on the expectation that Galen would contact him. The dark circles under Galen's eyes and the twitch in his left eyelid Krennic had observed during the recent dinner belied the scientist's declarations about being as happy as he had ever been, more grateful than he could put into words. Then there was the quickness with which he had embraced the idea of sending Lyra and Jyn halfway across the galaxy on a treasure hunt. Even the brightest of dreams-come-true had shadowy recesses. The tensions that Krennic had sensed at the facility were far from settled. So when the comm came from Galen he was prepared, and had suggested that Galen come to Imperial Energy Division headquarters in the Central District so they could talk face-to-face.

The Imperial Energy Division was new, but it, too, operated under the umbrella of Project Celestial Power. In fact, each separate department of the battle station project had its own cover name and cover agency, and Galen wasn't alone in working for a counterfeit division and having his research put to alternative uses. Scattered across the galaxy were teams of scientists working on conventional weaponry, tractor beam and hyperdrive technology, even hull cladding systems. Each project was concealed behind names like *Stellar Sphere*, *Mark Omega*, and *Pax Aurora*. But all those paled in comparison with research on the superlaser.

Krennic ushered Galen past bogus security personnel and employees and into his bogus office, which was adorned with holorepresentations of energy complexes and installations on dozens of worlds. Immediately they caught Galen's eye, and he asked about them.

"Facilities in various stages of planning and readiness," Krennic told him, relieved to see that the bogus holos could pass muster with someone of Galen's powers of discernment. "Have you heard from Lyra?"

Galen nodded in an unfocussed way. "She and Jyn and Nari are still acclimating to Alpinn, but they've already begun to investigate the cave system."

"That's good news. I knew they had settled into the archaeological camp, but I haven't had a chance to read Lyra's most recent report." He looked hard at Galen. "You must be lonely without them."

"At any other time I know I would be. But right now, I'm so involved . . . I haven't been much of a husband or father, in any case."

"I'm certain that Lyra understands the importance of your work. As long as everything's all right between you two."

"More often than not."

"I sometimes get the impression she thinks I'm a bad influence on you."

Galen's expression changed. "That's not true. She just doesn't understand our partnership."

Krennic laughed to ease the mood. "You know what I find interesting—or maybe ironic is the word. It's that each of us wants what's best for you. In a way, we're competing to make you happy, as old-fashioned as that sounds. And each of us has a different idea about what you should be doing. Especially now that you two have a child, Lyra wants you to be settled on a course that will mean the most for the family—fulfilled in a somewhat conventional way—and I maintain that you're meant for bigger things, and will continue to do whatever I can to bring opportunities to your attention."

Galen smiled thinly. "Don't think I don't appreciate it."

"Why shouldn't I be your advocate? I'm not a rival, like some of your jealous or envious peers. What's more, our relationship has profited both of us. Look where my supporting you has landed me! I'm like someone who discovered a wonderful artist and profits by being able to mingle with other exceptional talents."

Galen brushed aside the flattery. "I remember some of the conversations we had in the Futures Program. Trading ideas . . . Have you achieved what you set out to do?"

Krennic rocked his head. "More or less."

"You've never wanted a family."

"Seriously, Galen, can you imagine me a father?"

"You'd be quite the taskmaster, I'm sure. But serving the Republic and now the Empire has been enough for you?"

Krennic paced away from Galen. "How does an individual know what he or she is meant to do? I remember those conversations as well. But we grow up with dreams that sometimes aren't realized, so we explore different paths. If we're lucky we find something we're good at, and that gives us hope and purpose." He turned back to Galen. "I wasn't born brilliant or especially talented, but I'm capable and I'm driven, and that's brought me to where I am. I stumbled onto something I'm good at, so I'm fulfilled in that sense. But I'm up against some serious challenges."

"Anything I can help with? Schematics? Architectural plans?"

"At the moment, no. But I won't hesitate to ask if and when the opportunity arises."

Galen nodded, then gestured to the false holorepresentations. "I find all this encouraging. But—"

"Lyra's not the only one with doubts about the project."

Galen compressed his lips. "I don't want you to think I'm an ingrate—"

"Nonsense," Krennic cut in. "What's bothering you?"

"Reeva Demesne tried to contact me."

Krennic pretended surprise. "Reeva. How is she?"

Galen frowned at him. "You should know, shouldn't you? She's doing research for Celestial Power."

"Yes, she is. But I'm not in close contact with everyone involved."

"During the war she was doing shield generator research," Galen went on. "But before that she was always as interested in energy enrichment as I am."

"I'm not sure I see your point."

"If she's back to exploring energy alternatives, why isn't she working with me on Coruscant instead of doing whatever's she's doing on Hypori?"

Krennic knew from the surveillance recordings that that particular cat was already out of the bag, but Galen's mention of the isolated world set him on edge. "I can check into it. Why didn't you raise these concerns weeks ago?"

"I don't want Lyra to know that I have any reservations about what we're doing. She has issues enough about my working with kybers."

"That makes no sense. You're a scientist."

"Lyra and I are equally fascinated with the physical world. But she sees the kyber as symbolic of the Jedi Order and the Force."

"And you?"

"I don't think the Jedi went far enough in their use of the crystals."

"You'll get no argument from me."

"The Jedi were certainly aware of the tremendous potential, but they restrained themselves."

"Precisely what they did with the Force, as some have said. If they had made use of their full powers, the war would have ended in a heartbeat. And the galaxy would be in a different state entirely. For all their purported objectivity, they weren't scientists, they were mystics. For a thousand generations that sufficed. Notions of right and wrong can no longer be dictated by a select group to safeguard some personal vision of the truth."

Galen offered a narrow-eyed nod. "One thing I'll say in their favor is that they never made us fear them, when they certainly had the ability to."

"Perhaps they should have," Krennic said, then added: "We can talk history and philosophy until our heads spin. You still haven't told me what's bothering you. Do you need a break from the research—a sabbatical?"

"A sabbatical is the last thing I need," Galen said with a suddenness that took Krennic by surprise. "I'm on the brink of an important discovery . . . But I need to know that my research is yielding results, Orson, that my work isn't all theory without practical application. That it can be replicated. The power potential is nothing short of awesome, but the resultant energy needs to be properly harvested and stored."

Krennic lowered his eyes and his voice. "We were making headway."

"*Were?* If your teams haven't been able to reproduce my results, then someone isn't doing their job."

"Everyone has been giving their best effort."

"Then I don't understand."

Krennic snorted and raised his head. "Are you in a position to leave the facility for a couple of days?"

"I told you I don't need a break."

"This won't be a break. In fact, it bears directly on your concerns."

Galen searched Krennic's face. "Is this going to be

another instance of your showing me something I need to see, like you did at Grange?"

"You'll have to tell me."

Alpinn shone bright like a gemstone in deep space. Its high reflectivity wasn't due to ice and snow, but to mineral-rich seas that had dried up eons earlier, leaving behind sedimentary rock and crystallized elements that blanketed enormous areas of the principal landmass in dazzling white.

Has had had to pilot his ship through several lengthy jumps to reach the remote world, but by the time they set down at the archaeological station, Lyra had managed to shelve her suspicions about the mission and the Dressellian's part in it. She didn't need Has or anyone else looking out for her or Jyn, but she couldn't fault Krennic for being concerned for their safety. They were, after all, the wife and child of his chief researcher.

Alpinn's brilliance wasn't the only feature that distinguished it. In the dim past a group of spacefarers had discovered the ruins of an ancient civilization—vast structures built of immense blocks, statues, temples, and obelisks, all smoothed over by wind and eroded by seasonal rain—and archaeological excavations had been going on for nearly a standard century. With funding from the Republic before the time of Palpatine's chancellorship, a permanent camp had finally been established, consisting of prefab dwellings, wind turbines, a desalinization plant, and a small research center. The extensive ruins and the uniqueness of the terrain had prompted a team of scientists to petition for Alpinn to be declared a Legacy world, which would limit development, visitation, and the extraction of resources, but the entreaty was still pending Imperial approval. The archaeologists had accepted that the surveying and mapping Lyra and Nari were undertaking were integral to the mathematical resource estimation process, and in some ways that was true, as a find of kyber crystals would assure the planet's protection from corporate interests and exploitation.

Though glaring white—so white that humans and certain other species needed to wear protective goggles—the surface more resembled the bottom of a sea, and in most instances it took an expert to differentiate between artificial structures and what nature had created on its own: spires whipped by the winds into swirls that resembled sweet confections; hillsides embedded with fossilized sea organisms, corals, and shells; long-dry riverbeds and waterfalls that had recrystallized into marble; curving slides and deep gleaming basins. Close to the camp were a pair of sinkholes filled with the bluest water Lyra had ever beheld—as if lit from within—and in the crevasses of some hills grew a spindly vegetation that was as twisted and bleached as the spires themselves.

For Jyn, the world was an enormous white playground.

The mixed-species team of archaeologists was quick to make the new arrivals feel at home. Instantly adopted by everyone, Jyn—indefatigable as ever—reveled in being the center of attention, entertaining everyone with her antics, watching closely, learning.

In his eagerness to be useful, Has became the camp's assistant chef and helped prepare unusual but tasty meals from the limited stores, while Lyra and Nari—weighed down with packs, harnesses, and survival gear—made preliminary forays into the complex cave system in which kyber crystals might be hiding.

The data on the alleged vein were very imprecise. Lyra wondered whether the crude maps had been discovered in the Jedi archives or, as Orson maintained, had originated with the original spacefarers and languished for centuries in a Republic database. Whatever the case, Lyra had calculated, with some dismay, that completing a pre-feasibility study of the bedrock cave system of stalagmites, stalactites, and water- and bio-eroded tunnels was going to require weeks of exploration, mapping, and analysis, and she could only hope that Galen was making do without her.

She and Nari were exploring a wide, minor tunnel in the principal cave system when they chanced upon an enormous chamber whose curving walls and arched ceiling were coated with a bioluminescent lichen that imparted a yellow glow to the entire chamber. Has and Jyn had accompanied them and on entering the chamber all the four of them could do was marvel in wide-eyed delight.

Has glanced at Lyra as she and Nari were sitting down, as if to drink in every square centimeter of the lambent place, Jyn off on her own, though never far from Has's watchful gaze.

"The Jedi would say that the Force is strong here," Lyra said in a way that suggested to Has some sort of telepathic exchange with her friend.

Nari nodded and turned to him. "Can you feel it, Has?"

He took his eyes off Jyn to show her a perplexed expression. "What am I supposed to be looking for?"

"You're not *looking* for anything," Lyra said with a gentle laugh. "You're *feeling*."

He glanced around anyway. "I thought the Force disappeared with the Jedi."

Nari shook her head at him. "The Force could only disappear if all life in the galaxy perished."

Lyra was studying him. "Haven't you ever visited a world where nature is so profuse, so prolific and exuberant that it yanks you out of your thoughts? Not a world like Coruscant, where you're overwhelmed, but on some far-flung planet that sort of dazzles you into silence and reverence?"

"You can't help but sense the interconnectedness of all life," Nari added.

Has didn't want them to think that he thought they were deranged, and he certainly didn't want to think any harder about Samovar or Wadi Raffa, so he said: "I guess I've visited a few," and left it at that.

But Lyra wasn't satisfied with the answer. "And you never felt anything—even a sense of transcendent mystery?"

He shrugged. "I guess I was too busy working to notice."

"So the next time you find yourself on an unblemished world," Nari said, "you should remember this moment and try to allow yourself to feel the Force."

"Okay," he said. "Next time." Seeing Lyra turn suddenly to monitor Jyn, who was tapping a stone with a small replica of one of the hammers her mother carried, he added: "Don't worry, I'm watching her."

Hearing him, Jyn stopped her tapping and swung around. "Has is watching me."

"And don't you forget it," he said.

Lyra showed him a look of sincere appreciation. "You've been great with her, Has."

"That's because she's a trouper," he said loud enough for Jyn to hear. "In the best way, I mean."

The two women laughed. Then Lyra broke the ensuing silence to say: "I don't want to pry, Has, but how did you first get involved with Orson?"

Keep it simple, Has reminded himself. "He just makes use of me from time to time."

Lyra nodded. "He certainly has a talent for that."

"And you?" Has asked before Lyra could pose a follow-up question.

"Galen and Orson are partners of a sort in an Imperial energy program."

"On Coruscant?"

"In a facility that occupies what was the B'ankor Refuge."

"I think I heard something about that," Has said. "Must be exciting."

"Oh, very," Lyra said, eliciting a guffaw from Nari.

"Tell Has the truth, Lyra."

Lyra laughed with her. "Okay, so it's boring and I sometimes wish Galen had never gotten involved. But he's happy and the research could lead to a revolution in renewable energy."

"Well said," Nari remarked.

Lyra's laugh dwindled to seriousness. "I just wish the work didn't have to focus on kyber crystals."

Galen stood at the shuttle's viewport, gazing down on a ruined world. He had been wrong to surmise that Orson's plan was to echo the experience at Grange during the war.

This was far worse.

"What's the name of this world?" he asked Krennic.

"Malpaz, if it's of any consequence." The starship that had brought them there was in stationary orbit far above the shuttle. "It suffered invasions from both sides during the war, but managed to rebuild after each assault. Native population of sentient avians, but integrated with colonists from all over this sector."

"Reeva mentioned Malpaz to Lyra."

Krennic didn't respond directly. "Below is what remains of the capital city. You can see where we set up the power grid—that blackened area to the left. The facility itself crowned that hill, just where you see those walls."

Galen looked ill. "What happened here? I was very precise in my notes."

"The destruction had nothing to do with your research. We were preparing to connect to the power grid when the attack came."

"Who attacked?"

Krennic made a point of hesitating. "Galen, you're not going to hear this on the nightly holonews, but while the war is essentially won, it's not over. Not here. Not in many systems of the Western Reaches."

"I've heard reports of Separatist holdouts—"

"They're much more than *holdouts*. Call them what they are: anarchists. They want the Empire to collapse the same way some hoped the Republic would, only this time our enemies aren't rebelling in protest of Senate representation, trade routes, or taxes. They're intent on sowing chaos, on bringing everything down. They have no agenda—political, religious, or any other—beyond a desire to end civilization as we know it. The many attempts the Empire has made to improve the lives of those who suffered during the war have been thwarted by attacks. I could show you ten other worlds that have suffered this same level of destruction."

Galen spent a moment absorbing Krennic's words, then gave his head a mournful shake. "With the arsenal the Empire has—the stormtroopers, the Star Destroyers, and the rest—it has to be only a matter of time until all of them are vanquished."

"Each attack fosters another," Krennic said. "Populations that feel they have been betrayed or let down because the Empire isn't acting quickly enough, paying enough reparations, or rebuilding what was lost add their numbers to a growing storm. If it continues, we'll never succeed in realizing the Emperor's dream of uniting everyone."

"There has to be a solution."

"There might be." Krennic held back for a long moment. "Galen, I shouldn't be telling you this, and I won't even try to guess how many security oaths I've already violated just by bringing you here, but the Emperor has given his blessing to enlarging the scope of our energy enterprise. He has such faith in what you've already achieved that he has sanctioned mining operations on hundreds of worlds to provide materials for what will be needed to make Project Celestial Power a reality. Even as we speak ships are ferrying resources to countless star systems in preparation for the day the Emperor will reveal his plan to the public." He turned slightly so that he could confront Galen head-on. "He is determined to make an example of one world, in the hope that that world will serve as a kind of beacon and usher in the new age."

Galen held Krennic's gaze for a moment, then turned and paced away from him. "There's more that can be derived from the crystals," he said quietly without looking back. "Much more power than what we've harvested."

Krennic followed, placing himself in Galen's path. "Tell me."

Galen inhaled deeply and shook his head. "It's never been about power. I realized the potential of the kybers from the start."

Krennic's brow furrowed. "Then what's the issue?"

"Containment," Galen said, finally composed enough to look at him. "The kyber will submit to pressure up to a certain point before the output becomes impossible to harness. Untamable." He gestured out the viewport. "Even this level of destruction is trivial compared with the raw destructive power the crystals are capable of unleashing."

Krennic continued to watch him. "But you've discovered a way to coax that raw power from them."

Galen shut his eyes and nodded. "I'm on the brink. Very, very close . . ."

Krennic clamped his hands on Galen's biceps. "Then go after it, Galen. Don't concern yourself with matters of containment. I'll assemble a team to tackle that problem. What we need from you is the means to tap into that power. Give me solid evidence I can present to the Emperor and you'll have his unconditional support." He paused, then asked: "Will you do it? Will you do this for all of us? Not simply for the welfare of your daughter's generation, but for her child's generation and all that will follow. You are what the Empire has been seeking and needs. The entire galaxy will be nourished by your legacy."

Galen exhaled slowly. "We'll need to work in complete secrecy to avoid any information leaks. No one can know."

"That's right," Krennic said soberly. "No one can know."

20

DEEP TRUTH

THE SURVEY ON ALPINN WAS concluded.

It had taken Lyra and Nari almost twelve standard weeks to discover the vein. It lay deep in a constricted passage more than three hundred meters underground. Jetpacks dropped them to the bottom of a shaft, from which they'd had to squirm on hands and knees into a downsloping corridor, breathers gripped in their mouths and headlamps casting crazed shadows onto the jagged walls. Lyra used a small cutting tool to remove fragments of the vein, but in the end the field analysis kit Galen had supplied confirmed her initial suspicions.

"It's ranite, not kyberite," she told Nari when they were back on the surface and she had finished the analysis. "They're closely related, but ranite is denser and tougher. And true kybers are only found in veins of pure kyberite."

It was disappointing, but they weren't ready to give up. Using surveys conducted centuries earlier, they'd had Has fly them to areas of tectonic activity elsewhere on the principal landmass. But while some areas appeared promising, the rifts hadn't been produced by side-sliding faults, and the presence of additional veins of ranite substantiated that no kyberite would be found, since the two never occurred together.

By then the camp had become home, and the members of the archaeological team went all-out in throwing a leave-taking party. They lavished small gifts on Jyn, and made it clear that they were going to miss Has's culinary creations terribly.

Lyra revealed nothing to the archaeologists about the false kybers, since that wasn't supposed to be the purpose of her and Nari's expedition, and she presented the team with maps that indicated possibly overlooked ancient sites. Lost on Jyn was the fact that as close as all of them had become, there was little likelihood they would ever see one another again.

As Has was running a preflight in the freighter's roomy cockpit, Lyra said what had been on her mind for several days. "I almost wish we could lie about the kybers being false. Or at least tell Krennic that we need more time to explore and evaluate."

Nari and Has threw her questioning looks from their acceleration chairs.

"It's our obligation to the Force to protect worlds like this from exploitation," she went on, "the way the Jedi did with so many places. We should assume the responsibility in their absence."

Nari's smile was sad, wry. "Unfortunately, that's not our call to make."

Lyra nodded and drew in a stuttering breath, on the edge of tears, then made light of her emotional display with a laugh. "I honestly don't want to leave."

"Then say goodbye to Coruscant once and for all," Nari said. "Convince Galen not to renew his contract and get back to what you love doing."

Lyra snorted. "The only contract he has is with himself. Besides, he's doing important work. And even if that weren't the case I don't think the Empire would take kindly to our up and leaving—not after what's been sunk into the facility."

"What could the Empire do—sue you?"

Lyra glanced at her. "Who knows what they're capable of doing." She gazed out on Alpinn one final time. "Legacy status should be granted."

"It won't mean anything," Has muttered, almost as if despite himself. "Legacy status won't protect it," he added when Lyra and Nari had swiveled toward him.

"Since when?" Nari asked.

He continued to fiddle with the instruments as a means of avoiding eye contact. "Since the Empire came to town."

"The Legacy statutes are supposed to be inviolable," Nari said.

Lyra thought about it. "Yes, but so were the statutes protecting the B'ankor Refuge."

Has finally looked at her, then Nari. "Get ready to see just what the Empire's capable of."

"This can't be Samovar," Nari said when Has had dropped the ship out of hyperspace and the planet came into view. She glanced at Lyra, who had Jyn seated on her lap, the two of them gazing over the

CATALYST: A ROGUE ONE NOVEL   277

instruments at the despoiled world. "The northern continent was completely forested when I was last here. It looks like a desert."

"I can assure you that's it's Samovar," Has said. "The Empire works fast when it wants to."

The jump from Alpinn had been tortuous, but Lyra finally found herself in the Western Reaches. Has kept the ship distant from Samovar, but scanners showed hundreds of massive freighters in orbit and even greater numbers of smaller vessels feeding them whatever was being extracted from below. Far from the freighters the turbolasers of a Star Destroyer were denuding an entire landmass. The oceans and atmosphere of the northern hemisphere were brown with contaminants.

"A few conglomerates had concessions to mine limited amounts of ore," Has was saying, "but now the Empire is taking whatever's available, with former Separatists from all over this sector working as Imperial employees."

"Employees or slaves?" Lyra asked.

"It's a fine line. They come for the work, but end up in debt and unable to leave." He cut his eyes to her. "You'll see the same at Wadi Raffa. Deforestation, strip-mining, unchecked extraction."

"Why," Lyra wondered aloud, "with so many other worlds to choose from?"

"Bigger Star Destroyers?" Nari suggested. "Larger military installations?"

Lyra looked past Nari to Has, who suddenly struck her as far less guileless than he appeared. "What made you decide to bring us here, Has? Were Samo-

var and Wadi Raffa some of the places where Orson
made use of you?"

The Dressellian's expression neither denied nor
confirmed anything. Has merely said: "You aren't the
only one who didn't want to leave Alpinn. I guess I'm
just trying to get with the new program."

Galen's whiskered and drawn face was awash in
the glow of the computer room's displays and holo-
projections. Data swirled around him: calculations,
the results of recent electron diffraction experiments,
magnified views of kyber crystal vacancies, plaintext
excerpted from Jedi archival material.

He had signed and sworn to all the security oaths
Orson had pressed on him, which now made it a crime
for him to discuss the Emperor's expanded dream
project with anyone—even Lyra, for her own safety
as much as his. All that, though, would mean nothing
if he failed to find a way to amplify the research he
had been conducting for more than a standard year,
but which had fascinated him for half his life. Assuming he could coax greater power from the kybers,
would Orson's team be able to contain and deliver
the enhanced output? His personal legacy aside, how
could he not participate on learning that anarchy and
violence might doom the project even before it could
be implemented?

Of its own accord, his mind veered to thoughts of
Lyra and Jyn, and the need to safeguard their future. How could he have allowed them to leave Coruscant? How could Orson have permitted it, knowing

of the growing insurgency, the random raids on innocent worlds? Nightmares had plagued him for months following the battle droid assault on Lokori. Could he allow Lyra and Jyn to experience that again? Would he ever be able to forgive himself or Orson should something unthinkable befall them?

Vallt, Grange, Lokori, now Malpaz and so many other worlds . . .

He had to bring about change; it was his obligation to alter the circumstances.

He reached for the finger-sized kyber he had taken to carrying with him wherever he went. Each of the crystals was as unique as a snowflake or a human iris. It warmed as he curled his hand around it, but he knew from previous research that the crystal would show no change in temperature; and he knew also that it would not warm a sheath or a towel or any inanimate object. It responded only to life, even plant life. Which made the Jedi's use of it to power their lightsabers all the more ironic and mysterious.

He held the crystal up to the light of the displays, marveling at the kyber's mix of transparency and opacity—characteristics the ancient Jedi had referred to as "the water of the kyber."

The energy potential was a given; his team had proven as much in their earliest piezoelectric experiments. But an ignition facility or a power plant would have to be more than an enormous lightsaber, which, in addition to housing a crystal, was believed to incorporate an emitter matrix, modulator circuitry, plasma, and a superconductor that channeled energy back to the negative pole of the lightsaber's hilt. By rights lightsabers shouldn't have been able to cut through meter-thick durasteel and yet they could, which lent credence to the notion of their being augmented by the Force itself.

Acting through the kybers?

If the answers lurked somewhere in the former Temple archives, they had yet to be discovered, and probably never would be since many of the secrets of lightsaber construction had been passed down through oral tradition. Perhaps the answers resided in one of the Jedi Holocrons, but he had not been granted access to those.

Some of the kybers delivered to the facility had almost certainly been cut and faceted, perhaps to eliminate occlusions and thus intensify their power yield. Perhaps, then, the largest examples could be faceted in the same way gemstones were cut to maximize light refraction. Thus far the research team hadn't succeeded in pumping laser energy into the crystals without weakening their lattices, almost the way living cells were affected by radiation. A more pressing problem involved controlling the crystals' seemingly innate impulse to diffract power—treacherously and erratically.

He trained his gaze on the crystal.

Was it resisting him?

What sacrifices needed to be made to unlock its secrets?

Again his thoughts drifted to Lyra. How long would he be able to abide living a lie for a greater purpose? Was his fascination with the research blinding him? Had the crystals in some way imprisoned him?

Robust, immutable, inscrutable . . . Perhaps, as superstition had it, he could only unlock the kyber's secrets by facing in a certain direction at dawn or by watching mist rise on certain remote worlds. One Jedi commentator had called the kyber a somnolent stone that needed to be woken up to perform its purpose. But that same commentator had cautioned that the crystal was also easily insulted and a Jedi needed to take care.

Galen understood that he would never be able to interact with the kyber the way the Jedi had, through the Force, but as he had told Lyra, he had science on his side, and powerful machines that would address it atom-to-atom and *compel* the crystal to perform as demanded.

Early in their relationship, when Lyra was still doing freelance survey work, she and Galen sometimes wouldn't see each other for months at a time. Reuniting after those absences had always been a bit awkward, and finding their way back to being a couple had always taken a few days. It was something they had grown to accept, and neither of them made too much of it. Once Lyra had decided to put her career on hold so they could start a family, absences hadn't figured into their relationship.

The enforced separation on Vallt was entirely different.

Returning from almost four standard months with Jyn, Has, and Nari, Lyra wasn't sure what to expect, especially in light of what she had seen at Samovar and Wadi Raffa. The rampant devastation she had witnessed had affected her thinking about what the Emperor was saying publicly and what was actually happening far from the Core. She had been tempted to inform Galen immediately of what she had discovered, but decided to allow time for the three of them to grow close again before airing any of her concerns, if only to prevent the information from coming out in a crazed cascade.

Almost from the moment they landed on Coruscant, she felt that something was off. The familiar chasm loomed—and not only between her and Galen but also between Galen and Jyn. She wanted to ascribe his intense preoccupation to the demands of the research, but the more closely she observed his behavior, the more cause she found for disquiet. In the past he had never attributed an unwillingness to discuss the research to it being too technical for her to grasp. On the contrary, he would spout off in the most technical terms, knowing full well that she didn't understand the half of it, then go through his usual process of simplifying and simplifying until she could at least make some sense of it. That, too, was part of their dynamic, and why he was willing to entrust her with transcribing his personal notes.

Now all at once he couldn't explain what he was doing. She might have been willing to overlook it because she had her own summary field notes to compile for Orson—and more to the point, she didn't need to know *everything* in depth—had Galen not encouraged her to remain in the Central District apartment rather than return to the facility. He would commute back and forth, he told her. That way Jyn could attend an actual preliminary school rather than be tutored at home.

She said no to remaining in the apartment and had returned to the facility only to find the atmosphere greatly changed; differently charged. Galen explained in a vague way that the facility had suffered a breach while she was away, and that security had been tightened. The new measures dictated that formerly common areas of the complex were now accessible only to those with proper clearance. Data that had previously been sent to the oversight board through the HoloNet were now being sent through an Imperial intranet server.

Secrecy was ubiquitous.

Ultimately, however, she couldn't keep her concerns bottled up. Galen was holding her at arm's length and she needed to know why.

"Any regrets about encouraging me to take Orson's assignment?" she asked while they were clearing the table after a meal and Jyn was watching a holovid.

She had sneaked the question in when he wasn't prepared, and he took a moment to compose a response. "Only about having had to worry about you."

"I'm sorry you had to worry. We missed you terribly, Galen."

She hoped he would say the same, but instead he asked: "Why, are *you* sorry you went? It sounds like Jyn had the time of her life."

"I'm glad we went, but I'm feeling like you and I haven't reconnected." She searched his face before adding: "You just seem awfully far away, and I'm *still* missing you."

"It's not because you've been away," he said more forcefully than was necessary. "It's the work. I've been under tremendous pressure."

She was about to reach for his hand when he folded his arms across his chest. "That's what I don't understand," she said. "Why are you under pressure all of a sudden? It wasn't this way before I left. Is it because of the espionage attempt?"

Too late she realized she had furnished him with an excuse.

"Yes. No. Yes and no. The board expects results. There are funding issues."

"But you and your team were making progress," she said, trying not to sound like she was pressuring him. "What happened to change that?"

Clearly to give himself time to think, he pretended to check on Jyn. "The research has entered a new phase and I'm struggling with the data," he said finally.

"Is our being here that much of a distraction?"

"Of course not."

His rote answers were beginning to exasperate her, and her tone began to reflect that. "Come on, Galen. Are they demanding too much? Is that it?"

He stared at her. "What put that idea into your head?"

Lyra took a breath, determined to make a new start. An argument was the last thing she wanted. A warm embrace, a kiss could make the whole thing vanish.

"Can we back up for a moment? You asked if I had

any regrets about the trip. Again, I don't. But something came up that I've wanted to share with you for weeks." She forged ahead. "After we left Alpinn, Has took Nari and me to a couple of worlds in the Western Reaches that are being ruthlessly exploited by the Empire. Each has suffered widespread devastation because of unimpeded extraction."

He listened closely, almost in surprise, then forced a look of dismissal. "I understand how that might offend your sense of environmental justice, but the Republic was guilty of doing the same thing. Whenever there's expansion there's a need for resources. The Empire may be exploiting some worlds, but only to save many, many more." He all but scowled at her. "You're the last person that needs to be reminded of how many worlds are out there."

"But these aren't just any worlds. They're *Legacy* worlds, guaranteed protection by statutes going back generations. Just like here. The refuge, suddenly coopted."

"Also for the greater good," he said.

She failed to suppress a snort. "That's certainly the way Orson sold it."

Galen regarded her for a long moment, then asked: "What worlds?"

Encouraged, she told him. "Samovar. Wadi Raffa." She could almost hear him make a mental note.

"What does any of this have to do with us?"

"If the Empire is ransacking worlds in secret, how do we know you're not being lied to about what they're doing with your research?"

"I'm not being lied to."

"Because you trust Orson and the rest, or you have proof?"

Galen paced away from her, then spun around. "I've seen proof."

Lyra hadn't expected that. "When?"

"While you were away. I raised the same doubts with Orson, and we had a long talk. He agreed to show me in person that my research is being replicated and put to practical use. So we went to Malpaz."

She went from being surprised to dumbfounded. "You and Orson went to Malpaz while Jyn and I were on Alpinn."

"It was only for a few days."

"I don't care if it was for a few hours, Galen. You're just getting around to telling me this?" She paused to collect her thoughts and get a handle on her anger, then said: "Is that why Orson asked me to oversee the mission—just to be able to get to you without my being here?"

"Stop accusing him of manipulating everything," he said. "I went to him to discuss my—*our* doubts. I demanded answers, and he said I could see for myself, so I took him up on it."

"And the two of you jumped to Malpaz."

Galen started to avert his eyes from her gaze, but instead held it. "I should have told you sooner."

She took it under advisement. "Did Orson mention anything about Dagio?"

"Why would he mention Dagio?"

"Because Reeva said that Dagio had been conducting research on Malpaz, and that she hadn't been able to reach him. Is he still there?"

"No," Galen said, and was quiet for a long moment, pacing and shaking his head. "The facility that was responsible for replicating my results was destroyed before it could be used to supply energy to the capital city."

Lyra's jaw came unhinged. "Destroyed by who? By Separatists?"

"Orson prefers to call them anarchists. He broke his security oath to tell me."

"So Dagio might be *dead*?"

"He might be." Galen shook his head again. "I'm not supposed to be discussing any of this."

Lyra felt torn. Even though an apology might be in order, she needed to dig deeper. "Did you keep this from me because I'm not cleared to know?"

He nodded. "I swore to an oath."

"Then there's more you're not allowed to tell me?"

"Yes."

Lyra pressed her fingertips to her forehead.

"I don't care about the oath," Galen said. "But because of the destruction, I've had to double my efforts to find a way, some way . . ." He looked at her. "I wanted to tell you."

She tried but failed to assemble all the pieces, and felt suddenly bereft. "How did we come to a place where we're keeping things from each other, Galen?" She squeezed back tears.

"This is a critical time," he said, coming to her at last. "We have to trust that the Empire is doing what's best for the greater galaxy. There are forces trying to sow chaos and keep us in a state of perpetual war. The Emperor is determined to find a way to end it. He

wants to unite everyone and prevent another galaxy-
wide conflict."

Lyra hung on his every word. "I'm not used to
hearing you talk like this," she said, but she allowed
herself to be comforted in his arms. "You sound like
a convert."

"Providing power is the only way forward."

She wasn't entirely persuaded, but it was clear to
her that Galen had himself convinced.

21

SUBGROUPS

THE WANTON WELLSPRING HAD A small back room reserved for private parties and for stashing illegal substances during raids by authorities. In the past the local police would warn the owners about raids, but with stormtroopers garrisoned nearby, that was no longer possible. Seated around the main table were Has and more than a dozen smugglers, rogues, and scoundrels, some of whom he had known since well before the war—Yalli, Molo, the Dug, Dajo Koda, and a Twi'lek named Xosad Hozem among them— and others from war-ravaged worlds as distant as Onderon, who had made the seedy bar their unofficial headquarters.

The back room's ten-year-old holoprojector was normally used to run entertainment holos, but Has was employing it to display a midair map of the Salient star system, an autonomous region on the edge of the so-called Corporate Sector, three jumps from Rajtiri and the latest destination for deliveries of proscribed arms and matériel.

"Three worlds in the habitable zone of a red

dwarf," Has was explaining. "The moon of the outer planet, Epiphany, is owned by Zerpen Industries. That's our terminus." He indicated it in the holo. "Salient has a well-armed sentry station at the edge of the system, but our employers have agents working there who will breeze us through the checkpoint—"

"What's our guarantee they'll breeze us through," a deep voice interrupted.

Has didn't need to turn around to know that the remark had been uttered by the tall, imposing man from Onderon, Saw Gerrera. But he turned anyway. "That's the way it's always worked."

Saw shot him a dubious look. "And we'll take comfort in knowing that, I'm sure, when our hulls are riddled and our tails are on fire." Rarely without an opinion and frequently at the center of spirited conversations about galactic politics, Saw had become a popular figure in the Wanton Wellspring. "We need a contingency plan."

Has felt everyone's eyes on him. "I suppose you're right—for security's sake."

Saw shook his head and got up out of his chair. "I'm right because where most of you have spent your careers steering courses around confrontation, I've flown into the thick of it. I'm not saying that your skills won't come in handy, but if we're going to embark on a joint mission, the last thing we want is misadventure."

Has tracked Saw as he wound through the assembled group, punctuating his remarks with grimaces and commanding gestures. His hair was thick and black, but emboldened by a streak of color. He wasn't shouting, but he might as well have been, such was the force of his personality.

"All right, then, we'll work up a backup plan," Has said at last.

"My bailiwick," Saw said.

Has glanced around to see if anyone objected. "Now that that's settled—"

Saw planted his hands on his hips and launched a hearty laugh at the ceiling. "It's far from settled, Has. It's in the air; it's still *precipitating*." He fell briefly silent, then said, "What will we be carrying?"

"Most of our ships will be stocked with munitions and missiles, though some of you with larger freighters will be hauling armaments." Before Saw could interrupt again, Has added: "Saw will command that group."

The charismatic Onderonian vouchsafed a genuine smile as he reseated himself.

That the operation had resumed business so soon had surprised Has, and this time word had come directly from Krennic himself, whom Has was convinced had been supervising the appropriation missions from the start. Krennic hadn't admitted to that either before or after the star tour with Lyra Erso, her daughter, and her friend Nari, although Has hadn't asked. During a debriefing on Coruscant, Krennic had focused on Lyra, and whether she had discussed her husband's research. He had the reports Lyra had transmitted from Alpinn, but he was more interested in hearing about discussions that had taken place in the archaeologists' camp and aboard Has's ship. Has was baffled, but he did his best to provide all the details that wouldn't matter. For all he knew, the months on Alpinn had been part of the process of vetting Lyra for a security clearance, in keeping with her husband's Imperial research project.

Has had omitted mentioning the diversions to Samovar and Wadi Raffa. He had taken precautions to keep his ship from being scanned and he had purged the side trips from the log. But there remained a possibility that the ship's signature had been identified in one system or the other, and that his omissions would eventually come to light. In any case, it wasn't as if they had broken any laws. Environmentalist groups were a frequent presence in Wadi space especially, and Krennic might be willing to excuse Lyra and Nari's interest in seeing what was happening there.

Has had hoped that the debriefing would constitute a long-overdue end to their relationship, but Krennic had reached out, informing Has about Salient.

"Our insertion point for the Epiphany moon will be somewhere in this region." Has circled an area of the moon with his finger. "We'll be coming in with starlight at our backs, Epiphany on the far side." He enlarged the image of the moon and highlighted a spot on the bright side. "The landing is here, at Zerpen Industries headquarters. Your navicomputers will be provided the jump coordinates when the cargo is loaded and we launch from the depot pickup site. Once we've cleared the choke point, we're going to need to maintain a tight grouping. Imperial ships will be arriving in our wake, so our timing has to be precise."

Krennic had tendered the mission as Has's big score.

"Thanks, Has, for helping the Empire grab a couple of resource-rich worlds, and for spying on Lyra Erso. After this run you can retire in comfort from your many years of service as a useful idiot. And do bring all your friends and allies along, since there's plenty of profit to go around."

"So the mission is to land our cargo, wait for the Imperials to arrive, then stand aside while they accuse Zerpen of purchasing stolen weapons," Saw said.

"In so many words," Has said.

Saw narrowed his eyes and nodded in a conspiratorial way.

The landing zone might as well have been marked with the symbol for a double cross.

Galen sat at the console of the facility's dedicated server, which was linked through devious means to Krennic's communications hub somewhere in the Outer Rim. His forefinger hovered over the TRANSMIT key that would seal his deal with the Empire—and would mark his passing. It was one thing to have said yes to bleeding the kyber crystals of all their inherent power. Now he would be held accountable for doing so.

He wheeled his chair backward, stood, and paced away from the console.

Again.

As if getting over the moral hurdle hadn't been enough, he remained conflicted about having kept the true nature of his research from Lyra. He had revealed just enough to keep her from probing any deeper. But he was a terrible liar; he had no practice in the art. Never wanting to be involved in games, he had always spoken his mind. Where he was forever attempting to simplify his thinking, lying introduced complications. He said what he felt. Others certainly had a right to take offense, but no one could accuse him of lying. And here he had subscribed to a falsehood that could threaten his relationship with the family he was trying to support and protect.

He had acquiesced, and henceforth would be corrupted.

He cursed, ordered himself to come to his senses, and wheeled back up to the console.

How could anyone work when at the mercy of moral and emotional conflicts?

Once Krennic's team had succeeded in containing the energy output, his part of the project would essentially be complete and he would be able to speak freely with Lyra. For all he had promised Krennic, his real imperative had always been to protect her and Jyn, and be able to provide them with the peaceful future they were entitled to. Everything he had done was for them.

It had become a slogan he had been repeating to himself for the past several weeks, each time his guilt took him out of his work and the implications of his research rushed in on him like ravenous phantoms. But for them his breakthrough might have come sooner. Instead he had spent half the time grappling with whether he had been chasing an incorrect hypothesis or a false idea. He hadn't so much failed as found a thousand ways his theoretical approaches weren't going to work.

Then, that moment of pure discovery.

He had long suspected that the larger crystals needed to be faceted along certain planes, not only to eliminate occlusions and vacancies, but also to minimize diffraction resulting from the introduction of energy from a lasing medium. With the proper faceting, the pulse energy released by a crystal could be greatly amplified and, with the help of containment devices, directed into a collimating beam of incredible power. In theory, at any rate. It might also be possible to increase the energy yield by forcing the lattices to realign; by forcing the crystal to change its properties. Jedi commentators often referred to light and dark, day and night aspects of the Force. Realigning the lattices along a dark or nighttime axis might allow for greater control over the crystals' almost deliberate tendency to diffract. Technology had provided a method for getting the crystals to obey him; to surrender their awesome potential without destroying everything in close proximity.

That abundant yield could be siphoned off, contained, and made available as enriched energy. Without containment the same yield could result in a catastrophic event.

He and his team had run preliminary tests based on his computations. Reasons of space and security didn't permit them to construct a containment prototype at the facility, so a device based on his schematics was to be assembled by Orson's team wherever it

was headquartered, to determine if the results cor-
roborated Galen's predictions.

His scrutiny of the inner workings of the crystal
had become part of his waking and nighttime consciousness. Were the permutations in the kyber lattice
comparable to emotional shifts in a sentient being?
Could sentient beings compel what was inorganic to
pulse in harmony with their tempers and appetites?

Was there such a thing as a noble lie?

The Empire was lying to its citizens by suppressing
information about the worlds it was despoiling. Or
was it merely safeguarding an inconvenient truth?
Was his lie equivalent to the former, a kind of pillag-
ing: the sacrifice of some to save countless others?
And in the end, would a kyber-based facility make
real the Emperor's dream of renewable energy for one
and all? Which world might he choose to serve as an
example?

The only sticking point to all this was the data he
had collated regarding mining on the worlds Lyra had
visited on the return leg of her journey to Alpinn.
Contrary to what Galen had expected to learn, there
was nothing ordinary about the ores known to exist
in abundance on Samovar and Wadi Raffa. While
they were occasionally used in construction projects,
exfoliating doonium and dolovite were primarily employed to insulate the cores of immense hypermatter
reactors and to dissipate heat in the collimator shafts
of superlaser weapons.

Galen pushed concern from his mind and riveted
his gaze to the console's TRANSMIT key.

Would Lyra understand? Or would she accuse him

of being so driven by a need to measure up to the challenge that he had not only abandoned caution and scientific discernment, but also dragged her and Jyn down with him? What would his legacy be then?

Lyra might not see it as a noble lie so much as a grand betrayal.

Tarkin's blunt-nosed shuttle dropped like a raptor into the clear skies of Epiphany's exemplary moon. He sent his cadre of stormtroopers down the ramp ahead of him, then on descending found himself facing a Zerpen Industries representative backed by a uniformed security force several hundred strong arrayed in a formation as tight as might be expected of an Imperial battalion. Hopelessly outnumbered, as it were—except for the *Executrix*, which was ten thousand meters overhead with its complement of crew and soldiers at general quarters.

"Welcome to Epiphany, Moff Tarkin," the Zerpen rep stepped forward to say. He was a slender, hairless near-human dressed in tight-fitting purple clothing emblazoned with the company logo. "To what does Zerpen owe the honor of a visit by an emissary of the Empire?"

Tarkin had no patience for mincing words. "You may well consider it an honor, but I suspect you'll change your mind soon enough."

"I take it, then, that we're dispensing with official protocol."

"Why waste time?" Tarkin said. "We are in pursuit of a group of insurgents who were admitted through

your cordon and have apparently been given safe
haven here."

"Yes, so you explained when your Star Destroyer
entered orbit. But in fact, we only permitted your
shuttle to land as a courtesy. No foreign ships prior
to yours have arrived on our moon, and we have no
knowledge of this group of insurgents you seek."

"I suggest you dispense with coyness as I have cordiality," Tarkin said. "Do you think we would arrive
without proof? We have the tracking data. We know
precisely when and where the insurgents inserted."

The rep lengthened an already long face. "Your
data must be incorrect, Moff Tarkin." He indicated
the landing field and the hangars and buildings beyond. "As you can see, the only ships here belong to
Zerpen. You're welcome, of course, to conduct a search
of the hangar spaces, but you won't find what you're
looking for. What's more, I hope you will take it on
faith that the autonomous worlds of Salient would
never grant access to enemies of Emperor Palpatine."

"At least not since the war ended," Tarkin said.

"Ah, but wartime was another matter, Moff Tarkin. With the Republic and the Confederacy determined to vie for supremacy, our system was but a
sanctuary for those who wanted no part of the fray."

"Except that Zerpen brooked no issue with building and supplying weapons to anyone who asked—
to being equal-opportunity profiteers."

The near-human tilted his head to one side. "We
prefer to think of ourselves as mere entrepreneurs."

Tarkin, who usually knew what it took to get beings to give up their secrets, could see that he wasn't

getting anywhere with the Zerpen rep. Even with a Star Destroyer overhead.

"May I suggest an alternative explanation, Moff Tarkin?"

"You can try."

The rep proffered a calculated smile. "The Empire is using these alleged insurgents as a pretext for executing some hidden agenda."

Tarkin almost returned the knowing grin. It seemed that he and the rep shared the same skills. He was about to respond when his adjutant appeared by his side with a comlink in hand. "Urgent from the *Executrix*, sir."

Tarkin moved out of earshot of the rep and enabled the feed.

"Sir, the target ships have been identified and located. It appears that instead of landing, they completed an orbit of the moon and are now vectoring deeper into the system, all speed."

Tarkin took a moment to digest it. "Continue to track them, but do not fire. I'm returning to the ship." Without a further word to the rep, he spun on his boot heels and marched up the shuttle ramp, trailed by his adjutant and contingent of stormtroopers.

The shuttle extended its wings and began to ascend even before Tarkin was fully in his harness. It was clear that Zerpen had seen through the ruse, so perhaps they had denied the smugglers permission to land. But why then were Krennic's dupes making for Salient II rather than outbound from the system? It also occurred to him that the smugglers might have been killed on arrival and had their ships pirated. He had no sympathy for the smugglers one way or another. They were going to be treated as insurgents to help make the case against Zerpen. But if Salient had been so bold as to pirate the weapons instead of surrendering them—

"Sir, scanners indicate that Salient escorts from the checkpoint are en route to Epiphany," the shuttle's comm tech reported. "The ships are fast and heavily armed."

"Alert the *Executrix* to go to battle stations and reposition to protect us while we dock. If any of the escorts lock onto us, the commander has permission to destroy them."

He had barely gotten the words out when the tech continued: "The *Executrix* is receiving an incoming transmission from Salient Two Strategic Command."

Tarkin unfastened from the harness and moved to the communications board. "Have the *Executrix* redirect the comm to us."

He had to wait only a moment before the face of an avian humanoid appeared in the holo. "To whom am I speaking?" the Salient officer asked in a dulcet voice.

Tarkin identified himself.

"Moff Tarkin, you have been denied permission to remain in this system. Make no attempt to move your ship sunward."

"We are in pursuit of enemies of the Empire, General. I will make the determination as to where I can and cannot venture."

"We have the rogue ships on our scanners, Moff Tarkin, and we request that you allow us to deal with them," the Hiitian said. "Unlike the Empire, Salient still has a functioning judiciary."

"I'm afraid that won't suffice, General. Place them under arrest and we will see to the rest of it."

"You are violating the sovereignty of an autonomous star system. Withdraw from Salient or face the consequences."

Tarkin muted the feed and glanced at the enlisted-ratings tech. "Where are our quarries?"

"Still on course for Salient Two, sir."

"Inform the *Executrix* that I expect a complete assessment of this system's defenses the moment I arrive."

"Yes, sir."

"Do we have hypercomm?"

"We do, sir, although Zerpen is attempting to jam us."

"Then contact the battle group at Telos while we still can, and tell Admiral Utu that I want her to dispatch whatever assets she can spare to Salient soonest."

"Anything else, sir?"

Tarkin nodded. "Inform the *Executrix* to prepare for a microjump to Salient Two on our docking."

On Salient II the Hiitian officer who had spoken with Tarkin welcomed Has Obitt and his ragtag band of smugglers and mercenaries.

"The Imperials have refused to withdraw, Captain Obitt—exactly as you predicted. They demand that we arrest all of you and turn you over to their custody."

"That wouldn't be the worst idea . . ." Has started to say.

"Yes, it would," Saw broke in. "Because right now we're the allies Salient needs most. Besides, you've nothing to gain by arresting us, beyond delaying the inevitable. The Empire has Zerpen Industries and the rest of this system in its sights."

The Hiitian scrutinized him. "We are well aware, Captain Gerrera. Which is why Zerpen didn't simply blow your ships out of the sky the moment you inserted—although some in our government urged us to do just that."

Has accepted it. "If the Empire can't use us to make the case that you are harboring insurgents, it will find some other way to overpower you."

"Then why not simply invade?"

Saw forced a breath. "The Emperor's no fool. He's waiting to see if any of the local systems of the Corporate Sector come to your aid. Maybe he doesn't want to be seen as instigating another galactic conflict so soon after the last one."

The Hiitian nodded in agreement. "The word is already out, and we're expecting reinforcements from far afield."

"If you have a chance to fight, you take it," Saw said. "That's what we did on my homeworld when the Separatists took control."

The humanoid looked at him. "Were you victorious?"

"Eventually," Saw said. "But we paid a price—a terrible price."

Has and the Hiitian traded looks. This was Has's first face-to-face with Salient's commander, but they had communicated by holo shortly after Krennic had selected Salient as the Empire's next target.

Long before the war, the star system had become a headquarters for unsavory corporations, tax evaders, pirates, and arms merchants. Colonized by many of the species that had ultimately joined or sided with the Separatists, the system had been the site of incidents and skirmishes during the Republic era, and the confrontations had grown only worse in the lead-up to the war. Given the Empire's attitude toward autonomous systems, it was surprising that Salient had managed to remain independent for as long as it had, since absorbing it would net the Empire not only Zerpen Industries, but also a systemful of reprobate conglomerates loyal only to themselves. More, Salient would become the staging area for incursions deeper into a sector of the Outer Rim that was slowly coalescing into an entity all its own.

Has had considered rejecting Krennic's offer, but doing so would have meant running the risk of suffering an industrial accident of the sort that had eliminated Matese, or flight of a sort that would have left him looking over his shoulder for the rest of his days. Instead he had opted to make a show of playing along, when he had actually been busy informing Salient's leadership of the Empire's plan.

"I still don't understand your stake in this," the Hiitian general told the two of them, his gaze favor-

ing Has. "You said yourself that even without justification the Empire will find a way to rationalize its
actions here. So why not simply light out for as far as
your hyperdrive can take you?"

Has wasn't about to confess to having been Orson
Krennic's useful idiot, or to the effect that Lyra, Nari,
and Jyn had had on him. Since Alpinn he had been
rethinking the events that had brought him to a point
in his life where he was answering to people like Krennic, and all he wanted now was a chance to make
things right.

"What hope is there for freelancers like myself if
the Empire is determined to vanquish every independent system?" he said. Glancing at Saw, Molo, and
Yalli, he added: "All of us will end up Imperial employees, imprisoned, or dead."

Saw clapped him hard on the back. "That's the
spirit, Has. But there's more to it than that. To the
Empire we're nothing more than clots of dirt they'd
kick from their boots. Even Salient is nothing more
than a trial run. Not when the goal is subjugation
on a galactic scale. And that's where we come in, even
if it's just to rattle them some: to rebel against injustice."

Has heard him out. Like Lyra Erso, Saw was another glaring example of what he might have been.
But then, allies and partners often came along when
you least expected them.

"I stand with Captain Gerrera on that," he found
himself saying.

The Hiitian general returned a glum nod. "I'll tell
you this much: Salient has vowed to keep its resources

from being used as grist for the Emperor's voracious war machine. We'd sooner see our worlds reduced to ash than be swallowed up by the Empire."

Saw appraised him sadly. "Those eventualities aren't mutually exclusive."

The Hiitian nodded. "We'll defend ourselves until we're unable to."

"Even if it's not a fight you're likely to win?" Has asked.

"Even if."

Has said, "Another option would be to let the Empire have what it wants."

"Not an option," Saw said with force.

The Hiitian agreed. "Occupation? Captain Obitt, you've obviously visited worlds that have chosen that route. How is life there?"

Has smiled in solidarity. "I'd rather fight." Again he glanced at Saw and his fellow smugglers. "That's why all of us are here."

The humanoid flexed his feathered back. "What we fail to protect, Captain, we will leave in ruins."

The Star Destroyer that Krennic had requisitioned for use by his Special Weapons Group dropped out of hyperspace far from any known space lanes or jump points. No navigation buoys took note of its arrival, and there were no local HoloNet relays to provide easy communication with Coruscant or Geonosis or any other world.

In the middle ground of a perilous expanse of deep space, two collapsed stars were attempting to devour each other, the mated fields of their accretion disks resembling a mask, the black holes as cutouts for eyes. Warped by gravitational lensing, realspace swirled, making the nearby starfields appear to be rotating, dragged around the edges of the mask by unseen forces.

From the Star Destroyer's bridge, Krennic, Professor Sahali, Reeva Demesne, and other team members observed the dance of darkness in silence, the inspiraling energy prompted by supernova explosions.

Mas Amedda had wanted them to test-fire the experimental weapon closer to the Core, closer to home, but Krennic didn't want to chance a repeat of what had happened on Malpaz—even though the kybercrystal-assisted twin laser array had been carefully assembled and calibrated, and a misfire would likely mean going down with the ship.

"The Emperor doesn't want this," Krennic said, gesturing out the viewport toward the lasers. "You remember the former Palpatine. He resisted every attempt by the Senate to create an army, much less the push to wage war with the Separatists. But times have changed. Those he relies on for advice and guidance have proposed a revolution in military affairs, and it has fallen to us to lead the charge."

Krennic moved away from the viewport. "You look at the history of any sentient species and what do you find but a tableaux of violence and slaughter. It's finger-painted on the ceilings of caves and engraved into the walls of temples. Dig a hole deep enough on any world and you'll find the skulls and bones of adults and children fractured by crude weapons. All of us were fighting long before we were farming and raising livestock."

He held up a hand before anyone could voice an objection. "All of you are exceedingly well educated, and you're going to start rattling off the names of species and societies where that isn't the case. And my answer is that those aren't the beings or the star systems we need to worry about. It's the rest of them. Violence is hardwired into most of us and there's no eliminating the impulse—not with an army of stormtroopers or a fleet of Star Destroyers. That's why we've embarked on a path to a different solution. We have a chance to forge a peace that will endure for longer than the Republic was in existence."

"Peace through fear," Reeva said.

"Yes," Krennic told her, and let it go at that.

By rights it should have been Sahali who gave the countdown, but the scientist allowed Krennic to have the privilege, since he had been responsible for netting Galen Erso at last.

As Krennic counted down, everyone turned from the view of the internecine black holes to gaze at monitor screens, on which computers would depict what their eyes and optical sensors would be unable to perceive. Elsewhere, other computers and monitors would measure the discharged energy and compare the results with Galen's calculations.

When Krennic reached "one," Sahali called for simultaneous ignition.

Computer modeling showed the lasers' twin collimating beams racing away from the Star Destroyer. Then, captured by gravity, the beams become one, changing vector and accelerating beyond lightspeed as it disappeared into the mask's churning accretion envelope.

Krennic watched the monitor in naked awe, wishing there was some way he could screen the results for Galen without sending him into cardiac arrest or fleeing for the farthest reaches of the galaxy.

His legacy, in any case, his contribution to the greatest weapon ever constructed, was now assured.

22

EXIT WOUNDS

IN A COMMAND PIT BELOW the Star Destroyer's bridge, Tarkin viewed the data compiled by the ship's battle-assessment computers. In a move that was unusually cautious for him, he had ordered the *Executrix* to exit its microjump well out of range of Salient II's downside and orbital defenses. The smugglers' ships were known to have landed, but Tarkin had yet to learn whether the pilots and their crews had been arrested or given sanctuary.

"The planet has several massive shield generators, as well as ion cannons left over from the war," Tarkin's XO was saying. "It also has a couple of Zerpen-built turbolaser batteries capable of putting our deflector screens to the test."

Tarkin pinched his jaw as he mulled over the news. "Did the smugglers deliver any ordnance we need to take into consideration?"

The commander swung to a separate holo to access the information. "According to a report received from Lieutenant Commander Krennic, the smugglers' payloads consisted of pulse weapons and fission devices."

"And Salient One's fortifications?"

"Not as well defended on the surface, but home to the system's flotilla of warships, most of which are older-generation vessels retrofitted with Separatist weaponry—consistent with Salient's leaning during the war. Long-distance scans indicate that three ships separated from the home group and are presumably on their way to reinforce Salient Two. Hyperspace fluctuations suggest that they may have already taken up positions on the far side."

"Any word from Admiral Utu?"

"She's hoping to be able to send two Star Destroyers from Telos."

"Hoping."

"Apparently our assets are widely scattered at the moment."

Tarkin nodded, climbed the few stairs to the bridge walkway, and moved to the forward viewports to gaze on blue-and-brown Salient II.

No one had been expecting Salient simply to roll over, but the system's immediate shift to a war footing was surprising and unsettling, and was likely the result of the government having been forewarned. The idea had been to gain a toehold on the Zerpen moon and expand slowly into the system once the inner worlds had accepted occupation. It puzzled Tarkin that the same smugglers who had been instrumental in delivering worlds like Samovar and Wadi Raffa into his grip would suddenly change sides and attempt to compromise the Empire's strategy. Unless . . .

Tarkin allowed his thoughts to collect rather than follow a particular path.

Unless Krennic had engineered the reversal in order to keep him stalled at Salient—knowing full well that retreat would set a precedent that the Empire could be forced by autonomous systems to back down.

A chime from the comm broke his musings and he returned to the command pit, where a one-quarter holopresence of Salient's avian commander had taken shape above the holoprojector.

"We know that the insurgents have made planet-fall," Tarkin said without preamble. "Are you now prepared to surrender them to our custody?"

"We decline to do so, Moff Tarkin, as they will be crucial to exposing the Empire's subterfuge. Be that as it may, our leadership remains intent on finding a diplomatic solution to this deadlock."

"The time for that has passed," Tarkin said.

"Salient Two's ambassador wishes to know if you would be willing to receive him aboard your ship."

Tarkin gave quick thought to several possible scenarios. If the ambassador could be persuaded to capitulate, then perhaps Salient II could substitute for the toehold Tarkin had hoped to establish at Epiphany.

"Tell him he has my permission to come up."

"His shuttle is already in flight, Moff Tarkin, having anticipated that you would be open to exploring alternatives to open warfare."

"Sir," the XO said from behind Tarkin, "we have the consular vessel on course."

Again Tarkin climbed the stairs and stood for a

moment at the viewports, waiting for the ship to ascend into the light of Salient's red dwarf. On spying the glint of starlight, Tarkin swung to his executive officer.

"Hail the ship. Order the pilot to hold and await further instructions."

Tarkin waited.

"Sir, no response from the consular vessel. And something else: a slight delay in communications. Almost an echo."

Tarkin squinted at the distant speck of light. "Scan the ship for life-forms."

The response came quickly.

"Negative for life-forms, sir. It appears to be a drone. Possibly a ticking bomb."

"Engage the forward tractor beam to hold it fast," Tarkin started to say when alerts sounded from a separate duty station in the pits.

"Sir, three warships emerging from Salient's dark side."

Tarkin traded knowing glances with the XO.

"A deliberate provocation?" the officer asked.

Tarkin narrowed his eyes. Salient was determined to go down fighting.

"Ready the in-close batteries," he ordered. "It'll be a cold day in hell when the Empire has to be provoked into taking preemptive action."

"Congratulations are in order," Mas Amedda said, the blue Chagrian's holopresence larger than life above the holotable in Krennic's Geonosis quarters.

Krennic inclined his head in acknowledgment. "Preliminary results indicate that the energy released during the test-fire had the destructive power of the combined batteries of a qaz-class Star Destroyer."

"An encouraging beginning," the grand vizier said. "This is Galen Erso's doing?"

"Only in discovering how to conjure necessary power from the kyber crystals," Krennic said, playing to the holocam. "Credit for the rest—the lasers and such—goes to my team."

Amedda tipped his horned head. "I'll grant that you were right about Erso all along."

"I never had any doubts, Vizier."

"The Emperor has been apprised, and is most pleased. He has also approved your promotion to full commander."

Krennic restrained a smile. "His pleasure is reward enough—all that one could hope for—but I gladly accept the provisional promotion as well."

Amedda's lethorns stirred. "Provisional?"

"I maintain that rear admiral is a more fitting rank."

"You have conducted a successful test-fire, Commander. I suggest you now build the actual battle station weapon."

"Of course, Vizier." Krennic paused, then said: "Any further news regarding Moff Tarkin?"

Amedda scowled. "He remains embroiled at Salient."

"Most unfortunate," Krennic said, shaking his head. "I was anticipating his help with the next phase of the project."

"So were we, Commander. I will keep you updated."

Krennic waited for the holopresence to disappear before he allowed himself to smile. He had hoped to kill two birds with one stone—rid himself of Obitt and entrap Tarkin—and so he had.

There was an art to learning what individuals were made of, to analyzing how they were put together, and then—when the moment was right—lining them up just so and driving the point home, breaking them along predicted lines; faceting them like one of Galen's kybers. Obitt one way, Tarkin the other.

Once Krennic learned that Has Obitt had taken Lyra and Nari to the worlds he had helped ruin, he realized that he had lost the Dressellian to some sort of crisis of conscience; but also that he could be used in a more far-reaching plan. The chance that he would turn tail when offered the mission to Salient was great, but Krennic had gambled that Obitt would instead seek to redeem himself by coming to Salient's rescue. Obitt had even gone a step further by enlisting the aid of some of his disgruntled fellow smugglers.

As for Tarkin, Krennic needed only to review the man's personal history to devise an appropriate trap—his war record, his brutal actions in the Western Reaches, his missions with Darth Vader. Tarkin had proved himself incapable of retreating, of displaying the slightest sign of weakness. The tack he would take at Salient was obvious; and now ensnared there, he was no threat to Krennic's position in the battle station project. Perhaps even his relationship with the Emperor had suffered.

That left only one person who still needed to be broken.

On the destruction of the consular vessel, which was in fact an explosive drone, the trio of Salient warships had taken the fight to the *Executrix*. The Star Destroyer had responded with fusillades of its own, but the initial battle had raged for standard hours before the enemy cruisers had repositioned closer to Salient II. The Star Destroyer's shields had withstood the assault, but Tarkin had ordered the commander to keep the ship out of range of the massive turbolaser batteries planetside—at least until reinforcements from Telos arrived.

What was meant to have been a simple incursion had become a full-fledged battle.

Taken off his guard, Tarkin was willing to admit to himself that he had underestimated Orson Krennic, who was certainly the chief architect of the mess in which Tarkin found himself. He had also learned in passing that Krennic had managed to add another insignia square to his tunic, probably resulting from some measure of success in developing the battle station's primary weapon.

For Tarkin, the shenanigans at Salient offered further proof that Krennic was unsuited to supervise the project, and that realization was forcing him to reconsider the timing of the moves he would need to make to assume command—project setbacks and delays notwithstanding.

First, however, he was going to have to extricate himself from Salient.

Intent on giving Galen space, Lyra had returned to their Central District apartment, ostensibly to get Jyn started on classes in kinesthetics and tumbling. Their mutual admissions hadn't really cleared the air, but at least they were back to speaking. She didn't fully understand why the efforts on Malpaz— the practical use of Galen's research—had been classified top-secret, but with would-be insurgents still lurking about, she could accept that maybe there was a need for extreme security.

After class, Lyra had taken Jyn to a rooftop park of grass and trees and kids' attractions to work off some additional energy and recover from the fit she had pitched on being denied a silly little toy a Rodian merchant was hawking. From here Lyra could just see the spires of the former Jedi Temple, and it pained her to know that a massive remodeling project was under way there. She was catching her own breath on a bench when she heard her name called and turned to see Orson striding toward her, in white tunic, black trousers and boots, and a brimmed command cap.

"Lyra!"

Too surprised to speak, she returned an awkward wave. It wasn't impossible for beings to bump into each other on Coruscant, even as crowded as it was, but chance meetings usually didn't occur in the middle of the Central District.

"Galen told me that you sometimes take the child

here in the afternoon," Orson said by way of explanation. He raised his hand to point to an immense building adjacent to the park. "My office is just up there on the ninety-first floor. I saw you two and thought I'd come over to say hello." His eyes roamed the playground. "Where is she? I hope I'm not interrupting."

The thought of Orson watching them from his Imperial aerie sent a chill through her, but she didn't let it show. "No, of course not. Jyn's at the swings."

Orson followed her motion. "Still homeschooling her, or are you thinking about enrolling her?"

"We haven't decided," Lyra managed to get out before Jyn hurried over to them.

"Can I go on the grav-slip now?"

"Only if you promise to take turns this time," Lyra said, adding as Jyn ran off: "And no pushing!"

Orson tracked her, his upper lip curled in what seemed disapproval. "She's feisty."

"That she is."

"And growing up fast." He fell silent for a moment, then said: "Have you readjusted from your journey to Alpinn?"

"Finally, yes. Did you have any questions about my report?"

"Your notes were flawless. It's a shame you didn't find any true kybers."

"I know. Even so, I hope the Empire will be gentle with Alpinn. It really deserves Legacy status."

"I'm certain that the right decision will be made." Krennic paused, then said: "Samovar and Wadi Raffa weren't as fortunate."

Lyra gaped at him, unsure if she was angrier about

his knowing or the way he had decided to let her know. "You don't miss a trick, do you, Orson? Did you hear it from Has—your spy?"

"Actually, Captain Obitt neglected to mention the side trips. But he didn't have to. Visits to Imperial facilities are closely monitored. A scanner managed to grab the signature of his ship, despite his attempts to outwit it."

"He didn't mention anything to me or Nari about doing that."

"You wouldn't have tried to hide your tracks?"

"Why would we? Those worlds aren't off limits. Or are they?"

Orson shook his head. "Not the space around them. So you did nothing wrong."

Lyra showed him a livid frown. "I don't need you to tell me that, Orson."

His calm, calculating tone held. "Can I ask, though, about what prompted you to veer from your itinerary?"

Lyra considered the question before answering. "Nari told me that a couple of worlds she had surveyed were being exploited for resources. I wanted to see for myself."

"Not a pretty sight."

"That's something of an understatement, Orson. Why isn't the media reporting on any of it?"

"Do you really think anyone would care about a couple of remote worlds? What's more, everything being done on those worlds is in service to the needs of Celestial Power."

"Some might care. I care. Nari cares. Even Has seemed to care."

"Has cared," Krennic repeated, plainly amused by the idea.

"Is that funny?"

"Not really. He's always had a soft streak."

Done with the ride, Jyn hurried back to say: "Mama, I'm hungry."

"You'll have to wait until Orson and I are finished talking."

The little girl shook her head in defiance.

Lyra took a candy bar from her bag and gave it to her. "Don't eat while you're on any of the rides."

"Okay."

She waited for Jyn to leave, then turned slightly in Krennic's direction. "Orson, you didn't leave your lofty office just to say hello. What's on your mind?"

Krennic deliberated for a moment. "Can I assume you discussed your unscheduled stops with Galen?"

"Why do I get the impression you already know the answer?"

"Why would you think that?"

Lyra forced a breath. "I told him, and he pretty much dismissed it. Use up one, save a dozen others, that sort of thing. As you say, to serve the needs of Celestial Power."

"I think it's called seeing the bigger picture."

Lyra shrugged. "I suppose on some level the Empire is doing what has to be done."

"On every level."

Lyra smiled without humor. "Galen told me about

the clandestine voyage the two of you took to Malpaz."

Krennic narrowed his eyes but recovered quickly. "Clandestine? There was nothing secret about it." He smiled. "It's not as if we did anything wrong."

"Except that I wasn't supposed to know."

"Strictly speaking, yes, but I never expected that he would withhold the information from you."

"We try not to keep things from each other, Orson."

"Were you at all relieved to know that attempts are being made to put Galen's research to practical use?"

"To be honest, I was surprised."

"And relieved?"

She laughed shortly. "Orson, I feel like you're cross-examining me."

He swallowed what he had in mind to say when Jyn returned, her face a mess.

"Are we done?" Lyra asked him.

"Just one more thing. As a friend I need to remind you that Galen's work suffers when his environment becomes stressful."

Shock widened her eyes. "Are you going to lecture me on how I should behave around Galen, what we can and can't discuss?"

"I'm merely suggesting that you take into consideration the demands of the research and the importance of his being able to focus."

She shook her head in disbelief. "You think I don't understand that?" She waited a beat, then said: "So now that you've told me as a friend, is there anything you want to add as an Imperial officer?"

He flashed the briefest smile. "Officially it is incumbent on me to emphasize that Galen is involved in work that is critical to the security of the Empire, as well as caution you that continued interference could result in difficulties for you and your family."

Lyra covered her mouth with her hand. "Orson, how do you think Galen would react if he learned about this little chat?"

"I'm certain he would understand."

"He might, or he just might feel cornered. He's his own person, in any case, and whatever *stress* I introduce isn't going to cripple his concentration or interfere with his work."

Krennic made his lips a thin line and nodded repeatedly. "Obviously you underestimate your value to him. Which may be for the best." He stood and straightened his tunic. "Nice speaking to you, Lyra. Bye-bye, *Jyn*."

Watching him leave, Lyra put her arm around her daughter and pulled her close.

PART THREE

DEAD RECKONING

23

DERIVATIVES

Efforts had been made by Coruscanti who cared about such things to preserve some of the structures the B'ankora had built and lived in for more than fifty generations. In the rush to relocate the species' sole survivors and complete the construction of the Celestial Power facility, the request to create a museum had been denied. Regardless, some of the B'ankora's original paths remained, winding through gardened parcels, around landscaped areas, and past totemic sculptures and geometric assemblies of wood and stone. Since he rarely ventured outdoors, the paths were new to Galen, and he followed them without really taking notice, his feet and legs merely carrying him along. Neither was he aware of the day's heat, the slight breeze tousling his long unkempt hair, the tiers of horizontal traffic above him, the faint roar of the city-planet. Ten thousand beings might have been observing him from the surrounding monads and arcologies, but he gave them no thought. He moved somnambulantly.

Orson was still celebrating the fact that the power

yield of the altered kyber crystals had been amplified beyond any of his team members' expectations, and in accordance with Galen's calculations and prediction. When, however, Galen had asked for holo-footage of the test results and details regarding construction of the containment devices and storage capacitors, Orson had said that all that was still pending security clearance. Galen's request for information about the subsequent energy applications had met with the same specious, or at least equivocal, response.

At a right-angle bend in one of the pathways was a B'ankora sculpture of their sun symbol, seemingly floating at the summit of a tall column: a large disk from the perimeter of which radiated squiggly arms of various lengths, all of them ending in arrowhead shapes.

Contemplating the amalgam of stone and exotic woods, Galen felt as if he were confronting an exteriorization of his consciousness, and the scattered concerns that were bedeviling him.

Orson should have known better than to leave him to waiting and wanting, his mind restless and ravenous for data. In search of diversion he had turned to the facility's database, which housed exanodes of information regarding Project Celestial Power, including details on personnel, requisitions, credit allocations, even the names of subcontractors. Taking care to cover his tracks, Galen had wormed his way into the transportation hub in an effort to follow up on the mining operations that were under way in remote systems of the Western Reaches, and had been puzzled to discover that while some of the shipments of the unrefined ores could be traced from system to system, the bulk of the mined doonium and dolovite didn't appear to be ending up in any of the program's processing plants, or on any of the worlds on which Orson had maintained energy facilities were being readied. Instead it was as if the rare ores were vanishing into some sort of operational black hole. Which had left him wondering whether the records were being deliberately cooked to hide cost overrides and bureaucratic expenditures, or something more nefarious was occurring.

As he moved away from the sun sculpture, it began to occur to him that Lyra had probably run the very path he was following, and had certainly walked it with Jyn. But in fact any semblance of a shared path between her and Galen had disappeared in the same way the ores seemed to have. Since her recent return from the Central District apartment, Lyra had become as distant as she had accused him of being following the excursion to Malpaz, withdrawn and no longer interested in hearing about the research, even when Galen had tried to engage her; even after long sessions spent transcribing his personal notes, Jyn was caught between the two of them in a gulf her young mind couldn't fathom.

Had Lyra seen through his lie? Had she instinctively diagnosed the illness he had brought on himself, and decided to keep Jyn and herself safe from contagion?

Perhaps there was another B'ankora sculpture somewhere on the facility grounds that could furnish him with a way forward.

* * *

"Zerpen Industries and its moon are now the property of the Empire," Tarkin told the holopresence of Mas Amedda. "The local militias of Salient Two have been able to hold out longer than expected, but the tide has turned and we anticipate a complete victory there as well."

The vizier's delay in responding had nothing to do with the many parsecs that separated Coruscant and Salient. Amedda was turning the news over in his mind.

"Perhaps you should conclude your advance while you're still ahead, Governor Tarkin, since this incursion has already proved costly enough. Furthermore, it is our understanding that those beings who haven't fled deeper into the sector have been destroying the very mining operations and industries you have risked so much to acquire."

Tarkin had expected as much. The Chagrian would like nothing more than to see him withdraw. "Some of us complete what we begin, Vizier."

"A commendable quality, to be sure. But in this instance, we are not convinced that you should have started down this course in the first place."

Tarkin steadied himself for a reply, spreading his legs wider and planting his booted feet firmly on the bridge deck.

"Is everything in order?" Amedda asked before Tarkin could utter a word. "Your transmission is quite disrupted—as if the holocam is being shaken."

Tarkin managed to maintain his balance. "Salient

Strategic Command is still employing countermeasures to jam our communications."

Amedda grunted. "So long as you have the upper hand."

In fact, Tarkin's standard weeks at Salient had constituted some of the fiercest fighting he had engaged in since the Clone Wars, and had already resulted in more casualties than some of his campaigns in the Western Reaches to root out entrenched Separatists.

Outside the ship's viewports local space was crosshatched with destructive hyphens of energy and was strobing with short-lived explosions. Salient's warships were too distant to see with the naked eye, but the screens and holoprojectors on the Star Destroyer's bridge displayed four cruisers unleashing ion and turbolaser fighters against squadrons of ARC-170 starfighters deployed from the older-generation *Venator*-class Star Destroyers that had finally arrived from Telos to reinforce the *Executrix*.

It was true that Salient II had been brought to its knees, but months of combat against guerrilla groups might be necessary before an occupying force of stormtroopers could be garrisoned. Relentless hammering from the Imperial capital ships had ultimately overwhelmed the planet's defensive shields, and once the generators and ground-based planetary turbolasers had been destroyed, the government had sued for a cease-fire to forestall additional civilian deaths. As Amedda had pointed out, the locals had made matters worse for themselves and for Tarkin by obliterating almost everything of industrial, agricultural, or commercial value.

The same had occurred on Epiphany's moon, and there, too, Tarkin had been ill equipped to install an occupying army. Nor could he afford to leave a capital ship at Epiphany to serve as a kind of sentinel. Salient I, the innermost of the system's inhabited worlds, had only a few major population centers, but local militias were known to be gearing up for what Tarkin assumed would be a protracted ground war.

"With Salient Two on the brink, we need additional battalions of stormtroopers," he succeeded in saying without swaying too much as the *Executrix* was harassed by starfighter fire.

Amedda's enormous head was already shaking. "That's impossible, Governor. We simply haven't enough stormtroopers to allocate. Unless, of course, you are suggesting that we send cadets from the academies."

"And why not, Vizier? They need to be field-tested at some point."

Amedda started to stay something but changed his mind and began again. "Are you certain everything is in order? We're having trouble stabilizing your presence."

Tarkin realized that it was pointless to try to remain motionless on the bridge walkway. "The transmission will be better in one of the command pits."

Amedda made a fatigued sound. "Please be quick about it, Governor. I have much to attend to."

Like licking the Emperor's boots clean with your forked tongue, Tarkin thought as he negotiated the stairs leading to the nearest duty station. Once in position he supported himself against the console and wedged his boots beneath it.

"Still unstable, but somewhat improved," Amedda said.

Tarkin took up where he had left off. "An enduring occupation cannot be achieved without sufficient forces. If you can't spare stormtroopers, then send me a wing of TIE fighters."

Amedda lowered his horns in anger. "You ask too much. They are in even shorter supply than effectives."

Tarkin grimaced for the cam. "If I didn't know better, Vizier, I might almost think that you're attempting to undermine my efforts."

Amedda's blue eyes widened. "On the contrary. We are doing our level best to shore up your adventurism."

"Adventurism, is it?"

"Grandstanding, then. The Senate is up in arms."

"The Senate is a fiction, Vizier," Tarkin said with contempt. "The Emperor isn't facing a revolt. What's more, my grandstanding, as you call it, is part of the cost of moving the battle station project toward completion."

"That may be true," Amedda allowed, "but others involved in the project are seeing to their responsibilities without asking for the impossible."

Krennic, Tarkin surmised.

Amedda had become the engineer's champion. Perhaps the two were even in collusion to weaken him. Amedda was certainly unaware of the role Krennic had played in transforming Salient into a battlefield, but saying as much wasn't likely to serve Tarkin's interests.

"You have advocated that the moffs be entrusted with sector control," Amedda was saying, "when it appears that you are incapable of subduing a single star system without Coruscant's help."

Tarkin drew himself up, folding his arms across his chest. "All of Salient will soon belong to the Empire—with or without your help."

Amedda showed his pointed teeth. "I will be certain to reassure His Majesty, the Emperor."

"He doesn't require reassurance from you, Vizier. I'm certain you'll find that I have his complete support. Salient's resources, in whatever state we inherit them, are trivial against the necessity of sending a message to other systems in this sector that autonomy is at the pleasure of the Empire, and that that privilege can be revoked whenever the Emperor sees fit."

Amedda took a long moment to reply. "We concede your point about the importance of an enduring occupation, and will dispense what we can afford."

"Be quick about it, Vizier," Tarkin said. "I have much to attend to."

No sooner did the holopresence of the Chagrian vanish than Tarkin swung away from the cam and hurried back up the staircase to the shuddering forward bridge.

"Battle damage assessment."

"The shields are holding," the ship's commander updated.

While good news was always appreciated, it was clear that the battle in deep space was continuing to test the mettle of both sides. Salient's home group was made up of some twenty capital ships protected by powerful shields developed by Zerpen Industries, which therefore had to be challenged one by one. At the same time, Tarkin was deploying squadrons of starfighters to prevent the smugglers from delivering medical aid, arms, and even volunteer soldiers from neighboring star systems—the same smugglers who by rights should have been locked away in an Imperial prison helping to make the case for the Imperial appropriation of Salient. Each time Tarkin's task force of ships attempted to move closer to Salient I, they were forced to backtrack to put out fires, literal and otherwise, ignited by the resupplied militias.

Like guerrilla fighters themselves, Salient's ships— miscellanies of modules and wartime weaponry— would race in to exchange fire or destroy another wing of starfighters, only to jump to more defended areas of space. Without the requested reinforcements, Tarkin didn't see how he could take Salient I in six standard months, and that wouldn't do—not with Krennic still on the loose.

"Long-distance scanners are tracking a couple of smuggler ships inserting at Salient One," the commander said.

Tarkin turned to the command pit screens. "How is it that they are continuing to avoid our screening blockades and patrols?"

"Salient Strategic Command has to be providing them with hyperspace exit points unknown to our navicomputers."

Tarkin walked forward to the trapezoidal view-

ports to sight down the lancet bow of the *Executrix,*
as if by narrowing his eyes he could discern the rogue
ships. "This isn't a theater for amateurs. Tell me again
who's leading them?"

The commander called up a holo of a Dressellian
male from his datapad. "According to Commander
Krennic's data, it's the same smuggler who laid the
groundwork for us at Samovar and Wadi Raffa. Captain Has Obitt."

Salient's volunteer band of smugglers and mercenaries had maneuvered their freighters and cargo vessels
down into a wide valley that coursed along an enormous tectonic fault line in the western hemisphere of
the innermost world. Escarpments a thousand meters
high made of red and gray stone walled the valley on
both sides, and the broad floor was mottled with
shallow lakes that in the dry season were the gathering places for millions of birds. Farther south the
valley debouched into a vast savanna, interrupted by
stands of dense forest, the grazing grounds for rumi-
nants and other creatures who had that part of Salient I largely to themselves.

Stretches of the western escarpment had collapsed,
resulting in enormous falls of boulders and scree, but-
tressing sheer cliff faces. The gushing waters of a long-
vanished river had over the eons eaten deeply into the
base of the eastern escarpment, hollowing out a tall
and spacious indentation sheltered by an immense
overhang of rock and honeycombed with expansive
caves that ran for kilometers under the soaring wall.

It was on the sandy soil beneath the roof of rock that the smugglers' ships had set down, concealed from patrols of ARC-170s sprung from Imperial ships in deep space. From sectors as distant as the Tingel Arm, the volunteers had brought munitions, medical supplies, foodstuffs, and, in some cases, ragtag mixed-species groups of freedom fighters.

Light was late in arriving to the valley floor, but the air was already warm. A thin layer of mist hung over the shallow lakes, swirling and evanescing in the glow of morning. The cooling engines of the ships pinged, sweat bees bombinated, and the ground swarmed with black-bodied ants every bit as busy as the sentients and doing their best not to be crushed underfoot in the frantic bustle. Laser cannons had been hastily installed in the scree fields, and lookouts equipped with blaster rifles and rocket launchers were posted on the ledges above.

Despite the cargo hold's climate regulator, Has was sweating profusely under his enviro-suit, his puffy face beaded with drops of moisture as he wrestled crates from his ship and lowered them into the waiting arms of locals or droids, or set them atop repulsorlift sleds. Something was off in Salient I's mix of atmospheric gases, and he felt light-headed. Lines of humans and aliens and droids ran from the assortment of ships to the gaping mouths of the caves, in which much of the merchandise would be stashed until needed. Alongside Has was Saw Gerrera, doing the same at his own craft, shouting orders, organizing activities, making everything run smoothly and efficiently.

"You told the Hiitian commander on Salient Two that you'd done this sort of thing before," Has shouted to him between breaths.

Saw nodded and paused to mop his brow. "On my homeworld, during the war."

"Was it as bad as this?" Has asked, lifting his chin.

"Worse, because it was my own people fighting one another. But we had outside help in making things right. My being here is recompense."

"Did it work?"

"Did what work?"

"Defiance. Was that enough?"

"That wasn't the point."

"What was?"

"Believing that your actions mattered, and believing that a good end would come of them, even if you didn't live to see the results."

Has snorted. "Cheery thought. Throw dirt in your enemy's face, get crushed underfoot."

Saw stopped what he was doing and walked over to him. "Look at it this way, Has. If we can persuade enough people to start throwing dirt . . ."

Realizing that he was supposed to finish the thought, Has considered it, then said: "Eventually we bury them."

Saw grinned at him. "And folks say you're just a smuggler."

Has started to return the grin, then stopped. "Wait, what folks?"

Saw was still smiling. "Don't worry, you've made a lasting impression on Woana."

Saw's mention of Wanton Wellspring's captivating

barmaid cheered Has, but only for a moment. Then the reality of their situation rushed back in. What was happening now wasn't the same internecine fight Saw had fought, nor was it similar to what had happened during the Clone Wars. And Gerrera was right. The Empire was quickly becoming *the other,* a featureless gray enemy that species of varied sorts would be able to stave off only if they united, all differences set aside. It was almost heartening to witness the dawning of hope, as cautious and fragile as it was. If the oppressed could coalesce before the Empire's burgeoning military grew too strong or its forces too widespread, then maybe it could be foiled.

Has hauled a smaller, lighter crate to the hatchway and placed it in the arms of a waiting furred and bucktoothed aquatic sentient. The Tynnan hefted it into the arms of a skeletal insectoid, and the Kobok passed it to a bipedal felinoid Trianii, and so on down the line, toward the dark maw of the cave system.

Distant thunder echoed in the canyon, the sound of explosions from starfighter strafing runs. Has accepted that it wasn't a battle any of them could win, but assuming they could keep the Imperials tied up on a dozen fronts, maybe the Empire would ultimately give up the idea of occupying the system.

Was that too much to wish for?

Remembering the discussion with Lyra and Nari in the cave on Alpinn, Has paused and took a long look around him; then he shut his eyes and stretched out in his own way in an effort to experience the sense of transcendence and interconnectedness the two women had described. Feeling hot and sticky, he gave up the effort. Could the Force be felt even in the midst of conflict? Was it even available to one who had strayed as far from the noble path as Has had? Assuming he survived, he would have to contact Lyra at some point and ask her.

Has was shoving the final crate toward the hatch when a blond-haired human approached his ship.

"How do we keep this going, Captain?"

Has left the crate on the edge of the ramp. "He's determined, and Salient's battle group isn't going to be able to stop him. You're set on making this place unlivable, but my guess is that he'll be on the ground before you can bring that about. Unless we can keep delaying him with diversionary attacks. As more and more autonomous systems join the fight, he might think twice about establishing garrisons. We're arranging for you to be able to communicate with militias on Salient Two and on the Epiphany moon."

"We won't abandon the cause," the human said.

"Just remember to keep him guessing; strike, withdraw, and regroup," Saw added from nearby. "When his troops advance, you attack from behind. When he sends his ships to reinforce his troops on the moon, you open up new fronts on Salient Two or here. You need to keep him as off balance as you can, so he can't gain a foothold."

Has realized that where he and Saw should probably be saying *the Imperials* or *them,* they had personified the battle in the figure of the task force admiral, whose name Has had learned was Wilhuff Tarkin. A tall gaunt man, emblematic of the Empire, an outspoken propagandist, a true believer, former governor of his homeworld, close to Palpatine before the war and now one of his moffs. Worse than Krennic, who could say? But probably equally responsible for appropriating the worlds Has had helped manipulate into subjugation.

"You act like this is a personal vendetta," the human was saying. "Smuggler or a freedom fighter, which is it?"

Better to ask: pushover or nobody's fool, thought Has, but kept that to himself. "Started out one, became the other," he said without bothering to specify which came first.

Watching him from a distance, Saw nodded, then turned to the human soldier. "Either way, you have my word I'll be here till it ends."

24

CARDINALITY

A SECRET SEPARATIST DROID FACTORY founded by Techno Union honcho Wat Tambor had become a secret Imperial research station. Less than a hundred kilometers east was a narrow strait of such high salinity that a human could practically walk on the water, but here, more than sixty meters below Hypori's median sea level, the world had been painted fluorescent yellow and orange by the intrusion of magma into a vast lake of salt deposits. Sulfurous outcroppings, subaerial lava vents, and milky-green pools of brine and corrosive acids dotted the hellish hydrothermal landscape, all of it encircled by the jagged black walls of an ancient explosion crater. The hulk of a crashed *Acclamator*-class cruiser stood as a grim memorial to a pitched battle in which a group of Jedi Knights had been taken by surprise. Krennic, who had been privy to much eyes-only intelligence during the past standard decade, had wondered why the Baktoid Armor Workshop factory hadn't been reduced to rubble long before the end of the Clone Wars, or how Mas Amedda or the Emperor had learned of it since. But then each day brought instances of redacted information. It was on Hypori, in any case, that Krennic's engineering team was based; having been assimilated into Project Celestial Power, the focus of their work shifted from shield generation to weapons design and production.

It was also on Hypori that the prototype lasers had been assembled for test-firing, and in the wake of that event Krennic had asked the specialists to design a weapon fifty times the size of the ones they had discharged into the black hole binary known as The Hero Twins. The request had baffled all of them, but each had set him- or herself to the task and all were assembled now to present their findings in a building far from the actual droid factory that overlooked the largest of the putrid pools.

The room itself was not unlike the amphitheater on Coruscant where the Strategic Advisory Cell had met to plan the mobile battle station, except that there was no raised dais on which Krennic could pontificate as Mas Amedda had in those war years, imposing and high-handed, although a holoprojector occupied the center of the chamber, around which everyone stood. All save for Krennic, who had learned from the best— from the grand vizier and the Emperor—that when one was among underlings or those of lesser rank, it was best to sit. Even Tarkin knew as much. Aboard a ship under his command, Tarkin liked to remain on his feet, but anywhere else he would sit. And so Krennic—attired to suit his new rank of full commander in a white tunic with a white capelet, the outfit he would wear on his next visit to the Emperor's court—sat while one after another researcher weighed in on the proposed project. Krennic had yet to hear from Galen regarding further kyber breakthroughs, other than to relay his relief that his calculations had been substantiated and to request additional details about the energy generated by the faceted crystals. Regardless, Krennic had decided that the engineering team had enough data to move forward without Galen's direct input.

He sat with fingertips steepled and one leg crossed over the other while the first specialist spoke to budget; the next addressed the time constraints for completion; and the third dissected the materials that would be needed to produce energy inducers and focusing coils of suitable size. Another took up the thread to analyze what might be needed to fabricate adequate flux dampers, and stressed the importance of doubling the ratio of electrochemical cells that had been engineered into the prototypes.

Krennic's thoughts drifted.

How far he had come from those initial briefings—from sitting in the cheap seats to being close to center stage, the one in charge! All as he anticipated would happen. Now with Galen contributing unknowingly to the successful test-firing, there was just no telling how far he would go once the battle station superlaser was actually assembled. Certainly he would become a staple of the Emperor's court, and in command of a weapon that would give even Darth Vader pause and Tarkin a case of permanent envy.

Rear Admiral Krennic.

It was fated.

Throughout the summaries, he sat still and said very little, until Reeva Demesne took her place in front of the holoprojector to provide a breakdown of the laser weapon itself, concluding her summary with a request to pose an off-topic question.

"Go right ahead," Krennic said, leaning forward in interest.

"Does Kuat Drive Yards or Corellian Engineering have a new vessel under construction—something to succeed the Star Destroyer?"

"That is somewhat off topic, Doctor. Why do you ask?"

The Mirialan glanced at her colleagues as if for emotional support, all but Sahali and a few highly cleared others nodding in encouragement.

"It's obvious to all of us that a superlaser of the sort we're postulating would dwarf any present ship of the line, even the largest of the dreadnoughts. For a weapon fifty times the size of our prototype, the collimator shaft alone would have to be on the order of eight thousand meters in length." She laughed in nervous incredulity. "And that doesn't factor in the dissipaters, capacitors, or even the amplification crystal housing itself."

Krennic shrugged. "We're speculating, after all. But yes. Think of it as a new and improved capital ship."

Demesne's tattooed face furrowed in concern as her mind constructed such a vessel. "Then there is the matter of the crystal itself."

"What about it?" Krennic pressed.

"It would have to be enormous—the size of a small building."

Krennic feigned indifference. "The size is less important than the way the crystal is romanced and faceted."

"Is that Dr. Erso's thinking, Commander?"

Krennic fell silent.

"This is his research, isn't it?" Demesne went on. Again she glanced at her colleagues for support. "No one else could be responsible for this."

Krennic sat straighter in the chair. "Well, now we are wildly off topic, aren't we? Dr. Demesne, you'd do better to bear in mind that we—the entire engineering team—are only a single cog in a very, very large wheel. Dr. Erso can perhaps be thought of as an adjacent cog, but he is merely a theoretician. Of course our separate provinces of research and development occasionally engage, but he is not part of this evaluation."

Demesne started to speak, then paused and began again. "Which brings me to my final question?"

"Question or concern, Doctor?"

"Some of both—but on point rather than off topic, I think." She conjured a schematic of the proposed weapon from the holoprojector. "Given this facility's limitations, we're scarcely equipped to construct anything remotely this size. Are we to continue on here, or are we being transferred to somewhere adequate to execute the actual work?"

"In fact, you will all be moving on," Krennic said, abruptly jovial. "I'm not at liberty to reveal the destination just yet, but I think that it will come as a surprise to all of you. Consider it your just deserts, as it were, for the wonderful work you've done here."

The engineers exchanged looks, some excited, some clearly apprehensive.

"Speaking for everyone, we look forward to it," the chief of the engineering group said. "It can't be less hospitable than Hypori."

Krennic grinned at him. "One person's pleasure is another's displeasure. You'll need to decide for yourselves."

He got to his feet to signal that the meeting was concluded. "Major Weng will be arriving shortly to brief you on the next phase, as well as on the schedule for the coming weeks. If you will all kindly remain here while he makes his way over from the administrative building."

Outside the room waited two of his personal guard, who followed him as he hurried down the corridor.

"Your ship is standing by," the shorter one said when the door to the briefing room had sealed behind them. "Do you want us to accompany you up the well, Commander?"

Krennic waved in dismissal. "I'll go on ahead."

"And the others, sir?" the stormtrooper asked, with an over-the-shoulder motion of his helmeted head toward the briefing room.

Krennic kept walking. "See to it that they're permanently relocated."

How did people convince themselves to act against their nature; to do something entirely out of keeping with who they imagined themselves to be? How did they rationalize lying, betrayal? By claiming situational ethics, or in the belief that they were protecting someone they loved from pain, from hurt? Opening someone's eyes to what wasn't being seen or recognized? If she was trying to explain her actions to Jyn, where would she begin? Where did she need to look to find the words that would make her actions seem at least sensible, if not righteous?

She needed to remove Galen from the equation; erase him as she had so often seen him do to free-floating calculations with a swipe of his hand. What she was doing, she was doing for her own sake, though also for his and for Jyn's. But the need to know, the need to get to the bottom of her concerns was hers alone, and she would be fully accountable for her actions.

She had gone from distrusting Orson to fearing him; from merely disliking him to possibly hating him. He might have succeeded in getting her to stay out of Galen's affairs by simply expressing concern for Galen's work, but the implied threat to her and Jyn had brought everything crashing down. Now she was up on her hind legs, in combat mode.

She had been trying to outrun her disquiet for more than an hour, to sweat it out of herself, lap after lap around the grounds of the darkened facility, but to no avail. Each loop had only firmed her resolve to take action. For weeks she had been walking on egg-shells around Galen, hoping that he would pick up on her estrangement and confront her. Instead he had withdrawn an equal distance, maybe thinking that she was angry at him for not having told her sooner about the visit to Malpaz. Or disappointed. Or simply bored. Since her return from the Outer Rim, the months with Nari and Has, he had grown more absent and preoccupied than ever, putting his work above their marriage, even above bonding with Jyn.

She had no recourse. She wasn't built to hold things in; to be complacent or compliant. To anyone, let alone someone like Orson Krennic.

Committed to learning the truth, she broke out of her lap and jogged into the facility, gradually slowing to a fast walk, panting, sweating copiously, her hands akimbo on her aching sides. The building was quiet except for its ubiquitous, almost preternatural hum, its own rhythmic breathing. Jyn was at last asleep; Galen, who knew where. No one would wonder about her going to the communications suite, since she had made it her habit to do so, to establish a routine. To anyone watching it was nothing more than personal correspondence. Some of Orson's remarks had made her wonder whether she and Galen were under surveillance, or even whether her personal comlink might be bugged. But she didn't care either way. Orson may have drawn the line in the sand, but she would be the one to step over it.

Even so, she hoped that her suspicions proved false; that her concerns were exaggerated. More, that her need for dramatic weather and seismic shifts wasn't brewing a natural catastrophe. Should that end up being the case, then shame on her for being blinded by misgiving.

At the console, she logged in and accessed the facility's database for facilities aligned with Project Celestial Power. The list was thousands of names long, so she tasked the system to find Hypori, which popped on screen, along with a comlink connection. But when she tried to connect to the facility, there was no response, not even an occupied ping. A comp-voiced message stated that the connection was no longer viable or active. Had the facility been closed? First Malpaz, now Hypori? Had Reeva been relocated? She had promised to check in if that happened, but Lyra hadn't heard a word. So she ordered the database to find Reeva.

And it failed.

Reeva was no longer in the system.

Her heart pounding, she thought back to Reeva's concerns about the whereabouts of Dagio Belcoze. And now here was Lyra wondering about the whereabouts of Reeva. Had both of them quit the program?

Or had they been retired, and warned to cease all contact with Celestial Power employees?

She sat back in the swivel chair, chilled to the bone, to think through everything one last time. Then she reached for her personal comlink and entered a call. She didn't like drawing Nari into this, but the two of them were built the same and Nari would understand.

When a small-scale holoimage of her resolved above the link, Nari smiled.

"Hey, I was just thinking of you."

Nari asked about Galen, Jyn, even if Lyra had had any further contact with Has Obitt.

Forcing herself to speak as calmly as she could, Lyra responded succinctly, then came to the point. "Something's come up that I need your help with. Do you still have access to the survey company ship?"

"I'm aboard now," Nari told her. "Does this have something to do with our scouting mission?"

She hadn't told Nari about the conversation with Galen or his secret trip with Krennic, much less about Krennic's threat. "Indirectly. Could you possibly arrange jumps to Malpaz and Hypori?"

Nari frowned. "Possibly. But first you'll have to tell me where Hypori is. I've never even heard of it."

Lyra bent over the console's keypad. "I'm sending the coordinates now."

Nari's gaze moved to something out of cam range, then she spent a moment trying to make sense of what she had received. "Wow. I've never been anywhere near that sector."

"Do you think you can manage it?" Lyra said.

"It could be tricky. There are multiple travel advisories for those hyperlanes. I'll need to come up with an ingenious excuse." She paused, then said: "I can't promise you when I'll be able to make it happen."

"I'm sorry to have to ask."

"Don't be. But can I ask why you need a look at those worlds? Have they been appropriated like Samovar and Wadi Raffa?"

"It might be better if I don't explain."

Nari nodded, serious now. "Then I'll take the necessary safeguards."

25

THE STILL POINT IN
THE TURNING WORLD

ON THE BRIDGE OF THE *Executrix,* Tarkin paced while Salient II burned. With the Star Destroyer parked a hundred thousand kilometers out, the planet turned slowly below, rashed with ruin. Each rotation revealed new areas of fiery devastation, expanding explosions dissipating in the upper atmosphere, the starlit horizon gray and black with cycloning smoke. Tarkin's adjutant updated him from nearby.

"Most of the infrastructure is in ruins: dams destroyed, fusion and fission facilities smoldering, reservoirs poisoned, cities ransacked and on fire."

"I'm surprised they haven't attempted to melt the polar ice caps."

"They may yet. Many even took to smashing everything in their households before fleeing in response to the government's call for *a frenzy of annihilation.*"

Still in motion, Tarkin grunted. "I hope they took their pets."

"Apparently they did, along with herds of animals."

Tarkin came to a halt and laughed. "Indeed? What a wonderful myth it will make for the generations to come. The time Tarkin came to Salient!"

"Your legend grows, sir."

Tarkin sniffed. "And just where are the post-apocalyptic masses bound for?"

"Deeper in-sector. Farther from Imperial systems. Their exodus would be easy to hinder."

Tarkin walked to the forward viewports to gaze at the fleeing convoys of aged transports, yachts, and barely spaceworthy junkers of every variety. "Let them go," he said after a moment. "The smaller the population, the fewer troops we'll need to deploy to enforce an occupation." He swung back to his aide. "And at Epiphany?"

"The situation continues to deteriorate, sir."

The adjutant called up holos of the moon, which showed its surface to be pocked with bombardment craters and many of its life-support domes cracked open like eggs. Raked and ravaged by fire from Imperial capital ships and stung by starfighters, buildings had caved in, and debris clouds were forming in local space.

"Militia sappers managed to infiltrate Zerpen's complex and blow it to pieces," the adjutant added. "The consortium is said to be bringing suit against the Empire."

What price glory? Tarkin asked himself. "Stow that," he said, gesturing to the holo. "What else?"

"On the good-news front, the assault on Salient One has begun."

Tarkin compressed his lips, then flung his words

with abandon. "I don't want Utu's forces wasting their time softening things up. Order the commanders to initiate a ground assault before the locals commence their own frenzy of annihilation."

"Yes, sir."

Tarkin began to pace once more. "Are the militias still being replenished?"

The adjutant nodded. "The smugglers are supported by groups of Hiitians, Tynnans, Koboks, and others from elsewhere in the sector."

Tarkin arched a brow and tugged at his chin. "Throwing in with the losers, are they?"

"Apparently so."

"Well, then, let's accommodate them. Do we have intel on any of the resupply points?"

The adjutant consulted his datapad and summoned a holo of a broad, steep-walled valley dotted with small lakes and parcels of forest. Reconnaissance video taken by Imperial scout ships showed a pair of smuggler craft disappearing beneath a massive overhang of rock.

"So they've found respite under the mountain wall," Tarkin said.

The aide consulted his datapad again. "We have squadrons of starfighters in the vicinity. We could divert one."

Tarkin considered it briefly. "Are any of the Venators within range?"

The adjutant kept his eyes fixed on the pad's display screen. "Admiral Utu's ship is the closest in that hemisphere."

"Then why waste time with strafing runs? Relay

my request that she use her turbolasers to bring the entire cliff down on them." Tarkin grinned faintly. "Though we could say that the smugglers brought it down on themselves."

Sitting hunched on the couch in their residence in the facility, Galen looked up from his notebook in recognition of the fact that he and Jyn were actually occupying the same room—an infrequent event in the wake of renewed tension between him and Lyra. She had her sketch screen in her lap and was working furiously on creating an image of some sort, speaking quietly but animatedly to herself while she worked the controls and drew her forefinger across the screen.

Galen had his own small notebook in hand and was working on an equation he had been struggling with for weeks. Now that he'd found a way to alter the internal structure of the crystals, the kybers seemed in turn to have found a way to alter his. Despite not having heard from Orson, a new sense of urgency had crept into the research, as if someone or something were whispering to him to *hurry, hurry* . . .

Ever since he had transmitted the faceting data to Orson and his team, he'd felt as if he'd been running a low-grade fever, with some part of his mind fixed on solving a calculation that was veiled from consciousness. That it regarded the kybers he had no doubt, but the actual nature of the problem had yet to reveal itself. Plagued nonetheless, he had documented his dreams in the notebook. He had long ago mapped the

landscape of his subconscious and could usually decipher what his dreams were telling him, but his recent
ones seemed to be taking place off the map, set in
unknown regions of his mind. The dream journal ran
for several pages, with many of its entries written in
the middle of the night or immediately following a
nap, and broken here and there by sketches that ram-
bled into calculations, stray thoughts, microscopically
jotted notes he could barely untangle even now.

He raked his hair away from his face with his fingers and turned his attention from the notebook to
watch Jyn, still so completely absorbed in what she
was doing she might have been in a world of her own.
When she finally paused and sat back to evaluate her
drawing, Galen rose from his seat and went over to
her.

"Can I see what you've been working on, Stardust?"

Looking up at him in surprise, she nodded. "It's for
you."

Galen motioned to himself. "For me?"

She nodded again. "It's a picture of Brin trying to
get home."

Brin was the hero of her current favorite bedtime
holo, *The Octave Stairway*. On the screen was her
depiction of the stairway spiraling down through eight
levels to a concave area at the base where Brin received the magic powers that would enable him to
return to his home.

Galen had heard the story so many times he could
recite the passage from memory.

When at last they came to the castle, they walked under the big gate and went inside. In front of them they saw the stairway leading down into the ground. It was the fabled Octave Stairway that Brin and his friends had been searching for. They went to the top stair and looked down. "Eight levels," Brin said. "And on each we need to find a different piece of magic." Deep down at the bottom of the stairway Brin could see the Golden Bowl. Whoever was able to reach the Golden Bowl would have the power to fly straight up through all eight levels of the stairway, and clear through the ceiling of the castle into the sky beyond, all the way home.

Around the drawing of the stairway, adorning the edges of the device's rectangular screen, were strange signs and figures Galen immediately identified as versions of some of the mathematical symbols and talismanic doodles he would often leave about.

He looked closer at the drawing of the long-haired and somewhat disheveled Brin, wondering all at once if it was really meant to represent Brin or if Jyn had actually tried to draw *him*.

"Brin looks a little like me," he said.

She squinted at the drawing. "You can be Brin if you want."

Gazing down at her, Galen felt a sudden warmth well in his chest, and an outpouring of love that was as heartbreaking as it was joyous. He recalled the first time he had looked into her eyes in Lyra's bedroom chamber in the Keep, and how Jyn's flecked eyes had captivated him all over again on the day of his release from Tambolor prison. He thought of the many times she and Lyra had given him the strength to survive the cold lonely hours in his cell; the countless promises he had made to himself to provide them with wonderful and wondrous lives. His perfect daughter . . . How had he allowed himself to so imprison himself in his research that Jyn scarcely knew him any longer? How had he allowed himself to put the kybers first? His work was supposed to have been for them, and yet it seemed now to have been solely for him. All for the rapture of pure *discovery*.

Jyn almost jumped out of her skin when he pulled her into an embrace.

"I love you, Stardust," he whispered, using the heel of his hand to wipe tears from his eye. "I'm sorry for being so busy that I've forgotten to tell you how much you mean to me."

She nodded in his arms. "It's okay, Papa. Can we follow Brin home now?"

Krennic returned from Hypori to the orbital command habitat at Geonosis.

With increased funding, an army of improved labor droids, and advanced alloys arriving from appropriated mining concerns and foundries throughout the Western Reaches, the cladding of the battle station was increasing apace. Work had commenced on the hypermatter reactor and the sublight drives.

Shield projectors were under construction near the northern hemisphere focusing dish, and the orb's equatorial trench was being readied for turbolaser batteries and tractor beam generators. Even the Geonosian slave details had been spurred to accelerate the interior finish work.

The successful test-fire had been impetus for all of it.

At times Krennic could almost forget that he was constructing an exceptional weapon, for it seemed more the case that he was creating a world he would one day govern. A world of his own, replete with a power to rival that of the Emperor and Darth Vader; that of the Imperial Navy itself.

The challenge facing him now was the superlaser. As large as they were, even the orbital foundries at Geonosis were incapable of fabricating collimating shafts eight kilometers long. An appropriate remote site would have to be found; resources would have to be redirected; the results conveyed in secret to the battle station.

Then there were the kybers.

Krennic had expected more from Galen following the test-firing, and he wondered if the scientist's silence had anything to do with Lyra. Then he had learned that Galen—probably spurred by Lyra's suspicions—had been looking into the whereabouts of shipments of ore mined from appropriated worlds.

He had learned, too, that Lyra had tried to contact Reeva Demesne.

Had he erred in cautioning her to keep her nose out of Galen's affairs? People responded in different

ways to threats. Most were cowed, but she hadn't
been. A threat wasn't effective unless one was prepared to carry through with it, and Lyra presented
complications—not out of any fondness he felt for
her but because of what her disappearance would do
to Galen. His research could suffer more harm as a
result of Krennic's action than it might due to her ag-
gravating intrusiveness.

Was Galen to become the prize in a contest between them? Well, hadn't he always been that?

Could he safely assume that Lyra hadn't told Galen
about the implied threats?

The only way to know was to enter the arena and
deal with it. He had an explanation prepared for why
he had spoken to Lyra. He would say that he had
done so out of concern that Lyra's continued harping
might have caused Galen to break his security oath
and thus subject him to arrest by COMPNOR. He
had been trying to protect Galen—and Lyra as well—
but at the same time hadn't been able to reveal the full
truth to her.

Krennic merely had to turn the tables on her.

And if Lyra hadn't told him about the threats; and
if Galen had abided by his oath and avoided any mention of the lies Krennic had fed him about the Emperor's expanded plan . . .

Whatever the case, it was time to pay another call
on the Ersos, and, if necessary, to close the lid on them.

"I've finished transcribing everything," Lyra said as
soon as Galen entered the facility residence. She rose

from the desk near the comm station and met him halfway. "But I think you should take a look at what I've done."

Galen regarded her in confusion. He hadn't asked her to transcribe any notes; nor had she volunteered to do so.

"Just take a look at the early notes," she said, forcing a datapad into his hands that wasn't even the one they normally used.

At the top of the screen, she had written: *Tell me the notes are fine, then ask me to take a walk with you outside.* He had scarcely lifted his eyes from the screen when she said: "I can include more detail once you've had a chance to review everything."

Her eyes urged him to go along with the charade, and so he did. "How about if I review everything later on. Right now I think I could use some fresh air."

She forced a laugh. "You? Since when?"

"Just a quick walk."

"That's always fine with me."

Galen turned slowly and headed for the turbolift, then stopped. "Jyn—"

"She's fast asleep," Lyra said. "It took six bedtime stories, but Mac-Vee is with her now. I tasked him to comm us if she wakes up."

Galen directed a glance toward Jyn's bedroom, then nodded. Engaging in small talk, they took the turbolift to the ground floor, exited the facility through one of the side doors, and began to follow one of the secondary paths that wound through the grounds.

"What's all this about?" Galen asked quietly when they were some distance from the main building.

"I didn't want to risk talking to you inside," she said as they pretended to stroll.

"Risk?"

"I think we're under surveillance, Galen. That maybe we have been from the beginning."

He didn't try to hide his disbelief. "By whom?"

"Orson, for one."

"Why would he spy on us? We have nothing to hide from him."

"That might be true, but I'm convinced he's been hiding things from us." She linked arms with him so that she could snuggle against his shoulder and lower her voice. "I'm worried we're in danger."

"Here?"

"Yes, right here in this deluxe prison Orson engineered for you." She took a steadying breath, then said: "A couple of weeks back your Imperial benefactor paid Jyn and me an unannounced visit at the playground in the Central District. He warned me that I needed to be careful about undermining your work."

Galen whipped his head toward her. "He threatened you?"

"Not in so many words. But he implied that I was going to be held responsible if you failed to live up to the Empire's expectations. He said some things that made me suspect the Empire's been keeping close tabs on us."

Galen wrestled with it. "He couldn't have meant it like that. Not after all he's done for us."

"Oh, he meant it all right. And it gets worse. I

CATALYST: A ROGUE ONE NOVEL   361

think the Empire might be disappearing researchers
working for Celestial Power."

Galen had to force himself to keep moving. "First
it was Imperial ecocide, now it's disappearances?"

"You need to let me finish," she said in a way that
brooked no argument. "You remember I told you
that Reeva had promised to stay in touch with us
from Hypori? Well, her name has been erased from
the personnel database, just like Dagio Belcoze's, and
Hypori is no longer responding to comms. Could the
Empire be keeping researchers locked away to eliminate the possibility of information leaks?"

"That can't be the case. Anarchists are the threat."

"Refuse to believe it if you want, but you said
yourself that security is a huge issue. Look at this
place. Look where we have to have this conversation
out of fear of being overheard."

"*Your* fear of being overheard," he said, though
in a controlled way. "Maybe you're looking for
problems where none exist. Hypori might have been
phased out, and for all we know Reeva left the program."

"I tried to convince myself of that, but I couldn't,
so I asked Nari to go to Malpaz and Hypori and report on what she finds."

Galen fell silent. She kept waiting for him to accuse
her of having lost her mind, take her to task for using
the facility comm, come to the Empire's defense, sing
Orson's praises for having helped them time and again.
Instead, he seemed to be listening without judgment,
his coolheadedness almost worrisome in its own right.

"How soon can we expect to hear from her?" he said at last.

Lyra glanced at him in surprised relief. "She needs to find a way to justify the trips. Would you at least be willing to evaluate whatever data she sends—even if it's just to reassure me?"

"We need to get to the bottom of it," he mumbled in reply.

"The bottom?" She brought them to a halt, so she could turn to him fully. "Galen, after everything we've been through the past couple of months, I . . . I guess I expected you to be resistant to all this. What happened?"

In the light of the distant buildings, his eyes narrowed slightly. "I have suspicions of my own."

26

EXPONENTS

HAS CAME SLOWLY TO CONSCIOUSNESS, his head throbbing and his vision blurred.

"Enjoy your soak?" a male voice asked.

With effort he focused on the tall, gaunt Imperial officer who was standing a few meters away.

"Where am I?" Has asked weakly.

"In the prisoners' medbay of the *Executrix*," the officer said, "currently in stationary orbit above Salient One." The human closed on the foot of Has's cot. "You've spent a week in a bacta tank, and here you are, nearly as good as new."

Has realized that he was in red prisoner's garb, his hands and feet secured in electrocuffs.

His still-bleary eyes went to the blue-and-red rank insignia squares affixed to the officer's gray tunic. "You're Moff Tarkin," he said.

A brief look of surprise tweaked Tarkin's severe features. "I'm encouraged to learn that your brain remains in working order."

"What's left of it," Has managed. "No thanks to you."

Tarkin studied him openly. "Admiral Utu's strike on the valley wall was very precise. Her turbolasers stitched a line of destructive energy along the eastern escapement that brought the roof down on all of you who had been sheltering beneath it. Initially I wasn't concerned with possible survivors, but in the interest of seeing what we caught I ordered Utu's rummager droids to have a look around. You were discovered in a cavity that had formed in the rubble and carried out to the valley floor, where of course you were promptly airlifted and taken into custody."

Has had no memory of any of it. "Why did you bother going to so much cost?" he asked, motioning with his chin to the bacta treatment ward.

"In the interest of speaking with you before you begin what will undoubtedly be a lengthy prison term."

Has was too weak to care. "In that case, prepare yourself for a one-sided conversation."

Tarkin shrugged. "Noted. But let's see how we do. I'm curious to know if the actions you took at Salient—for all they accomplished—were at the behest of Commander Krennic."

Has regarded the moff for a long moment, wondering just how much he knew.

"Sudden amnesia?" Tarkin asked.

"Weighing my options," Has said carefully.

"That suggests to me that you may still be under Krennic's orders."

"I'm not under anyone's orders."

Tarkin frowned. "All those back-and-forth supply runs undertaken selflessly? For a system that now belongs to the Empire?"

"Good luck with your detoxification and reseeding efforts."

Tarkin allowed a grin. "If nothing else, Salient will serve as a jumping-off point for further strikes into the sector."

Has felt his strength returning. "The Empire won't stop until it reaches the edge of the galaxy, is that it?"

"Why stop there?" Tarkin asked. He paced away from the cot, then turned. "The rest of your little band of mercenaries managed to escape, but we'll eventually root them out."

"Don't be too sure. They're very good at what they do."

Tarkin's smile straightened. "Assuming you're being honest regarding Commander Krennic, I'd be interested to know what swayed you to join the other side after what you helped bring about at Samovar and Wadi."

Has winced. So Krennic and Tarkin had been in league from the start. "What difference does it make?"

"Did Commander Krennic betray you? Or is it that you fell out of favor with him?"

Has's laugh became a harsh cough. "There's a way of looking at it where he's responsible for my change of heart," he said when he could. "But since you're so curious, what changed me was a trip I took with a couple of human women."

Tarkin came to a full stop a meter from the foot of the cot. "Now I am intrigued. These two women somehow helped open your eyes, your heart, what part of you?"

Has decided not to deny it. "To the effect the Empire's actions are having on the lives of people who still care."

Disappointment pulled down the corners of Tarkin's mouth. "Please, Captain. Let's try to refrain from naïveté. Where did you and your human companions venture on this life-altering voyage?"

Has began to wonder if Tarkin had drugged him with truth serum. Even if not, there was a chance, however slim, that honest answers could buy him leniency. "We started at Alpinn."

"I'm familiar with Alpinn."

Has wasn't surprised; Tarkin seemed to have a handle on everything. "The women did some surveying and mapping. They expressed an interest in visiting a few Legacy worlds, so I took them to Samovar and Wadi Raffa."

"Took them to see what you had done, you mean." Tarkin grinned. "How self-cleansing that must have been for you!"

"Their reactions forced me to take a hard look at myself."

Tarkin gazed at him. "I honestly don't know whether to laugh or shed a tear. Here I've been thinking of you as a talented smuggler and able mercenary, and now I learn that you're more a sentimental chaperone."

Has tried to prop himself higher on the cot. "The chaperoning was Commander Krennic's idea."

Tarkin's brows quirked in renewed interest. "Whatever for?"

Has gave up on struggling against the cuffs. "The idea was to make sure they didn't get into any trouble. One of them is the wife of an important scientist, and I had history with the family."

"What scientist?" Tarkin said, hardening his gaze.

"His name is Galen Erso."

Tarkin's eyes widened in genuine revelation, and he brought his fingers to his chin. "The energy specialist."

Has didn't answer immediately. Had he lucked onto finding common ground with the moff? "You know him?" he asked finally.

"What history do you have with the Ersos?"

"I assisted in rescuing them from Vallt during the war. That's when I first met Commander Krennic. I didn't know that Erso was still involved with Krennic, because it seemed to me at the time that Erso wanted no part of anything military."

Tarkin didn't bother to mask his surprise. "Galen Erso is working with Commander Krennic?"

"Lyra—his wife—said so."

Tarkin blinked. "So it's *Erso* who's responsible for that new set of rank squares on his tunic," he said, mostly to himself.

Has instantly regretted his disclosures. Had he put Lyra and Jyn in danger by shooting off his mouth? Whatever the source of the obvious rivalry between the two Imperials, Galen Erso seemed to be a part of it.

Tarkin was grinning at him.

"You and I have both been played by a rather brilliant strategist. Commander Krennic reconnected you with Lyra Erso to spur your treachery at Salient, and your treachery here has drawn me into Krennic's duplicity."

Has's thoughts raced. Was there some way to warn Lyra? Tarkin was regarding him once more, clearly in the midst of doing some strategizing of his own.

"You've caused me a good deal of trouble, Captain," the moff said at long last, "but I'm going to give you a chance to redeem yourself."

In Jyn's room, which Galen had swept for listening devices, he sat in concentrated silence at the compact computers and holoprojectors he had relocated from elsewhere in the facility.

Lyra paced nervously behind, waiting for him to deliver a verdict. A standard week had passed since their hushed conversation on the footpaths, and Nari's holodata reports regarding Malpaz and Hypori had arrived only standard hours earlier. In Lyra's brief conversation with her friend, Nari had said that Hypori was as far a jump as she had ever taken, and not a world she was eager to revisit, using the words *vile* and *corrupt* to describe what she had seen. But Nari hadn't speculated on any of the images or readings recorded by the survey ship's sensors, and Lyra hadn't asked. Nari was already too deeply involved in what might be construed as a conspiracy or espionage, and Lyra didn't want to provide her and Galen's unseen watchers with more ammunition than they already had.

"Hypori wasn't phased out," Galen said finally. "It was destroyed."

"Anarchists," Lyra started to say when he cut her off.

"Not by anarchists or Separatist holdouts, but by Imperial Star Destroyer–grade turbolasers." Galen turned away from the humming, chirping devices to look at her. "It's more accurate to say that the installation was *scoured*."

Lyra had come to a standstill and was regarding him in astonishment. "But we know it was a Celestial Power facility."

Galen's nod confirmed it. "There's no doubt about that."

"Then why would the Empire destroy one of its own installations? Was there some sort of contaminant leak?"

Galen motioned to the bank of instruments. "There's no evidence of that."

"Maybe to keep the place from falling into the hands of insurgents."

Galen nodded again. "It's a pleasant fantasy." He gestured to a holo running above one of the holoprojectors. "Hypori hosts a former Baktoid Armor droid factory that might date to ten or maybe as many as thirty standard years before the war. That facility is still more or less intact, possibly even operational, but everything around it—including a couple of newer, retrofitted structures—was laid to waste."

"Can you tell when it happened?"

"Recently—so recently the area is still hot. I'd guess within a couple of standard weeks. Not more than a month." Galen fell briefly silent.

Lyra recalled the Star Destroyer she had observed

at Samovar, bringing its turbolasers to bear on vast areas of pristine forest. "Malpaz also?" she asked hesitantly.

Galen's expression went from disconsolate to angry. "Malpaz's destruction is owed at least in part to kyber crystal diffraction."

She gaped at him. "But you told me—"

"I know what I told you. The same thing that Orson told me: that anarchists were responsible. But it was all a lie." He gritted his teeth. "They've been attempting to weaponize my research."

"Galen," she said, as if all the air had gone out of her.

He swung back to the screens and holoprojectors. "Neither Malpaz nor Hypori was an energy facility. They were weapons research sites. The comps have been able to recognize what were once the collimator shafts of immense lasers, focusing coils, and energy inducers." He shook his head back and forth. "But it's all beginning to make sense now. The vanishing shipments of dolovite and doonium, Orson's delay in furnishing me with data on the energy experiments— the test-fires, for all I know—perhaps even his mention during the war of the unique military installation he was working on." He shut his eyes and blew out his breath. "I've been a fool, Lyra."

Equally distraught, she rested her hand on his shoulder. "You couldn't have known. *We* couldn't have known."

He shot her a look. "No? If I hadn't been so blind . . ."

"Is it possible that even Orson isn't aware of some of this? Or is that wishing for too much?"

Galen stood and strode away from the devices. "He's coming here," he said with sudden force, pivoting to face her. "He made it sound like just another social call, but I think he wants to check on us. If you're right about surveillance, then he knows that both of us have been trying to get to the truth."

She took her lower lip between her teeth. "What can we do?"

He thought about it, then said: "We can allay his suspicions."

"How?"

"I think we can safely admit to having some concerns, but we don't theorize about disappearances. We underplay everything." Galen narrowed his eyes at her. "Can you do that?"

Lyra firmed her lips. The destruction visited on Malpaz and Hypori didn't explain the disappearances of Dagio and Reeva. Was that Galen's ultimate fate? Was it theirs?

"I'll certainly try," she told him.

27

END OF PROOF

KRENNIC ARRIVED LATE AND WITHOUT any bottles of vintage wine, but in the company of two stormtroopers who remained at the facility landing zone with the airspeeder. On seeing him, Jyn refused to leave her room, so Lyra left her in the care of Mac-Vee. She might not have been able to articulate her reasons for disliking Krennic, but her wariness was plain as day.

"All-Species Week has made the traffic even worse than normal," he said by way of explanation and apology once the three of them were seated in the residence's upper-story sitting room, Coruscant's cityscape sparkling outside the tall windows. "I only hope I haven't ruined the evening entirely."

"No problem, Orson," Galen said. "We appreciate your visiting."

Krennic lifted an eyebrow and dumped the friendly tone. "Do you? As busy as both of you have been?"

Galen forced a smile. "The research and Jyn keep us on our feet."

"Yes, how is the child?" Krennic asked, all but sneering. "Into everything, I'll bet."

Lyra spoke to it. "She's very inquisitive."

Krennic smiled without showing his teeth. "So like her parents."

"I'm thinking about taking her to visit my mother on Aria Prime," Lyra went on.

Krennic looked at her. "Indeed. Well, be sure to let me know if you require any assistance in arranging travel. Even though the space lanes are essentially safe, one should take care where one ventures."

The subtext wasn't lost on her. "With anarchists and all," she said. "I tried to convince Galen to come along, but he won't leave his work."

Krennic nodded gravely in Galen's direction. "The Empire values dedication. Especially when it's unswerving." His gaze returned to Lyra. "Still, it's important to make time for family and friends."

She kept her response neutral. "Where would any of us be without friendship."

"Speaking of which," Krennic said, "were you ever successful in contacting Reeva Demesne? I recall your asking after her, Galen, and I haven't been able to track her down."

"It's the strangest thing," Lyra answered for him, "but she's nowhere to be found."

Krennic appeared to ponder it. "I wonder if she left or was dismissed from the program."

"Dagio Belcoze, then Reeva," Galen interjected. "I guess research isn't for everyone."

"Certainly not for the faint of heart or the unfaithful," Krennic told him. "If memory serves, Reeva was on Hypori last."

"That's where she was when she commed us,"

Lyra said, unable to stop herself. "What sort of facility does Celestial Power have there?"

Krennic glowered at her. "At the moment, none. An industrial accident required that it be shut down."

Lyra feigned surprise. "That's terrible."

"Quite," Krennic said. "The Empire had a lot invested in the place."

Lyra locked eyes with him. "Any luck in identifying the ones responsible for destroying Malpaz?"

"Not yet. Why do you ask?"

"Curiosity."

"Hardly an appropriate justification for discussing matters of Imperial security."

"I know what I risk by asking," Lyra said before Galen could cut her off.

Sudden color mottled Krennic's face. "I'm finding that harder and harder to believe."

"I'm just wondering if we're in any danger," Lyra said.

"You personally?"

"As employees of Celestial Power, I mean."

Krennic put his elbows on his knees and leaned forward. "Are you actually frightened, Lyra, or is this another ploy to undermine the work Galen is doing?"

"She's not trying to undermine anything, Orson," Galen said. "She's simply concerned."

Krennic kept his eyes on Lyra. "As what—a mother, a wife, or a troublemaker?"

"Orson—" Galen started to say.

"I'm sorry, but we're not playing some parlor game tonight. I arranged for the expedition to Alpinn because I wanted Lyra to feel included in the program. But instead of confining herself to the assignment, what do she and her friend do but jump around the Western Reaches visiting worlds the Empire is mining for resources critical to Celestial Power. And now she's worried about anarchists." He riveted his eyes on her. "Lyra Erso, galactic detective. You should know better." He glanced at Galen. "Both of you should know better."

"Just assure us that Dagio and Reeva are safe," Galen said.

Krennic touched his chest. "Are you implying that I had some hand in removing them from the program?"

"Of course not," Lyra said, "but Reeva wouldn't simply leave without telling us."

Krennic firmed his lips. "I honestly can't say where she is."

"Can't say or don't know?" Lyra pressed.

"Enough of this," Galen said in a rush. "Lyra, Orson isn't obliged to breach his security oath just because we have questions." He looked at Krennic. "Still, you can't blame us for having concerns."

"Perhaps if I was convinced it was mere concern," Krennic said.

Galen shook his head. "I don't understand."

"Don't you see what Lyra's really trying to do? She's using these alleged concerns to persuade you to abandon your research. Her goal is to keep you to herself—to stand in the way of your legacy."

"Legacy?" Lyra repeated in genuine bafflement.

"Orson, please," Galen said, completely unnerved.

"We only want to be reassured that we're not being lied to and that we're not in any danger."

Instead of responding to Galen, Krennic addressed Lyra. "You have no idea what you're fooling with. This is much bigger than me. This is much bigger than all three of us. I warned you not to go down this path."

"Then I guess another warning is in order, Orson," Galen said.

Krennic was taken off his guard, but not for long. "So you confided in him that we had a chat."

Lyra shrugged. "I told you that we don't keep things from each other."

Back on track, Krennic nodded. "Precisely the reason I approached you." His gaze shifted to Galen. "I knew that Lyra had reservations about your research with kybers, and I was worried that her concerns might prompt you to compromise your security oath as a means of justifying your work. I couldn't abide the thought of you ending up in prison—again—so I cautioned her that prying could lead to questions regarding her loyalty. But I did so only for her own sake."

"You should have come to me," Galen said, sounding more dejected than angry.

"You have my deepest apologies," Krennic said in a calmer voice. "I sensed that you were nearing a breakthrough, and I was merely trying to keep you from being distracted." He paused for a long moment, then added: "I was wrong to interfere. And had I known you were setting a trap for me, I certainly would have postponed this visit."

Galen rose to prevent Krennic from standing. "This wasn't meant to be a trap, and I understand why you took the actions you did. We needed to have this talk to clear the air." He turned to Lyra. "Can we be done with this now? I'm sure that Orson was only doing what he felt was right."

Krennic relaxed somewhat. "Thank you for your trust, Galen. I give you my word that I'll put all your concerns to rest."

Lyra allowed a nod. "I feel so much better," she said straight-faced.

Traffic was crawling, almost at a standstill, even in the sky lanes reserved for authorized vehicles. Fireworks displays erupted overhead and lasers crisscrossed on the sides of buildings. Blaring, grating sounds issued from vehicle horns and wind instruments, and songs in two dozen tongues competed with one another. Glittering metallic confetti rained down from rooftops and balconies, and beings danced with abandon wherever they could find space.

Krennic brooded in the backseat of the open military speeder, his two stormtroopers up front, while from all sides came celebratory hoots and hollers from Twi'leks, Gran, Rodians, Ishi Tib, even some humans. The cacophony of nighttime Coruscant at the climax of All-Species Week mirrored his internal chaos: angry one moment, betrayed the next, concerned, cornered, vindictive.

The evening hadn't gone as planned.

Galen had diffused the situation before it had

turned too ugly or explosive, but the damage had been done, and Krennic could only hope that it wasn't irreparable. Lyra had truly outdone herself, gone from being merely annoying to potentially dangerous in one fell swoop. Despite that, she could be handled. Her suspicions would never see the light of day, and if Krennic had his way neither would she. Her allegations could be turned against her, and COMPNOR would take care of the rest. But what of Galen? Even if he could find it in himself not to hold Krennic accountable, would he be willing to continue his work? Would he be capable of finishing what he had started, and one day be brought into the battle station project?

Galen's departure from the project would be on his watch. COMPNOR's intelligence chiefs would say that he should have been keeping closer tabs on Galen and Lyra. He would be reprimanded for having sent Lyra to Alpinn; for not having reported on her activities at Samovar and Wadi Raffa; for failing to have restricted her access to the Celestial Power database. Even in the face of support from Vizier Amedda and other powerful Imperial players, he might be stripped of his rank and ostracized.

He closed his eyes and refused to consider the implications.

There had to be a way forward. He wondered how far he was willing to go to resolve matters. Could Lyra and Jyn be quietly removed? Could Galen be relocated? What if an accident of some sort occurred? What if—

He shook his head as if to clear such thoughts from

his mind. As he did, the stormtrooper in the front passenger seat turned to him.

"Commander, incoming from Governor Tarkin."

Krennic hid his consternation. Of all the times for *Tarkin* to contact him; Tarkin, who would be the first to gloat if Krennic went down.

"Governor Tarkin," he said toward the backseat microphone, forcing himself to sound relaxed, even cheery. "What a surprise to hear from you. I only just learned of your victory at Salient."

"Hard fought but accomplished, Commander. You're on Coruscant, I see."

"And mired in traffic. The culmination of All-Species Week."

"Unfortunate. But I'm glad to find you there, as something of interest has come to our attention."

Krennic adjusted his posture in the pleated bench seat. "Something I can help with?"

"We hope so. It concerns your Dressellian operative, Has Obitt."

Krennic uttered a short laugh. "Hardly an operative, Governor. More a dummy. And a traitor, I understand. I would be relieved to learn that he and his fellow smugglers have been eliminated or placed in custody."

"We thought we had him cornered," Tarkin said. "But he managed to commandeer a small ship and escape."

Krennic took a moment to appreciate the fact that reversals weren't exclusive to him. "I never would have thought him clever enough to outwit you, Governor. But I'm certain he'll turn up in one haunt or another. His kind always do."

"Then you're done with him?"

Krennic frowned. "Of course I am. What would lead you to think otherwise?"

Tarkin was quiet for a moment. "We intercepted an Imperial-frequency message transmitted from the stolen ship. We haven't been able to identify the person or persons at the destination end, but it seems that Obitt is en route to Coruscant."

"He's coming here?"

"We wondered whether he was still in your service as a double-agent and might be meeting with you to receive new orders."

"With me?" Krennic's irritation was genuine. "After what he pulled at Salient I want no part of him."

"Have it your way, Commander. The transmission was garbled, but we were able to deduce that he is arranging to meet with unknown parties at some pre-assigned location."

"I'm afraid I'm drawing a blank, Governor. But I will do what I can to locate him."

Krennic sat in silence with the information, his thoughts loud enough to drown out the raucous partying in nearby vehicles. On the run from Tarkin, Obitt was racing to a prearranged location on Coruscant. Either he was desperate to connect with cohorts or—

A sinister feeling took hold of him.

Could Lyra have reached out to the Dressellian for help? Had Galen and Lyra tricked him? Had the evening been set up simply to satisfy their curiosity, when in fact they had already made up their minds to bolt?

Krennic rubbed one hand across his mouth while the other went to the comm; then he reconsidered. Ordering the facility into lockdown might tip them off. Plus, if he was rushing to judgment, a lockdown would only give Lyra another reason to distrust him. A better course would be to show up unannounced. He would say that in thinking through the conversation he realized that he hadn't explained himself adequately. He could apologize again; state that he couldn't leave things the way they were. In the interest of saving their relationship he would even be willing to violate his security oath . . .

That just might do it.

He tapped the stormtrooper pilot on the shoulder. "Get us out of this jam. We're returning to the facility."

"They've gone," Lyra said as she watched Orson's airspeeder lift off from the facility landing zone and insert into one of the crowded traffic lanes.

Galen was sitting on the couch, his head in his hands. "All he did was counterattack and talk around everything we brought up. Instead of denying everything, he deflected. Even when he claimed not to know where Reeva and Dagio are." He looked up at Lyra. "He's complicit, if not responsible."

"I'm sorry, Galen," she told him. "I know how much this facility means to you. But at least we're closer to learning the truth."

He shook his head. "There is no one truth. We're both right; we're both wrong. There are truths and falsehoods on both sides. It's irrelevant whether he had any part in what happened to our friends or to the facilities. We're never going to learn the full story. There's simply too much at stake—" Galen stopped mid-sentence, then added: "What matters is that I can't do this anymore."

"What choice do we have?" Lyra asked carefully.

"There comes a point where an oath's not justification enough for silence." Galen shot to his feet and stormed away from her.

"Galen," she said, following him.

He came to a stop, but kept his back to her. "I'm the one who provided them with what they needed to weaponize the research. I played into their hands."

"You? When?"

"After Malpaz. After I bought into Orson's lie about anarchists and the Emperor's dreams for sustainable energy. I agreed to go deeper into the research than I knew was advisable. I trusted Orson when he said that his teams were working on ways to contain the power yield, when in fact they were merely working on ways to *channel* it into a delivery system. To harness the full force of the kybers' destructive power for use as a weapon." He raked his hair back from his face. "The Jedi were right."

Lyra felt the blood drain from her face. "Star Destroyers and dreadnoughts aren't enough for the Empire?"

"Who knows what order of weapon they're working on, or who they're planning to target. Krennic said that the Emperor wants to make an example of one world. Maybe that wasn't entirely a lie."

Lyra forced a weary exhale. "It must have been some sales pitch, Galen, for you to betray your own sense of caution and respect for the crystals."

He turned to face her. "I had myself convinced that I was doing it for you and Jyn and to safeguard future generations. Instead I failed as a husband, a father, and a scientist." He snorted in a sad way, then said: "I can't do anything about being a failed scientist, but I can correct the rest—if it's not too late."

She smiled in encouragement. "Don't be an idiot. I didn't fall in love with your research, Galen. I fell in love with *you*."

He took her into his embrace and held her tightly, saying into her ear: "I love you and Jyn. You're all that matter to me."

He's back, she thought, resting her head against his chest. "I know I made matters worse with Orson. We may be in more danger than before."

"That's why we're leaving."

She pulled away to regard him.

"We need to go now while it's the last thing Orson would expect us to do," Galen said. "I refuse to live my life under terms dictated by the Empire."

She swallowed hard and looked into his eyes. "I wasn't going to say anything until you'd made up your mind."

He let his puzzlement show. "Say anything about what?"

"We may have a way out."

Galen waited for the rest.

"A friend contacted me. It seems I'm not the only one who's worried about our safety."

"You trust him?"

"Completely."

"He contacted you here? Through the facility comm?"

"Through my personal comlink."

"Then we have to work fast to arrange things," Galen said. "Where is it?"

Prizing the comlink from her pant pocket, she handed it to him, and he went immediately to the facility console, where he began inputting data.

Lyra came to his side to watch him. "Galen, Orson will know if you delete or alter anything."

He nodded while he entered commands. "That's the idea."

Even screeching sirens and threats of physical violence weren't enough to speed their return to the facility. On the landing pad, Krennic ordered the stormtroopers to seal the exits and hurried into the darkened building. Despite the late hour, researchers and droids were still about as he made his way to the turbolifts that accessed the residential area, and from those he went directly to the Ersos' apartment. His explanations and apologies rehearsed and committed to memory, he straightened his shoulders and tunic and signaled the security cam to announce him. A long moment passed before the door slid aside and a humaniform MV droid appeared in the doorway.

"Are the Ersos still awake?" he said.

"They may well be, sir," the droid told him.

Krennic stepped into the suite. "Tell Galen that I'm here."

"I am unable to, sir, as I am unaware of Galen's current whereabouts."

"And Lyra?"

"None of the Ersos are here, sir."

Krennic activated his wrist comm. "Check with security to see if anyone has left the facility in the past three hours," he said when one of the stormtroopers answered. "If no one has left, then conduct a search of the grounds."

He shoved past the droid and began a search of his own. The two bedrooms were empty, but the closets and drawers were filled with clothing and nothing looked disturbed except Jyn's bed. He returned to the main room and hurried to the communications board. The console had just acknowledged his clearance when his wrist comm chimed.

"The Ersos left the grounds two hours ago, Commander, by way of the front gate," the stormtrooper said. "They told the guards that they were going out to join in the celebration."

"With a child, at this hour?" Krennic grated.

"It's what they told the guards, sir."

"Widen your search. Download their images into your comlink and get the local authorities involved. I don't want them apprehended. Just monitor them and await further orders from me."

"Yes, sir."

Krennic was trying to keep from fearing the worst, but his instincts told him that Galen was in flight. Quickly he read through the comm station's message

queue for the previous two standard weeks. The
queue listed Orson's calls to Galen, and multiple calls
placed by Lyra: to her mother, to her friend Nari, to
other friends, to Hypori—

Krennic ground his teeth in anger. Then his gaze
alighted on a text that had been received a day earlier
from an unknown sender. Recalled to a screen, it
read: *If you're at all interested in embarking on another tour, I'm at your disposal. If you wish, it can
be a family outing this time.*

The log showed that additional messages had been
exchanged, but they had been purged from the system—
which only Galen had the clearance to do.

Krennic whirled away from the console and went
to the living room, his eyes moving from the couch to
the chairs in a replay of the evening's conversation, all
three of them in a time warp of his imagining. Then
he thought about Has Obitt and the preassigned location he was bound for.

He ran through the possibilities. Had Galen and
his family left from the local spaceport? Had they
hired a private speeder? No sky-cab would have been
allowed to land on the grounds or the rooftop landing zones; it would have to have been waiting outside
the entrance. All the while he had been bogged down
in traffic, the Ersos had been crawling toward the
Central District to meet with Obitt.

Again he activated his wrist comm.

"The facility is to be placed on full lockdown: no
one in or out, and no one is allowed access to any
internal or external communications or databases.
Alert COMPNOR that we're going to need a team of

expert slicers to extract everything we can from the research computers."

"Will we be remaining onsite, Commander?"

"Negative," Krennic told the stormtrooper. "We're heading soonest to the Central District spaceport—in low orbit if we have to. And order the rest of the squad to meet us there."

Galen couldn't recall a time when he had seen more people on the walkways, the rooftops, the balconies and terraces, everyone celebrating without restraint. Lyra had Jyn in her arms, the poor kid still in pajamas and struggling to remain asleep, despite the welter of tongues, the fireworks and general revelry.

Caught up in the sweep of the crowd, he said: "I guess there's no fighting it."

"That's Coruscant for you."

"We'll never get there on time."

"On time only means getting there without being caught," Lyra said. "Otherwise he'll wait for us. That's the plan."

"Just how long have you been working on this?"

"Since yesterday."

"How could you be sure it wasn't a trap? Something Orson set for you."

"I wasn't sure at first. But he convinced me everything was on the level."

"You told me what you and Jyn had to go through when you left for Alpinn. Getting off Coruscant isn't going to be like walking out of the facility. We might be on a no-fly list. We don't even have travel permits."

"I was told not to worry, and that everything would be arranged—even at a moment's notice. This isn't going to be Vallt all over again."

Galen absorbed her words as the crowd moved them along. "The bigger mystery is how you knew I'd be willing to go along with it."

"I hoped our conversation with Orson would convince you to leave. If that failed, then I was going to try to talk you into it." She paused, then asked: "Do you think he'll find the message?"

"It's Orson. Of course he will."

"And the ones you altered?"

"Some of them. He'll bring in forensic specialists to help."

"And the kyber research?"

Galen tapped the side of his head. "That's in here. And here," he added, tapping the notebook in the pouch pocket of his trousers.

"You could have at least made him work to get the current data."

"He's welcome to whatever he finds. I could have sabotaged everything, but I don't want to give the Empire a reason to hunt us down. We're simply dropping out—although covertly. Besides, what I left will keep them occupied for a while."

"Revenge was never your style."

Galen considered it. "Orson may have worked me, but he didn't force me."

They continued to edge through the crowds, Galen employing a program on his comlink to alert them to police activity and fixed and mobile facial-recognition cams.

"Will they have enough data to build a super-weapon?"

Galen shook his head. "Not without me."

"You realize that he's never going to stop looking for you, Galen. You're in his blood, crystal research or no. He's never going to let go of you entirely."

Galen took a long moment to digest that. "Then we'll have to travel far," he started to say before coming to a sudden halt and frowning at the comlink's screen. "The program has crashed."

"Crashed or—"

She cut herself off on seeing her and Galen's faces resolve ten times larger than life on a nearby building's newsfeed screen.

Gazing around to get her bearings, she said: "We need to go down three levels, turn right, then left, and turbo up to Republic Plaza. It'll be easier to mix in there."

"You've been mapping the territory?" Galen asked as he followed on her heels.

Lyra hefted Jyn in her arms. "Long walks were the only way I could get her to sleep."

Galen kissed Jyn on the forehead. "Don't ever change, Stardust."

The last thing they saw before disappearing into the turbolift was a police speeder spiraling down out of the busy night sky to set down fifty meters away.

Cleared for landing on Coruscant, Has, flying solo, maneuvered the ship toward a hangar on the outskirts of the Central District spaceport. Traffic was heavy in every direction at every elevation, but the Zerpen-built craft, outfitted with a superb hyperdrive and military-grade deflector shields, was more agile than the one Imperial forces had buried under metric tons of rock on Salient I. As he drew closer to the hangar from which he, Lyra, Jyn, and Nari had embarked for Alpinn so many standard months earlier, he asked himself why, on leaving Salient, he hadn't simply jumped to the farthest reaches of Tingel Arm instead of returning to the Core. He wanted to believe that the answer had something to do with being true to his word, but it was more a case of being caught between Tarkin and Krennic. Betraying one or the other could lead to imprisonment or worse, so his options were limited indeed.

Tarkin's terms of redemption called for Has to talk his way back into Krennic's good graces and serve as Tarkin's inside man and listening device, rightly assuming that Has wouldn't risk double-crossing the moff by lighting out for the Rim. Has, though, had persuaded him to send a message that would make his return to Coruscant appear credible. That much accomplished, he had jumped the Zerpen ship directly for the Core, putting other plans into play while en route.

Trusting the ship to autopilot, he relaxed into the pilot's seat, working the kinks out of his shoulders and running through the next few moves. Thanks to the time he had spent in the bacta tank, he was back to feeling healthy and strong, but he was going to need to be sharper than usual to succeed. Krennic wasn't just astute; he could see around corners, and there was no telling how he would react to seeing his own stooge again.

The ship eased through the hangar's open-irised roof and settled on its landing gear. He waited for the systems to shut down before shrugging out of the harness, then left the cockpit for the boarding ramp, which was already lowering.

His boots had just hit the hangar's concrete floor when Krennic appeared from around the stern of the ship, backed by a squad of stormtroopers with BlasTechs raised. Has let his jaw drop as the Imperial officer approached.

"Clearly you're surprised to see me, Captain."

"You have that right, Commander," Has managed.

"Not the passengers you were expecting."

Has tilted his head in question. "Passengers? I wasn't expecting anyone to be waiting. How in the world did you know I was coming?"

"Governor Tarkin intercepted your transmission."

Has cursed under his breath. "And here I thought I'd made a clean getaway."

"Of all beings, Obitt, you should know that there's no escaping the long arm of the Empire."

"You're right, Commander. But I'm awfully glad to see you just the same."

Krennic mimicked Has's earlier head tilt, signaled for his cadre of troopers to lower their weapons, and took a few steps toward the ship's ramp. "Admit that you've come here to assist the Ersos in leaving."

"The Ersos?"

"I know that you've been communicating with Lyra."

"Lyra? I haven't exchanged a word with her since the expedition. Why would I?"

"You're denying that you offered her assistance?"

Has shook his head in bafflement. "I wouldn't know how to find her even if I wanted to."

Krennic scrutinized him. "Then why are you here?"

"To see *you*, Commander." When Krennic didn't respond, he added: "I'm in desperate straits. I need your protection."

Krennic continued to regard him. "You dare come to me after your betrayal at Salient?"

"But I didn't betray you," Has said in a rush. "None of us did. Zerpen refused to allow us to set down on the Epiphany moon and dispatched some of their fighters to scuttle us. Then Tarkin showed up and sicced his starfighters on us as well. We spent the whole of his campaign at Salient being chased all over the system, from moon to planet and back again. In the end he nearly caught up with me, but I managed to seize this ship and escape."

Krennic tried to digest it. "Who was on the receiving end of your transmission about coming here?"

"One of my confederates. Just another smuggler. We've a date to meet at a level-five cantina. Then I was hoping to find some way to contact you."

Krennic called one of his stormtroopers forward and ordered him to check the ship's log.

"I had no other choice," Has went on. "Oh, I suppose I could have tried to hide, but I'm not interested in living out my days as a fugitive. I thought maybe you could help me—for old times' sake."

"Old times' sake," Krennic said.

"For services rendered. However you want to label what I did during the war and since."

Krennic was chewing it over when the stormtrooper reappeared.

"The log's clean, Commander. No commo with Coruscant. Only the original transmission monitored by Governor Tarkin."

Krennic listened, then shot Has a gimlet look. "You're lying to me, Captain."

With a downcast look, Has gestured broadly to the hangar. "If I am, Commander, then where are the Ersos?"

Galen was carrying Jyn in his arms as the three of them arrived at the small spaceport that had been built close to the former refuge to serve the needs of the Celestial Power complex. Travelers of many species were huddled at the terminal entrances and exits, most of them heading for or returning from distant parts of Coruscant now that the weeklong celebration was finally winding down. Three times the normal number of police had been deployed to deal with the throngs, but stormtroopers were circulating as well, seemingly on the search for beings of interest.

Galen and Lyra kept to the thick of the crowds. His eyes darting left and right, up and down, he would signal her when they were within range of a facial-recognition cam or a probe droid, and they would bow their heads and allow themselves to be carried on the living tide. They came to a halt well short of the first security checkpoint and extricated themselves to a parcel of open space along the terminal's front wall.

"I don't think we can risk going through," Galen said, shifting Jyn in his arms. "If our absence has been reported, our identichips will trigger alarms all over the terminal. What was the plan?"

"There was no plan other than to reach the spaceport."

"No destination concourse or hangar?"

Lyra shook her head.

"That leaves us no choice but to go through security. What's the worst that can happen? It's not like we're breaking any laws."

"Orson may have something to say about that, Galen. Besides, there are ways to avoid going through security."

"Then I'll tell him we were frightened," Galen went on, as if he hadn't heard her. "We panicked and decided to spend time in the apartment."

Lyra offered a faint smile. "That actually sounds reasonable. But he'll see through it. There'll be consequences."

Galen nodded. "We'll still have one play left— *me*. If they want my help, they'll need to play by my rules."

"I wouldn't count on it."

He squeezed her hand and kissed her on the cheek. They were two steps from merging with the crowd streaming toward the checkpoint when a tall, thin human with a streak of color in his thick black hair stepped into their path.

"I'm a friend of Obitt's," the man announced in a self-assured voice.

Galen looked at Lyra.

"You're from Onderon," she said, as instructed.

"Onderon it is." The man smiled broadly. "I'm called Saw Gerrera. You're Lyra, Galen, and . . ."

"Jyn," Galen said, stroking his daughter's hair.

"Good to meet all of you."

Lyra directed a glance at the security checkpoint. "Do we go through, Saw?"

He frowned and shook his head. "We need to find some other way."

"Where did you put down?" Lyra asked.

He motioned with his chin. "The ship's at the eastern edge of the field."

"Near the Warsi Tower or closer to the Salss skyway terminal?"

"The tower," Saw said.

Lyra narrowed her eyes in thought, then nodded. "I know a route."

Saw grinned broadly. "Has told me I could count on you." With Galen's permission, he took Jyn into his arms and motioned for Lyra to assume the point. "Just don't lose us."

Smiling at him over her shoulder, she said: "We have a ship to catch," and hurried off.

Krennic stormed from the hangar into the air of nighttime Coruscant and passed a long moment gazing at the traffic lifting off, arriving, traveling to distant areas of the planet.

Had he been tricked, or had he tricked himself? The Ersos hadn't returned to the facility. Thus far their images hadn't been captured by any facial-recognition cams and their identichips hadn't been scanned at any stores, facilities, public transport stations, or security checkpoints. Was it possible they had simply gone out for the night?

He knew better than to hope.

They had escaped out from under him.

Beings had been known to hide on Coruscant for a lifetime, but Galen wouldn't be one of them. He wouldn't be able to stay away from his research. He would have a change of heart. He would turn himself in. He would reach out . . .

The anger and despair he had felt in the airspeeder returned and settled on him like a great weight.

"Galen," he said, as if orphaned. Then: "Galen!" shouting it to the busy sky.

28

TRANSPOSED

RETURNED AT LAST TO HIS old stomping ground, Has sat quietly with his drink, deciding that even the music sounded good.

Rumor had it that he had died at Salient, so on stepping into the Wanton Wellspring he received what had amounted to a hero's welcome, friends and former shipmates insisting on buying him drinks and his lovely Dressellian dream girl surprising him with a kiss that lingered.

Even now, after months of traveling about, he wasn't sure to whom he owed his good fortune; perhaps to the Ersos, or Wilhuff Tarkin. In some ways, Krennic figured into things as well. But probably Tarkin most of all. If Tarkin hadn't been willing to trust that Has would willingly serve as his spy, he would never have been able to contact Lyra, and arrange for Saw to remove them from what Has perceived as danger born of Tarkin's obvious competition with Orson Krennic.

Krennic, however, hadn't simply allowed him to leave Coruscant after their reunion at the spaceport hangar—at least not immediately. He had kept Has locked away until the story of his escape from Salient could be substantiated, and Tarkin had been only too happy to oblige, since by then he had come to think of Has as his inside man. In short order, then, Has was back in the commander's employ and tasked with hunting down the missing Ersos, progress on which he had furnished to both Krennic and Tarkin, confident that the two would never have cause to compare notes.

The Ersos had been identified by cams at a spaceport near the former B'ankor Refuge, but there was no record of them having passed through security. A thorough study of departing traffic had revealed that a starship had launched shortly after cams had acquired the Ersos' images, but the ship's signature was unknown and no trace of it had been found. The fact that the ship had been ID'd multiple times at Salient by Tarkin's forces had clearly escaped Krennic's notice, probably owing to Tarkin's reluctance to share information of any sort with his rival in the Corps of Engineers—or in whatever branch of the military Krennic was actually enlisted.

Several messages had been teased from the Celestial Power communications suite, but the most tantalizing of them—those exchanged between Has and Lyra—had been relayed through so many HoloNet transceivers that the origin sources couldn't be pinpointed. Krennic, however, had focused on Lyra's friend Nari Sable as the person most likely to have helped the Ersos complete their flight.

In keeping with the search for the Ersos, Has had located Nari, but the comely surveyor had been able to provide her Imperial investigators with an alibi and had been released soon after being questioned. So Has had devoted the next several standard months to following up on leads as to the Ersos' whereabouts, which in fact had meant applying himself diligently to not finding them—even going so far as to avoid having any contact with former Onderonian freedom fighter Saw Gerrera, out of concern that Has's communications were being secretly monitored by Krennic or Tarkin.

Sipping from his drink, Has wasn't entirely convinced that he had accomplished something worthwhile, but it sure felt that way. More, he was close to being back on his own after years of executing the commands of others, and as free as anyone could be in the ever-expanding Empire, despite being unemployed, without a crew, and still having to transmit the odd lack-of-progress reports to Krennic and Tarkin.

Lyra had been right when she told him during their final communication that the Force worked in mysterious ways.

Finishing his drink, he stood and walked to the bar, where the Dressellian server who had kissed him was busy trying to chat up a customer. Sidling up alongside her, he said: "What would you say to my taking you away from all this?"

Turning immediately from her target, she said: "It's about time, Obitt."

Her smile said the rest, and with arms linked, the

two of them left the Wanton Wellspring in search of new horizons.

Tarkin and a contingent of stormtroopers arrived at Sentinel Base in his personal ship, the *Carrion Spike*. A wind-scoured gray moon, the base and several others in the vicinity supervised supply shipments bound for Geonosis, where the battle station was still under construction. Some in the Imperial court wondered why the Emperor had assigned one of his top moffs to control space traffic, but Tarkin wasn't there to safeguard the battle station so much as to keep an eye on Orson Krennic, who, despite recent obstacles, remained in charge of the Special Weapons Group.

Wind-driven grit assaulted the cockpit viewports as Tarkin brought the ship down on the base's target-like landing field. As inhospitable as Sentinel was, the moon was preferable to the Western Reaches. Adjusting to a downside life after so many years spent aboard Star Destroyers would be the difficult part of the assignment. But gazing out on the complex of interconnected domes and hangars, Tarkin knew that he could endure a standard year or two there if it meant furthering his goals.

Has Obitt was still reporting to him on what he could glean of Krennic's activities, and of course on the seemingly futile hunt for Galen Erso and his family. When the truth had emerged that Erso's research into kyber crystals had been weaponized without his knowledge, Tarkin wasn't surprised; nor did he feel any real sympathy for the situation in which the scientist had placed himself. The need to serve the Empire superseded personal goals, and sometimes personal morals also. More to the point, Erso should have seen through Krennic, the way Tarkin had. That Erso's disappearance would delay completion of the battle station superlaser was certainly regrettable—and would have to be remedied immediately—but not the fact that Krennic had been somewhat crippled by the scientist's unexpected departure. The headstrong and impulsive commander had been gaining too much prestige and influence with Vizier Mas Amedda and other advisers, and Tarkin was gratified to see him taken down a notch.

Fortunately, the Emperor agreed.

Tarkin wasn't certain that Krennic's team of researchers and engineers would find a way to equip the battle station with a suitable weapon on their own, but that wasn't his concern at the moment. He would execute his new role and bide his time. Having succeeded in the Western Reaches and at Salient, he was a step closer to assuming command of the entire project.

"I refuse to accept a demotion to lieutenant commander," Krennic told Amedda in no uncertain terms.

The pair were in the vizier's temporary office in one of the original spires of the Jedi Temple, which was undergoing extensive renovations designed to transform it into the seat of the Imperial court, complete with auditoriums, conference centers, and private landing fields. It was precisely the sort of project Krennic would have been supervising were it not for the battle station, and during the long walk to Amedda's headquarters he had recognized many of the current crew chiefs and foremen.

"It is hardly within your purview to reject a reduction in rank," the Chagrian told him.

Dressed in a white uniform that included a cap, capelet, and black gloves, Krennic was moving through the room like a storm. "Few involved in the project are aware that the Ersos have disappeared. Therefore a demotion will be interpreted as my having committed some sort of blunder. Which is an outright fabrication. I was Erso's handler, not his keeper."

Amedda considered it. "Have you been able to learn anything?"

"Only that the entire family managed to slip out under our very noses, and that there has been no sign of them since."

Amedda's lethorns stirred. "What will you do without Galen?"

Krennic came to a sudden stop. His mouth was open, but no words emerged; then he managed to say: "He's not the Empire's only genius crystallographer."

"That contradicts what you were telling me four years ago."

"Erso didn't tamper with any of the research data. Professor Sahali and Dr. Gubacher are confident that they can take up where he left off."

"At least they are still with us," Amedda said, fixing Krennic in his gaze.

"Trust me, Vizier."

"We have, and perhaps beyond your abilities. There are some who think you should be here, in this building, supervising the renovations."

Krennic didn't believe it for a moment, and decided not to dignify the remark with a response.

"An overseer is certainly in order," Amedda added.

Krennic snorted. "Is that why Tarkin has been assigned command of the Sentinel bases?"

Amedda spread his large hands. "He is merely there to safeguard against further setbacks. It pleases the Emperor to keep him close to you."

"That's Tarkin's job—to monitor me?"

"Not entirely. But should the need arise."

"It won't."

"Then the Emperor will be even more pleased." Amedda paused, then said: "Finish what you started, Commander."

Krennic marched from Amedda's office with four stormtroopers falling into formation behind him. A shudder went through him as he passed teams of droids at work in the wide, colonnaded hallway.

He could hope that Amedda had been persuaded to accept that the Special Weapons Group was picking up the slack. The fact was that work on the superlaser was stalled, and Galen's insights were needed more than ever. After all he had done for Galen! Fame would have come to him. Grandeur. Legacy. Without his science, Galen was a nonentity.

And Lyra . . .

Flushed with anger, he peeled his gloves off as he

walked and threw them violently to the polished floor.

He would leave no stone unturned in the search for them.

Jyn stared out the front window of Saw Gerrera's spaceship. There were too many lights to count. But she knew that some of them were balls of fire— stars—and that others had houses and buildings, inhabitants. Planets.

"Which one?"

"It's too far away to see," Saw said.

"But we can go there?"

"If your mom and dad want to."

"Through hooperspace."

He smiled at her. "Hyperspace."

She corrected herself. "Hyperspace."

"Should we go tell them what we found?"

"You can tell them."

She unfastened the restraints and put her boots on the deck. When Saw stood up from his seat she reached out to take his hand, her small pink one in his big brown one, and they walked out of the cockpit together.

Mama and Papa were standing by a window in the large cabin. Mama's arm was around Papa's waist, and his arm was around her waist. They smiled when they looked at her and Saw, and Papa bent down, opening his arms to her.

"Come here, Stardust," he said.

She hurried to him and he picked her up, so that

she was almost as tall as he was, but not as tall as Saw was.

"I think I've found the perfect place," Saw told her parents. "Remote. A bit desolate, but tranquil." He nodded his chin toward Jyn. "Plenty of room for this one to run around." He pulled his datapad from his pant pocket and showed them the image of a green, black, and blue planet with a wide ring. "It's called Lah'mu."

Papa looked at the image and said, "It looks unspoiled."

"It's getting harder and harder to find worlds the Empire hasn't swept into its grasp," Saw said. "More and more star systems are knuckling under; more and more planets are being ravaged and sucked dry for resources. Lah'mu is one of the exceptions."

Papa carried her away from the window. "What do you think, Stardust? Should Lah'mu be our new home?"

"Can Saw come and live with us?"

Papa looked at Saw and smiled. "Saw is a very busy pilot. But I'm sure he'll visit us. Right, Saw?"

Saw nodded and made his eyes smile. "Someone needs to keep an eye on you three." He looked at Papa. "I applaud you, Galen. I applaud all of you for taking a stand. You're my heroes. It's people like you who continue to inspire me to play a part in exposing the Empire's machinations." He considered for a moment, now looking down at Jyn. "Not everyone understands the sacrifices necessary to stop them. If we don't use every opportunity, every secret, every weapon available to stop them, how can we face our

children? How can we hand them a future filled with
such injustice?"

Saw turned to Mama and handed her a flat metallic card like the ones Papa used in his work. "In the
meantime, take this comm card. It will allow you to
contact me if you ever need my assistance."

Jyn thought about her old bedroom on Coruscant.
"I miss Mac-Vee, Mama."

Mama stretched out her hand to move the hair
from her face. "I miss him, too, sweetheart. Maybe
we can get a new Mac-Vee."

Jyn nodded, still thinking about the old Mac-Vee.

Mama looked at Papa without smiling. "I guess
we're just not cut out to be nomads, after all," she
said.

Papa nodded. He also wasn't smiling. "Funny to
hear you say that. But we're a team. We'll get through
this."

"No regrets?" Mama asked.

Papa said: "None."

Jyn watched them and listened. She didn't know
what the Empire was or who the Empire was, but
Mama and Papa and Saw didn't like it. In some way
the Empire had made them leave behind all her toys
and Mama's and Papa's clothes and other things. And
Mac-Vee, too, who would have nothing to do without them there. But she felt warm and safe in Papa's
arms, and Saw was a new friend.

Mama and Papa were good and so was Saw. And
so was she. Good like Brin was in *The Octave Stairway*. If they tried hard enough, maybe they could find
the home they were looking for.

Saw went back to the cockpit, and Mama and Papa and she stood at the window.

Soon after, the lights in space shifted slightly, then turned to long lines, and Saw's ship jumped and disappeared into swirling gray hyperspace.

ACKNOWLEDGMENTS

Thanks to polymath Ronie Lavon for the crash course in lasers, crystals, and synthetic diamonds, and to Tim Lapage of Safari Experts for some last-minute inspiration. Thanks also to the members of the Lucasfilm Story Group for bringing me aboard; and to Elizabeth Schaefer and Greg Kubie, of Del Rey books, and Mike Siglain, Jennifer Heddle, and Frank Parisi, of Lucasfilm, for their help and support along the way.

Read on for the short story

VOICE OF
THE EMPIRE

BY
MUR LAFFERTY

This story was originally published in
Star Wars Insider #170.

DON'T SAY A WORD. Stone-faced HoloNet News editor Mandora Catabe didn't say it out loud, but the message was clear.

Calliope Drouth's eyes flicked from Mandora, seated at her desk, to the man standing behind her, smiling widely, hands clasped behind his back. Mandora's face was set, grim, her eyes fixed on Calliope's.

That's an Imperial smile. Calliope had hoped to be called in to hear about the promotion she'd asked for, but that hope died when she saw Mandora's face.

"Calliope, sit down," Mandora said, indicating the chair opposite her desk. "This is Eridan Wesyse. I wanted to tell you first: I'm retiring, effective immediately, and Mr. Wesyse will be your new editor in chief."

Whereas Mandora was small and shrewd, suspicious of anyone and everyone, Eridan looked as if he would always listen sympathetically, smile kindly, and report whatever fit the kind of story he wanted to tell; Calliope knew the type.

She nodded. She'd seen the man around doing Imperial PR. "Nice to meet you, sir," she said. "I've seen you at some events, haven't I?"

He nodded, smiling wider. "You do have good eyes," he said. "Mandora said you'd be my star reporter. Yes, I've done some work for the Empire, and I will continue to as Mandora's replacement. You see, the Empire wants to have a tighter—" He paused, searching for the word. "—*connection* to HNN. We'll want to keep on all of the loyal staff, though, so you shouldn't worry about your job."

Calliope couldn't help glancing at Mandora.

"No, I'm the only one leaving. I was already contemplating my retirement," Mandora said, her eyes indicating no such thing. "The Empire just made me an offer I couldn't refuse."

"How generous," Calliope said, her mouth going dry. "What plans do you have for HNN, Mr. Wesyse?"

"We're going to start by giving you a promotion!" he said. "We're promoting you to senior reporter and calling you the Voice of the Empire. We were so impressed with your work on the Wookiee threat."

Calliope froze. Her piece on the Wookiee "threat" had been heavily edited by Imperial censors, removing the main point of her story entirely and nearly causing Calliope to quit.

"Based on your noteworthy history with HNN," Wesyse continued, "it's obvious we want to promote you. It's quite an honor to be the one person on cam that countless citizens will watch to get their news!"

"That is an honor," Calliope agreed, using the smooth voice she used on sources she knew were lying. "Thank you for the promotion. I'm looking forward to the new direction you will take us in, Editor Wesyse."

She wanted to take Mandora aside and ask her what was going on, why was this happening, but Mandora's normally animated face was set, which scared Calliope more than anything.

"As our newly appointed Voice of the Empire, we're throwing you at your first story, actually," Wesyse continued. "You are to cover the Imperial ball tonight. We got you an invitation, which was no easy task." He paused here, as if to give her a chance to thank him, but she pulled out a small keyboard and started taking notes, nodding for him to continue. "You are to go and interview the dignitaries, report what people are wearing, mention how good the food is, and so on. Your job is to show the Empire in a way the public doesn't usually get to see. Make it more accessible. When you give them the inside view, the Empire becomes *their* Empire. Understand?"

Before Calliope could protest that investigative journalism was her preferred area of news, Mandora pushed something across the desk at her. "I'm giving you Zox. I won't need it after I retire. It's yours now." She patted the little droid, an elderly X-0X unit about the size of her hand. "It's been very good to me, and I know it will serve you the same."

The droid was dome-shaped, and its original color was probably red or orange, but it was hard to tell, as the paint had worn off with age. It extended three spidery legs and rose from the desk, wobbled, and fell over on its side. It beeped plaintively until Mandora righted it.

"It will probably be better on your shoulder, now that I think about it," she said, smiling fondly at Zox and ignoring Calliope's confusion entirely.

"But an Ex-Oh-Ex doesn't transmit, it only records," Calliope said. "Why can't I take one of the newer droids?"

Wesyse frowned. "Unfortunately, the military did a recall all of the transmitting droids reporters were using. Turns out there were some technical problems."

Calliope wanted to laugh, but her spine had turned to ice. Did he know how transparent he was being? Stifling the press by removing their ability to transmit video feeds would drive the press in a direction Calliope didn't want to go. She opened her mouth, but Mandora interrupted her.

"Anyway, I'm retiring and it needs a good owner. I know you will treasure it as much as I always have." She gave it another push, her steely blue eyes locking onto Calliope's. *Take the droid.*

Calliope's mind raced as she put her hand over the small dome. They were balanced on the edge of something very sharp now. "Thank you, Mandora. I'll treasure it."

Much of the HNN staff had plans to go to the terrace of the HoloNet News building to watch the Empire Day parade below. Thousands of officers and soldiers marched by, flanked by the Empire's machines of war. They were followed by small vehicles showing off the new Imperial TIE striker, designed for both suborbital flight and atmospheric flight, using state-of-the-art technology in navigation and speed.

Calliope shook Mandora's hand, wishing she could talk to her and find out what was really going on. She waved to her co-workers and left during the parade. She was hardly dressed for an Imperial ball, as she had been expecting an average day at the office, and had to rush home to change.

Calliope spared a look over her shoulder as the new TIE fighters were displayed to the crowds. She had hoped to do a story on them, but doubted she'd ever get the chance now if she was doing shallow interviews of famous people.

Calliope rummaged in her closet for her few pieces of fancy clothing. She had reported from the front lines of wars, from the bridges of starships, from high atop a tree as she observed a raid on a droid manufacturing plant. She'd endured a broken arm, several burns, and one cut on her cheek, which she refused to surgically remove, as it was a reminder to all about how seriously she took her job.

And now she had to pull out the ivory gown that she had worn to her sister's wedding. She had to admit it was beautiful, woven with smart strands of synthetic fiber that gave off shimmers of different colors depending on the angle of the light on the dress. The ivory contrasted well with her dark skin and delicate features, although accessorizing with a rusty droid would be challenging.

Finally dressed, she put X-0X on her shoulder. It beeped inquisitively at her, though its beep was more like a strangled chirp; this droid had been around for decades, and her boss had never replaced it.

"Why Mandora insisted I bring you, I'll never know," she said, and then stopped abruptly. X-0X whirred in a way that sounded much like the newer, sleeker droids, and its scratched ocular lens glowed. Had it been modified?

A hologram appeared in front of Calliope. Mandora paced within the small circle of X-0X's beam, showing finally the energy and fierceness that Calliope expected.

"Calliope. I don't have much time. As of right now, the Empire is taking over HNN. I'm out, but you can still stay in. They will censor you. They will silence you. They will enrage you." Mandora stopped and jabbed her finger at Calliope, spitting out one word per jab. *"But I need you to stay where you are."*

The hologram began pacing again, just a few steps, to keep within the ability of X-0X to record. "This will be my last message to you. I'm leaving Coruscant. The fight against the Empire is bigger than we ever expected, and I'm going to help them however I can."

"Against the Empire?" Calliope whispered. She'd found evidence of resistance while researching some of her stories, but Mandora had stopped every attempt to report on it. They didn't have enough to broadcast yet, she'd said.

"You have a few choices. I'm sure if you do what Eridan Wesyse wishes you to, you will be rewarded.

Voice of the Empire. The Empire does appreciate loyalty. But you're better than that. You're smarter than that. And my . . . *friends* could use you. The second option available to you is dangerous and—" She paused and smiled. "—subversive."

Calliope listened to the second option, hope and excitement blossoming within her. This was the kind of reporting she could get behind.

X-0X clung to her gown, and she didn't even mind it crushing the fabric. It burbled and beeped at her as she approached the Imperial Palace. "What exactly did she do to modify you, anyway?" she asked. It remained silent.

Calliope walked past the dozens of Imperial Guards, and then the helmeted troopers, who always made her shiver. She showed her press credentials and invitation to the stern-faced guard at the top of the staircase. He frowned, casting a suspicious eye on X-0X. "That a recording droid?"

"It is," she said, smiling. "It's vintage, mostly for show. It's here with HNN editor in chief Eridan Wesyse's blessing." Recognizing the name, he gestured her through.

She thought of the impoverished people on far-off systems and wondered who among them would want to know which designer a diplomat from Alderaan would be wearing. But she went dutifully to find out.

Oddly enough, Alderaan had sent a junior diplomat, who looked as if his suit was very uncomfortable. She joined him at the bar.

"You look like this is your first Empire Day," she said to him, smiling. "I'm Calliope Drouth, HoloNet News."

His pale eyes scanned hers, and he swallowed. "Pol Treader. I recognize you. And what you're really asking is why Alderaan sent someone so young to such an important day."

She laughed. "If you're going to succeed in diplomacy, you're going to have to be much less direct." She took the drink offered by the bartender.

"Diplomacy isn't my usual job title," Pol said, pulling at his waistcoat. "I'm here as a favor to the Organas. They couldn't make it."

That was interesting. "Why not?"

He shrugged and looked irritatedly at her. "They don't tell me things like that. I'm just an assistant in antiquities." He wandered away.

"Who did your suit?" she called after him, but he was gone. She stopped herself from chasing after Mr. Antiquities when someone new swept into the room. All eyes fixated on the newcomer, and some young Imperial officers at the bar began whispering in hushed tones. Calliope edged closer to them.

"I don't believe you," one said to the other. She was tall, nearly two meters, with dark skin much like Calliope's.

Her companion was shorter and pale, his cheeks ruddy from already enjoying the flowing alcohol. "Fine, don't believe me," he said. "Doesn't make it any less true."

"You were there, with him? For Project Celestial Power?" she asked.

He shushed her frantically, his head swiveling around to see who had overheard. Calliope kept watching the new man who had entered the room, tall, pale, with a long white cape that shone in the light. Everyone seemed fascinated with him, but he gave attention only to the high-ranking Imperials drinking from thin flutes in the corner.

"Yes, I was with him, now be quiet about it. If we're overheard I could be demoted!" He fingered the insignia of rank on his chest. "And I just got this."

"Yes, you said so. About five times," his companion said, sounding bored.

Calliope noticed their uniforms as if for the first time, and approached. The pale officer looked worried but stood his ground.

"Calliope Drouth, HoloNet News," she said. "Everyone is impressed with that man who just came in, but I can't place him. Who is that?"

"That is Commander Krennic," the tall woman said. "He's the architect behind some of the emperor's greatest projects."

"All classified, I would expect," Calliope said, smiling.

"Of course," the pale officer said.

"I would love to find out more about him, Officer . . ." She raised her eyebrows and waited for him to supply his name.

"Tifino. Officer Tifino," he said. He indicated his companion. "That's Officer Wick."

Wick bowed, looking amused. Calliope decided she liked her.

"I'll get the next round," she said. "Incidentally, what do you two think of the fashion here tonight?"

Once she had the officers talking, Calliope managed to steer the conversation toward the various dignitaries flaunting themselves in the ballroom.

"Now, that is Ambassador Oaan from the third moon around Jaatovi," Wick said. The ambassador was tall and thin, with long black hair cascading down her back, and she moved with grace through the crowd. She reached Commander Krennic and began speaking with him.

"She is so subtle she could step through a lightning storm and not get zapped," Wick said. "I'd watch out for her."

"Or interview her," Calliope said, winking. She took a testing step away from her new friends, and they began protesting.

"You can't leave, you just got here!" Tifino said. "You can talk to her later!"

Everyone likes the woman buying the drinks, Mandora had always told her, and she returned to them and got another round. If she could make these officers feel they owed her something, so much the better.

Calliope pointed to Tifino's insignia of rank. "It looks as if you made an impression on Commander Krennic," she said, handing the bartender credits for the drinks. "It sounds like he's doing highly classified things. You could be heroes and few would ever know. What does that feel like?"

Tifino finished his drink in one gulp and focused on Calliope, blinking a few times. His eyes fell on the silent droid on her shoulder. "He's already a war hero," he confided. "I—I can't tell you why."

"Of course you can't," Calliope said, nodding. "That's not the action of an officer who's caught the commander's eye. Speaking of which, where did he get that amazing cape?"

She'd guessed right; neither officer felt like following her lead about fashion. Wick brought up how she could be transferred to Tifino's ship.

"We need scouts more than anything," he said. "How's your tracking?"

Wick made a face. "I'm a pilot. I haven't spent time in any terrain but a city since I was a child."

"What do you need with scouts?" Calliope asked. "I'll bet the Emperor is looking for a place to spend a holiday!" She tapped on X-0X and frowned when it did nothing. Then she pulled her small keyboard from her bag and began typing. "Where is he looking to vacation?"

Tifino frowned. "No, it's not like that. Who'd want to spend time on Jedha for fun, anyway?"

"Who'd want to scout there?" Calliope said. She got another round of drinks. Tifino excused himself to visit the lavatory.

Wick sighed when he was out of earshot. "That guy. A screwup through the Academy. I carried him, you know. And then luck hit him and missed me, and he's under Krennic and I'm, well . . ." She looked down at her empty glass and Calliope gently removed it and put a full one there.

"I'm doing shuttle runs," she finally said.

"Shuttle pilots can scout," Calliope said. "You have a wider view of the terrain. You need to seize opportunity, tell them why they need you. You've got hot hands at the helm, right?" Wick nodded, realization dawning on her face. "You've got sharp eyes, right? Sharper than Tifino's?"

"Much sharper," Wick scoffed.

"Then you tell your superiors that shuttle pilots can be just as good at scouting as troops on the ground. Better. You can see lights, smoke, the movement of groups. The Empire needs you to look for hidden enemies."

Wick had been nodding fervently at her, and then frowned and stopped nodding. "No, they're not looking for enemies. They're looking for some kind of crystals. What were they called? Cyder? Kyber? Hyper? Something like that. Anyway, Tifino's team just found a huge stash of them. That's what got him his new rank."

"And you carried that guy!" Calliope said, eyes wide with outrage.

"And I carried that guy," Wick said firmly, nodding. They clinked glasses and drank.

Tifino returned with a confused smile. "Wait, I want in, what are we toasting?"

"To Wick's future," Calliope said, raising her glass again.

"Who carried you through the Academy," Wick reminded him. "Who may just be the next hot officer to find the commander some of those fancy crystals!"

Tifino looked meaningfully at Calliope, who listed

toward the wall and fiddled with X-0X, which was still unresponsive. Wick waved a hand, dismissing her. "She's as drunk as we are. Besides, her recording droid died a while back." She gulped and stood a little straighter, looking at Calliope. "You aren't going to mention this, are you?"

"Depends," she said. "Are you going to tell me who made the commander's cape or not? Because that's the story I'm chasing."

They laughed, and Calliope mock-frowned at them. "No, really. If I don't report that, I'm going to get into serious trouble with my new editor. Everyone on Coruscant is going to want one!"

The officers laughed, and Wick launched into a very funny joke about bartenders on planets with high seawater content. Suddenly X-0X gave a strangled chirp and tumbled off Calliope's shoulder, landing hard on its dome and bouncing a meter away. Calliope went to retrieve it, and as she reached out, a black boot settled gently on the droid's still-rolling body and stopped it. She straightened and looked up into the face of Commander Krennic.

"Is this yours?" he asked, picking the silent droid up swiftly. Calliope groaned inwardly.

"Yes, it's not the most reliable," Calliope said, glaring at the little droid. She looked up and met Krennic's eyes, blue and searching. She held out a gloved hand and he looked at it for a moment, and then shook it instead of giving X-0X back. So she introduced herself.

"Commander Krennic, it's an honor. I'm Calliope—"

"Drouth, yes, with HoloNet News," he said. He scrutinized the droid. "I was under the impression we would supply our reporters with better equipment."

"Actually, we just heard the military recalled our newer droids. Anything to serve the Emperor's cause, but that leaves us with, well . . ." She indicated X-0X's sorry state.

"How old is this droid?" he asked.

"I don't know," she said. "It was a gift from my former editor. I keep it mainly for nostalgia purposes. And recording, when it works."

"Nostalgia and connections to loved ones," he mused. "Some would consider it a weakness."

"While others would consider it a comfort," she said.

He smiled slightly. "I would definitely think the inability to record things is a weakness for a reporter. You may just miss something that could make your career. Or you could be lucky enough to miss something that could destroy your career."

Calliope thought of the data that Mandora had sent her. She hadn't erased it from the droid yet, and now it was in Krennic's hands.

She smiled back at him. "I try not to rely on it too much."

"Then how will you gather your information to report on the Imperial ball?" he asked. "Surely you're missing all the gossip by fiddling with a broken droid."

"I'm getting gossip at the bar, sir," she said. "I just found out your tailor's name. Do you know that you're setting fashion trends?"

Krennic focused on the officers behind her, who were frozen at attention. "Tifino," he said. "Are you making the most of your shore leave?"

Tifino nodded, unable to speak.

"Good." He looked down at X-0X, held in his long, gloved fingers. "If you'd allow me to borrow this droid, Ms. Drouth," he said. "I know some tinkers who can fix it right up."

Calliope knew that if she protested too much, she'd make herself look suspicious. She glanced back at Wick and then looked meaningfully at Krennic. *Come on,* she mouthed. *Now's your chance.*

Wick swallowed and then lunged forward, stumbling slightly. "Commander," she stammered, putting a hand on his white coat and then pulling it off as if she'd just remembered herself. "Officer Ianna Wick, sir, and I wanted to make my case for joining your next mission."

Krennic frowned at her, then opened his mouth, but Wick forged ahead. "I'm a shuttle pilot, best in my class at the Academy, and Tifino says you need scouts . . ."

Calliope had no love for the Empire, but she'd developed a soft spot for Wick. She prayed the Imperial wouldn't blow it by saying too much in front of Calliope. Lucky for all involved, X-0X chose that time to come back online and buzzed, vibrating in Krennic's hand, its sensor glowing again and beeping in a confused way.

"There you are," Calliope said, interrupting Wick. She reached up and took the droid from the distracted Krennic, who frowned at her. "He's working now, sir, thanks for your offer, but you have more important things to do at this ball. Like listen to this young woman discuss her career with you." She made a play of looking around the room and focusing on the miserable nobody from Alderaan. "I see an ambassador I need to talk to, I hope you both have a lovely evening." She nodded to them both, passed behind Krennic, and then gave Wick a thumbs-up. The woman smiled at her before making her case to the stern commander.

"She did carry Tifino, after all," Calliope muttered to herself. She put X-0X on her shoulder, where it gripped her as tightly as before. "Let's circle the room once or twice and then get you home and into a good oil bath that will scrub you clean of *everything.*"

Calliope faced the cam, smiling with experienced ease as the transmission to countless planets concluded. She deftly double-checked the monitor to ensure that her hands were still visible in the feed.

"We here at HNN hope you enjoyed your Empire Day. Last night, I was afforded an inside look at the elegance and finery of the Imperial ball." The monitors showed the footage X-0X had gotten before it malfunctioned, panning around the room and focusing on the well-dressed dignitaries. "I can report that the fashion of Coruscant is going to be taking its lead from the attendees! From the sharply dressed dignitary from Alderaan to the elegant dress uniforms of the upper echelon of the Imperial forces, these attendees showed not only their diplomatic and military might, but also their fashion sense. Our Imperial forces are, well, a *force* to be reckoned with, both on the battlefield and in the ballroom! You can find some of the superstar tailors who dressed our dignitaries listed on your screen. You'd better get your call in soon! This is Calliope Drouth, your Voice of the Empire."

The light above the cam died, and Calliope sat back and sighed, forcing her shoulders to loosen. Eridan Wesyse hurried up to her, beaming. "Even better than your script, so vivid!" he sang. "I'm going to put you on all the society stories!" He frowned. "I would have liked more interviews with the who's-who of the Empire, though."

"My droid malfunctioned halfway through the night," Calliope said truthfully. "I did what I could."

He clapped her on the back and rushed away to converse with another reporter. She finally unclasped her hands. *I got away with it.*

Now the question was: Would anyone hear her true report? Mandora's message had included a file on code phrases and cyphers, which Calliope had used to carefully select the words in her transmission. The position of her hands during the broadcast would clue the subversives in to which algorithm to run on her seemingly vapid report. With any luck, they would be on their way to Jedha within the hour. Calliope didn't know what kyber crystals were, but if they were important enough for Krennic to go after, they had to be important enough to report.

If what Mandora said was true, Calliope was one

of many spies gathering information against the Empire.

She thought of Officers Wick and Tifino: possibly invisible "heroes" in the Empire's eyes. She knew how that felt now.

No one would ever know her work, not if she did her job right. No one but X-0X, which sat on her desk in her office, beeping quietly to itself.

She was growing fond of the little nuisance.

Read on for an excerpt from the thrilling
novelization of *Rogue One: A Star Wars Story*

ROGUE ONE:
A STAR WARS STORY

BY
ALEXANDER FREED

Published by Del Rey Books

As the shadows of the Empire loom ever larger across the galaxy, so do deeply troubling rumors. The Rebellion has learned of a sinister Imperial plot to bring entire worlds to their knees. Deep in Empire-dominated space, a machine of unimaginable destructive power is nearing completion. A weapon too terrifying to contemplate . . . and a threat that may be too great to overcome.

If the worlds at the Empire's mercy stand any chance, it lies with an unlikely band of allies: Jyn Erso, a resourceful young woman seeking vengeance; Cassian Andor, a rebel commander on a mission of assassination; Bodhi Rook, a defector from the Empire's military; Chirrut Îmwe, a blind holy man and his crack-shot companion, Baze Malbus; and K-2SO, a deadly Imperial droid turned against its former masters. In their hands rests the new hope that could turn the tide toward a crucial Rebellion victory—if only they can capture the plans to the Empire's new weapon.

But even as they race toward their dangerous goal, the specter of their ultimate enemy—a monstrous world unto itself—darkens the skies. Waiting to herald the Empire's brutal reign with a burst of annihilation worthy of its dreaded name: Death Star.

PROLOGUE

GALEN ERSO WAS NOT A good farmer. That was only one of his many flaws, but it was the reason he was still alive.

A man of more diverse talents—a different Galen, a Galen who could intuit what colonial crops would thrive in an alien world's soil, or who could check a withered tree for rot without peeling away its bark—would have grown bored. His mind, left idle in the fields, would have returned to subjects he had forsworn. That Galen, consciously or by habit, would have sought out the very work that had driven him to exile. He would have stared into the hearts of stars and formulated theorems of cosmic significance.

In time, he would have *drawn attention*. His obsessions would surely have killed him.

Yet an unskilled farmer was anything but idle; so the true Galen, the one who inhabited the realm of reality instead of idle fantasy, had no trouble filling his days on Lah'mu without succumbing to temptation. He took bacterial samples off boulders left by prehistoric volcanoes and looked in awe at the evergreen moss and grass and weeds that seemed to sprout from every surface. He surveyed the endless crooked hills of his domain, and he was grateful that he had yet to master his new profession.

He constructed these thoughts like an equation as he looked out the window, past his orderly rows of budding skycorn and toward the black soil of the beach. A tiny girl played near the rows, sending her toy soldier on adventures in the dirt.

"Is she digging again? I swear she didn't learn the words *stripmining* from me, but we're going hungry next year if she keeps this up."

The words breached Galen's concentration slowly. When he heard them, understood them, he smiled and shook his head. "The agricultural droids will repair the damage. Leave her be."

"Oh, I never planned to do anything. That girl is all yours."

Galen turned. Lyra's lips curled until she smiled. She'd started smiling again the day they'd left Coruscant.

He began to reply when the sky rumbled with a boom unlike thunder. One portion of Galen's mind narrowed its focus and was aware of only his wife before him, his daughter on the beach. The other portion processed the situation with mechanical precision. He was walking without conscious intent, striding past Lyra and the cluttered kitchen table and the worn couch that reeked of clove aftershave. He passed through a doorway and reached a device that might have evolved in the junkyard of a machine civilization—all cracked screens and loose wires, apt to shatter at a touch. He adjusted a dial and studied the video image on the screen.

A shuttlecraft was landing on his farm.

Specifically, a *Delta*-class T-3c, all sharp angles and bare metal. It busily broadcast active scans of the landscape as its broad wings folded in for landing and its sublight engines tapered their thrust. Galen studied the associated readouts and let the specifications settle into his memory—not because they might be useful, but because he wanted to procrastinate for just a moment. To shut away the implications of what he was seeing.

He squeezed his eyes shut and gave himself three seconds, two, one.

Then it was time to accept that his family's life on Lah'mu was over.

"Lyra," he said. He assumed she was near, but didn't turn to look.

"Is it him?" she asked. She sounded unafraid, which frightened Galen more than anything.

"I don't know. But we have to—"

"I'll get started," she said.

Galen nodded without looking from the console.

Galen was not prone to panic. He knew what needed doing, had rehearsed it on those rare days when the farm tended to itself or on those less rare nights when sleep eluded him. Such preparations were the only obsessions he permitted himself. He turned to another machine, tapped in a code, and tore a series of cords from the wall with swift jerks. He began another countdown in his head; if the data purge did not complete in five minutes, he would begin physically destroying components.

He heard footsteps at the front door, quick and light. He turned to see Jyn dash inside, brown hair matted and face touched with dirt. She'd left her toy in the fields. Galen felt an unexpected pang and feared—absurdly, he knew—that the loss of Stormy would distress her once she was far from the farm.

"Mama—"

Lyra stepped away from the bundle of clothes and datapads and portable meals she'd piled on one chair and knelt before the girl whose pale, slender features mirrored hers. "We know. It's all right."

Galen approached the pair, waited until his daughter had seen him. He spoke softly but somberly. "Gather your things, Jyn. It's time."

She understood, of course. She always did, when it mattered. But Galen had no time to be proud.

He turned back to his machines as Jyn sprinted to her room. The data purge had not completed. There were other files he had to handle as well, files he should have erased on Coruscant but which he'd brought to Lah'mu instead. (Why had he done that? Was it nostalgia? Misplaced pride?) He opened a drawer stuffed with spare droid parts and removed the arm of an agricultural unit. He flipped open a small panel, dug his fingertips between wires, and extracted a datachip.

"The scrambler, please?" he said.

Lyra passed him a metal orb the size of his palm. He inserted the datachip and—before he could doubt himself—pressed the toggle. The orb heated and produced a smell like burning hair. He tossed it in the junk drawer and felt a tightness in his stomach.

"If there's anything else, make it quick." Lyra's tone was clipped. A light blinked faster on the sensor console.

"Set the rendezvous and take Jyn," he said. "I'll finish here."

Lyra abruptly stopped double-checking her bundle of provisions. "That wasn't the plan, Galen."

"I'll meet you there."

"You have to come with us."

Her eyes were hard. Please smile, he thought. "I have to buy you time," he said.

The sensor light went dark. A fault seemed unlikely.

Lyra just watched him.

"Only I can," he said.

It was an argument impossible to refute. Lyra didn't try. She stalked into the kitchen and tapped at the comm unit as Galen made for Jyn's room. He caught just a snippet of Lyra's words: "*Saw—it's happened. He's come for us.*"

Jyn stood with her bulging satchel at her feet. Galen surveyed the tiny chamber's remaining contents: a few toys, the cot. Easy enough to hide. Enough to buy a few more minutes. He pushed a doll out of sight before returning to the doorway.

"Jyn. Come here."

He considered what he might say; considered what impression he wanted to leave Jyn if everything ended in disaster.

"Remember—" He spoke with deliberate care,

hoping to etch the words in her bones. "Whatever I do, I do it to protect you. Say you understand."

"I understand," Jyn said.

And this time, of course, she didn't understand. What eight-year-old could? Galen heard his own foolishness, his ego echoed by her voice. He wrapped her in his arms, felt her slender, warm body against him, and knew a better memory to leave her with.

"I love you, Stardust."

"I love you, too, Papa."

That would be enough.

He looked to his wife, who stood waiting. "Galen," she began, all the harshness gone.

"Go," he said.

She did, coaxing Jyn with her. Galen allowed himself the luxury of watching, heard his daughter offer a last confused, "Papa?" Then they were gone from the house, and he resumed his work.

He collected objects out of place—more toys, Lyra's clothes, unwashed dishes from the kitchen—and stashed them in niches he and Lyra had prepared long ago. He checked the unfinished data purge, returned his mind's eye to his mental countdown. A few seconds past the five-minute deadline. That meant he could keep busy while he awaited his visitors.

By the time Galen heard muffled voices approaching the farmhouse, two of his homemade data processing units billowed acrid smoke as their circuits melted. He stepped out the front door to greet the new arrivals under the cloudy sky.

A company in bleached white and gleaming black advanced toward the doorstep. The leader was a narrow man of Galen's own age in a spotless ivory officer's uniform, head high and movements stiff. The breeze failed to disturb the sandy hair beneath his cap. His cohorts wore armor like a scarab's shell, bore pistols and rifles as if ready for war. The troopers stepped when their leader stepped, matched his pace; to Galen, they seemed to exist only as extensions of their superior.

The man in white halted less than three meters away. "You're a hard man to find, Galen," he said, not quite smiling.

"That was the idea." Galen did not quite smile, either, though he could have. He could have let the farm and sky fade, let the troopers become shadows, and conjured an office on Coruscant around him; allowed himself to believe he was sparring again with his friend and colleague Orson Krennic.

There was no point in nostalgia, however. Orson surely knew that as well as he.

Orson was tugging at his gloves as he studied the fields with an exaggerated crane of his neck. "But farming? A man of your talents?"

"It's a peaceful life," Galen returned.

"Lonely, I'd imagine."

With those words, Orson had declared his game and his stakes. It did not surprise Galen.

"Since Lyra died, yes," Galen said.

The corner of Orson's mouth twitched, as if he were taken aback. "My sincerest condolences," he said, then gestured to the troopers and spoke more sternly. "Search the house. Shut down any machines—we'll want them examined by the technicians."

Four of the troopers obediently, rapidly, made for the doorway. Galen stepped aside to allow them past.

"I don't imagine," Orson said, "you've laid any traps? Nothing that would harm a patriot doing his duty?"

"No."

"No," Orson agreed. "I've always found your constancy refreshing. Galen Erso is an *honest* man, unaltered by stress or circumstance."

Troopers called to one another in the house behind Galen, and he stifled the impulse to turn. "Honest, perhaps. Still just a man."

Orson spread his hands, conceding the point. He moved as if to join the troopers in the house, then stopped. "When did she die?" he asked.

"Two, three years, I think. It's a bit of a blur."

"She was a wonderful woman. Strong. I know you loved her very much."

"What is it you want?"

The words were a mistake. Galen barely hid his wince as he heard himself, recognized the edge to his voice. The longer he played, the longer Lyra and Jyn had to escape. Instead he'd grown impatient.

Orson was replying carelessly, feigning the blunt honesty of a man too worn to lie. "The work has stalled, Galen. I need you to come back."

"I have the utmost confidence in you. In your people."

"You don't," Orson snapped. "You were never that humble."

"And you have too little faith in your own skills," Galen said easily. "I told you that when we were practically children. You could have done everything I did, but you preferred to dabble; to shepherd people instead of nurture theory. I always respected your decision, but don't let it narrow your world."

All of it was true. All of it was also designed to hurt Orson, to pry at his insecurities. Galen kept his tone measured, casual. Infuriatingly so, perhaps, but Orson's fury did not frighten him. He feared focus, efficiency, speed; not wild rage.

Orson only grimaced—a forced smile that didn't take. "You will come back."

So much for that sidetrack. Galen straightened his back. They were coming to the end. "I won't do it. This is where I belong now."

"Scratching the dirt with a shovel? We were on the verge of greatness, Galen. We were this close to providing peace, security for the galaxy."

Behind Galen came the sound of ceramics shattering as the troopers continued their search. He mentally cataloged dishes and ornamental vases, then dismissed the list. Nothing in the house mattered. "You're confusing peace with terror. You lied about what we were building."

"Only because you were willing to believe."

"You wanted to kill people."

Orson shrugged, unmoved by the argument. "We have to start somewhere."

Galen almost laughed. He remembered when he could laugh with Orson, instead of feeling nothing but hollow defiance.

Snapping sounds from the house. Furniture being

broken apart, hiding places revealed. Orson would have his proof momentarily.

"I'd be of no help, Krennic." *Needle him. Deny all familiarity.* "My mind just isn't what it was." And now he could only talk, not try to persuade or to enrage or do anything more than buy a few more seconds, a few precious moments for Lyra and Jyn. "I thought at first it was only the work—I would sit some nights and remember equations and theorems, but I couldn't hold them in my head anymore. I chalked it up to exhaustion, to forgoing the habits of a focused intellect . . ." He shook his head. "But it's more than that. Now I have trouble remembering the simplest things."

Orson wove gloved fingers together, eyes glittering with cruel amusement. "Your child, for example? Galen, you're an inspired scientist, but you're a terrible liar."

Orson didn't need his troopers to report an extra bed or a toy left out in the fields. There would be no more delays for Galen, no hope of hiding his family's presence on Lah'mu.

He prayed that Lyra would fare better. She had never failed him before.

Galen put aside even that thought to picture his daughter in her arms.

Lyra ran, her fingers wrapped around the fragile wrist of her daughter. She pulled without tenderness. She heard Jyn whimper in pain, felt the girl stumble beside her, and longed to hoist her in both arms, carry her across the rocks and clutch her to her breast.

She longed to, but she couldn't carry her daughter and crouch low enough to take advantage of the concealing hills. She couldn't add another twenty-five kilograms onto the supplies she carted on her back and still maintain her speed. Lyra loved her daughter, but love wouldn't save them today.

Lyra had always been the practical one in the family. *Damn you, Galen,* she thought, *for sending us away.*

She caught a flash of motion out of the corner of her eye, turned to confirm that it wasn't the wind, and tugged Jyn down as she dived onto moist soil. Her stomach already hurt from the run. The cool dirt felt good on her body, but her forehead prickled with sweat and fear. She peeked around the rocks to watch a half dozen figures—black-clad Imperial troopers led by a uniformed officer in white—stride rapidly toward the farmhouse.

No, not just an officer in white. *Orson Krennic* was leading a death squad to the farmhouse. Toward Galen.

"Mama—" Jyn was whispering, tugging at her hand. "I know that man."

That caught Lyra by surprise. But Jyn had her father's mind, if not his obsessions. Her memory was better than Lyra's had ever been.

That's your father's special friend Orson, she wanted to say. *He's a lying bastard who thinks he's a visionary.* Instead she whispered, "Shh," and pressed two fingers to Jyn's lips before kissing her on the forehead. "We need to keep going. Don't let them see you, okay?"

Jyn nodded. But she looked terrified.

They moved together, as swiftly as Lyra could

manage while squatting out of sight. Her hips were cramping as she led Jyn around the base of a comm spire and stopped again to peer toward the farmhouse. She couldn't make out Krennic past the troopers, couldn't see if Galen had emerged, but the group had halted near the front door. Lyra suddenly pictured the armored figures raising flamers, reducing the house to ash and charred metal while her husband screamed inside . . .

She knew better. So long as Krennic was in control, Galen would stay alive long after the rest of them were dead. He would have no choice but to work for that man until he was old and feeble, until his intellect began to fail him and the Empire determined he was no longer useful.

Lyra realized she'd made a decision.

She unslung her bag, rooted through the contents until she found what she needed. She set a bundle of clothes in the grass and placed her hands on Jyn's shoulders. The girl was trembling. She met her mother's gaze.

"You know where to go, don't you?" Lyra asked. "Wait for me there. Don't come out for *anyone* but me."

Jyn didn't answer. Lyra saw the moisture in her eyes. A voice told Lyra, *If you leave her now, she's done. You've taken all her strength away.*

But Lyra had committed herself to a path. Her husband needed her more than her daughter.

She hurriedly reached to her own throat, pushing away coarse cloth until her fingers caught a fraying string. She pulled off her necklace, watched the pendant swing in the breeze. The jagged, cloudy crystal was etched with writing on one side. Gently, she put the necklace over Jyn's head. The girl didn't move.

"Trust the Force," Lyra said, and made herself smile.

"Mama—"

"I'll be there," Lyra whispered. "Now go."

She wrapped Jyn in her arms—*Don't hold her too long, don't give her time to think*—and turned the girl around, pushed her away. Lyra watched her daughter stumble amid the rocks, disappearing out of sight.

It was time to refocus. Jyn would be safe. Safer if Lyra did this, safer still if she succeeded, but safe either way. She looked back to the farmhouse and the group gathered around the doorstep, lifted the bundle of clothes, and walked back the way she came. She kept her body low, picked up her pace as she saw four troopers enter the house and reveal Galen and Krennic standing together. She heard their voices, faintly. Krennic unctuously declaring We have to start somewhere.

She hadn't expected to see an opening so quickly. She'd wanted more time to plan. But there was no guarantee she'd catch Krennic with fewer bodyguards anytime soon. She straightened and hurried, kept the bundle clutched close.

Krennic saw her first, though he spoke only to Galen. "Oh, look! Here's Lyra. Back from the dead. It's a miracle."

Galen turned in her direction. She'd rarely seen such pain on his face. "Lyra . . ." But he was looking past her, searching the fields for Jyn.

Lyra almost wanted to smile.

The black-clad troopers raised their weapons. "Stop!" Krennic snapped.

Lyra let the clothes fall from her arms and raised the blaster she'd concealed beneath the pile. She aimed the barrel at Krennic, felt the chill metal of the trigger under her finger. She didn't look at the troopers. If they killed her, all she needed to do was twitch.

The troopers kept their weapons low. Krennic smirked at Lyra. "Troublesome as ever."

"You're not taking him," Lyra said.

"No, of course I'm not. I'm taking you all. You, your child. You'll all live in comfort."

"As hostages."

She'd lived that life before, or close enough. She had no desire to do it again.

Krennic seemed unperturbed. "As 'heroes of the Empire.'"

Lyra heard Galen's voice to one side. "Lyra. Put it down." The concern in his tone felt like a weight on her arm, a hand on her wrist. She kept the blaster up anyway, ignoring her husband.

Krennic wasn't smiling anymore. Lyra let the words, the threats, roll out. She'd imagined this before, made speeches in her mind to the man who'd ruined her life again and again, and the actuality felt, in turn, dreamlike. "You're going to let us go," she said. "You're going to do it because you're an egomaniacal coward. And I'm sure if your superiors let you live you'll come after us again, and that's fine. But *right now* we go free. Do you understand?"

Krennic merely nodded and said, "Think very carefully."

She sensed the troopers tensing. She knew, somehow, that Galen was staring at her in horror. And she suddenly realized that she'd misjudged Orson Krennic's cowardice—that he'd changed in the years since she'd known him, or she'd never understood him even in the old days.

Jyn would still be safe.

Maybe she could still save her husband.

"You'll never win," she said.

Krennic cocked his head. A patronizing gesture to an outmatched opponent.

"Do it," he said.

Lyra pulled the trigger, felt the blaster jump even as light flashed nearby and hot pulses ravaged her chest. She heard the troopers' shots only after she felt the pain—dull, almost numb pinpricks up and down her body, each surrounded by a halo of excruciation. Her muscles seemed to vibrate like plucked strings. Galen was shouting her name, rushing toward her as she fell, but she couldn't see him. All she saw was Krennic, clutching a black and smoking shoulder as he snarled through pain.

If Lyra could have screamed, she would have screamed not in agony, but in rage. She could not scream, however, and she went into darkness bitterly.

Her last thought was: *I wish Galen weren't here to see*.

The last things she heard were Galen shouting her

name and a furious voice calling, "They have a child. Find it!" But she was too far gone to understand the words.

Jyn wasn't a bad girl. Jyn didn't like to misbehave. When her parents told her to do something, she almost *always* did it. Not fast, but eventually (almost always eventually). She didn't deserve to be punished.

She knew she shouldn't have stayed to watch her mother talk to Papa and the man in white. But she couldn't have known what would happen. She couldn't have known what the troopers would do . . .

Had they been talking about her? Was it her fault?

Mama wasn't moving. Papa held her in his arms. Jyn couldn't stop herself from crying, but she held back a scream because she had to be brave. She *had* to be.

She'd seen how scared Mama had been. Whoever the strangers were, Jyn knew they would hurt her, too.

And she knew what she was supposed to do. She needed to behave now. She needed to make things better.

She had trouble breathing as she ran. Her nose and eyes streamed, and her throat felt swollen and clogged. She heard voices in the distance, electronic voices like droids or garbled comms. The troopers were coming after her.

She was wheezing with a high-pitched sound that would give her away. Her face felt like it burned hot enough to see for kilometers. She knew where she was going, though. Papa had tried to pretend it was a game, all those times he asked her to race and find the hiding spot, but she'd known better. She'd asked Mama about it once; she'd held Jyn's hand and smiled and said, "Just pretend it's a game anyway. It'll make your father feel better."

She wanted to pretend now, but it was hard.

She found the spot Papa had showed her among the piled rocks. She dragged open the hatch cover embedded in the hillside, almost shaking too hard to tug it free. Inside, a ladder led to the lower compartment, but Jyn stayed by the cover and pulled it shut. A sliver of light escaped through the hatch, illuminating the dusty gloom.

She pulled her knees to her chest and sang one of her mother's songs, rocking back and forth, ignoring her tear-streaked face and filthy hands. This was part of pretending, too. All she had to do was wait. That was all she'd ever been told to do in the hiding spot.

Mama or Papa would come for her.

She smelled smoke, and the smoke stung her eyes worse than her tears. She could see the shapes of troopers moving among the rocks, but even though they went back and forth and back and forth they never noticed the hatch. Never saw her shelter. When the daylight began to fade, they left and Jyn climbed down the ladder.

The lower compartment was too small for comfort, made cramped by stockpiles of food and machines and containers, but she could sit. She found a lantern and watched its feeble light wax and wane through the night as she listened to the rumble of a storm outside and the splashing of rainwater down the hill above her. She tried to sleep, but she never slept for long—raindrops crept into the cave and tapped at her forehead and sleeves no matter how she arranged herself.

Even her dreams were about that insistent tapping. Those wet, random strikes. In her dreams, sometimes Mama fell down when the raindrops hit Jyn.

When morning came, she woke to the sound of metal scraping above her. For an instant she confused dreams with reality and thought Mama or Papa had arrived at last—she believed what she'd seen the day before was a nightmare, and that this was another of Papa's games.

But only for an instant.

She looked up. The hatch opened, and silhouetted above her was an armored figure with a dark face graven with scars. The man looked down at Jyn with eyes that gleamed in the lantern's light and spoke in a voice of command:

"Come, my child. We have a long ride ahead of us."

Orson Krennic observed Galen aboard the shuttlecraft and wondered when the man would finally pry himself from the gurney where his wife's corpse sprawled. "We'll bring her home," Krennic said. "I promise."

Galen said nothing and stroked his wife's hand.

What more did I expect? Krennic wondered.

Lyra would have survived if not for her own foolishness. Krennic had risked his life for Galen and his family, given Lyra every opportunity to stand down rather than immediately signaling his troops to fire. *That* would have been the safest bet—his death trooper elites were *unkind* men who, given their druthers, would have ended the standoff far less mercifully.

She'd *shot* him!

He'd tried to spare Lyra for Galen's own comfort, out of an understanding that genius worked best without distractions—and yes, out of a desire to honor the cordiality, if not friendship, he and Galen had once shared. Yet self-imposed exile had changed Galen: He was no longer a man of dispassionate contemplation, able to interpret facts without prejudice. Whatever Krennic said, every action he took, was to be interpreted by Galen as the ruthless ploy of a scheming powermonger.

This irked Krennic—of course it irked him, to have the rapport of years so neatly dismissed—but he could use it. If Galen refused to readjust (perhaps a man who changed so swiftly once could swiftly change again?), then Krennic could play the monster to ensure his cooperation.

The bandage around his shoulder rendered his arm immobile. He'd need weeks, if not months to fully recover, with who-knew-how-many hours spent immersed in medicinal bacta tanks. The pain would be considerable once the analgesics wore off, yet he could forgive that; not so the loss of time.

Any debt he owed Galen was now repaid.

"We will find the child," he said, more insistent.

Galen did not look away from Lyra's body (another gift from Krennic—who else would have brought her home for a proper funeral?). "I think if you haven't found her already," Galen murmured, "you are very unlikely to succeed."

Krennic bristled, but there was truth to the words. Jyn had clearly received outside aid—the signal sent from the farmhouse suggested as much—and Krennic was not prepared to underestimate her rescuer's competence. He hoped investigation of the comm stations, no matter how badly Galen had damaged them, would reveal the particulars; the results would determine how he turned the situation to his advantage.

If Galen was unsure of his daughter's fate—if he'd sent out a general distress call or offered a reward for retrieval to every smuggler or bounty hunter in receiving range—then Krennic's dogged pursuit of the girl would incentivize Galen to cooperate. Galen would never admit to it, of course, but he would be soothed by the certainty of knowing his daughter was in Imperial hands.

Conversely, if Galen knew exactly who had rescued Jyn, then perhaps it was best to leave well enough alone and use the threat of Imperial interference as impetus for cooperation.

All of which, Krennic realized with a start, was a worry for another day. He'd been so consumed by his mission that he had failed to appreciate his own victory.

After a long search, Galen was back in his hands. The scientific setbacks, the engineering problems plaguing Krennic's teams would soon vanish. The constant needling from men like Wilhuff Tarkin—bureaucrats without any true sense for the *scope* of Krennic's accomplishments—would soon be over. These were truths worth celebrating.

Krennic smiled at Galen and shook his head fondly. "Your wife will be honored. We'll have the service as soon as we reach Coruscant. But meanwhile . . . shall we discuss the work?"

Galen finally turned and looked at Krennic with loathing.

Then, almost imperceptibly, he nodded.

SUPPLEMENTAL DATA: REBEL ALLIANCE INTELLIGENCE UPDATE

[Document #NI3814 ("Situational Analysis Regarding Jedha, et al."), time-stamped approximately thirteen years after the conscription of Galen Erso by Orson Krennic; from the personal files of Mon Mothma.]

There is no hard evidence of an inter-planetary engineering project consuming Imperial resources (living, financial, and material) on a massive scale. That remains the bottom line, as it has since our investigation began.

Yet as before, we consider this statement insufficient and our situation grave.

Major tactical deployments of Imperial forces to strategically insignificant worlds continue on Jedha, Patriim, Eadu, Horuz, and twelve others of note. Frequent communications blackouts make analysis of these deployments exceedingly difficult, and we strongly suspect our list is neither accurate nor complete. Nonetheless, we know that a majority of the worlds in question contain facilities for resource harvesting, manufacturing, or scientific research and development. More recently, we have learned that several of these worlds share a set of nonstandard security protocols far exceeding the Imperial norm.

We have intercepted multiple communiqués sent to Orson Krennic, the Empire's advanced weapons research director, from these worlds. We are not yet able to decrypt them.

We have intercepted multiple communiqués sent to one "Galen Erso" from these worlds. We are not yet able to decrypt them or confirm that the "Galen Erso" referenced is the former head of multiple high-energy research projects (including "Celestial Power"–see notes) once housed on Coruscant.

We have intercepted multiple communiqués referencing a future weapons test of indeterminate scale. Our attempts to surveil Imperial activities related to this matter have resulted in the loss of several operatives. We request additional personnel. Attempts to obtain the cooperation of Saw Gerrera on Jedha have been ended at the recommendation of General Jan Dodonna.

We understand that our concerns are considered controversial inside Alliance council leadership. We do not dispute that intelligence resources should be focused on the Senate if there is to be any hope of a peaceful political resolution to the larger struggle. Several analysts have declined to attach their names to this document for fear of giving it "undue credibility."

But this is not a conspiracy theory, and ignorance will not protect us from whatever the Galactic Empire is building.

Full report is attached.

CHAPTER 1

THE RING OF KAFRENE WAS a monumental span of durasteel and plastoid anchored by a pair of malformed planetoids within the Kafrene asteroid belt. It had been founded as a mining colony by Old Republic nobility, built for the purpose of stripping every rock within ten million kilometers of whatever mineral resources the galaxy might covet; its founders' disappointment, upon realizing that such valuable minerals were scarce at best in the Kafrene belt, had earned it the unofficial slogan that arced over its aft docking bay in lurid, phosphorescent graffiti: where good dreams go bad.

Now the Ring of Kafrene was a deep-space trading post and stopover for the sector's most desperate travelers. Cassian Andor counted himself among that number.

He was already behind schedule, and he knew that if he hadn't drawn attention during disembarkation he was certainly doing so now. He moved too quickly down the throughway, shouldering aside men and women and nonhumans of indeterminate gender who

had the proper, plodding gait of people sentenced to
live in a place like Kafrene. Between the road and the
distant rock warrens stood a thousand sheet-metal
shacks and shoddy prefabricated housing units recy-
cled from foreign colonies; outside the main through-
ways there was no plan, no layout that didn't change
almost daily, and even the workers proceeding home
in the artificial twilight stuck to the major arteries.
Cassian tried to moderate his pace, to ride the crowd's
momentum rather than apply force. He failed and
imagined his mentor's disappointment: The Rebel Alliance taught you better than that.

But he had been traveling too long, from Coruscant to Corulag and onward, tugging at the loose
threads of an elaborate tapestry that was outside the
scope of his vision. He had paid dearly in time and
credits and blood for precious little intelligence, for
the reiteration of facts he'd already confirmed. He'd
spent too much to return to Base One empty-handed.
His frustration was starting to show.

He cut across the street and smelled ammonia waft-
ing from a ventilation shaft—exhaust from an alien
housing complex. He suppressed a cough and stepped
into the gap between one tenement and another,
working his way through a maze of corridors until he
reached a dead-end alleyway barely wider than his
arm span.

"I was about to leave," a voice said, full of nervous
irritation. The speaker emerged from the shadows: a
human with a soft round face and hard eyes, dressed
in stained and fading garb. His right arm hung limply
in a sling. Cassian's gaze locked on the man even as

he sorted through the distant sounds of the street: voices, clattering merchandise, something sizzling, someone screaming. But no commotion, no squawking comlinks.

That was good enough. If there were stormtroopers hunting him, they weren't ready to shoot.

"I came as fast as I could," Cassian said. He stashed his paranoia in the back of his brain—out of the way but within easy reach.

Tivik started toward Cassian and the alley mouth, wiping one palm on his hip. "I have to get back on board. Walk with me."

"Where's your ship heading?" Cassian asked. "Back to Jedha?"

Tivik didn't stop moving. In another moment, he'd have to squeeze past Cassian to continue. "They won't wait for me," he said. "We're here stealing ammo—"

Cassian shifted his weight and broadened his stance, blocking Tivik's path; he wasn't a large man, but he knew how to feign *presence*. Tivik flinched and took an abrupt step backward.

As informants went, Tivik was one of the more maddening Cassian had worked with: He was, for all his faults, a true believer; he was also an abject coward, forever looking to escape the moral responsibilities he assigned himself. He responded well to pressure. And after the past few days, after rushing to extricate himself from Corulag based on Tivik's oblique message, Cassian was in the mood to press.

"You have news from Jedha?" he growled. "Come on . . . I came across the galaxy for this."

Tivik met Cassian's gaze, then relented. "An Impe-

rial pilot—one of the cargo drivers on the Jedha run?
He defected yesterday."

"So?" Low-level defectors from the Empire weren't
uncommon. They made up half the Rebellion's foot
soldiers, give or take. Tivik knew that as well as Cassian.

"This pilot? He says he knows what the Jedha mining operation is all about. He's telling people they're
making a weapon." Tivik spat the words out like bitter rind. "The kyber crystals, that's what they're for.
He's brought a message, says he's got proof—"

Cassian sorted through the barrage of information, cross-referenced against what he already knew,
and reprioritized his concerns. This was why he'd come,
but it wasn't what he'd expected. There had been
leads about a weapon before, and every one—on
Adalog, in Zemiah's Den—had turned to dross.

His pulse was quickening. Maybe he wouldn't return to Base One empty-handed after all.

"What kind of weapon?" he asked.

Voices rose in the street, distorted by echoes down
the alleyways. Tivik somehow shrank into himself,
the small man making himself smaller. "Look, I have
to go."

"You called *me*. You knew this was important—"

"You shouldn't have come late!" Tivik snapped.
His eyes were glassy with distress.

Cassian hoisted Tivik under both arms, dug his fingers into the sling and coarse cloth and soft flesh. The
man's breath had the scent of cinnamon. "What kind
of weapon?" Cassian repeated, louder than he'd intended.

"A planet killer," Tivik whispered. "That's what he called it."

Cold crept down Cassian's spine.

He tried to bring to mind old reports, speculative intelligence documents, tech readouts, anything to put the lie to Tivik's words. A planet killer was a myth, a fantasy, an obscenity dreamed up by zealots who viewed the Emperor as a wrathful deity instead of a corrupt tyrant.

Along with the cold came a shameful mix of excitement and revulsion. Maybe for this, any price would be justified.

He set Tivik down as gently as he could. "A planet killer?"

"Someone named Erso sent him, sent the pilot. Some old friend of Saw's."

That much fit the puzzle. "Galen Erso?" Cassian asked, trying to tamp down his own intensity. "Was it?"

"I don't know! I shouldn't even have said this much." Tivik shook his head. "The pilot, the guys who found him, they were looking for Saw when we left."

Saw Gerrera. A defector pilot. Jedha. Kyber crystals. A weapon. A planet killer. Galen Erso. Cassian sorted through them and found it was too much to deal with, a hand built of too many playing cards. Tivik was on the verge of bolting, and Cassian didn't have time to figure out the right questions. "Who else knows this?" he asked.

"I have no idea!" Tivik leaned in, his cinnamon breath coming in quick little bursts. "It's all falling apart. Saw's right—you guys keep talking and stalling and dealing and we're on fumes out there, there're spies everywhere—"

Tivik didn't finish the sentiment. As he stared past Cassian's shoulder, Cassian heard movement behind him and turned to face the alley mouth. Positioned to block the entrance, as Cassian had blocked Tivik, were two figures in white armor with helmets like stylized skulls: Imperial stormtroopers, rifles hoisted casually and aimed in Cassian's direction.

Cassian cursed silently and made himself smile.

"What's all this?" The stormtrooper's voice buzzed with distortion.

He was curt, authoritative, but not scared. Cassian could use that.

"Hey," Cassian said, and gave an exaggerated shrug. "Just me and my friend. If we're bothering someone, we'll get out of the way—"

"You're not leaving." The second stormtrooper spoke now, impatient. "Come on, let's see some scan-docs."

Cassian kept his eyes off Tivik. There was nothing he could do to coax the man into playing along, to urge him to *make no move*. He kept smiling his small, reassuring smile at the stormtroopers, even as his blood pumped fiercely with the promise of a *weapon,* a *planet killer.* "Yeah, of course," he said. "My gloves?"

He indicated a pocket with a gesture. The stormtroopers didn't object. Thieves were common on Kafrene, and they'd doubtless seen stranger hiding spots.

Neither stormtrooper reacted in time as Cassian reached down and touched the cool metal of his pistol's grip. He barely moved his wrist and squeezed the trigger twice, averting his gaze just enough to avoid the glare of the energy discharge. The electric noise was low and sickly, muffled by an illegal silencing device that was *almost* effective.

A moment later the stormtroopers lay dead in the alleyway. It was a miracle, Cassian thought, that the silenced blaster bolts had penetrated their armor. In a fairer world, he would be the one lying in filth with a burning hole instead of a heart.

"No . . ." Tivik was shaking his head. "What've you done?"

Cassian caught another glimpse of white, heard a garbled voice beyond the alley mouth. There would be more troopers coming, many more, and next time they wouldn't hesitate to fire. He seized Tivik by the elbow, hurried deeper into the alley, and scanned the walls. There were no exits, no air shafts or back doors, but the rooftops weren't more than a meter or two out of reach. Unaided climbing wasn't his specialty; still, he could be up and over in seconds, and he'd disappear in the labyrinthine depths of the Ring of Kafrene.

Tivik recognized his intent. "Are you crazy? I'll never climb out of here." He tugged himself away from Cassian's grip—Cassian released him after a moment—and adjusted his sling. "My arm . . ." He rotated his body awkwardly to watch the alley mouth.

Cassian heard footsteps and a distant, distorted yell. He looked Tivik up and down and realized that, in all likelihood, the man was right: He really couldn't make it up the wall, not without help and not swiftly.

In the best-case scenario, by the time both he and Cassian were up on the roofs, the stormtroopers would already have identified them and initiated a cordon.

"Hey," Cassian said, and touched Tivik's shoulder—gently now, his voice stripped of all force. "Calm down. Calm down. You did good—everything you told me, it's real?"

"It's real," Tivik said. His voice was the voice of a confused child.

One more payment.

"We'll be all right," Cassian said. And for the third time that day, he squeezed the trigger on his blaster. He heard the sickly electric squawk, smelled burning fibers and worse as Tivik fell to the ground. The informant let out one last little groan, like he'd been troubled in his sleep, and lay still.

They would've caught you, Tivik. You would've broken. You would've died. And neither of us would deliver your message.

Cassian's hands were shaking as he pulled himself up and over the wall, grabbing at handholds along pipes and stained sills, kicking at the surface for support. He heard the stormtroopers behind him counting bodies and hurried on, chest flat against the rooftop.

Less than an hour later, he was on a shuttle departing the Ring of Kafrene. His face and beard were dripping where he'd wiped them with a cold sponge in the sanitation station—not just to hide the sweat on his brow, but to shock himself back into focus. He had a lot to occupy his mind, and farther to go before he could transmit it to Draven and Alliance Intelligence.

He closed his eyes and sorted the cards in his hand:

Jedha. The pilgrim moon. A wasteland world intimately linked to a vast Imperial project only visible through its ripple effects.

The kyber crystals. Jedha's only natural resource of any value. The Empire had been shipping crystals offworld, their ultimate destination unknown.

A defecting pilot carrying a message to Saw Gerrera. Possibly trustworthy, possibly not.

Saw Gerrera. Nominally part of the Rebellion. In practice, not so easily categorized.

Galen Erso. The legendary scientist, connected—again—to the Imperial mega-project whose existence the Alliance could only speculate about. The man whose message the pilot supposedly carried.

And the weapon. The *planet killer*. The galaxy's nightmare, designed and built and polished to shine by Erso and his cronies.

It was more than Cassian had hoped to bring back from this mission; a treasure hoard of facts and speculation and possible connections, enough to keep the analysts busy for weeks or months or years.

If he was lucky, it would even be enough to keep him from replaying—over and over in his head, on the long shuttle ride to safety—the last dying groan of the man he'd murdered.

Bodhi Rook had only ever doubted himself, and today was no exception.

His captors hadn't hurt him. Threatened him, yes; refused him food and water and left him with a headache that seemed to squeeze his skull tight around his swollen brain, yes; but they treated him more like an object than a man. They rarely spoke as they dragged him across the frigid Jedha desert, grasping him by the arms and marching at a pace that he—insulated by the Imperial flight suit he wore under a loose kaftan—couldn't quite match. His soles touched sand twice for every three steps his captors took; and so every three steps he flew, and their grip became painfully tight.

He could survive this, he told himself. He'd chosen right, found the right people. And when he delivered his message, they would all understand. They would accept him as a good man, a brave man.

He could only hope that was all true.

"How much farther?" he asked.

His captors stayed close around him, so close he couldn't see much of the wasteland: just pale and freezing sun, low mountains that formed the borders of the valley, and the occasional crumbling monolith of one of Jedha's great statues—a stern humanoid head with lips worn smooth over millennia, or a pair of broken legs embedded in the cracked and rusty valley floor. When the wind rose, loose wisps of long, dark hair drifted before his eyes.

"I know you're being careful," he said, struggling to sound reasonable. "I know that's smart—you think I could be a spy, and spies have to be a worry for people like you."

Don't make them think about spies! He told himself that, even as another part of his brain assured him: *Hide nothing. Only honesty will save you.*

He fought to regain his train of thought. "But—but!" He spat air through dry lips. "You also have to give me a chance. Not for my sake, but for yours. I want to help you . . ."

His captors—five revolutionaries in ragged local attire, each armed with an illegal blaster rifle—yanked him hard, and he scrabbled over the dust. No one met his gaze. Instead scarred, unwashed faces watched Bodhi's bound hands or the endless desert.

An interminable time passed before he spoke again. "Do you have a family?" he asked a towering man with a blade half concealed in his boot.

For his troubles, he got the briefest of glances.

"*I* have a family," Bodhi said, though it was only somewhat true.

The revolutionaries began to spread apart, wordlessly changing formation to put Bodhi at the center of a broad semicircle. With his newly expanded field of vision, Bodhi now saw a second group standing ahead of them in the wastes—small, dark figures on a bright horizon.

"Is that him?" Bodhi asked, and received no reply.

The semicircle closed the distance to the second band. The newcomers resembled Bodhi's captors but carried their ordnance more conspicuously: A white-furred Gigoran hoisted a rotary cannon, while the humans wore bandoliers and detonator belts. At the fore of the newcomers was a Tognath: a lanky figure dressed in dark leathers, whose pale, skull-like head was set in the vise grip of a mechanical respirator. The

Tognath turned his sockets onto Bodhi and said in a thickly accented dialect, "It's the pilot. Look alive!"

The Tognath gestured once, and the two bands merged with swift and soldierly precision. Bodhi flinched under the Gigoran's glower and felt a flush of shame; nonhumans hadn't made him nervous before he'd signed on with the Empire.

He made himself focus. "Okay, so you're—you're Saw Gerrera?" he asked, more in hope than genuine belief.

Someone snickered. The Tognath examined Bodhi with an expression that might have been disdain.

"No?" Bodhi shook his head. "Okay, we're just wasting time that we don't have. I need to speak to Saw Gerrera! I keep telling them—" He lifted a shoulder at one of his original captors. "—before, before it's too late."

He thought he heard another snicker. It might have been the wind playing on sand, but it was enough to raise his ire.

They need you. You need to make them understand.

"We need to get to Jedha City. We're out here in the middle of nowhere—" His voice rose to a shout, thick with frustration. "What part of *urgent* message do you guys not understand?"

He saw the shadow above him, then felt coarse cloth drag over his hair, catch on the goggles perched on his forehead, and slide tight against his nose, mustache, and beard. He saw the glow of the sun through the stitching of the sack over his head. "Hey!" he said, trying not to bite the fabric. "Hey—we're all on the same side, if you just see past the uniform for a minute . . ."

You always talk, his mother had said, *but you say so little! Learn to listen, Bodhi Rook.*

Talking was all he could do now.

"I've got to speak to Saw Gerrera," he cried. He was pleading as one set of hands released his arms and new hands, the terribly strong hands of the Gigoran, took their place. "You know what? Just tell him—tell him what I told you, and then he'll want to speak to me."

I gave up everything to come here. I'm here to help!

Someone pulled the sack tight around his neck. It scraped at his throat when he breathed.

Bodhi Rook thought about the reason he'd come back to Jedha and found himself hating Galen Erso.

Jyn had been at the Empire's mercy before. Sometimes she'd even deserved her troubles—she couldn't blame some petty dictator for ordering her dragged off the street and slammed into holding when she really, truly was planning to blow up his ship and steal his guns. She'd had rifles pointed at her, felt stun prods deliver jolts to her spine, and generally suffered the worst a stormtrooper was authorized to deal out.

What made her circumstances different now was that, for the first time, Jyn had no escape route. No partners outside the prison walls waiting to bust down the doors; no in with a greedy security officer she could promise (lying or not) to pay off; not even a knife she could hide where the guards wouldn't find it.

She'd run out of *friends*. She'd come to Wobani Labor Camp alone. She expected to die there that way and, very likely, it wouldn't take long at all.

She opened her eyes, flinched away her thoughts as a drop of filthy water smacked into her forehead and took a circuitous route down the side of her nose. She smeared it away with her palm and glanced about her cell as if it might have changed since lights-out. But there was no gap in the wall, no blaster tucked discreetly beside her slab. The blanket-draped lump of her cellmate moaned and wheezed, loud enough to wake Jyn even if she did manage to sleep.

She waited for the stormtrooper on patrol to pass her door, counted to five, then slid to her feet and crept to the bars. Outside was an endless march of more cell doors, more prisoners sleeping or, in a few cases, feeding their own private demons—clawing their arms or sketching invisible mandalas on the floor. Wobani didn't care about treatment or rehabilitation any more than it did about punishment. Order and obedience were the priority; everything else was left to rot.

"Bad dreams?" The moaning and wheezing had stopped. The voice sounded like claws on slate.

"Not really," Jyn said.

"Then you should not be up," her cellmate huffed. The tentacles protruding from her pinched, wormlike face writhed in irritation.

The woman called herself Nail. The other prisoners at Wobani called her Kennel, for the parasites she hosted in the filthy cloth jacket that half covered her leathery chest. Only the guards called her by her real name, which—along with her species and actual gender—Jyn hadn't bothered to learn.

They both fell silent as the patrol came around again. Jyn returned to the slab that served as her bed, considered rising a second time solely to irritate Kennel, then decided against it. If she was going to pick a fight, better to be awake enough to enjoy it.

"Do you want a warning?" Kennel asked. "Before I do it?"

"Not really," Jyn repeated.

Kennel grunted and rolled from one side to the other. "I will give you one anyway. Next work crew we are on together. I will kill you then."

Jyn laughed breathily and without humor. "Who's going to keep you company?"

"I like a quiet cell," Kennel said.

"What if I kill you first?" Jyn asked.

"Then I hope you like a quiet cell, Liana Hallik."

Liana Hallik. Not Jyn's favorite name, but probably her last. She twisted her lips into a smile that her cellmate wouldn't see.

"Were you always like this?" she asked after the stormtrooper had passed by. "Before Wobani? Back to when you were a kid?"

"Yes," Kennel replied.

"Me, too," Jyn said.

Neither of them spoke again. Jyn lay on her slab and didn't sleep and toyed with the necklace tucked under her shirt—the crystal she'd managed to keep, smuggled into the prison when she should have been worried about weapons or a comlink. She didn't think much about her would-be murderer, knowing that if Kennel didn't kill her something else would.

No one survived Wobani for long. Jyn was supposed to serve twenty years, but anything more than five was a death sentence. All she could do was try to pick the most interesting end possible.

The next morning, the stormtroopers gathered up the work crews, selecting prisoners at random (supposedly at random, though everyone knew the guards had *favorites*) for their day on the farms. Jyn preferred work to sitting in her cell—she handled strained and quivering muscles better than agonizing boredom—and she'd almost given up hope when a guard waved a rifle at her cell door. A short while later she and Kennel were chained by the arms to a bench in the back of a rusting turbo-tank, bouncing and rocking with three other convicts as a trio of stormtroopers looked on from the front.

None of the prisoners looked at one another. Jyn took that as a good sign: If Kennel was planning to kill her, at least she didn't have allies.

The transport stopped so suddenly that Jyn whipped forward, the metal of her shackles raking the flesh of her wrists. There was shouting outside. Curiosity wormed its way into Jyn's brain; they'd been in transit too little time to be at the farms. The other prisoners shifted restively, glancing at the stormtroopers and the forward door.

"Nobody moves!" a trooper snapped. His two partners had their weapons up. All three turned to face front.

Jyn heard the dull *thunk* of something metallic and a faint, high-pitched whine. One of the other prisoners was looking up now, grinning with excitement like he'd figured it all out.

Then the front of the transport exploded.

The roar of the detonating grenade—it had to be a grenade, Jyn knew the noise too well—made her ears throb and turned the screams and shouts and blaster shots that followed into a tinny, incomprehensible buzz. Smoke carrying the odor of ash and burning circuits flooded the rear compartment, stinging Jyn's eyes and nostrils. She tried to follow what was happening, watch the movements of the stormtroopers, but it hurt to look and she had to blink away grit. She kept her gaze on the floor. In her peripheral vision she saw the stormtroopers die one by one, felled by a barrage of particle bolts that burned through their armor and sparked against the transport walls.

"Hallik!" a muffled voice called, barely audible above the ringing in her ears.

Jyn lifted her chin with a jolt and turned toward the front of the turbo-tank. Three armed figures in battle-stained attire picked their way among the bodies. They wore no insignia, but she knew them by their movements, by their uniformity of manner and their scowls.

They were professionals. Soldiers.

They weren't with the Empire; that made them rebels. They'd *found* her.

She couldn't stop the thought. It leapt into her head, demanded that she fight, that she *run*. But it made no sense. Why would they even be looking for her? Maybe it was a coincidence, maybe they were after a different prisoner and she'd misheard . . .

"Liana Hallik!" the leader—a man so thoroughly covered in gear that his exposed face seemed out of place among the cloth and leather—called again.

Jyn slowly lowered her gaze to the chains around her wrists. Her hands were shaking. She gripped her seat to make them stop.

"Her," another rebel said, and gestured in Jyn's direction.

Her deafness was abating. She waited, half expecting a blaster bolt to the head. She wondered how it would feel. People died fast from blaster bolts; she'd seen it enough. She didn't think it would hurt much.

"You want to get out of here?" the rebel leader asked. His tone was neutral, guarded—as if he was as cautious of Jyn as Jyn was of him.

Jyn tried to imagine what had brought the rebels to her. Had Saw decided to bring her back? Had one of his people decided she knew too much?

She nodded at the man, lacking any better option.

One of the rebel grunts fumbled with her shackles, finally unlocking them with a key from a stormtrooper's corpse. Jyn snapped upright, dizzy from the smoke and the blood rushing to her head but determined not to show it. Her rescuer started to say something when, from the other side of the transport, a prisoner called, "Hey! What about me?"

The rebel standing over her turned away. Jyn recognized it as an opening.

She was halfway across the transport floor in a second, her foot driving firmly into the leader's soft gut to slam him against the wall. Momentum kept Jyn upright as she spun toward a second body closing in. She swung a fist, landed a solid blow to the newcomer's face, felt his teeth through his cheek. She stumbled forward, still light-headed, and grabbed the first weapon she could find among the farming tools stored nearby: a shovel, solid and long enough to give her reach. She'd seen the damage a shovel could do in a prisoner's hands.

She let the shovel's weight carry her through her first swing, gave a solid, fleshy *smack* to the leader as the man bounced back from where she'd kicked him into the wall. She swung again to strike the rebel who'd unshackled her as he came up from behind. Jyn saw a clear path to the front of the transport and dashed for the twisted and broken doors.

The world was a blur, but she was *out,* feet striking the gravel trail.

She could find a way off Wobani. Forge new scandocs. Retire *Liana Hallik* and start over yet again, pick whatever name she wanted, one the Empire wouldn't care about and the Rebel Alliance would never *find*—

"You are being rescued," a voice said. It was electronically distorted, but too high-pitched to be a stormtrooper. A cold metal hand snagged her collar, hoisting Jyn until she was wriggling half a meter in the air. Before her towered the spindly chassis of a sunlit security droid, black as night save for the Imperial insignia on its shoulder plates and the dead white bulbs of its eyes. "Congratulations."

The droid flicked its arm and tossed her to the ground. Pain flashed up Jyn's spine, crashed through her skull. Tilting her head back, she saw an angry, bloody-mouthed rebel pointing a rifle at her chest.

Damn Saw Gerrera anyway. Damn the whole Rebel Alliance.

THE STORY CONTINUES...

ROGUE ONE
A **STAR WARS** STORY

READ THE EPIC NOVELIZATION BY ALEXANDER FREED

FIND OUT MORE AT RANDOMHOUSEBOOKS.COM/ STARWARS

DEL REY

Disney | LUCASFILM